The Iron Hammer

Book Six of the Iron Soul Series

J.M. Briggs

Contents

To the Montana Mythcreants.
You people are weird,
but I'm glad to know all of you,
especially during November.

1

Magical Path

Magic was complicated. There were a lot of strings attached to it and many aspects of her experience with it that Alex had yet to fully process. She was worried about just what she'd find and how she'd feel when she did stop to take a look into that potentially bottomless pit. Reincarnation and destiny seemed to be part of the price of magic and yet it wasn't all bad.

Her own magic was dancing over her skin in small flickers of gray light as she called more and more forth. She'd kicked off her tennis shoes and socks as part of an experiment and squeezed the grass with her bare toes. Beneath her, Alex could feel a pulse of magic rippling over the surface of the ground that sent a wave of giddiness through her. It was a bit like she'd just taken a shot of liquor that she couldn't handle and for a moment the world spun though she didn't move. Alex took a deep breath and sidestepped onto the edge of her family's patio, allowing the warm wooden planks to insulate her from the rush of magic a little. Her head cleared and she breathed a bit easier.

"Alex?" Aiden called with a hint of worry behind her.

"It was just a bit much." She nibbled nervously at her lower lip.

Alex looked around the large yard carefully. Her family's home in Spokane, the very house she'd grown up in, was surrounded by a tall privacy fence that she hoped would be enough to keep out prying eyes. Magic was powerful, but not as convenient as it was in the stories. While Merlin could erase someone's memory, Alex knew she lacked the control needed for that. Alex forced herself to focus on the task at hand. She hadn't come back to Spokane from her university town of Ravenslake to ponder the role of magic in her life or the likelihood of her killing someone because she tried to erase their memory.

Calling on the magic again, Alex smiled in relief when it came forth around her, but didn't overwhelm her mind as it had before. More gray sparks of magic swarmed around her right arm. Alex licked her lips as she slowly brought her left arm up. There was an iron dagger with a sharpened edge clutched in her hand that she fought to keep from shaking. She hadn't gotten used to this yet, but grit her teeth and quickly cut a slice into her right palm, careful not to go too deep. Her blood on the edge of the blade began to glow for a moment as her magic jumped into the iron-rich liquid.

Holding out her right hand, Alex let the blood gather in her palm. Gray sparks of magic were pouring into it and making it glow a dangerous bright red color. Around her, everything was becoming hazy as a thick fog of magic swept around her and closed Alex off from the rest of the world. Sounds were muted, though she could hear her friends behind her on the deck and a few nearby birds, but the magic was taking over. As before, a rush of energy rolled through her body, making every nerve flare. It wasn't painful, but the air was forced from her lungs and her heart began to race as the blood still running through her veins became soaked in magic. She was grateful that her bare feet weren't touching the grass anymore.

Stepping forward, Alex brought her hand out over the grass and tilted it. The first brightly glowing drop of blood rolled out of her palm and hung at the edge of her hand for a moment. Staring at it in fascination, Alex felt a tingle of excitement roll up her spine. This was an unusual way to spend sophomore spring break, but as she watched the magic gather as her desire to protect this area sank into it, Alex couldn't argue. The droplet fell from her hand, glittering in the sunlight before striking a blade of grass and rolling down the green stalk to the ground. Her magic in the droplet connected with the earth below violently, pulling magic from all around them to fuel her spell.

Magic rushed out of Alex's body, her knees shaking as her heart skipped too many beats. It was like standing in a downpour as energy flowed over her skin and into the blood still dripping from her palm to the ground. The world slowed down. Ripples of bright red rolled across the yard like waves on a pond after a rock was thrown in. Prying her eyes off the grass, Alex fought to retain awareness of the moment. To her eyes, the world gained a reddish hue. Her childhood yard bathed in a strange almost fiery glow. She could hear their golden retriever Anne whimpering, the sound cutting through the haze.

Regaining more awareness of what was happening, Alex pushed the magic out of her body, forming a short glittering gray thread between her chest and the pulsing orb of spinning blood red and gray that began to form in her hand. Holding it out, Alex moaned as the pressure in her chest eased and tilted her head curiously as she watched the magic flow out of the orb and down to the ground, creating another longer thread of magic. Alex willed the magic to connect outward, trying to visualize it doing what she'd done only days ago in Ravenslake.

When Arthur had attacked them with a force of Sídhe creatures under the control of the warped magic of the Iron Chain, Alex had taken both his and the surrounding magic and used that for the blood spell instead. Her mind continued to clear and she watched as sparks of magic flew into the orb from the air like a magnet attracting tiny flecks of metal. A smile tugged at her lips. This spell was dangerous. Merlin and Morgana had made that clear and yet... the tension in her body was fading quickly as she was no longer the focus of all that power.

She kept pulling on more and more magic, watching the air shimmer around the orb like waves of heat were rolling off of it. This might be dangerous, gathering up and forcing so much magic into her own blood as it kept dripping off her palm and carrying more of the magic into the ground. Inwardly she kept chanting for it to protect Spokane, to protect her home, and her family, tying that wish into the magic as tightly as she could. The city was far larger than any of the towns other mages had ever used this spell to protect, but she didn't care.

Alex's hands trembled as the orb's soft gray color darkened into a metallic sheen, like iron metal, and the vibration around it increased. Breathing slowly, Alex shifted her hands over the orb before pushing the whole burst of magic down into the ground with the blood splatter. Everything around her shook, though Alex wasn't sure it really did and the orb shifted form, becoming a flood of magical sparks falling to the ground like pouring water. The blood gleamed a sharp red color before turning white for a moment. Then it vanished and the last flickers of magic faded from the air. Around her, the world smelled sharp and clear like a thunderstorm had rolled in, but the sky remained a clear blue.

Her knees were giving out. The odd thought consumed her mind yet Alex didn't feel her body trying to do anything to prevent it. Her nerves were raw and there was definite exhaustion clawing at the edges of her awareness. Yet she wasn't unconscious which was a victory. A giggle escaped her. There was an ache in her chest where the flow of magic had been. Maybe not unconscious, but she'd be feeling it for a bit.

"Alex," Bran called. He jumped forward and caught her right arm as her legs finally gave out. "Easy, easy."

"Wow." Aiden's brown eyes were bright with excitement as he caught her left arm. "You looked so calm and in control."

"Not completely." Alex brought up her right hand to push some of her blonde hair out of her face, completely forgetting about the blood on it. "But I do think this method works well."

"Well, you're still on your feet," Nicki said. "That's something."

Lance was kneeling down with one hand holding the collar of Anne and the other gently stroking the dog's fur. He offered her a warm smile, his brown eyes bright with relief. Next to him, Jenny pulled one of the deck chairs closer. Bran and Aiden half lifted half dragged her over to the chair and set her on it. Someone took her hand and Alex looked over to find Nicki inspecting it, but instead of a long cut, there was a thin white line surrounded by pink.

"You healed yourself." Nicki sounded surprised, turning her hand over with a slight frown. "That's new."

"Really?" Alex's mind began to re-engage with what was happening. "That's... neat I suppose."

Nicki smiled at her and patted her hand before releasing it and standing up. She moved over to join the boys as they looked down at the grass. The red glow was gone now and Lance released Anne who scurried over to her and nudged her hand. Smiling, Alex rubbed the top of Anne's head. Her body made a small shudder as the last of the magic in her veins settled.

Alex took advantage of the others giving her a little space and eyed them all. Everyone seemed calm and in good spirits which was a gift given how challenging the last few days had been. The reminder of how brief a time it had been made Alex's head spin. They had been on the last day of midterms, though thankfully everyone had finished theirs early, and suffered a major attack at the hands of Arthur. A small army had marched on them and yet here they all were healthy and alright. It hadn't been something she'd anticipated being worried about when she started college almost two years ago, but then again, she hadn't known the truth then.

"Alex," a voice called tentatively from the house.

Climbing to her feet, Alex was pleased when she remained steady and gave her friends a small wave when Aiden took a step towards her. The others lingered outside in the warm spring air while Alex pulled open the screen door and stepped into the kitchen. Turning to the right, she found her mother standing at the counter and chopping vegetables for the lunch salad. Alex really wished that her mom hadn't had today off, but they'd rushed up to Spokane too quickly for her to even check that. Her mom looked older than even a year before. They'd had the same long blonde hair, but the gray was fast taking over and the worry lines gained in the past few months were far more than even her years as a doctor had given her.

"Did everything go okay?" her mom asked in a forced cheerful tone.

"Yeah, there's now blood protection extending out around the house," Alex said. "It'll keep any Sídhe or Fae from coming after you."

"And you really thought that was a problem?" Her mom looked out the window of the kitchen and into the yard.

"You're my family." Alex shrugged weakly, rubbing her left arm nervously. It really didn't need any more explanation than that. "I care about you, for the Queen that may be enough."

Her mother's frown tightened and Alex again wondered if telling them had been the right course of action only to dismiss the doubts. She'd told them the truth so that if she died or was injured, they'd at least know why. It was a sobering thought and one Alex knew shouldn't have been a part of her life when she couldn't even legally drink yet, but it was there.

"Will you be able to stay long enough to see your father?"

"Uh... yeah, we can stay tonight, but then we're getting on the road tomorrow for Eugene and Portland. I want to get the blood protections down as soon as possible."

"Alright, well it's nice to have you home now." Her mom smiled and reached over to hug her. Alex heard an intake of breath from her mom as she prepared to say something more, but nothing more came. "Anyway, let's get you mages fed," her mom said a moment later as she released her and stepped back.

Still braced for more to be said, Alex helped her mom put all the sandwiches on a large platter. Her younger brother Ed looked over at her uneasily as he was called into the kitchen to help. The excitement that had been present in his eyes when she'd first revealed her magic had dulled. They'd probably talked about it since that day; quiet conservations here in the safety of their own home as they tried to understand just what to make of it all. Alex felt sorry for her parents, their only daughter was a mage doomed to fight back the things that didn't belong on Earth.

Still Ed gave her a smile and moved to follow their mom's instructions by taking the food out onto the porch with Alex falling into step behind him. Setting the bowl of salad on the table next to the plate of sandwiches, Alex gave her friends a real smile. The sun was shining down on them and while it wasn't the best circumstances, she was getting to see her family during spring break. Everyone grabbed the plates and made their way to the table before spreading out amongst the various porch chairs. In the corner of her eye, Alex thought she still saw a soft shimmer of red rolling over the grass and was filled with a sense of relief. Magic might have complicated her life, but at least she could use it to protect those she loved.

"So, Jenny's your ex-wife," Ed said with a mischievous smirk. It earned him a warning glare from their mom as he picked up his sandwich.

"Suppose so." Alex balanced her plate of salad and half a turkey sandwich on her lap. "But then again apparently I've got other ex-wives."

"True," Nicki said. "Could be funny to have Jenny meet Sif."

"I'm pretty sure that marriage vows don't extend into the next reincarnation," Bran offered with a cautious glance towards her family. "But it's something we're dealing with."

That remark got an odd look from her mom and Alex rushed to explain. "Bran's a reincarnation too. He and I were mages and friends in another life too. Wales... uh..."

"About 2,300 years ago," Bran told them quickly.

"Wow, that's got to be a head trip." Ed gawked with wide eyes. "What about you two?" he asked looking at Aiden and Nicki. "Are you reincarnations too?"

"Not that we know of." Nicki shrugged lazily. "Might be though. We don't really know how that works. Bran established a link with his previous life so we could find the Iron Chalice and Merlin and Morgana have observed Alex, Lance, and Jenny be reborn, but that's what we know on that topic."

Looking down at her plate and her feet, Alex tried to ignore the talk of reincarnation. She still hadn't really adjusted to the notion that she was the current life of the three-thousand-year-old soul that had inspired the mythology of King Arthur and had been the historical basis for the Norse

God Thor. She wasn't sure just how many lives she'd had, but recently there had been the uncomfortable revelation that one of her lives had been a slave ship captain and had used his magic to bind others to his will. Add it all together and it was becoming more and more uncomfortable. Not to mention that for some reason she was the first known female incarnation and as much as Alex wanted to be proud of that or wanted to believe it meant something important, she was at a loss.

"You can understand why we're worried," she heard her mom say. Alex forced herself to focus on the conversation around them. "It's just a frightening thing to know that your child is fighting monsters." Her mom's frown deepened. "And the concerns about what will happen if you're discovered." Alex wanted to say something, to reassure her mom, but her mouth was painfully dry.

"We'll look after each other," Aiden promised. He met Elizabeth Adams' gaze calmly. "The others found the Iron Chalice and saved me. We know that we can accomplish more together and I promise that you don't need to be worried about the loyalty of those present."

If her mother's eyes jumped over at Jenny and Lance for a moment they didn't flinch back from the look. Alex could understand her mother's fears. Everyone, at least everyone in the Western world, knew the story of Lancelot and Guinevere. It was the sort of story that everyone knew, even if you couldn't remember when you first heard it.

"Just be careful," Alex told her family with a forced smile. "There's now a blood protection spell around Spokane. Sídhe and most of their descendants shouldn't be able to come here."

"Shouldn't?"

"You'll be safe," Alex assured her with a smile, reaching over to squeeze her mom's hand. "But if you see anything strange then let us know right away."

"We will," Ed agreed with a nod and a serious look that surprised Alex.

"We will." Her mom gave a slight nod of her own and squeezed Alex's hand in return.

Taking another bite of her sandwich, Alex did her best to push away her worries. Her family would be safe now. The blood protection spell was one of the most powerful and raw magical spells known even to Merlin and Morgana. She'd bound her desire to keep this city safe from invaders into the very soil, into the plants, and even the human-made structures of the city. Yet she couldn't quite ignore that there was a lingering fear at the back of her mind. Some sort of suspicious and frightened shadow seemed to have settled there and Alex was at a loss of how to banish it.

2

Walking the Old Path

Merlin rather liked Norway. The landscape was still raw like it had been all those years ago when he and Morgana had been training the young and rather stubborn Thor. Even from his place up the hill, he could still hear the waves crashing below and the glimpses of towns that he could see were distant and small. It wasn't like England which was so changed by the years that he sometimes doubted it was truly the same place. He could still remember when London had been nothing but a Roman fort town; it made him feel every bit his almost three thousand years. Norway on the other hand still smelled like it should. The people had shifted away from their Viking culture back to a calmer and more community-centric one like it had been when he'd lived in the area.

Chuckling softly, Merlin shook his head at his own thoughts. He was sounding old indeed; much older than the simple, if a touch eccentric, literature professor Ambrose Yates should. He chuckled again, this time amused by his own modern name. It was always bittersweet to create a new identity, but there was often an element to fun to the process.

Breathing in the air, Merlin noted the taste of salt and kept moving. His walking stick clinked against the rocks and Merlin tightened his fingers around the well-worn wood. The staff stood as tall as him and the warm brown color and smooth finish was interrupted by small symbols carved into it. They circled the top few inches and appeared seemingly random down the rest of the staff. It wasn't his original staff, that one had been destroyed long ago in Wales. During Gofiben's lifetime if he remembered correctly.

Wales: that thought struck a chord with him and made him pause. There were still wild places in Wales in the crags of the valleys and mountains high above the rolling farmland and calm pastures. After all the young generation of mages had found a Dragon hidden deep beneath Dinas Emrys, guarding a fallen white Dragon and the Iron Chalice. There remained so many questions. The origin of the local legend of a blond person with blue eyes finding a hidden cavern with a treasure within was a mystery to him.

"Perhaps I should visit the Dragon this summer," Merlin remarked thoughtfully to himself, relishing the way his voice echoed against the rocky outcropping. "He must be lonely for company and conversation."

It would certainly be one of the more interesting conversations and moments in his life and given the length, there were many remarkable ones to choose from. His foot almost slipped on a loose rock and Merlin sternly reminded himself to pay more attention to his surroundings. Shifting to the right, Merlin looked around critically at the nearby rock formations. He was almost there and followed the ridge of rocks down to a small narrowing crevice.

The dark local stone was spotted and covered with a thin layer of dirt, dust, and some vegetation trying to grow. Putting his hand on a warm rock side, Merlin moved further down the slope into the small ravine. His eyes scanned the hillside, trying to find the right section of rock. Then he spotted a sunken area with a pile of rocks collapsed around it. As he stepped towards it, Merlin's phone suddenly rang and he pulled it out at once.

"Ambrose Yates." Leaning forward, he examined the half-collapsed area. He was confident that this was the right way.

"Ambrose, Morgana," a very familiar voice greeted.

"Ah, Morgana, how are you? Nothing wrong I hope."

"No, Ambrose," she replied in an even tone. "Nothing is wrong. I'm just checking in."

"You needn't worry so," Merlin teased with a smile tugging at his lips. He could just imagine his counterpart frowning as she narrowed her green eyes. "I'm almost to the Iron Hammer now. I'll have it within an hour. Though please keep in mind that the phone will not function once I'm below ground."

"I'll remember," Morgana answered, but there was a hint of something in her voice. Merlin remained on the line even as he kept walking, just waiting. "The mages have left Ravenslake. They were in Spokane today."

"The blood spell?" Merlin was unable to suppress the small flare of worry in his chest. "Morgana, was that wise?"

"They are all together," Morgana assured him quickly. "They are planning to visit the cities around here where they have family: Spokane, Eugene, and Portland."

"That spell is dangerous."

"Not so much for Alex," Morgana reminded him with a hint of pride in her voice. Merlin frowned at that, worried that Morgana was allowing her fondness for the reincarnation of her beloved younger brother Arto to cloud the issue. "Her ability to collect the magic of the others and even traces in the air makes it much less dangerous for her."

"Using that spell can kill mages," Merlin protested.

"You taught Arto how to use it."

"I trained Arto from a very young age, Alex has been training barely a year," he countered as he came to a stop, far too distracted to keep moving. "It isn't about power, Morgana, I acknowledge that the girl has that, but she lacks experience."

"None the less they are casting the spell. Aiden checked in with me and the spell in Spokane went smoothly. Alex was a little shaky on her feet, but she was fine."

"Still-"

"I remember you and Arto hiking through the night after he cast the spell at Glastonbury and creating Cathanáil before he had any rest," Morgana told him sternly with a definite hint of disapproval. "He was fine and you weren't so worried then. Alex may be fairly green still, but she has the determination and her endurance is improving. Only time and practice will improve her skills now, Merlin."

She was irritated with him now, Merlin reflected. Morgana made a point of calling him Ambrose, though he had to admit she'd been slipping more and more lately. The younger mages had long since adopted Merlin over Professor Yates and she seemed to have followed. A sigh escaped him and Merlin held his staff in the crook of his arm so he could rub between his eyes.

"Very well, Morgana," he said. "I have faith that you'll keep them safe."

"I will. Keep us up to date on your progress and I'll do the same. They should be back about the same time as you'll return with the Iron Hammer."

Tightening his grip on the phone, Merlin tried to articulate his thoughts. There was a bad feeling creeping up his spine that he didn't quite understand and wasn't sure how to communicate. It was foolish. The children had been successful in finding the Iron Chalice in

Wales over Christmas break mere months ago. He'd gone looking for the legendary chalice himself centuries ago with no luck and they'd been successful.

"I see," he finally forced out, fighting down the wave of worry. "I'll be in touch then." Making himself smile, Merlin added. "I've found the entrance to the tunnels."

"Good, stay safe, Merlin."

She hung up on him, probably sensing that he was trying to find some argument against Alex leaving Ravenslake. Though she had already. Merlin wasn't sure what it was that bothered him so much. He'd grown up in a rather egalitarian society and known Morgana for three thousand years so he was fairly certain that this wasn't based on Alex's gender. Still, he couldn't put his finger on why he was so concerned about this Iron Soul. Certainly, he was always a bit protective of them, but he liked to think he'd gotten better over the centuries.

Shaking his head, Merlin shoved those thoughts away to ponder another day. Apparently, Morgana had cleared the young ones to leave her side and given how protective she was then she must not be very worried. Instead, he turned his attention back to the matter at hand: recovering the Iron Hammer.

Rocks had shifted over the small cave entrance, half burying the thing beneath the weight of the hill. Rather than feel irritation, Merlin smiled in relief. At the time the Iron Hammer had been placed here the underground had been firmly in the hands of allies. Yet that had been a very long time ago. Merlin glanced around and listened for a moment just to be certain that he was alone. When he found no sign of anyone else, he raised his staff dramatically into the air and called forth his magic.

The familiar leaf green magic flared around his fingertips, flowing freely from his chest through his arms. Twinkling green sparks spun around his staff and settled into the wood in a well-practiced action. Merlin allowed himself a small puff of pleasure in the simple calling of magic before he turned his staff towards the hillside. Mentally he commanded the magic to move the rocks and open the way. In his mind's eye, he could see the old tunnel that had led into the hidden chamber and commanded it to be shown to him. Pushing his will into the magic, Merlin focused on his desire and urged the magic to make it reality.

Green streams of magic burst forth and spun into the rocks. Merlin waited with a small smile as his magic caused the whole hillside to shift. Rocks were scooped out of the hidden tunnel and flung out into the ravine like a great invisible hand was at work. Magic continued to spin around Merlin lazily and he fondly traced one of the symbols carved into his staff. Then the feel of magic brushing over his skin eased, the task he had set his magic to completed. With the stones and dirt dug away, Merlin could clearly see a long tunnel stretching into the earth ahead of him.

Opening his left hand, Merlin called on more magic and watched calmly as the green sparks appeared once more. They fused together to form a perfect orb. The green color faded to white as the orb began to glow and cast a soft light around Merlin, brightening the shadows cast by the walls of the ravine. Merlin brought the orb up to the top of his staff and the magic-laced itself around the top of the wood, fixing the light securely to the top. With that sorted, Merlin stepped into the small tunnel and began to follow the worn stone path deeper into the earth.

The tunnel only went in about thirty feet in a slow slope. Runes were carved into the walls. Nothing special in his eyes, but they were bits and pieces of Thor's story: descriptions of his relationship with Sif, Odin's affection for the young man, his powers over lightning, and more importantly a description of the Iron Hammer. It was a dramatic description to be sure, but Merlin could understand the awe that Thor's Hammer would have created. His ability to summon storms and call lightning down had been impressive even to a seasoned mage like him.

Merlin paused to look at the runes and wondered if these runes had played any part in the rise of Thor's myth. He was certain that the man he'd known would be tickled to know that he was remembered as a god. Though Merlin could not figure out where Loki had come from in the mythology. Then again, he knew that humans loved their stories and they often grew in the telling. Hence why a mage could become a god and he and Morgana could vanish from the story completely.

Following the tunnel further into the hillside, Merlin became aware of the drop in temperature as he ventured far beyond the rays of the sun. As the air became staler, he used a quick wave of magic to clear it and kept moving. Merlin hummed softly to himself as he allowed the old memory to guide him through the tunnels. Everything was still and quiet with the musty smell of stone surrounding him. Gone was any sound of the Dvergr at work and Merlin felt a twinge of mourning for the long-gone beings. This had never been their world and they had been all too happy to lock themselves into the old Dark Elf tunnels. Time had done the rest. At least he could reassure himself that while Brokkr and the others were gone that their home world remained.

There were small collapsed tunnels leading off the main one, but Merlin ignored them in favor of following his current path. The lower tunnels were long abandoned and he doubted there was much to find deep in Svartalfheim after all this time. Instead, he stayed focused on this tunnel and followed it until it widened into a small room. It was a small cavern cut in a roughly round shape with two stone pillars supporting it.

Stepping further into the room, Merlin found himself holding his breath. He reminded himself that Thor wasn't buried here. Sif had taken her late husband's body into the water with her and there was nothing waiting here except for the Iron Hammer. Merlin walked further into the room and lifted his staff to cast more light through the space. The beams filled the room and Merlin turned his eyes to the pedestal.

Merlin was still in the passage doorway as he took in the sight of the old cave. The elegant carving of the Tree of Reality filled the back of the cavern and one only mildly familiar with Norse mythology might have mistaken it for Yggdrasil if they did not stop to note that there were far too many worlds. But the stone pedestal that had been the resting place of the Iron Hammer was empty. It was gone.

3

Lord of Thunder

Thor moved one calloused finger over the smooth flat surface of the Iron Hammer, studying the plain form intensely. His fingertip glowed a bright almost white-blue color as he carefully poured his magic into the Hammer. The iron was resisting him. Thor frowned and glared at the smooth shimmering surface of the Hammer in his hand. It fit perfectly in his palm, even more so than when it had simply been his primary forging hammer. One end of it was thick and large with the other end tapering into a narrower head. He'd always found it solid with enough versatility to start any project and finish most of them, but now the magic in the metal was pushing back a little against him.

Huffing in irritation, Thor tried to relax as Morgana had instructed him in the past. It wasn't an easy thing for him. He was a man of action, a man who liked to just get his work done so a moment of silence and inaction was uncomfortable. However, he could feel the hum of magic in his chest growing stronger as the spark flared to life like an ember fed with fresh, dry kindling. Sparks jumped across his fingertips, illuminating the small alcove of rock that he'd hidden himself in to work far from his still reeling village.

As the bright pale blue of his magic flowed into the Iron Hammer, Thor smiled when the shimmer of magic within the metal increased. He could feel small jolts of lightning arcing off the metal and onto his fingertips. Rather than being frightened or worried, he found the sensation pleasing and exciting. Thor quickly pressed his finger against the warm metal of the Hammer and summoned up the design he wanted to add in his mind. Right now, the Iron Hammer was too plain for an object of such power.

Slowly the iron shifted beneath his fingertip, melting and reshaping ever so slightly. Thor's smile widened and he carefully moved his finger along in the desired design. The smooth curves of a triskele appeared and Thor could feel the magic in his chest flaring at the sight of the symbol. Morgana and Merlin had tried to explain the significance of the symbol as the mark of the magic of the Iron Realm, but he hadn't fully understood. None the less at the moment he could feel something settling in his bones as if it was a relief to have the Hammer thus marked.

Unsure of what to make of that, Thor pushed his confusion aside and decided not to dwell on it. After all, it was magic. He didn't think he was really supposed to understand it. As the magic began to fade and left a three spiral arm design on the side of the Hammer, Thor nodded in satisfaction. It was far neater than he'd expected: there were no rises of melted iron. Instead, the symbol appeared to have been perfectly carved into the metal. Turning the Hammer over in his lap, Thor leaned back against the cool stone and repeated the process on the other side.

Soon he had the triskele on both sides of the Iron Hammer. He hefted it a few times to test that the balance was still correct. It was. The Hammer still fit perfectly in his hand and Thor knew that with some force, the weight of the front half could easily turn deadly. He'd shaped weapons, pots, and tools with this Hammer and now it was so much more. With that thought, Thor shifted and fastened the Hammer into the leather loop he'd added to his belt. The weight against his hip was still unfamiliar, but he was confident that he'd get used to it.

With a sigh, he looked up and turned his gaze towards the ocean. His home village was built near the shores of the pounding waves amongst the rocks and small inlets. It was a rough area: full of rocky hillsides, small ravines, and small trees around the fields that they've managed to scrape out. His farmer brother was out there no doubt, hands in the dirt and hard at work. Thor sighed; he should be too. There were plenty of orders that needed to be filled throughout the village and he was the only blacksmith now that Erlendr was dead. Snorting, Thor mentally amended that thought: he was the only human blacksmith.

Brokkr was a smith and a very good one. Not as gifted as he was, of course, but the Dvergr was very impressive. Ever since they'd helped him escape from the Dark Elf tunnels, he'd been all but locked up in Thor's forge. It was a bit small for the two of them even with Brokkr's small size. They needed to make another forge for him to work in as Brokkr wasn't exactly helping to meet the village's needs right now. With Erlendr's old forge destroyed in the last attack, they needed a second anyway. Thor was making weapons, lots of weapons, but his father had been all too happy to remind him that life went on.

Yet while he could still see the collection of wooden homes and small work yards, Thor couldn't deny that the village had been changed by the recent events. When he'd been a child there had been no need for the half circle of long wooden houses to be enclosed by a wall, but the Dark Elves had made it necessary. The twisted and poisoned Sídhe creatures that had forced their way into his world were paying for it dearly. Yet, they'd still gotten into the Iron Realm despite the Iron Gates and the best efforts of Merlin, Morgana, and this previous Iron Soul life Arto. Thor didn't think much of his first life whose life's work had failed, but would never say such to Morgana.

He shook his head and pushed himself to his feet. Dusting off his tunic, Thor reached up to check that his hair was still neat. It needed a good combing when he got home but was clean enough. Wringing his hands for a moment, Thor debated heading for home or seeing if he could take back his forge from Brokkr. The latter option was certainly preferable but seemed unlikely as the Dvergr was throwing himself into work with a ferocity that astonished him. He chuckled under his breath, rested his right arm on the Hammer, and started down the hill.

It didn't take him long. Thor's feet were familiar with the landscape surrounding his home. As a boy, he'd relished any chance he had to flee the village for a short time and explore. He'd gotten into plenty of trouble, such as the time he'd fallen into a deep crevice in the mountain. Shuddering, Thor pushed the memory aside even as his stomach tightened at both that incident and the worry that he'd be returning underground soon to face the Dark Elves. Their great weakness to the sun forced them to stay in the caverns beneath the mountains in a twisted little realm that his father had already begun to call Svartalfheim.

Thor paused at the doorway of the long wooden house he shared with his family. The smell of the livestock hung thick in the air and the pounded dirt floor beneath his feet was stable and familiar. However, his stomach turned a little as he caught sight of the expressions on the faces of his father and brother. For a moment no one said anything as his brother Arvid's eyes dropped to the Hammer hanging on his belt. By some instinct, Thor shifted his hand over the Hammer and gave his brother and father a small smile. He walked over to one of the long wooden benches that lined the walls of the house and quickly located a large bowl of water beside a carved comb.

He started by splashing some water on his face and did his best to ignore the heavy gaze of his father and brother on him. Combing out his long, bleached hair and carefully cleaning his short red beard, Thor took several deep breaths to calm down. His family meant well. He knew that of course. They couldn't understand how it felt, what it was like to feel the power of the world rushing up through you and making your visions real. How could they even begin to comprehend being a mage and knowing that the world depended on your power and your choices?

Releasing a shaky breath, Thor nodded to himself and splashed some of the cold water on his face to ensure the grime of the day was gone. He studied his hands for a moment. They were strong hands and showed signs of his work as a smith. There were small burns scattered about on his palms, the backs of his hands, and up his arms. There were scattered cuts from his earlier days when he hadn't been so careful sharpening the new blades and axe heads. These were good strong smith hands and now they were the hands of the Iron Soul.

Thor didn't even bother trying to temper his sense of pride. He didn't understand why he should. He had power and a stronger connection to the Iron Realm than even Merlin and Morgana. He'd poured so much magic through his Hammer that he'd imbued it with great power. It was a bit embarrassing that he hadn't realized the significance of what he had created at first. A strange thing for a blacksmith.

"Thor?" his father called, breaking the silence hanging in the long-house.

"No, Father, not tonight," Thor said. "Brokkr is just fine where he is."

"Thor," his father tried again. "Surely you can understand our hesitation. Those beings aren't human. That... thing using your forge, just beyond this wall, is not of this world!"

"We're just concerned that you haven't thought through all the repercussions of these actions." Arvid laid a calming hand on their father's arm.

"I understand that you're worried." Thor schooled his features into a neutral expression even as his hand moved to touch the warm metal of his Hammer. "And you are right to be. This is all very strange and dangerous, but it is necessary."

"Why?" His father straightened up in challenge. "The Dark Elves attacked first, yes, that's true, but since then they'd kept to their caves. They can have the below and us the surface."

"You can't be serious?" Thor demanded, pleased to note that his brother looked a touch alarmed by their father's suggestion. "They are not shifting to peace, Father, they are rallying themselves and preparing for war!"

"Thor," his father half scolded-half scoffed. "Do you imagine that you are going to save the world? That you will stop these Dark Elves?"

"Yes." Thor squared his shoulders. "With the help of Odin, Sif, Frea, Merlin, and Morgana. I have allies, Father. It isn't some impossible task."

"It sounds impossible," Arvid muttered giving Thor a doubtful look. "What strategy do you have?"

"Brokkr is going to help us." Thor didn't like the tone of the conversation and his patience was slipping away. "He's been in the tunnels. His people are still being held there."

His father and brother exchanged a look and Thor pushed down a flush of anger. They'd clearly been speaking together and planning how this conversation should go. Did they honestly think that just ignoring the Dark Elves was the answer?

"What would you have me do?" Thor demanded. Distantly, he heard the roll of thunder as his fingers tightened around the Hammer. "What is your solution, Father? Just ignore them. Their very presence has an impact on our world!"

"So do those other creatures," his father said. Arvid made a sharp move to step between them. Both Thor and his father ignored him. "The gods!"

"They aren't gods," Thor heard himself say with a scoffing laugh that surprised him. He was channeling Morgana now. "And yes, they impact our world's magic, but they make an effort to remain peaceful."

"Thor!" Merlin's voice snapped from the doorway behind him, making Thor hiss in alarm at the realization that the other mage had snuck in behind him. "Calm down!" Merlin ordered and Thor spun to face him just as a flash of lightning illuminated the house. "You're calling up a storm."

Blinking, Thor's anger and frustration vanished as he listened to the howl of the wind. He'd heard the thunder before but suddenly realized that he could smell lightning in the air and hear rain beginning to pound down on the roof. Merlin's shoulders were wet and the man's curly hair was flattened to his head. Thor looked down, surprised to find that at some point he'd pulled the Iron Hammer from the loop on his belt and was grasping it tightly.

"You need to calm down." Merlin gestured to the Hammer in Thor's hand. "When you hold that... well, its ability to call a storm seems very tied to your mental state."

"You see?" Thor looked back at his father and brother with a slight smirk. "I hardly have a choice in the matter."

The thunderous expression on his father's face that faded into worried resignation made Thor hesitate. He offered his father and brother a quick nod before turning and striding to the door. Merlin stepped aside to allow him to move out into the cooling evening air. Sucking in a deep breath, Thor walked further from the house as dark clouds churned above them.

"Your family means well," Merlin murmured. Thunder rolled in the distance after a sharp crack. "This is never easy."

"What was your family like?" Thor asked, grasping for something to get his mind off his own storming emotions and being careful to keep his hand off of the Iron Hammer.

"My mother was a priestess." Merlin's staff hit the ground as they moved through the rain which was easing quickly. "She was not a mage, but was capable of using some magic through rituals."

"And your father?"

There was a long pause and Merlin coughed lightly. Thor was certain that there wasn't going to be an answer even as he perked up in curiosity at Merlin's reaction. Morgana insisted that they were quite old so how would it possibly matter?

"My father was a Sídhe Rider," Merlin said with a sigh. "My birth was very unusual in that regard, normally no children are produced from such a... union." Shaking his head, Merlin didn't look at him and added, "Needless to say I have no idea of which individual Síd it was. I suppose I might have siblings in Sídhean, but I suspect that any Sídhe connected with me have long since been executed."

Thor had not expected that answer and dozens of questions flew to his mind, but he could tell it was a dangerous subject. Deciding not to think about it, Thor drummed his fingers on the leather wrapping of his Hammer. He could feel the hum of the magic through it and focused on that. With a nod to Merlin, he stepped into the house the older mage shared with Morgana and braced himself for a lecture.

4

Sense of Dread

Alex had never spent time in Eugene. It was the sort of town that she'd driven through with her family on trips before and maybe stopped for lunch, but nothing more than that. Now she found herself at Bran's small house that was located right behind his family's bakery near one of the major streets of the town. The smells of the bakery seemed to have seeped into the wood walls of the one-story green house because Alex would have sworn that she smelled fresh sweet rolls as they sat in the living room. Under better circumstances, she'd have teased Bran about growing up in a place that smelled like this all the time, but there was a nagging sense of worry that she couldn't shake.

It was a bit odd to be popping in for a visit with Bran's mother after all but driving through Portland that morning without giving Lance a chance to see his own family. They'd stopped only long enough to cast the blood spell and thankfully that had been enough for Lance. With a little luck, they'd be back in Ravenslake tonight and get some news from Morgana. Her fingers twitched just at the thought. Alex desperately hoped their theory that the Iron Hammer, made by her previous life Thor, would be able to break the connection between the dark power of the Iron Chain and the enslaved Sídhe creatures would prove true.

Just thinking about it made Alex feel ill. She could remember the confusion when she'd first pulled on the magical connection only to use the power to destroy it a few moments later. The knowledge now that she'd killed something that had just been freed from a spell was bitter. No wonder one of them in Wales had asked her what she'd wrought. Her previous life as a slave ship captain had created something truly horrible with his low levels of magic, but it was enough that it was haunting them now. The knot in her stomach tightened and Alex leaned forward to put her elbows on her knees in an attempt to suppress the discomfort.

"Oh, Bran," a high sweet voice called. "Help me with these sandwiches. You mustn't be a poor host!"

Alex was pulled from her darker thoughts with relief and looked up to see Bran rushing into the kitchen just off the small living room. He returned only a moment later with a large jug of bright red punch and a stack of glasses. With an amused smile, he set them on the small table that all but filled the space between the long couch beneath the window, the love seat, and the pair of armchairs stuffed into a small nook in front of a massive bookcase. Alex offered Bran a smile as he pushed a loose strand of his dark hair out of his face.

"I need a haircut," he muttered before sitting down on the couch.

"Right there with you, bro." Aiden tugged at a longer strand of his own brown hair that was hanging into his face. "Maybe we should do what Lance does and just get a buzz cut."

Lance raised a dark eyebrow at them and chuckled from his place on the loveseat next to Jenny. "I'm not sure you two could pull it off."

Soft laughter from the doorway made Alex look towards the kitchen doorway as Bran's mother entered. Jinsung Fisher was a blend of adorable and terrifying. The small pretty Asian woman with gray beginning to appear in her hair and warm brown eyes was apparently a fierce hugger. While she wasn't aware of the full story about magic, she knew enough to be grateful for her son's leg being healed. She set the tray of sandwiches down on the coffee table next to the jug of punch with a beaming smile before sitting down on the couch next to her son.

"It is so nice that you all stopped by for a visit," Jinsung said. "I haven't seen you since that BBQ that Aiden's parents hosted." She looked over to Aiden and asked, "How is your family? That scare you had at Christmas must have been horrible for them."

"It was," Aiden agreed. "But they're doing alright now."

"It's just horrible, something no parent should go through," Jinsung insisted with a pained expression before turning her gaze towards Jenny and Lance. "And now I get to meet your other friends." She paused and glanced at Bran asking, "Are they…"

"No," Jenny said. "We're not mages, nonmagical friends."

"Yeah," Lance agreed. "We're just traveling with them while they do the protection spells." Bran's eyes widened, but Lance didn't catch the look. "We just finished the one here before we came over."

"A protection spell?" Bran's mother straightened up and looked at her son with alarmed eyes. "Why is that necessary?"

"It's just a precaution, Mom," Bran said quickly. "We aren't the only beings with magic and some may react violently towards us or our families."

A frown appeared on Jinsung's face and her eyes darted over to the mantle of the fireplace where a photograph of a man, who had a strong resemblance to Bran, and a folded American flag were displayed. Bran shifted uncomfortably and Alex was reminded of why Bran hadn't wanted to tell his mother about the magical war, the Sídhe, or Arthur. She'd already lost her husband to a human war and would no doubt be terrified of losing her son to a magical one. Lance seemed to catch on and gave Bran an apologetic look.

"I just want the peace of mind of knowing there is a protective spell around you," Bran assured her, taking her hands with a forced smile. "And there is one in Ravenslake so you don't need to worry."

"I suppose." Jinsung gave her son a searching look. Her eyes dropped to his leg and she nodded. "Well, it can't be bad, can it? That vision you had in the car saved our lives and now your leg is healed." Her smile returned and she reached over to pat her son's cheek. "Are you going to play soccer again?"

"Maybe, I'm going to start with fencing club next year actually," Bran replied with a smile. "All the others are in it... well, not Lance and Jenny."

"I'll probably join next year," Lance said with a shrug. "Won't be able to do much during football season, but it sounds like a good idea."

"I've got spirit squad," Jenny added with a small smile towards Lance. "But yeah, it might be nice for the spring."

Alex straightened up and fought back a smile. They hadn't talked about next year and last time it had come up with Jenny, the other girl had been talking about transferring. She'd tried not to let the idea bother her. After all, Jenny and Lance had been through a lot the last few years. As the reincarnations of Gwenyvar and Luegáed, the inspirations for the story of Guinevere and Lancelot, they'd been used by Arthur as part of his charade that he was the Iron Soul. The news that Jenny was considering staying in Ravenslake made Alex shiver in relief. Her former roommate caught her eye and offered her a small smile, probably aware of her reaction to the announcement.

They settled into a calm conversation about the rest of the year and plans for next year. It was going to be their junior year, but Alex was having trouble processing that fact. In some ways, it seemed like an eternity ago that she had started college with concerns about making friends and doing well. That had fallen apart quickly with much greater problems taking its place. Alex rubbed her hand over the thin pale red mark left from her casting the blood spell earlier. It had been even easier this time and yet there was a sense of foreboding that she couldn't pinpoint.

Shifting uneasily, Alex bit her bottom lip before licking it again. She could already feel them becoming chapped, but couldn't explain the worry weighing down on her. Rationally, she could connect it to the odd peace they'd had the last couple of days. Since Arthur's large-scale attack and their decision to protect their home cities nothing unexpected had happened. Yet she didn't have the sense that she was waiting for the other shoe to drop. This was more like something was tugging at the back of her mind, like something fluttering around in the corner of her eye. It was driving her crazy and she was at a loss.

So, she stayed silent after polishing off half of a sandwich, turning over the problem and trying to sort it out. Of course, she was worried about Arthur. There was a permanent knot in her gut that she knew would be there until he was dead. She wasn't sure who would kill him, but Morgana and Nicki were both certainly contenders alongside her. No that wasn't it, she conceded with a soft sigh. There was an odd sense that she was forgetting something teamed with worry over what Arthur and the Queen were up to now that his last attack had been such a failure.

The ringing of a phone cut into her deep thoughts making her flinch. It took her a moment to realize that everyone was looking towards her. After another moment she recognized the ringtone as one of hers and the sound as coming from her pocket. Alex pulled out her phone with an apologetic look. Looking down, Alex sighed in relief when Professor Yates' name appeared on the phone. Arthur hadn't called her since his last attack on Ravenslake and while Alex was dreading it, she knew it was only a matter of time. She stood up and nodded to the others, moving into the kitchen of the small house before answering.

"Hello, Merlin," Alex greeted only to be met by fast breathing. "Are you okay?"

"Out of breath," the older mage told her. "Alex, listen to me, the Iron Hammer is gone."

"What?" Alex asked in disbelief. "I mean... are you sure?" She could feel her own heart pounding and a nervous sweat beginning to break out on her forehead. "Merlin-"

"I'm sorry, but yes the Iron Hammer is gone," Merlin told her with a quiver of resignation in his voice. "I'm going through the tunnels just to make sure, but I'm seeing some signs that someone has been here recently."

"Okay, how recently are we talking?" Alex gripped the edge of the counter with her free hand in an attempt to stay calm. "I mean centuries or-"

"Not that long ago, but the tunnel entrance had been filled in with rocks and rubble so I'd say at least fifty years. Maybe less if a local filled it in."

"Would anyone in the area have known what was down there?" Alex was a bit lightheaded as she struggled to control her breathing. "Any local myths?"

"I'm checking into that," Merlin said. "But I will not be returning with the Iron Hammer I'm afraid. You and the others need to return to Ravenslake quickly. Stay near Morgana and keep practicing your magic."

"What are you going to do?" Alex asked frantically, unconcerned with her volume. "Merlin, what is your plan?"

"As I said I will check on the local myths and try to contact the Norse Old Ones and see if they are aware of anything. I suspect that at least one of them is waking up."

"Can we do anything?"

"No, Alex," Merlin said. Bran came to the doorway of the kitchen with a frown. Alex could see Aiden and Nicki behind him looking similarly worried. "Just return to Ravenslake. I'll be in touch. Stay safe."

Then he hung up on her as Alex was trying to come up with an argument. Pulling the phone away from her ear, Alex glared at it. "Wise old advisor my ass," she muttered.

"Alex?" Nicki called, shifting next to her and eyeing the phone. "Bad news?"

"The Iron Hammer is missing," Alex forced out before nervously rolling her lips as her stomach churned and a terrible ache settled into it. "Merlin went to its resting place, but it was gone. Someone took it, he thought in the last fifty years or so," Alex explained in a frantic rush.

Alex leaned against the counter and placed her forehead against the cabinet above. Her knees were shaking and there was a building pressure in her chest that was making it hard to breathe. Sucking in some air, Alex felt a cold sweat trickling down her spine and shuddered as Merlin's words echoed in her head. The Iron Hammer was gone. It was supposed to be safe and hidden and yet it was gone. Maybe Merlin would find it, maybe he wouldn't or maybe Arthur had already beaten them to it despite Merlin's thoughts on the timeline. Or maybe he was just trying to make her feel better.

"I think she's having a panic attack!" Bran hissed just before a pair of arms encircled her waist helping to keep her upright. "Easy, Alex."

"Shit!" Nicki cursed. "What do we do?"

"Bran?" Jinsung's voice called. "Is everything alright in there?" Alex managed to turn her face just enough to see the woman coming into view.

"Mom, please," Bran begged as he shifted between his mother and Alex. "Just give us a few minutes. Alex is just feeling overwhelmed and she doesn't know you well."

"Overwhelmed?" Jinsung repeated with concern. "Bran, what-"

"Just some bad news on classes," Nicki lied. "Give us a second."

She lost track of things as her throat tried to close up once again. Vaguely, Alex was aware of being turned so she was no longer facing the cabinets. Bran's face swam in front of her and Alex blinked her eyes to clear the tears she realized had gathered.

"Easy, Alex." Bran wrapped an arm around her shoulders. "The Sídhe don't have the Iron Hammer."

"How can you be sure of that?" Her lips were so dry they felt ready to crack.

"If the Iron Hammer can truly break the hold of magic, then they would have already tried to use it against the Iron Gates," Bran said. "Instead, Arthur and the Queen focused on Cathanáil."

"Exactly, Alex," Nicki agreed. "I doubt that the Sídhe have it. Merlin said that it's been gone for a while and if they had it then they would have used it to break the Iron Gates by now, right?"

"I suppose so." The words penetrated the panicked haze trying to keep its claws in her. She couldn't imagine Arthur and the Queen not using the Iron Hammer if they had it. "But then where is it?" she demanded as another spike of fear rolled over her.

"Maybe archeologists found it," Bran offered as he extended a glass of water to her. "Or locals found the cave. It might be in someone's barn or in a chest in someone's attic. It's too early to tell, but we need to stay calm."

"That's possible." Nicki squeezed her shoulder. "We found the Chalice after all and even Merlin had gone looking for that artifact."

"And we found a Dragon," Bran added with a smile.

"Just rub it in why don't you," Aiden pouted, giving them all a glare. "Tease the guy who was stuck in a coma."

Alex managed a smile at the words and a soft chuckle escaped her. "If you hadn't been in a coma we wouldn't have gone after the Chalice." She brought the glass to her lips and took a sip of the water. "Okay," Alex said a moment later. "I'm okay." She exhaled slowly and straightened up. "You're probably right. Merlin will find it."

"And even if he doesn't, we know that you and Bran can do the tag team magical item tracking trick," Nicki reminded her.

"Convenient that," Bran said. "Speaking of which, we should see if we can find Cathanáil on the equinox. We've figured out how to work together on that."

"Maybe," was all Alex could offer in reply as her stomach tightened at the idea. The last time she'd teamed up with Bran like that she'd discovered the Iron Chain which had been created from suffering and only added to the power of their enemies. She wasn't sure that she was ready for whatever else she might find in her past. "We'll see what happens with the Iron Hammer first."

"You sure you're okay?" Aiden asked her. "You still don't look so good."

"Yeah, I'm fine, bit embarrassed," Alex assured them with another forced smile. "Just wasn't ready for that. Sorry to worry you."

"Nicki, Aiden," Bran called softly. "You go and reassure Lance, Jenny, and my mom that Alex is okay."

"Should we tell them-"

"No, don't freak my mom out. We'll tell Jenny and Lance later."

Then Bran was moving her away from the counter and to the small breakfast table in the corner of the kitchen. It was right next to a window that looked out into the small yard between the house and the bakery. Looking outside, Alex smiled at the sight of the green grass and the small path made of large flat stones that cut through the yard and led to the back door of the bakery.

"This is a nice house," Alex told him, earning a concerned look in return.

"You didn't hit your head, did you?" Bran asked, sounding like he was only half teasing.

Giving him a look in response, Alex raised the glass again in a silent toast before draining the last of it. The worried and tight expression didn't leave Bran's face and made Alex want to say something, but she couldn't find any words. Instead, she stood up and started moving back towards the door.

"Alex," Bran said in a low voice as he caught her arm. "I know what a panic attack looks like. Mom had enough of them after Dad's death so..." he trailed off and shook his head for a moment. "Look if you want to talk then we're here for you, but really try not to worry. Merlin will find the Iron Hammer and with luck, by spring equinox we'll have struck a literal blow for our side."

Holding in a sigh, Alex tried to adopt the more optimistic views of her friends. They had a point; they'd found the lost Iron Chalice so how hard could it be to find the Iron Hammer? Yet the cold sense of dread in her stomach remained as if someone had camped out on her grave, but Alex still had no idea of the source of the foreboding. Still, she offered Bran a small smile and a nod. Then she headed back into the living room before Jinsung Fisher could become too suspicious.

5

Destination of Dreams

Astench of human waste, sweat, and salt washed over her, crashing down like a tidal wave and making her knees shake. Alex's lungs constricted as revulsion overwhelmed even the need to breathe. Even worse was that she instantly knew where she was. That realization was enough to make her feel physically ill. And yet her body was stiff and completely unaffected by her emotions or physical revulsion. Even as she sought to back away, close her eyes, and cover her nose, Alex remained held in place by a body that was not her own.

She knew what was happening and was powerless to fight against it. The memories had pulled her back in, trapping her inside a terrible nightmare, but she did not have the benefit of Bran's magic to help her take control. Nevertheless, Alex desperately pulled at the flicker of magic she could still feel in her chest. There was a pitiful flare in response instead of the rush of power that she needed. Still, she let it flow through her and tried to order the limbs to obey her. Tried to make herself blink on her own command, but there was nothing.

Beneath her, the wooden floor was shifting up and down. Thankfully her eyes closed a moment later as a large hand came up to rub her eyes as if seeking to banish a headache. She inhaled deeply against her will as the hand dropped back to her side. The stink hit her again along with the confirmation that she was back on the ship. That terrible ship that she'd hoped never to see again in any dream or memory. Before her were racks of wooden shelves built into the sides of the hold. Half hidden in the shadows were hundreds of captive Africans crammed into the tiny spaces between the wooden planks. Long clinking chains bound them all to one long chain running down the center of the hold. Alex could see a soft black shimmer of magic running across the chain. Her stomach tightened at the sight. That magic was binding the... slaves to the will of their master, to the captain of the ship. Her previous, horrible life that Alex wished she could forget.

"Captain Allard," a voice called before the ship jolted sharply. "The storm-"

"I know!" Alex's lips moved but a much deeper voice came forth.

She turned without any control over the body and began to lurch up the small stairs leading from the hold. The sky above was dark and stormy with flashes of lightning illuminating the horizon. She hauled herself up onto the deck as members of the crew shifted back as if there was a dark aura around her that they dared not touch. Fear hung in the air around them and whatever relief Alex felt about being out of the hold was almost eclipsed by the discomfort those looks created. They didn't linger around her and resumed their rush to secure the ship's rigging and brace for the storm around them.

Lightning flashed as she strode across the slippery deck. The ship churned on the ocean, but her body didn't stop moving. Cuthbert Allard just kept moving confidently as if he expected the world to just bow to his whims. Anger and shame warred in Alex as her too large hand griped the rail of the stairs. He hauled himself up towards the helm where two sailors were holding tight to the wheel and keeping watch.

She-he- they did not stop moving. Alex was uncertain of how to think of Captain Cuthbert Allard while caught in his memories. Nothing in her life had prepared her for the knowledge or the burden of reincarnation. She was pulled back to the matter at hand as Allard pulled open the door to his cabin and stomped inside to escape the storm. They shrugged out of their dripping coat as another roll of thunder echoed beyond the window on the far side of the small room.

Sitting down at the desk, a large masculine hand reached for a cabinet stuffed in a corner below the chair. They pulled out a bottle with a heavy cork that the captain opened easily. The liquor burned her throat on the way down even as Alex felt an alien rush of satisfaction that she knew wasn't her own. Then they leaned back in the uncomfortable chair with a satisfied sigh that made Alex want to strike out to hit something, preferably Allard's face even if she would share the pain.

His eyes slid closed leaving Alex in darkness, but she could still hear the storm churning outside and wondered how the man could be so calm. She could hear the sailors, but a strange calm seemed to have fallen over the ship leaving Alex feeling uneasy. An odd wave of exhaustion rolled over her despite her racing mind and Alex was being pulled under like a strong wave had a hold of her.

The sting of the wind on her cheeks pulled her back sharply, but not to a familiar scene. Weapons, pots, and tools were sailing through the air, a fierce wind howling as magic pulsed around her. There were shouts and screams. She was at a loss for what was happening. The smell of salt had been replaced with smoke. Alex began to look around in surprise and confusion only to find a strangely familiar landscape with rocky hillsides before her. Then a sharp burning in her side forced the air from her lungs and her whole body trembled.

"I'm actually sorry that your wife ran off and left you," a familiar voice said, the words almost lost in the wind and the haze of pain.

A hand moved to her side and she felt coarse fabric now moistened with a warm liquid that seeped out over her fingers. The sense of familiarity became sharp as a knife and for an instant, Alex thought she might be back on the lakeside. But she wasn't, this was someplace and sometime else. That thought frantically clawed its way past the rising panic, reassuring her that this had to be another dream and she'd be alright when it was over.

Turning her head, Alex found a man with long dark hair bound up in a knot. Dark eyes stared at her while the lips curled into a smirk. Alex could do nothing but stare at him even as his mouth kept moving. The words were lost on her as the agony in her side spread further and further through her body.

"Medraut?" The name escaped her lips without a thought except the voice was not her own.

Medraut kept talking, but Alex was unable to fully grasp the words. The pain in her side and the glimmer of magic across the ground around her was too distracting. Her mind raced to catch up. If this was Medraut then this was a memory of Arto, the first Iron Soul. As Medraut was speaking, Alex was studying the arrogant smirking man before them. His features were different from Arthur's. That was to be expected. Arthur would have nothing in common genetically with his prior life. And yet Alex could clearly see him looking back at her. Those brown eyes were strangely similar to Arthur's blue ones when he'd been gloating above her. Perhaps just as Jenny and Lance had been caught in repeating events there was a part of Medraut in Arthur that just couldn't help himself.

Then Medraut turned away and bent to pick up a sword discarded on the ground. Alex recognized it. Medraut's fingers brushed over

Cathanáil's hilt and white magic burst forth from the blade, striking Medraut. He was thrown back with a shriek of pain as the magic covered him with lightning. When he didn't move, Alex hoped he was dead even as their body convulsed in pain.

Blood trickled from her side, but she didn't stop moving. Everything was aching and cold. It took her right back to that lakeside when Arthur had stabbed her with Cathanáil. Swallowing, she desperately fought back the strange thirst that was overtaking even the pain as her blood trickled away.

"Luegáed." Blood trickled from her mouth and tears spilled down her face. "I needed you here." The world was growing hazy. Fear punched Alex in the chest. What would happen if she was connected to Arto like this when he died? "Gwenyvar..."

Suddenly the pain eased and magic rolled over her, tugging her sharply from Arto. It was like falling. Alex had just enough time to realize that before her lungs constricted and she sucked in a greedy breath. Her eyes snapped open and Alex found herself looking at an unfamiliar wall. Alex stared at a small spot where the paint was wearing thin as her eyes adjusted to the darkness. There was some faint light from a window somewhere, but she was at a loss for where she was. She was thirsty still, but it wasn't the consuming thirst of losing blood. Her hand went to her stomach and then her side, tracing over the warm uncut flesh beneath her shirt.

"Alex?" Jenny's voice suddenly called to her. "Are you okay?"

A light was turned on, illuminating the wall and making the bad patch of paint less obvious. Alex remained still even as a tentative hand was placed on her shoulder. She forced her body to relax before turning towards the voice. Jenny was leaning over her with a worried frown and for a terrible moment, her features were replaced by those of another woman, the one she had been a very long time ago.

"Where are we?" Alex started to sit up, realizing that she was on a couch.

"Bran's house," Jenny said gently. "In the basement. You fell asleep on the couch and his mother wouldn't hear of us waking you. Lance brought you downstairs."

"Oh," Alex muttered, swinging her bare feet off the sofa. She knocked her feet against her shoes that were waiting on the floor. Nicki stepped into her view, coming to stand beside Jenny. "What time is it?"

"Late afternoon," Nicki answered. "We were talking about if we should just stay the night here."

"You should have woken me," Alex grumbled. "Let's get going." She began to stand up only to have Nicki catch her shoulder.

"Hold on," Nicki ordered. She gave Alex a suspicious look. "Alex... we came downstairs because we heard you talking."

"Really?" Alex asked uneasily as she flashed back to the nightmare. "Anything interesting?"

"Yes actually," Nicki replied with a hint of irritation. "You were speaking what sounded like that language Morgana and Merlin speak sometimes. You know the one that is probably ancient proto-Gaelic."

"Oh." Alex scrambled for something to say or do to make them stop looking at her like that. Nicki's frown deepened and the redhead nodded a bit to herself. "What are you doing?" Alex asked as Nicki pulled out her phone with an intense expression.

"Calling Morgana," Nicki answered before Alex could protest.

Forcing herself off the couch, she made a grab for the phone, but her body seemed too light and she began to tumble. Jenny caught her with a soft gasp of alarm and dragged her backward from Nicki who was looking at her with wide eyes. They fell back onto the couch and Alex struggled for only a moment, discovering that despite Jenny being several inches shorter than her, she was very strong.

"Alex!" Jenny scolded. "That isn't normal and you know it!"

"There's enough to worry about," Alex grumbled, trying to twist away from Jenny.

"Sit on her," Nicki commanded, looking torn between irritation and amusement. "Hi, Morgana. It's Nicki." There was a pause and Alex made one last attempt to reach the phone before her churning emotions gave up fueling her. She collapsed back against Jenny who shifted around her and did as Nicki suggested, sitting down on her lap sideways to keep her pinned.

"That wasn't necessary." Alex groaned, falling back against the couch cushions.

"No, that's okay," Nicki said in reply to something Morgana had told her. "The reason I'm calling is because Alex started speaking what sounded like that language you and Merlin use sometimes. She was asleep."

Alex remained still and silent, straining her ears in an attempt to hear Morgana's reply. Her heart was pounding and the noise of her own blood pumping was too loud in her ears. A moment later Nicki shifted the phone away from her ear and tapped the screen.

"Alex?" Morgana's voice called out on the speaker, sounding half frantic. "Are you alright?"

"Other than the fact that Jenny is sitting on me I'm fine."

"I'm just going to ignore your attempt to distract me-"

"No, she really is sitting on me," Alex insisted earning her a dark look from Jenny.

"Alex, what were you dreaming about?"

"Does it matter? I was just reliving a memory, I suppose and was talking in my sleep. That's probably a normal reincarnation thing."

"That hasn't happened with the other Iron Soul lives." There was something in Morgana's voice that Alex couldn't read. She hated not being able to see Morgana. "What was it, Alex?"

Alex hesitated. Arto, the first Iron Soul, had been the beloved little brother of Morgana. She'd loved him so much that it had cut through the years of programming she'd undergone as a captive of the Sídhe. Telling her that she'd been reliving what was probably the day Medraut killed Arto was a bit much.

"The making of the last Iron Gate I think," she finally settled upon. "I saw Arthur, I mean Medraut."

"Both names are accurate I suppose," Morgana answered softly. "Alex, are you alright? Truly? Those events can't have been easy to see. Especially not in light of what Arthur-"

"It was just a nightmare!" Alex was too aware of how pale Jenny had suddenly gotten. "It may not have been a true memory, Morgana," she said. "It may have been just a nightmare bringing together everything that's happened."

"She had a panic attack earlier when Merlin called to tell her the Iron Hammer was missing," Nicki said. She met Alex's angry gaze calmly. "Had trouble breathing and almost fell over."

Alex wanted to argue, but the fight drained out of her as Jenny turned her sad brown eyes towards her. Alex let her eyes fall closed and tried to push the uncomfortable thoughts away. There was a hum under her skin that was disquieting and her mouth tightened like she was going to be sick.

"Don't hurry back to Ravenslake," Morgana told them. "Take a few days, return to Portland and enjoy some of the sights. You are on spring break."

"But-"

"Alex, there is nothing to be done here," Morgana said calmly. "Timothy is doing very well and whatever wish you bound into the blood spell seems to still be keeping it from harming him."

"Are you enjoying having a Brownie?" Nicki asked with false cheer.

"Not really," Morgana answered with a soft chuckle. "I'm a bit uncomfortable around him, to be honest, but I am convinced of his well-meaning nature. I'd have no objections to him living with you as I believe that is his wish. He seems very much under the impression that he owes Alex his life."

"Except it was my magical chain that bound him to the Queen in the first place."

"It was not your Chain, Alex," Morgana insisted sharply. Alex could feel Nicki's eyes boring into her. She kept her eyes closed and stayed still. "I'm very serious, Alex," Morgana said. "Try to relax, spend some time with your friends. For a moment try to be a college student on spring break. These dreams are likely being brought on by stress and you using magic subconsciously. Try not to worry and relax a little."

"Yeah," Alex heard herself reply in a voice full of surrender. "Okay, maybe that's a good idea."

Jenny made a small sound of relief and Alex sighed softly, trying to ignore the continued conversation between Nicki and Morgana. The sound of her previous sister's voice washed over her even as the meaning of what she was saying was lost. It was oddly comforting. Her eyelids grew heavy again but she fought off the urge to sleep. She wasn't ready to find out when, where, and who she'd end up this time.

6

An Odd Gathering

16 C.E. Sør-Trøndelag, Norway

At some point, this small glade had become their place of council. Thor wasn't sure how or when that been decided, but none of the parties seemed to wish opening their homes to the others. Over his head, a wind rustled the leaves of the trees and disturbed the spot of shade he had retreated into. The summer sun was hot on his back and he moved further into the trees.

"Sit down, Thor," Merlin called to him with a chuckle. "They will be here soon."

Thor turned around to find Merlin resting amongst the roots of a tree that had valiantly grown around a large rock. Morgana was perched on the top of the rock with her green eyes scanning the forest carefully. Thor glanced towards their fourth member, Brokkr who was paying the rest of them no mind. They were an odd company to be sure. Merlin and Morgana were mages who were far older than they looked. While Merlin's curly hair was gray and he had soft wrinkles about his eyes, he was much older than he seemed and Morgana with her long dark hair and minimal frown lines looked younger than his own father. Both of them wore long cloaks with small amulets hanging around their necks.

Brokkr was a strange creature from another world who was suddenly their guest and ally though Thor was still a bit unsure what to make of him. The Dvergr was a little under five feet tall with earthy skin that carried a faint green hue. His eyes were dark and sunken in comparison to a human's. Wrinkles were spread across his face yet Thor had the distinct impression that he was not elderly. Wild black hair that faded to brown at the tips framed his face and a long beard was secured into his belt. He was seated off to the side with a newly forged axe in hand and was carefully sharpening the long, curved cutting edge. Thor admired the weapon for a moment. It was plain, but the workmanship was excellent.

Holding back a sigh of boredom, Thor shifted to the right and leaned against a tree standing firmly in the shade. He closed his eyes for a moment and told himself to enjoy the silence. Thor focused on the rustling of the leaves and compared it to the sound of the ocean, but found his fingers tapping against the bark of the tree. He was saved from his boredom or a lecture from Morgana by the snapping of a stick to their right.

He turned quickly to find several figures moving in on their position. His hand was dropping to his Hammer before he caught up with what he was seeing. These figures were familiar and Thor relaxed, lazily dropping his arm on his Hammer. A large figure in gray moved out into the glen, joining them in the cool shade of the trees. Pulling back his hood, he revealed an older face that still shone with energy and long gray hair that was tied back neatly in a braid. His left eyelid drooped a little into the empty socket that Thor longed to ask about, wondering if the story of the Well of Wisdom was true. In the branches above two ravens landed and cawed loudly in greeting. Two more figures emerged: one tall and strongly built and the other shorter and slighter. Thor instantly turned his attention to the smaller figure.

Thor smiled when Sif took her place beside Odin. Her long golden hair was flowing over her shoulders with small braids framing her face. As always there was a soft glow around her that Thor knew must be connected to her magical nature, but seemed so much... more than the aura that surrounded her father Odin or her brother Baldr. She was beautiful as always and he felt a soft flush overtaking his cheeks as she met his eyes with her startling green ones. They glistened and he fought down a foolish grin, grateful that his brother did not attend these meetings.

They came closer, Odin nodding in greeting to all four of them. His good eye lingered on Brokkr for a moment, but the Dvergr ignored the attention. Soon enough the Old Ones that Thor had grown up revering as gods were beside them. Sif was the only one who he hadn't known and who didn't inspire an instinct to bow. Thor tried not to shift uneasily next to Baldr, but the tall being made him feel a bit small. He was tall with the same bright golden hair as his sister which made his own bleached hair look dingy. Though to be fair, his red hair was beginning to show. Sif offered him a kind smile as her cheeks colored just enough to fill him with excitement. Baldr then caught his eye and rather than looking irritated the Old One simply looked amused. Thor was at a loss for how to take that.

"How are you?" Merlin offered in greeting.

"We are well. As is the rest of our family," Odin replied. Thor looked curiously at them, wondering how many of them there were. He'd heard stories, but he couldn't help but want more details. "Sadly, we have little news to offer. The Dark Elves have been keeping to their underground tunnels since our last encounter."

"Indeed," a soft chiming voice declared, making them all turn.

Another figure, this one in a dark blue cloak moved through the trees with silent steps. He quickly identified the figure despite her hood shadowing her face and relaxed.

"Greetings to you, Frea," Sif called pleasantly.

"Greeting to you, Sif," Frea returned politely as she joined them, lifting her head a bit.

Thor almost chuckled as he watched Frea linger in the shade of the trees next to Sif. A person might look at Sif and mistake her for a mortal though she was a bit too beautiful. Frea was another matter entirely. She was tall, slight, and fair, but while Sif made him think of the sun, Frea made him think of the moon. Frea's skin was pale and translucent, catching the small amount of light reaching her face in odd ways. Large violet eyes met his and she offered him a deep nod which caused some of her pale hair to spill out from beneath her hood. She quickly pushed it back under the hood and pulled it further over her face to keep the sun from her eyes. It also hid the small nubs of horns that she had from sight.

"Those things have longer horns," Brokkr said as he studied Frea without any concern for her discomfort, even as her hand shifted towards the sword hanging at her side. "You're a bit different. Thor said you were related to them."

"Indeed, over the last few generations, our horns have gotten shorter and shorter. I suspect that they will vanish within a few more," Frea replied. "It separates us from the beings still residing in Sídhean."

"I had not properly noticed that." Merlin studied Frea with renewed interest and less hostility than he had in the past.

"I assure you, good Dvergr, that my people are not associated with the Dark Elves who captured you," Frea said quickly, straightening up and fighting to regain her composure. "We are just as determined to see them driven back."

"I don't think driving them back is an option, missy," Brokkr informed her with a laugh, seeming far more amused by her statement than relieved. "They seem interested in taking their home realm." He paused and shook his head. "But in the meantime, they mean bad things for this world and my kin."

"Has anything new been discovered as to how you came to be here?" Sif asked. She shifted a little away from her father and brother, moving closer to Thor who smiled. "Any more portals?"

"Nothing as of yet," Morgana answered for Brokkr. "We haven't been able to find where he and his fellows fell through or confirm how it opened."

"We still believe that it is tied to the Sídhe breaking through the Iron Gates," Merlin added. "While not in this area, their magic extends across the world and grants it protection. Whatever the Sídhe did to... circumvent that protection backfired on them and seems to have torn connections between worlds that otherwise do not connect."

"Have you ever seen anything like that before?" Odin asked, running a hand over his beard thoughtfully.

Morgana and Merlin exchanged a glance that Thor could not properly read. Then Merlin shook his head. "There were rumors, but we have never been able to confirm such a thing. However, I believe that these holes seal up quickly as we have not located them, possibly from the magic of our world trying to protect the Iron Realm from even more outsiders."

"Well, from what I've seen it seems that your inner worlds have more magic." Brokkr shrugged as he kept inspecting the metal of the axe he'd been working on. "More life too. There are so many creatures everywhere in your world." He beamed at Thor, revealing his sharp teeth. "Good for eating."

"Many of them are yes," he tentatively agreed.

A look of discomfort bordering on disgust crossed Sif's face but vanished quickly. Frea tilted her head in a gesture that was half nod and half consideration. Thor kept silent, unable to say much on the subject as his people kept domesticated animals and hunted in the surrounding area.

"I'd suggest you keep your distance from Huginn and Muninn," Odin told Brokkr with a chuckle. "They are clever things and I don't think you'd find it worth the trouble."

Brokkr looked up towards the birds in consideration. He must have seen something in Odin's words because he nodded and turned his attention back to the others. There was a strange surprised silence over the group for a long moment which was broken by a weak chuckle from Sif. Thor caught her eye and barely contained his own laugh. An odd group indeed.

"Does anyone have anything new to report?" Merlin asked to shift them back to the more serious matter at hand.

"My scouts haven't seen any Dark Elves leave the caverns for several days," Frea said as she tightened her cloak around herself. "There has been no movement at the tunnel entrance you collapsed, no sign of anything being shifted. We've patrolled the area, but haven't found any other entrances as of yet."

"They may be trapped or they may be getting more cautious," Morgana said with a frown. "I wonder if there is any chance of them just starving to death down there." That remark earned her an irritated look from Brokkr, but he said nothing.

"There is too much we do not know." Odin shook his head. "Brokkr has been able to provide us with some basic information on the tunnels, but too much remains a mystery."

"The journey into our world changed them, but we don't know if they will keep changing," Morgana added as she twisted her fingers together. "We can't just wait and see. We need to address the threat. Who knows what they are turning into down there?"

"And what of the Sídhe and these tunnels?" Baldr asked. "Can we expect more of these creatures to come forth?"

"We can hope that the Sídhe are aware of the danger now and will not seek to enter the Iron Realm any longer," Sif said. She blushed slightly when the others turned their attention towards her.

"I doubt that." Merlin shook his head with darkening eyes. "Their rulers are petty and vicious things."

"Agreed," Morgana said. "They might fear these corrupted Sídhe, but it is also a good way of destroying rivals for power."

"Are they truly so vicious?" Sif asked and Thor found himself wondering the same thing. It all seemed a bit too much.

"The Sídhe... they are a race that has embraced the enslavement of others," Morgana said. Her tone was sharp and final. "They do horrible things to those they take. I will not burden you with the details, but the fates of those taken during the War were terrible and there was no escape."

An uneasy silence engulfed the group and Thor eyed Morgana carefully. He wasn't sure where that statement had come from, but it sent a shudder down his back. It was probably something Arto had known, he reflected with a spark of irritation.

"At least we have the advantage of sunlight over the Dark Elves." Merlin drummed his fingers together. "Though they are aware of that now and will be more cautious," he said.

"We may need to consider a major action against them," Odin told them all sternly. "With our combined power we could bring that mountain down."

"Right on the heads of my kin!" Brokkr shouted. He leapt to his feet, gripping his axe, and glaring at Odin.

"And we might not get them all, Father," Sif said, reaching over to touch Odin's arm. "That is a hasty action and not one to rush to. The mountain is their domain and we should assume they have fortified it by this point. Not to mention its destruction would also harm Thor's people."

"We cannot wait forever," Morgana said, looking straight at Brokkr. "They may be changing down there. They may be starving and already eating your kin, Brokkr. They may already have new tunnels to the surface and are hiding from us. They may have reconnected with Sídhean and are increasing their numbers!"

"What do you propose then, Morgana?" Odin asked, looking at her with a small frown.

"We reopen the tunnel together, and pour as much magic down there as we can. We find out what is happening and address it. The longer we wait the worse things may be becoming."

"And if we find them dying?" Merlin raised an eyebrow slightly.

"Then we reseal the tunnel and leave them to die," she said. "We cannot risk leaving them alone and them turning it to their advantage. Our ignorance might be the opportunity they need and surely a force of us together would prevent them from escaping. We go during the day so escape onto the surface isn't possible and push on until we know what we are dealing with."

Thor glanced towards Sif who had a small frown marring her features. He wanted to say something clever and propose a new and better plan.

The problem was that they knew too little. Even he recognized that. Beneath his feet, Thor could feel a soft hum that he'd come to associate with magic and yet there was something strange about it. Something just a little bit off. He couldn't explain it and didn't like it, but as he focused on that odd feeling Thor had to admit that Morgana might be correct about not leaving the Dark Elves alone for too long.

7

Interlude in Portland

Alex didn't have anything against Portland. She was just already wishing that Nicki and Jenny hadn't been so fast to agree with Morgana and tell the boys. Nicki was in the driver seat and following Lance's truck at a safe distance as they navigated into a nice quiet looking neighborhood. Some kids were out playing in a small park and partially in the street forcing them to slow down. Alex felt an itch of irritation.

"Stop sighing, Alex," Nicki scolded. She turned her head just enough to give Alex a warning look. "Lance is totally allowed to want to see his family."

"Yeah," Jenny agreed from the back seat though there was a nervous quiver in her voice. "You'll be able to look through your books soon enough."

Alex made a small sound of agreement but didn't say anything as she shifted her feet. They hit the large paper bag of books beneath her and there was an odd flare of excitement and resignation in her chest.

"How are you?" Nicki asked. "Are you nervous, Jenny?"

"I'm not sure I'll be introduced as his girlfriend," Jenny answered, slightly out of breath.

Alex straightened up and turned in her seat to offer Jenny a soft smile. The other young woman returned the smile uneasily, her hands tugging at the hem of her long aqua green shirt.

"I hadn't thought about that," Alex admitted apologetically. "This is your first-time meeting Lance's family."

"Lance said we're just going to stop in for a few hours." Jenny forced a laugh, but her nervousness was still clear. "This really isn't the time to introduce me as his girlfriend."

"Yeah, but even only meeting them as a friend he's on a short road trip with, you'll still want to make a good impression," Nicki said. "Anyone know what Lance told them?"

"Not sure." Alex turned to face the front and watched the back of Lance's truck once more. She could see the outline of the three boys inside, moving around slightly and wondered what they were talking about. "We'll have to figure out if we're telling them we're staying locally."

"And if we really are," Jenny added. "Or if Alex is going to demand heading back to Ravenslake tomorrow."

Alex pouted a little and looked back at Jenny, but couldn't be too angry as she observed the spark of amusement in Jenny's brown eyes. Next to her, Nicki chuckled a bit and glanced her way knowingly.

"Morgana wants me to take a vacation," Alex said, tapping her fingers on the door. "I can give it a shot."

"That's the spirit," Nicki cheered. "Lots to do in Portland: great music scene, Oregon Museum of Science and Industry, Portland Art Museum, and an IMAX theater."

"You sound like a commercial," Alex informed her, fighting back a smile.

"I'm just saying that if nothing attacks us and we don't get summoned back to Ravenslake, we should be able to have a decent Spring Break," Nicki said. "It isn't Cancun or anything, but it'll work."

Lance's truck turned onto a short dead-end street that opened into a cul-de-sac of suburban homes. They were all rather alike: two stories, pastel or white paint, sloping rooflines over gable windows and neat yards with small white fences around them. Yet the one he stopped in front of stood out with cheerful yellow trim and a raised herb garden beneath the front windows.

"Oh boy," Jenny groaned in the seat behind her.

Alex couldn't help but smile. "Relax," she said. Reaching back, she offered Jenny her hand for a quick squeeze. "One, this isn't an official meet my girlfriend visit and two, they'll love you when the time comes."

"Maybe," Jenny murmured as Nicki pulled the car into the driveway behind Lance's truck. "As long as they never learn the whole story."

"Jenny, honey," Nicki laughed. "They'd never believe the whole story."

"Don't worry about it," Alex said. "You and Lance are working it out and that's what matters, no matter how it all turns out."

"You are such an understanding ex-husband," Nicki teased. She unbuckled her seatbelt and leapt out of the parked car before Alex could hit her.

"Jenny." Alex unbuckled her own seatbelt and twisted to look back at her friend. "Ignore Nicki. Just ignore everything she says."

That remark got a small smile from Jenny. Alex watched her check her long wavy hair one more time before she reached for the door handle. Holding back a sigh, Alex glanced down at the bag of books and wondered if it would be horribly rude to bring them in. She just wanted to start the research, but this was important to Lance. Alex reached down and fished out one of the books to shove into her shoulder bag before climbing out of the car.

"Nice place." Aiden's eyes scanned the house as everyone gathered by the front door.

Alex's eyes landed on a pile of dirty shoes by the front door and a pair of bikes leaned up on the side of the garage. Lance must have noticed because an affectionate chuckle escaped him. "I've got two younger siblings," Lance said with a glowing smile. "Chris is six years younger than me and Kelly is eight years younger. They're in that early teenager stage, but I swear they're good kids."

Alex nodded; she was pretty sure that Lance had told her that before but couldn't remember any details. Then again many of her early 'getting to know you' conversations had been around Arthur. It was hard to admit, but she could, that back then she hadn't paid much attention to anyone other than the handsome blond man with the great smile. She shook her head as the brief memory of his smile morphed into the crueler one she'd come to know.

"Early teens huh." Jenny chuckled nervously beside her as Alex forced herself to pay attention. "That's got to be fun."

"Well, I do find myself missing the times when all they wanted was to talk my ear off about their toys," Lance admitted with a nostalgic sigh.

"I know what you mean," Aiden said, clapping his hand on Lance's shoulder as they moved up the walk.

"Aisling is awesome," Nicki protested.

"Yeah, she is, but you can't argue that she wasn't easier to deal with before the pop music and boys stage."

Nicki grumbled lightly but didn't argue which just made Aiden's smile widen.

"Dad's probably home," Lance informed them as he dug out his keys. "He works from home part-time."

"Oh, what does he do?" Jenny asked, twisting her hands nervously once again. "You've never said."

"He does freelance website design. He loves it and it lets him be at home."

"So, your dad was the stay-at-home parent?" Aiden asked, blinking in surprise before he grinned. "Awesome!"

"A bit yeah," Lance said. "Though when he and Mom first married, he worked full time. He didn't switch to part-time until Chris was born." Lance shrugged as he put the key into the lock and twisted it open.

Alex found herself holding her breath and standing straighter. She was braced for something, this meeting was important, but she was suddenly uncertain as to why. Frowning at herself, Alex relaxed her shoulders and eased her almost military rest position. She didn't understand her own reaction. Sure, meeting Lance's family was important and it was better for everyone to make a good first impression, but it wasn't that serious. Confused, Alex shrugged it off and focused on the house as Lance led them inside.

The entryway was very clean for a house with teenagers with a woven rug in front of the door that was slightly faded from the sun coming through the windows. There was an old-fashioned wooden hat stand filled with coats, a couple hats, and scarves in the corner next to the door. A staircase in front of them led up to the second floor with a small hallway alongside it leading towards the back of the house. The large archway to their left opened into a spacious living room. To the right was a large room with a long wooden dining room table that led into the kitchen. Sunlight was streaming through a long row of windows, bathing the house's wooden floors in a warm glow. It was different from her own home, but there was a sense of peace in the place that helped Alex relax a little.

"Dad?" Lance called, moving further into the house and leaning over to look into the living room. There must not have been anyone because he walked across the entry hall and looked into the dining room.

"Lance?" a deep voice called up from what seemed to be below them. "That you?"

"Yeah, it's me. I brought some friends too," Lance shouted back, heading down the hallway by the stairs.

There were footfalls from beyond the staircase and a moment later a beaming man dressed in jeans and a faded concert t-shirt appeared. Lance's father was even taller than Lance with bright brown eyes that swept over them. His look of confusion morphed from surprise to genuine pleasure at the sight of Lance. Alex watched as he laughed and grabbed Lance in a hug. Aside from them sharing African descent, Alex couldn't see any features in common. Lance's father's eyes were a lighter shade, his skin was darker and they had different noses and different jawlines. It took her an embarrassingly long time to remember that this was Lance's step-father.

"Lance! This is a surprise, a welcome one, but a surprise."

"Sorry about that, Dad," Lance apologized with just the right blend of apologetic and amused. "My friends and I are on a short road trip around the region and thought we'd stop by."

"Well, you're very welcome. I'm afraid your mom is working late tonight, Chris and Kelly are out with friends, but should be back soon."

"We're not in a hurry," Nicki assured him with a smile.

"Ah, you must be Nicki." He chuckled before looking at them all in turn. "Uh let's see Bran?" he asked as he pointed to Bran who nodded. "Aiden and Alex," he said as he pointed to them. "And Jenny."

He said her name completely calmly though there was a spark of interest in his eye that hinted that Lance might have told his dad a bit about their complicated relationship. She hoped for Jenny's sake that he hadn't gone into too much detail.

"Nice to meet you," Jenny answered in a voice that went higher than usual.

"And it's nice to meet all of you," Mr. Taylor said. "I hope you've had a safe trip so far."

"We have," Alex agreed. "Thank you, Eab-" Alex began to thank him only to stop suddenly when she heard the wrong name coming from her mouth. "Thanks, Mr. Taylor."

"Not a problem." Lance's step-father smiled warmly. "It's nice to have a chance to meet Lance's friends." His smile became slightly comforting like he was trying to calm a wounded animal. "And you can call me Peter. I'm glad you kids stopped by." He gestured vaguely over his shoulder towards the back of the house. "We were going to barbeque and you're welcome to stay."

"Sounds great, Dad," Lance replied with a nod. "Thanks!"

Alex vaguely listened to the conversation between Lance and his father. There were questions about their plans, but Alex was barely aware of them. She allowed the others to move ahead of her as they began a quick tour of the house. Not trusting herself to speak, she stayed silent and struggled to hold back a tingling chilled sensation that was creeping up her spine. Finally, they finished the tour of the house which ended with Bran and Aiden teasing Lance about some poster in his room. Alex slipped away from the group to breathe.

She found her way back into the living room and shuddered, trying to shake off the odd sensation of dread plaguing her. The voices of the others in the kitchen were irritating rather than soothing and Alex swallowed a rush of bile. Sitting down on the couch, Alex relished the moments of silence. She was very aware of how rude she was being and how awkward this would make things for Lance, but she couldn't just—Alex shook her head.

Something was wrong. Eaban: that had been the name she'd tried to say. Alex slowly mouthed the name, careful not to say it out loud. It rolled off her tongue easily despite Alex being certain that she'd never used that name before. Of course, how was she so certain that it was a name at all? It was a bit similar to Ethan she supposed, but that wasn't the name of Lance's step-father. She had a bad feeling that she knew the real source of the name.

Luegáed's father must have been Eaban. The name of Lance's father in the other life. First, she'd had that dream and been speaking in what was probably the ancient Gaelic tongue and now this. A shiver went through Alex as she pulled out the book on Norse mythology. It was an older book and was frayed at the edges of the old hardcover. As a used book they'd gotten it for only a few dollars, but Alex hoped it would prove more valuable in helping her understand just who Thor had been and that maybe it would distract her.

"There you are." Nicki strode into the living room with the bag of books in hand making Alex jump. The others were right behind her. "We told Lance and Peter that we'd give them a little time. He seemed a bit embarrassed but pleased."

"Oh," Alex managed. Nicki sat down on the sofa next to her and Bran sank into an armchair.

"You okay?" Nicki asked in a softer voice as Aiden sat down on her other side.

"Fine," Alex replied with a nod. "Just wanted to start reading." She held up the book in her hand.

Nicki gave her a searching look and Alex glanced towards the others to find similar expressions on their faces. She noted that Jenny was absent and wondered if she was still with Lance and Peter, but didn't trust herself to ask. The last thing she needed was to call Jenny Gwenyvar.

"Okay, so Norse mythology this time," Nicki muttered as she picked up the first of the books they'd bought. "It's so sad. I was in one of the biggest bookstores in the world and I could only shop one section."

"We'll go back," Alex promised though she was already flipping through the heavy used book of Norse stories.

"I'm not sure we'll find anything to explain the Hammer's current whereabouts," Bran told Alex, his voice carefully gentle as if he was worried she'd snap at him.

"I know," Alex admitted with a sigh. "But I just want to familiarize myself with the information. From the little I know, it seems like that it is probably the life where the myths are the most accurate. I just need to know some basics."

She looked down and started to read, fully aware that the others were exchanging worried glances over the top of her head. Biting the tip of her tongue, Alex fought down another shiver and focused on the words. They blurred slightly and she closed her eyes for a moment to fight back the unbidden tears. First the... panic attack and now trying to cry for no good reason. Alex wanted to scream at someone, what was going on. Was this a side effect of the reincarnation thing? Was it a bad thing that she'd connected to her other lives or was this something that happened which Morgana just hadn't warned her about yet? It was confusing, frustrating and the knot in her stomach was getting worse. Something had changed and now there was something wrong with her.

8

Waking a Goddess

Frustration was a familiar companion to Merlin, but never a welcome one. At almost three thousand years old he'd been confronted with many circumstances that angered him and left him feeling helpless. His long-standing decision to interfere as little as possible in politics or religion outside of the lifetimes of the Iron Soul often made him grumble to himself when he disliked the current leaders or despaired over the ability of normal humans to remember history. This frustration, the sort that came from ignorance was the worst. He didn't have to feel it often, but it seemed that since the newest generation of mages had arisen that he'd been feeling it more than he had in the last century.

He pushed the thoughts away, unsure of what to do with them now. When he found the Iron Hammer and returned to Ravenslake he could sit down with Morgana and a cup of tea and have a long overdue chat. One of those uncomfortable times to lay everything bare to each other was coming up quickly, he could feel it.

The terrain dipped before him, forming a small basin among the ridges. A small lake or perhaps a large pond filled the lowest area. He hesitated for a moment, reminding himself that she might not even be sleeping here anymore. Yet he forced himself to keep walking and followed a small trail down to the edge of the water.

Merlin paused in front of the small lake, his hand tightening around his walking stick. The water was calm with only the slightest ripple on the surface from the small trickle of water feeding it and the wind. His eyes searched the water though he knew it was silly. The Old Ones were beings made up of energy and that energy spread out while they slept. There was nothing to see in the water until she woke.

Raising his left hand in front of him, Merlin tightened it into a fist and exhaled slowly. He pulled on the familiar spark of magic. The power of the Iron Realm rushed through him, being fed by the ground below his feet and the air all around him. There was another moment of hesitation. Perhaps he should wait and return to Ravenslake. Alex and Bran had been able to locate the Iron Chalice and perhaps they could find the Iron Hammer. Then again, the skull of Bran's prior life had been with the Chalice to make certain they'd find it.

"Blast the magic keeping these things hidden," Merlin grumbled to himself.

He opened his hand and let the magic rush out across the water. The green sparks formed a mist above the surface of the lake and then slowly sank into the water, sending tiny ripples across it. Stepping back, Merlin tried not to shift as he waited, but it was difficult. Minutes ticked by without any sign of Sif and Merlin licked his lips as his nerves began to fray.

Just when he was debating turning around and leaving, backtracking to see if he had come to the wrong spot, the surface of the water began to shimmer anew. There was no rush of water and for that Merlin was grateful. Sif and others of her kind merely slept in the waters of the world to keep themselves pure, none had bonded themselves with it as completely as Cyrridven. Merlin's chest tightened at the memory of his mentor, wishing that he'd had a chance to speak with her and thank her. He'd never thanked her enough, but he supposed that was normal.

Sif's form did not rise from the lake, but rather tiny pricks of light appeared on the surface as if they had bubbled up from below. They glittered for a moment and then swirled into the air. Like flakes of metal drawn to a magnet they all gathered above the water. Merlin watched with detachment as a female form began to take shape. The lights dimmed and colors appeared as Sif's long golden hair solidified.

She was unchanged. Sif's long hair was in a braid that hung over one shoulder and she was dressed in a simple white gown with a small golden circlet around her head. There was a glow about her that marked her as something distinct. Her skin was rosy but lacked the darker bronze hue of Cyrridven or the absolute black of Chernobog's. She almost looked human and was regarding him with surprise.

"Merlin?" she greeted as her eyes scanned the area around him. "I- it is good to see you," she said. "I'm surprised to see you," Sif admitted a moment later. "Are you well?"

"I am," Merlin replied with a nod. "Morgana is not with me, but she is in good health."

"That's good."

"Thor's Hammer is missing," he announced, forcing himself to get it over with. "I'm hoping that you took it."

Sif's pale face would have reddened with anger if she'd been human. Her green eyes widened only to narrow at him a moment later as her lips pressed together. Merlin stepped back instinctively, wondering if he was about to see the temper that Thor always swore she had.

"Missing," Sif repeated in a low tight voice. "What do you mean, Merlin?" The accusation in her voice echoed in the small valley

"It is no longer in the cavern," Merlin confessed. A nervous knot formed at the base of his spine. "I take it that you have not removed it then." The last flicker of hope he'd been holding onto vanishing.

"No," Sif all but spat at him. "I don't have the Hammer nor do I know where it is." She set her eyes on him and frowned. "If you recall, Merlin, I wanted it to stay with me."

"I know," Merlin agreed quickly. "But at the time we agreed that having it in the tunnels where another Iron Soul could access it was for the best. The Dvergr were able to watch over it."

"The Dvergr have been dead for years and humans dig below the surface." Sif looked out across the rocky landscape. "We can hope it is in the possession of humans."

"Most likely," Merlin replied, aware that he didn't sound very confident. "The Sídhe have not made any sign that they have it."

"One of my kind may have it." Sif raised an eyebrow and gave him a harsh look that made Merlin miss the younger Sif who had been much calmer and quieter. Thor had been a terrible influence on her. "Just to be safe I will wake my trustworthy family members. We will make inquiries."

"That's not necessary," Merlin protested only to receive another look.

"The Iron Hammer was created by the mortal man I chose to marry," Sif snapped. "I allowed you to decide its hiding place against my better judgment."

"Respectfully, Sif," Merlin cut in. "It never belonged to you. It was an artifact of the Iron Soul and belongs to them in all lives."

They stared at each other. Merlin could almost feel the irritation rolling off of her, but then he sensed her surrender. She could be mad, but apparently, Sif still had enough sense to know it wasn't really him she was angry at. Merlin almost sighed in relief but kept his facial features calm.

"Then we should stop arguing and make sure that it finds its way back to the Iron Soul." Sif said a moment later and shook her head. "Is there anything else I should be aware of, Merlin?"

"Humans have changed a lot."

"I've been dreaming of the world," Sif assured him with a tiny smile. "The rise in magic had already begun to wake me, but you already knew that."

"Still, I think the technology may throw you a bit," Merlin told her before pausing. "Your family is rather popular in human memory." Sif smiled at that which made more of the younger Sif shine through. She nodded and visibly relaxed. "Otherwise... well, there have been many battles since you and your family went into the water."

"I'm sorry we couldn't help," Sif apologized.

"Don't be," Merlin said. "It is important that your people remained uncorrupted by the Iron Realm. We don't need more insane Old Ones." He shook his head. "Honestly even after all this time, I'm never sure what I'm going to experience with your kind."

"That's fair I suppose," Sif agreed though she looked a bit insulted. "Yet remember, Merlin, that while many were exiled here, for some of us it is the only home we have ever had, even if it does not always welcome us as I wish it would."

There was a long moment of silence and Merlin nodded his understanding. "That's fair," he finally agreed. "I should not cast aspersions on you and your family. My own nature is only half human."

"You have done well for the Iron Realm," Sif assured him as if sensing the change in his mood. "What other news is there, Merlin? What more should I know and alert my family to?"

"Cyrridven is dead." Merlin lowered himself onto the shore and stretched out his legs as the joints protested the hike. He just felt old and groaned slightly as Sif gasped in horror.

"What?" Sif demanded with wide eyes. "When? How?"

"Recently I'm afraid, only a few months ago. Chernobog woke, his insanity was as strong as ever and he went after the Iron Soul. Cyrridven intervened to save her and-"

"Her?" Sif cut in, tilting her head curiously. "The Iron Soul is female?"

"Indeed, in this life, it is," Merlin agreed with a small smile. "The first female incarnation as far as I know."

"About time."

"You sound like Morgana," Merlin said. "Her name is Alexandra Adams though she goes by Alex. A talented girl with interesting powers, but I'm a bit worried about some of the things occurring around her."

"From what I have seen, the life of an Iron Soul is always strange," Sif said. Her expression softened and turned sad.

"That would be fair," Merlin agreed carefully. "Alex is a good girl. I dare say that you would like her."

"And what is the threat?" Sif asked. "Chernobog?"

"No, Alex was able to destroy him." Satisfaction flashed through Merlin at the way Sif's eyes widened in surprise and maybe a touch of awe. "I'm afraid that our ancient enemies the Sídhe have returned." He held up a hand to stop the question he knew was coming. "And no, the magic of the original Iron Gates has decayed to the point that they are coming through untainted. The Dark Elves have not risen again."

"I see, but surely in the modern era making new Iron Gates is not a challenge." Sif folded her hands in front of her.

"There is a... complication," Merlin replied, unsure of how he could even begin to explain Arthur. "The old Sídhe Queen Scáthbás survived in the magic of the Iron Gates. I still don't understand how, but she has created a half Sídhe-half human being similar to Morgana and myself. He has proven to be a vicious enemy and knows a great deal about us."

Merlin settled with that, unable to confess how badly he and Morgana had erred in assuming that Arthur Pendred was the current Iron Soul. Just the reminder that he'd once been certain that the strong handsome young man had been Arto's reincarnation made him feel ill thanks to his current knowledge of what the boy was truly like. Sif must have sensed something was wrong because she gave him a long searching look as they fell into silence.

"Anyway." Merlin coughed when her gaze became too heavy and started reminding him too much of Morgana's. "I'm afraid that Scáthbás is using another artifact of the Iron Soul to bind the various creatures of her branch of the Tree of Reality to her will. I was seeking the Iron Hammer to break that connection."

"What artifact would have such a power?" Sif asked him with a frown. "That does not sound like Thor at all."

"It was an accidental creation," Merlin offered with a forced, almost painful chuckle. "I'm afraid that Morgana and I were not even aware of that life as there was no magical threat."

"I shall join you in seeking Mjǫllnir," Sif said. "My father still considers Thor family and we will not allow his artifact to fall into the wrong hands."

"Thank you, Sif," Merlin replied gratefully. "The current center of magic is Ravenslake, a town in Oregon in America. I trust you can find it?"

Sif raised an eyebrow at him and smirked, "Our Vikings were the first Europeans to find that land, Merlin. I'm sure that I can manage." She paused and eyed him carefully. "Where will you go now?"

"Back to England," Merlin found himself replying honestly. "There is something I need to retrieve."

"What?" Sif asked in a sharper tone.

"Something that I never thought I'd need." Merlin met her calm green eyes, surprised at the hint of defeat in his voice. Shaking his head, Merlin cleared his throat and added, "Take care, Sif. I appreciate your help."

He turned quickly and walked away, pleased when the Old One did not call after him. Those words must have inspired questions and yet she was giving him space. The tightness in his lungs eased even as his grip on his walking stick became so hard that his hand ached. As he climbed up the slope of the hill, he heard a rush of water and turned back to see a spinning whirlpool forming in the air.

Merlin stopped and watched Sif leap into the water and vanish from sight, leaving him alone in the quiet countryside. He exhaled slowly and gave himself a moment, feeling the ache in his bones. The years were all pressing down on him and he debated the words he'd said to Sif. They filled him with dread, but it indeed seemed like it was time to return to England and recover the cache.

9

Svartalfheim

16 C.E. Sør-Trøndelag, Norway

It was a beautiful morning. The sun was already rising as last night's rain settled into the soil. The world smelled fresh and it was almost enough to make Thor forget that they were going back into the Dark Elf tunnels. Almost. There was a cold sweat gathering at the back of his neck. He was leaning against one of the larger boulders by their meeting point, torn between impatience and nervousness. Part of him wanted to get this mission over with, while the other feared going underground again. Thor shuddered at the very idea and tried to calm his suddenly racing heart.

His hand brushed the Hammer and Thor paused as a spark of magic ran up his arm. It was enough to distract him and he looked down at the heavy loop on his belt that held the magical hammer. So far it had been a strange adjustment to carrying around his Hammer like he would a sword, but there was a sense of rightness to the weight that surprised him. Thor looked back at Morgana and Merlin before pulling the Hammer from its resting place and hefting it thoughtfully.

Thor pushed a tiny trickle of magic into the Hammer and it hummed a sweet tune that settled in his bones in response. Grinning, Thor watched as the small jolts of lightning jumped over the surface of his Hammer. Thor eyed a nearby large rock that had fallen off the cliff side. A dangerous thought was running through his head and he risked a glance down the hill to where Morgana and Merlin were talking.

He wasn't sure how much longer they'd be waiting for the Old Ones and Frea. His eyes moved to Brokkr who was sitting a short ways from him, chewing on some smoked venison and didn't seem to be very concerned about leaving too soon. Looking back at the boulder, Thor wondered if his Hammer was really strong enough to take on an impact like that. He knew that it would help him summon lightning and that he could tap into the reserve of power woven into the metal, but he wasn't sure of its limits.

Thor licked his suddenly very dry lips. The sensible part of him cautioned against damaging the Hammer while another part of him was whispering for him to try it. Thor stepped closer to the boulder and tested the weight of the Hammer before he swung. Slamming the Hammer down, Thor's chest tightened with a frightened certainty that this was a mistake, that his Hammer was about to shatter. He could already hear Morgana's angry voice echoing through his head along with the sharp ring of the metal against the stone. But then the Hammer shook and the rock cracked sending rock dust into the air. It fell apart into three large pieces, their ragged edges showing where they fit together.

"Impressive!" Thor spun to find Brokkr standing behind him, rubbing his hands together gleefully as he inspected the boulder. "Crusher! Excellent! There's the weapon's name!"

"Crusher," Thor repeated carefully, looking down at his Hammer with a thoughtful expression. "Mjǫllnir. It means grind, like grind stone."

"Suit yourself. Mjǫllnir is a bit fancy, but it has a certain flare to it I suppose." Brokkr stepped closer to Thor and held out a hand. Thor hesitated a moment before he handed Mjǫllnir to Brokkr. He watched silently as Brokkr studied it, checking the weight, the balance, and ran a long dark finger over the symbol. "A fine weapon." Brokkr said, handing it back gently.

"What's going on?" Morgana's voice called up the hill.

"Lad was just testing the Hammer!" Brokkr shouted down to Merlin and Morgana.

Thor could see a slight scowl on Merlin's face at the words, but whatever the elder mage had been thinking to shout in response was delayed by five figures stepping out of the trees. Thor grinned as he caught sight of a long golden braid over the shoulder of one of the figures. He glanced towards Brokkr who had a look of mild interest on his face and began moving down the hillside.

Thor strained his ears to hear as Merlin and Morgana moved to greet Odin and his party. Looking into the trees, Thor wondered how soon Frea would arrive and how many she'd bring with her. His eyes shifted back to the Old Ones and he eyed the two unfamiliar figures. For a moment he lingered and realized with irritation that he was waiting for a signal from Merlin or Morgana. Marching forward, Thor pushed that realization to the side and told himself that it was ridiculous.

Then he stopped as the shortest of the figures stepped away from the group and started up the path towards him. Sif smiled, her hood falling back as she looked towards him. Odin was already speaking with Merlin and Morgana with Baldr at his side. The other two figures were dressed in odd shimmering armor and waiting a few steps back.

"Sif, it's a pleasure to see you. I wasn't expecting to see you today."

"Oh?" Sif asked with a tilt of her head. "Why might that be, Thor? You knew we were all meeting up for the examination of the tunnels." There was a note of challenge in her voice that made Thor feel uneasy and certain that he'd offended her somehow.

"It's just that-," Thor stuttered, desperately trying to school his features. "I thought only warriors were coming."

"Warriors," Sif repeated slowly, raising an eyebrow and giving him the universal look of acceptance that men were fools. "I'll forgive you for that as you've never seen me fight."

"Uh... what sort of magic do you have?" Thor asked, searching her hands and belt for a weapon and finding nothing. "I mean uh-"

"I'm rather good with vegetation actually. I'm not as impressive as Merlin or Morgana or my brother, but I can help with this." She shifted and Thor caught sight of a sword strapped to her belt which gave him a sense of unease.

"Is it just the five of you?" Thor glanced towards Odin who was speaking with Merlin intently.

"No, of course not, but not everyone has control over their powers," Sif admitted carefully, dropping her eyes and fidgeting. "While we're born here, we still don't completely belong. Only a few of us have family connections, but we and others like us all try to be civil and work together." Sif paused and blushed. "Oh, you meant for today... yes. Father felt that we were the best suited to help today."

"Oh," Thor murmured. He was a bit unsure as to why she bothered with that whole explanation, but quickly focused on her red cheeks. "Are you blushing?"

"No, of course not!" Thor couldn't help it, his smile widened and Sif's soft blush only deepened. "I'm not," she insisted. "I'm a being of energy. I only have a physical form because I wish to."

Thor didn't really understand what she was talking about. Merlin had tried to explain it to him. They were magic bound together by will, but with Sif's soft blush reddening her cheeks and a few strands of her golden hair falling into her face it was difficult to focus on that.

"I suppose I shouldn't be surprised." Thor watched her expression carefully. "You are a remarkable being."

"Remarkable being?"

"I have a feeling that if I tried to say you were beautiful that you'd think me shallow," Thor offered with a wider smile. "And to be fair that wouldn't quite capture the essence of what makes you so... fascinating to me."

"Would you be talking with me like this if you weren't the Iron Soul?" Sif asked with a teasing smile.

"Probably not," Thor admitted with a grin. He leaned against the rock face, hoping he didn't look too silly. "But I am."

"And I'm a being of energy that originates from a very different world."

"You were born here."

"Ah, but my physiology isn't human. I only look this way. It doesn't mean that this is what I truly am." Sif grinned at him, her green eyes sparkling. "And for a man who was stumbling over himself when I first arrived you are suddenly very confident."

"You smiled and blushed. Reassured me that I'm not a complete fool."

"You are a fool, Thor." Sif's expression turned sadder and she gestured between them. "This isn't wise. You barely know me."

"I'd like to get to know you better. And what I do know about you is impressive. Beautiful, smart, powerful, and carries a sword." For a moment neither said anything as Thor enjoyed the warmth of Sif's smile.

"Thor!" Merlin called out, drawing Thor's attention away from Sif's face. "Frea has arrived!"

Thor turned back to Sif and offered her his hand. She blinked in surprise, but he could see her smile as she took his hand and he carefully led them down the path. A noise behind them made Thor turn sharply with his hand falling to his Hammer. It was only Brokkr, trotting along behind them. He met Thor's eyes with a small smirk on his features that made Thor feel a rush of embarrassment. He'd completely forgotten that Brokkr was there.

"I've given my Hammer a name," Thor informed Sif as they approached the others in an attempt to distract himself from Brokkr's knowing gaze. "Mjǫllnir."

"Mjǫllnir," Sif repeated thoughtfully with a smile tugging at her lips. "I like it."

That statement pleased him far too much, but Thor fought back the smile. Morgana was watching them with a dark look in her green eyes while Merlin looked torn between amusement and worry. He was sure that he would hear about this soon, but today they had a different priority.

"Greetings, Frea," Thor said with a nod to the Sídhe. All of them were armed and wearing cloaks with their hoods shading their eyes against the harsh light of the sun.

"Thor," Frea greeted. "Are we prepared?"

He was a bit surprised that she was asking him, but Thor nodded as his eyes swept over their group. They had three mages, five Old Ones, and five allied Sídhe. If they hadn't been heading underground, he might have been excited. He nodded sharply and led them to the cavern entrance. Merlin looked towards him with a pleased smile before green magic flared around his staff. Thor's stomach turned as the magic seeped into the rocks and began shifting the earth out of their way, revealing the dark opening.

Merlin headed in first with Frea at his side. Thor hung back to let them all enter ahead of him. The moment he stepped inside, the dark tunnels were already threatening to close in around him. Light from floating orbs of magic shimmered on a smooth water worn stone and he told himself to breathe. At least he could feel the open air behind him as they descended.

Cold sweat rolled down his back and Thor barely held back a shudder. The back of his tunic was beginning to stick to his back and his chest was far too tight. Everyone was silent. A group of beings that didn't know each other were depending on each other to make this mission a success. Thor dropped his right hand so it rested on Mjǫllnir. The slight hum of magic in it was reassuring as they turned another corner and followed a slick slope further into the ground. A ragged breath escaped Thor and he found himself fighting the urge to run back the way they'd come. For a moment he felt lightheaded and had to leverage a hand on the rock wall to stay upright.

"Thor?" Sif put her hand on his arm. "Are you alright?"

"I don't like being underground," Thor said weakly. "I fight with lightning, remember? Under the sky is where I belong."

Sif's hand on his arm made it easier to take another step forward. Yet his fingers tightened on his Hammer like a lifeline. Like it could save him if the countless pounds of mountain above him collapsed. It was foolish, but he couldn't force himself to let go. Up ahead were faint glittering lights as they rounded another turn. Morgana's light orb suddenly dimmed sending a rush of fear through Thor. Sif's hand tightened on his arm and he thought he heard her make a soft soothing noise that sounded like how his mother had calmed him as a child.

There was enough light for him to see the passage opening wide. The stone above his head vanished and Thor could feel more open air around him. Sif's hand fell from his arm leaving a sting of cold in its absence, but he understood as they slowed and carefully moved towards the Dark Elf stronghold.

The small city had changed since the last time they'd been down here. Thor's eyes widened as he took in the small buildings that had been carved into the side of the mountain. It was rough work, but strong and far more organized than he'd wanted the Dark Elves to be. Small flames were burning in stone bowls scattered near the path and cast enough light to reveal there weren't any Dark Elves present. For a moment Thor allowed himself to hope that they were all dead. That they'd died when the tunnel collapsed of starvation or suffocation. But then he realized that someone was still here and alive to light the flames.

The group began to spread out, though Thor stayed near Sif and smiled when Brokkr came with them. Everyone remained in sight, but risked small glances into the structures. Yet there were no Dark Elves to be seen. Thor shifted protectively towards Sif, hoping she wouldn't notice. She did and snorted lightly.

"My kin must be near," Brokkr whispered gruffly.

"How can you be sure?"

"Listen," Brokkr ordered, holding up a hand. "I can hear them."

Thor strained his ears, but at first, he only heard their breathing and the occasional drip of water. Then he caught the soft strain of a song. It wasn't coming from the small city, but past it in another cavern. They followed the sound to a staircase down carved into the stone that was already showing signs of wear from use.

The lower cavern was smaller or at least appeared to be so. Piles of rock surrounded them, filling in large holes between the stalactites and stalagmites. Thor struggled to keep moving, driven forward by his fear of being left in the dark underground alone. There was a long tunnel leading deeper into the mountain, but the walls were lined with tool marks and there was a strange shimmer on the stone.

Thor could hear the song of the Dvergr more clearly now, but there was a mournful tone to it as it mixed with the ring of metal against stone. The sound of the singing and the working of the stone suddenly stopped, leaving them all in darkness and silence. Suddenly the smooth stone walls of the circular tunnel began to glow violet. Frea moved forward first with two of her men trailing after her. The light was enough that they could now see the Dark Elves who were lined up with their hands pressed against the wall. None of them seemed to notice they were being watched.

The Dvergr were seated in the center of the tunnel, tools discarded to the side with their heads bowed low. Next to him Brokkr made a sound of relief and anger, but thankfully didn't storm forward. The glow in the tunnel grew brighter, and Thor's stomach shifted uneasily when he noted it was originating from the hands of the Dark Elves. Across the surface of the stone the violet light formed strange bands of different shades of purple. His skin tingled uncomfortably and he shuddered as the desire to run was replaced with a frantic need to make this stop.

Thankfully Morgana and Frea seemed to have decided they were finally close enough. They knelt down behind a pile of rock near the tunnel mouth. Kneeling down next to Frea, Thor looked over at the Síd. Frea's face was impossibly paler and her violet eyes were wide with fear.

"Frea?" Morgana turned to Frea with dark angry eyes. "Are they doing what I think they're doing?"

"They can't be!" Frea twisted to peer over the rocks. "They can't reconnect to Sídhean!" There was a long pause and nobody moved. "Can they?"

"I... I'm not sure," Merlin answered slowly. "I did not believe they had any magic, but we know too little about them."

The violet magic rolling over the walls of the tunnel began to fade to darkness. Still, no one moved, and he risked a glance at Morgana before the last of the light vanished. She looked uneasy, but opened her palm to conjure another orb of light.

"Perhaps this is a good thing," Morgana suggested with a spark of glee in her eyes. "If the Dark Elves march to war against Sídhean then we'll be rid of them and the Sídhe will suffer some damage."

"Morgana, we don't know what they are doing," Merlin reminded her in a tightly controlled voice. "They may be planning to kidnap and corrupt more Sídhe to expand their numbers." Merlin gestured into the tunnel. "This, all of this, is unnatural. This is not what was intended by Arto's magic and we need to focus on keeping this realm safe from more... unpleasant events."

"Merlin is correct." Odin's good eye glowed with a tiny spark of magic. "Should they manage to break through from our world into the Sídhe world there is no telling what the result would be." He looked pointedly to Morgana. "After all, they would be breaking through your brother's protective magic as well and who knows what that would cause going into Sídhean."

"It might destroy them."

"Or make them more powerful," Odin retorted with a frown. "And if it did what you hope, then a world would die. I fear what the ramifications from that would be for the Tree of Reality." Odin's words made Morgana fall silent and she cast her eyes down.

"What do we do?" Thor asked, uncertainty churning in his gut. "They have some kind of magic?"

"Weak magic." Sif raised her chin and looked over the rock piles. "Not much alone, but they're combining it. This tunnel is some sort of... focus for them."

"I'm not sure we can defeat them all," Merlin said. "There are dozens of them and with the rock..." he trailed off and looked meaningfully up at the ceiling while Thor barely kept his breakfast down.

"We need to help my people," Brokkr huffed, looking at them with dark stubborn eyes.

"Brokkr-" Odin protested, but Brokkr spun away from the rocks.

Rushing towards the Dark Elves, Brokkr raised his axe and gave a war cry. It did the trick; the Dark Elves turned their attention away from the walls. An unfamiliar curse escaped Merlin, but he stood up with Morgana only a second behind him. Thor almost sighed in relief. This wasn't good, but it was better than sitting in the dark worrying about the roof falling in. He pulled his Hammer free of his belt and pulled on his magic, letting it flow through his arms and into Mjǫllnir.

Snarls echoed into the cavern as Dark Elves drew their weapons and rushed towards them. Around them, Thor could see the Dvergr beginning to move. He hoped they'd take the chance to run. The Dark Elves met them half way through the cavern and Thor stopped as one narrowed its focus on him. Tightening his grip on his Hammer, Thor brought it up and watched the creature begin to circle him. It lunged for him and Thor swung Mjǫllnir. He grunted as it impacted with the Dark Elf's chest and lightning arched off the smooth metal and into its body. The Dark Elf was sent hurtling back against the wall and struck it with a thunderous crack. A pained shriek escaped it as its body began to dissolve into dark dust.

Another Dark Elf dashed forward. Long talons raked across his arm, slicing through the rough material of his shirt. Thor hissed, but held back a cry. Smashing the Hammer forward, Thor felt a rush of vindication as the Dark Elf collapsed backwards with a scream of pain. The Dark Elves kept coming towards them. He hit two more with Mjǫllnir, but dared not summon lightning in the small space. Exhaling slowly, Thor ordered his heart to stop pounding so hard. He was certain that everyone could hear it. Another Dark Elf was on him and he swung Mjǫllnir again. Another small flash of lightning and it fell to dust.

"Fall back!" Merlin's voice echoed through the cavern.

Thor was happy to comply and started shifting back. In the corner of his eye, he saw Sif stab a Dark Elf through the upper chest. As it fell, she freed her sword and slashed with a vicious shout at its neck. The ground beneath his feet rumbled and Thor's knees quivered as green magic spun around Merlin.

"Fall back!" Merlin shouted again.

The piles of rocks began to shift, carried into the center of the room by waves of green magic. Sif grabbed his free hand and began to pull him back towards the stairs. It was dark before him until Mjǫllnir hummed with magic and began to glow, illuminating the way. They were running now as the sound of shifting rocks echoed behind them. He could hear Brokkr calling for the others to hurry. Tunnels twisted around them, but Sif's grip on his hand didn't waver as she guided him.

Stumbling out into the sunlight, Thor gulped in a greedy breath of fresh air and turned his face up into the light. Sif steered him further away from the entrance as the others came out. Looking over his shoulder, Thor quickly counted as the others came out. Everyone was there. Thor's shoulders slumped in relief. Sif's grip on his arm tightened, forcing him to look down at her. He met worried eyes.

"I'm alright."

"Stop trying to be alright when you aren't, Thor!" Sif hissed, her green eyes flashing.

He stopped struggling. Sif watched him for a moment before she reached into a pouch on her belt and pulled out a few strips of clean cloth. Without another word, she pulled away the torn material of his shirt and began wrapping his arm.

"I'm sorry I can't heal it."

"Merlin and Morgana have explained why that's dangerous." Thor's mouth was dry as he breathed in Sif's presence. She smelled earthy which surprised him. He'd expected a being from another world to smell different, but she smelled like the world after a solid rainstorm. Fresh, sharp, and rich. "But thank you," he added, dropping his eyes.

There were other things to worry about he told himself as he saw Brokkr embrace another Dvergr in the corner of his eye. There was a small group of them gathered together. Yet Thor couldn't bring himself to turn his attention away from Sif.

10

The Red Flag

Smoke filled the square, drifting up over the shouting horde that packed the open area amongst the unfamiliar stone buildings. Everything was illuminated by the flickering light of the flames. There was nothing pleasant or inspiring here, only a scene that he could feel burning into his mind. A stray tear escaped his eye and he quickly brushed it away before it could be seen. Thankfully no one was paying attention to him. He wasn't worth their notice, but caution was necessary as dread rolled over him.

People were marching forward, rushing to the pyres like children fleeing the school at the end of the day. Armfuls of books were tossed to the fire and with each new flare as the flames devoured the paper another cheer rose from the crowd. He swallowed, uncertainty, horror, and disgust churning in his chest. How was this happening in the 20th century? How had the party whipped the population into this?

A flag fluttering on the far side of the crowded square caught his eye and the knot in his stomach tightened. Bright bloody red with that horrid four-legged black sign in the white circle. The world shimmered and convulsed. Alex shuddered, falling away from the dream as the sight of the swastika on full display stunned her. The scene around her snapped back into full detail. She looked around in shock at the cheering crowds.

Troops were placed around the square in parade rest, looking impressive and frightening. If the crowd was displeased there was no sign of it. No, everyone looked excited and enthralled with the flames. Alex shifted nervously. The body reacted to her emotions, but it refused to move from its position. She felt the stiff collar around her neck and her heart stopped for a painful moment. To her right and left were soldiers in the tan uniforms she'd seen in her dad's war movies. All of them had armbands that prominently displayed the Nazi swastika.

Her eyes were drawn to the symbol against her will, staring at the four bent black lines that made her think of a spider as she tried to ignore the thick smell of smoke and the noise. Then something shifted. The noise of the crowd dimmed. Before her eyes the swastika began fluttering and moving, becoming smaller until she blinked and closed her eyes tightly. The smell of smoke was gone, replaced by a blend of dust, food, and dozens of tiny hints of things she couldn't name. Opening her eyes, Alex found herself staring up a small Nazi flag atop a huge metal structure.

It fluttered innocently in the wind with a bright blue sky behind it and only a few wisps of clouds at the edge of her vision. Frowning, Alex dropped her eyes from the flag and took in the metal structure only to gasp. It was the Eiffel Tower. She struggled for air, trying to overcome the rush of confusion swamping her.

Hammer, she thought stubbornly. I want to know about the Hammer. She tried to say the words out loud, but the body refused her commands. Alex's eyes wouldn't move away from that flag. Regret and loathing churned in her gut, but she wasn't sure if she was the source or this person. Once again, she repeated her wish to see the Iron Hammer.

If she had to be plagued by these strange dreams then at least they should be useful.

"Eckstein!" someone shouted in a thick accent behind her. The call was followed by cheerful laughter up the street.

Alex felt her body starting to turn despite her own desire to stay still. The name echoed in her head, tugging at something deep in her memory that Alex already knew really shouldn't be there. Then another voice, a louder one started calling a more familiar name.

"Alex!" Nicki's voice called, overwhelming the other voices. The smell of the city around her was fading and she heard the call again. Her eyes were dry and heavy, but Nicki's voice kept calling to her. "Alex! Wake up!"

Forcing her eyes open, Alex found herself looking at a frowning Nicki in the low light of the hotel room lamp. Her friend's freckles stood out more than usual in the dim light and her long red hair was hanging in a messy braid over her shoulder.

"Nicki?" she asked in a hoarse voice. The sound of someone else in the room made her look over towards the other side of the bed.

Jenny was sitting on the other side of the bed, her long wavy hair now a wild mane around her worried face. "You were speaking in another language again," Jenny told her softly, holding onto her phone like a lifeline.

"Shouting was more like it." Nicki stood up and gave Alex more room. "You kept saying the same thing over and over again. You were damn near yelling when we got you to wake up."

"It sounded like German I think," Jenny said.

"German or another Germanic language," Nicki agreed with a nod, glancing towards Jenny's phone. "Did you get it?"

"Some of it," Jenny answered with a small nod.

"Wait what?" Alex asked as the confusion began to lift. "Got what?"

"Jenny recorded you speaking in German," Nicki said calmly, reaching over and putting her hand on Alex's forehead. "You don't feel feverish so this is probably tied to magic."

"You recorded me?" Alex repeated dumbly looking at the phone.

"Just a little bit," Jenny assured her.

"We thought it was a good idea to find out what you're saying," Nicki explained. She patted Alex's cheek with a wide overly cheerful smile. "Maybe you're saying something we need to know. Like I said you kept repeating the same couple of sentences over and over."

"I doubt it," Alex grumbled. "The dream...." She shuddered.

"The dream?" Nicki pressed. "What was it about?"

"I don't want to talk-" Alex started to say only to sigh when she saw Nicki's stubborn face. "I was a Nazi. I was at a book burning."

"Nazi?" Nicki repeated while Jenny's eyes widened. "That's a bit different, isn't it?" She offered Alex what was supposed to be a reassuring smile. "Look we'll call Morgana about it."

"That wasn't everything," Alex said, sitting up and swinging her legs out of bed. "The dream changed..." she clung to the memory. "There was the Eiffel Tower. I was only there for a moment."

"That fits," Jenny said. "You said Paris."

"As part of a sentence." Nicki reached over to squeeze her shoulder. "We didn't understand the rest of it." Nicki paused and tilted her head. "Well at least I don't think we understood it."

"That's part of what I recorded," Jenny said. "So, we can get it translated and find out what you were saying."

"I don't remember saying anything in the dream," Alex protested weakly, trying to remember any helpful details. "I was just... there. Just an observer."

"Well... the person you used to be may have been just observing so you didn't really have control," Nicki suggested as she stood up from the bed to give Alex more room. "But that doesn't mean that part of your mind wasn't processing it and trying to tell you something."

"Nicki, you don't get it. I was in that line! I was standing with the soldiers..." Alex trailed off in horror as her stomach turned. "Oh god I was a Nazi!" She jumped up, suddenly trapped and cold. "I remember Merlin and Morgana saying that there was an Iron Soul alive during World War II, but they didn't say they were on the wrong side!" She was ranting now, pacing in the small hotel room. "As if being a slave trader wasn't enough-"

"Alex!" Nicki grabbed her arms to still her. "Calm down!" she ordered in a softer voice. "It's okay."

"It is not okay," Alex gaped at her. "Nazi, Nicki!"

"I get it, but it isn't you. No more than you're Arto or Thor or Gofin."

"Gofiben," Alex corrected automatically with a frown as irritation flared in her chest. "How can you be so calm about this?"

"Because you are jumping to conclusions after one dream," Nicki told her sternly with a sharp glint to her blue eyes. "Alex, World War II was a complex mess of events and people. There's no telling what you were actually like then as a person. For all you know he might have been a spy or someone who ended up betraying the Nazi party."

"Besides the bigger question is why are you dreaming about him now?" Jenny added.

Frowning at the question, Alex stayed silent and considered it. She'd had dreams of her slaver life because it connected to the Iron Chain, because those dreams while as unpleasant as they were had provided information. Bran had visions of his past life in order to help them find the Iron Chalice. With the Iron Hammer missing and her waking mind filled with thoughts of it she'd expected to dream of Thor.

"Anything, Alex?" Nicki pressed, looking at her thoughtfully.

"No," Alex forced out, shaking her head. "No, I don't think I dreamt anything about Thor."

"Still…" Jenny muttered with a look towards Nicki who nodded in agreement.

Nicki went over to the dresser and retrieved her own phone from where it was charging. Alex licked her dry lips and looked over at Jenny, noting the uncomfortable, but slightly hopeful expression on her face. Alex wondered just what she had said that were making the pair so twitchy. They said that they hadn't understood any of it except for Paris. She was so deep in thought that she missed Nicki calling Morgana up until she started talking.

"Morgana," Nicki greeted carefully, blushing a little and suddenly looking hesitant. "Uh sorry to wake you."

"I assume it is important," Morgana said with a hint of impatience over the speakerphone. "I'm guessing from your greeting that you are not in immediate danger."

"No, we're not," Nicki answered with a slight smile in Alex's direction. "I didn't think about the time, sorry. Look Alex just woke up from another dream and she was talking in another language again."

"I see."

"We recorded it this time," Jenny chimed in helpfully before her eyes widened and she shied back from the phone.

"Excellent." Morgana now sounded pleased and more awake. "Play it for me," she ordered, suddenly sounding far too excited for Alex.

Jenny hit the play button and Alex leaned towards the phone as if it would help her understand. They hadn't been lying that she was almost shouting the words. It was creepy hearing her own voice, but not understanding it. Alex frowned as she caught what sounded like 'hammer' in the almost mad rant that seemed to repeat itself, but wasn't sure. Somehow her American accent had vanished, replaced with a full thick German one. She glanced towards Nicki who nodded in shared understanding as hope threatened to bloom in her chest. Maybe, just maybe....

Then the recording was done and silence rang in the room with its sudden absence. Alex silently mouthed one of the long phrases that had been repeated, but the words were heavy and alien on her lips. She turned her gaze towards the phone, noting that Morgana was silent on the other end.

"So, what did I say?" Alex asked, joining the conversation for the first time.

"There's bits of pieces of names," Morgana answered thoughtfully. "But the clearest section is the most interesting. You said the Ahnenerbe found the Hammer and Gottfried Eckstein took it." There was suddenly the clicking of a keyboard in the background. "And you said 'in Paris' several times."

"The Ahnenerbe," Nicki repeated thoughtfully. "I feel like I should know what that is. It sounds familiar."

"The Ahnenerbe was a society created by Himmler in the days before World War II," Morgana explained in a distracted voice. "They were tasked to study the cultural and archeological history of the Aryan race. It would make sense for them to seek out Thor's Hammer and other artifacts from the Norse I suppose, but I don't recall them ever doing an expedition to any of the Scandinavian lands."

"Maybe they covered it up after they located the Iron Hammer," Jenny said. She sat down on the bed and put a hand on Alex's shoulder. "To keep anyone from discovering that they found it and lost it."

"What about Gottfried Eckstein?" Alex pressed, remembering the name someone had called to her. "Was that the Iron Soul?"

"I'm not sure," Morgana answered. The clicking stopped. "At the time our scrying confirmed that there was a current Iron Soul, but magic wasn't very strong and the signs pointed to them living in Germany. There was nothing too unusual. Merlin and I made a couple of attempts at locating them, but it wasn't a good era to be moving in and out of Germany. We never determined their exact location and were unable to make contact. After confirming that no magic was at play in World War II, we turned our attention to other things."

"But if Gottfried Eckstein was the Iron Soul, then it might explain why he took the Iron Hammer," Jenny suggested, toying with a strand of her hair. "Magic may not have been powerful, but if he came into contact with the Iron Hammer and felt a connection to it, then he may have been driven to take it. Things from prior lives can manifest in weird ways," she added softly with a flush of embarrassment.

Morgana made a thoughtful noise and Alex looked quickly between Jenny and the phone, uncertain if she should say anything. "That's possible," Morgana finally agreed. "If, and this is all still speculation, a reincarnation did come into contact with the Iron Hammer, it may have caused a magical reaction that affected him. We can only hope that he had good intentions if Alex's words are correct and this Eckstein took the Iron Hammer."

"But maybe not," Nicki muttered with a grimace. "Himmler was also the leader of the SS and those weren't good people. If this Eckstein had access to the Hammer, then he may have been one of them."

Alex flinched at the idea of not only being a Nazi in another life, but also SS. She wasn't an expert on history, but those had been the ones running the death camps. Still, she remembered standing in formation with those other Nazis in the dream.

"It is a possibility," Morgana agreed calmly. "I need to see if I can find anything on this man, but at least your dream has provided us with a potential lead on the Iron Hammer."

"Yeah," Alex offered weakly. The tight tingling in her jaw made her worry she was going to be sick.

Morgana must have heard something in her voice because a moment later she gently added, "Alex, also keep in mind that the SS was one of the larger organizations. They did more than just the death camps, they were also an intelligence organization and if Paris does hold the key, then he would have likely been an administrator there. Potentially doing historical research for the Ahnenerbe if he was one of them."

It was a stretch and Alex knew it. They didn't know a thing about this guy other than his name and that he'd been a Nazi. Still, she remembered the distress she'd felt during his memory of the book burning. That didn't guarantee that he was any good, but maybe he hadn't been a total monster.

"Also," Morgana continued after a moment. "A lot of people were trapped by the Nazi regime. If you had a family or couldn't get out in the early days, you were under a lot of surveillance. Not to mention that once the party took over, depending on your profession it was required that you were a member of the party. A lot of people faced bad choices between being Nazis and the safety of their families."

Jenny squeezed her shoulder again and Alex wondered how accurate what Morgana had just said was. It was hard to imagine, but then again, she did come from a culture that painted all Nazis as evil for the sake of having straightforward enemies in movies. The party leadership had been evil, but maybe, there was some gray here and there. She could hope.

"So do you think the Iron Hammer is actually in Paris?" Alex asked to distract herself.

"It would explain why you started dreaming about this life," Morgana reminded her gently. "Your magic is reaching out to find it."

"Have any of the others ever had dreams? Like mine?"

"No," Morgana admitted carefully. "But we've usually put the artifacts in safe places and recovered them as needed. You're the first Iron Soul that has needed to use your magic to find them. It is a different set of circumstances." A loud sigh came through the phone before Morgana added, "I need to do some research and see if I can find anything. You girls get some sleep and bring the boys up to speed. Tomorrow we'll sort out a plan."

"What do you think is going to happen, Morgana?" Nicki asked, voicing Alex's own question.

"I'm not sure yet, it depends on what I find. If there is any evidence that Eckstein was real and had a connection to the Ahnenerbe then it will change what happens next. As I said for now try to get a couple more hours of sleep."

That wasn't much of an answer and Alex wanted to protest, but the call ended. Jenny dragged her back into the bed as Nicki put her phone away. Both of them gave her reassuring smiles and Alex sighed in silent surrender. Putting her head back against the pillow, she waited as Nicki turned off the lamp and went over to her own bed. Jenny's hand found hers and gave it a reassuring squeeze.

Alex just stared up at the ceiling as her eyes adjusted to the darkness. She wondered what Morgana thought she was going to find about some random World War II soldier in one night. Tomorrow they'd plan, but Alex already had a strange sense of what they needed to do. She remembered the sight of the Nazi flag atop the Eiffel Tower and couldn't help the excited flutter in her stomach. Paris, she'd always wanted to go there.

11

Finding the Way Forward

There was not enough coffee in the whole of the west coast to make her feel better. And Alex knew that with Seattle only three hours north that was saying something. Her whole body ached and she was certain that she could still smell the smoke of the book burnings. There was a dull pain in the back of her head, but she couldn't seem to turn her brain off. She didn't want to think about anything at all, but the memories of the dream kept whispering to her like a siren song that she knew meant horrible things.

The weight of her phone in her pocket was difficult to ignore as the temptation to start looking up when the book burnings had taken place and try to learn more about this person she'd probably been eighty years ago taunted her. Of course, she knew from experience that she might not like what she found. It was all a far cry from the ideal of the reincarnated King Arthur who would always be good and save people.

"Here you go." Jenny said. She set a steaming cup of coffee in front of Alex with a soft clink. "Drink up."

Alex blinked at the sound of the voice as the scent of the coffee hit her. It was a simple large deep brown mug that looked handmade with hints of blue around the rim and handle. She found the earthy color oddly reassuring. Grumbling at Jenny's overly cheerful tone, Alex obediently picked up the warm cup and took a drink. The bitter taste hit her tongue, but the rush of caffeine was already doing its job.

"You know," she said after swallowing a few sips. "I'm not sure if coffee is the best or worst thing we ever created."

"What?" Nicki chuckled and slid into the seat next to her. "An addictive not restricted substance that millions can't get through a day without? Surely not."

"Don't start, Nicki." Aiden groaned as he sank into his seat at the large corner table holding his own mug. "Not this morning." He sighed happily after his first sip.

Alex nodded her agreement and took another long sip of the coffee as she looked around. The coffee shop was fairly quiet thanks to the initial rush of the day being over. It was a pretty, old building with the brick exposed on the interior. Local artwork hung from small chains from the ceiling and small cards with prices were next to them. A display of baked sweets was next to the register and the staff was moving fluidly around each other behind the counters. There were a few groups scattered about that alternated between older folks and people their own age. She was so lost taking in the environment that it took Alex a long moment to realize that the others were watching her and waiting.

"I don't want to talk about it," Alex told them firmly as she looked into her mug of coffee. "Nicki brought you up to speed this morning and that's that."

"Not really, Alex," Bran countered kindly. "It's the best lead that we've got. You've probably been thinking about the Hammer so much that your mind and magic reached out to find it." He offered her a soft smile though his green eyes were a bit sad. "That's something to be grateful for, even if it is a bit rough for you."

Bran's explanation didn't make her feel much better, but it did ease the worry about why she'd suddenly started dreaming about yet another life. Seeing and feeling Arto die hadn't been a picnic and hadn't been useful, at least this had the potential to be. She stayed silent and took another sip of her coffee, looking into the brown swirling liquid rather than at her friends.

"And Morgana is right that you shouldn't make assumptions about this former life," Aiden said. "World War II and Nazi Germany was a mess. Efficient on the surface, but a lot of issues. There were resistance groups and depending on the circumstances you- he may not have had a lot of options."

"I really don't want to talk about it guys," Alex snapped. Then she sighed, putting down the coffee cup and forcing herself to look at them. Vaguely she wondered how messy and tired she looked. "I get what you're saying, but I don't want to get my hopes up." Shaking her head, she groaned a little before adding, "I mean I've already got a slave ship captain former life. There's no getting around the fact he was a nasty piece of work. I was just hoping that I wouldn't find out I had another nasty life so quickly."

"I get it, Alex," Lance said gently, giving her a smile as he rested his elbows on the table. "Reincarnation is a bit uncomfortable. Jenny and I know that."

"It's not the same thing," Alex reminded him. Leaning forward herself, she looked between the pair of them. "You weren't Nazis." The word tasted bitter on her tongue and Alex was sure it was the years of history, culture, and movies and not the coffee.

"Maybe." Jenny said, tugging at a strand of her hair. "Might have been. It could have been one of our lives, who knows? The point is that you certainly aren't a Nazi." Jenny reached over and brushed her hand over

Alex's for a moment. "It isn't you, Alex. Not anymore and it doesn't affect this life. Remember?"

"You can't obsess about this," Lance said firmly. "It'll mess with your head." Alex almost flinched at the words, remembering the panic attack she'd had in Bran's kitchen. Her stomach tightened and a chill swept over her. "But denial doesn't help either."

"You two do realize that this doesn't seem that convincing from you," Alex huffed as a strand of blonde hair fell into her face. "You are dating now so clearly there is some carry over."

"Which didn't start until we'd taken some time to process things," Jenny pointed out with a frown, obviously a little offended by her point.

"Look, I appreciate that you two have experience on this crazy issue," Alex forced out, trying to keep her voice calm though she could hear a quiver. "But it's the memories more than anything. I..." She faltered for a moment, all too aware that the others were waiting. "I enter their head; I feel things with them and it isn't always pleasant. It's not really about if this guy was a Nazi, it's just... sharing headspace even in a dream is weird."

Understatement, but the others' expressions softened. Alex was aware that they were all exchanging worried looks and was reassured that they got it, at least to a point. She felt a little lighter and inhaled deeply even as her knees turned to jelly beneath the table. From his place on her left side, Bran reached over and squeezed her hand. He caught her eye and gave her a small smile.

"I know," he murmured to her and Alex was reminded that to a certain extent Bran did. Unlike Jenny and Lance, his visions had actually put him into some sort of contact with the original Bran. "We'll back off," he promised. "Just tell us what you need."

"If you want to talk then let us know," Nicki added, looking uncomfortable. "We're your friends, Alex."

"Exactly," Aiden agreed with a smile. "Yours, not Arto's or Thor's or Gottrich-"

"Gottfried," Alex corrected with a chuckle. "Honestly what is it with you and Nicki and names?"

She got what they were saying. It sank in and Alex knew that at least on most levels they were right. Yet if the dreams didn't stop... what then. Jenny caught her eye and gave a small nod of understanding. At least Jenny and Lance did know that it would take some time to process. She wondered if this cold knot in her stomach was something they'd experienced, but didn't want to ask. Now wasn't the time. They didn't really have time for this.

"I should get the tablet set up," Bran said. Turning in his chair, he reached for his bag. "Morgana should be calling at any moment."

"That isn't necessary," a crisp slightly accented and very familiar voice said behind them.

"Morgana!" Alex squeaked, almost falling from her chair in surprise. "Uh-"

"I said that we'd speak." Morgana raised an eyebrow as she came to a halt next to their table and stared right at Alex.

"I thought you'd call," Alex told her. Lance stood up and grabbed another chair from a nearby empty table and set it across from Alex. "I wasn't expecting you to be in town."

"Just arrived," Morgana said, sounding a touch out of breath. She took the seat and nodded to Lance. "I felt it was better to do this in person."

"You didn't water travel, did you?" Nicki asked quietly, looking around the coffee shop as if she expected to see a fountain or pool of water.

"No, Nicki," Morgana answered patiently. "I drove up an hour ago and scryed for you."

"You can get it that detailed?" Bran questioned with wide eyes. "So exact?"

"I could see the coffee shop name," Morgana explained gently with a soft look of amusement. "Then I used Google."

Pressing her lips together, Alex almost laughed when Bran's expression faltered as his brain processed her statement. Nicki wasn't able to hold in the giggle and Aiden grinned. Jenny looked surprised and a bit thrown off by Morgana actually showing a sense of humor around her and shifted a bit closer to Lance.

"Now if that is settled," Morgana chuckled affectionately as her eyes traced over all their faces. "We have things that need discussing."

"Is Merlin back yet?" Alex asked. "Any news?"

"I'm afraid that Ambrose has not contacted me as to his plans," Morgana said. She shrugged out of her light jacket and hung it over the back of her chair. "He told me that he was going to seek out Sif and confirm that she didn't have information about the Iron Hammer. He has yet to confirm that he is on his way back to Ravenslake."

"Can't you call him?" Nicki asked with a deep frown that made Alex nervous.

"I have attempted to, but he seems to be out of range," Morgana answered. As they began to ask more questions, she sharply brought up a hand to motion for silence. "Don't panic, he may very well still be in the mountains looking for clues. Service can be unreliable in rural areas."

"Is this unlike him?" Alex asked uneasily. The idea of Merlin simply dropping out of contact frightened her a little, though after three thousand years she expected that he could look after himself. "He'll be alright, won't he?"

"It's not unlike him, Alex, so try not to worry. He's been known to follow his own path at times, just usually not when there is an active

Iron Soul life." Morgana paused thoughtfully and gave a little shake of her head. "Merlin has lived through much worse things and he has magic right now," Morgana assured her with a slight smile. "He'll be fine, it just means that he is not going to be a part of this conversation. I'm sure that he's just trying to follow some trails on the Iron Hammer."

"So, what are we going to do?" Aiden asked, leaning forward and lowering his voice. "You wouldn't have come all the way to Portland just for a chat if you didn't have a plan."

Morgana gave Aiden an approving look, but said nothing as one of the servers came over with her mug of coffee and croissant. She nodded to the server and made them all wait as she took a sip of her drink.

"I called on a friend in Germany, a fellow history professor," Morgana explained. "Called in an old favor. He wasn't able to find much on Gottfried Eckstein, but confirmed that Eckstein was a professor of linguistics in Cologne before the Nazis took power. He was married with four children, two sons and two daughters. His family lived in an old village a little outside the city."

"And?" Alex pressed, her heart racing. "Anything else?"

"Johann did me a favor and only had a few hours, Alex," Morgana reminded her sternly. "He was lucky that Eckstein's name could be found in relation to the university. Any information on his career in the party is going to take a great deal more time and honestly a lot of luck to find. Many records are long since destroyed."

"But hey he was a language expert," Aiden said, giving her a smile. "That would explain why the Nazis may have sent him on an expedition for the Hammer. Probably means that he wasn't part of the fighting or..." he trailed off with his smile falling.

Morgana said nothing. Alex was grateful that her professor wasn't in a hurry to offer potentially false reassurances. Her mind turned over the information of the four children nervously. She'd never heard of an Iron Soul having kids before and with them being from World War II she might have grandkids- Alex stopped that train of thought with a sharp little shake of her head. Sitting up straighter she took a deep gulp of her coffee and pretended not to notice Morgana's gaze.

"So, is this friend of yours going to keep looking?" Nicki asked Morgana to Alex's gratitude since she wasn't sure she could get her mouth to work.

"No," Morgana said. "I don't want to draw too much attention to it. The last thing we need is Arthur catching wind of what we are looking for. He's already proven that he's happy to use cell phones to track you, I don't doubt that he'll try to monitor what Merlin and I are doing."

"I don't remember him being that tech savvy," Jenny muttered, gripping her mug tightly and clenching her jaw.

"He might have kept it a secret or he might be working with some Sídhe descendants," Aiden offered with a tilt of his head. "I mean if you think about it, they look albino, but too many of them in one place would attract attention. They may work behind the scenes jobs."

"You think they have jobs?" Lance asked. Then he pressed his lips thoughtfully and nodded. "I suppose that some of these creatures must have some sort of income."

"A topic for another time," Morgana cut in smoothly though Alex thought she saw a glint of interest in the older mage's eye. It was weird to remember that Merlin and Morgana didn't necessarily stop and think about things like they did. "We have more pressing matters to discuss. Alex's dreams are most certainly the result of her focusing on wanting to find the Iron Hammer. Gottfried Eckstein isn't a great lead so far, so I will keep digging and see what we can find. Alex's words about the Iron Hammer being in Paris are our best lead and we need to follow it. There was a lot of chaos in Paris during the Nazi occupation and a lot of effort was being made to preserve historical sections of the city. If Gottfried Eckstein did get his hands on the Iron Hammer, then Paris would have been a good place to hide it."

"So, what do we do?" Alex asked, dropping her head forward to lean it on her hand. "What exactly is your plan, Morgana?"

Green eyes met her own and the world shifted a little. Some old instinct had her holding her breath and waiting. Morgana sighed, the sound somehow echoing through the whole coffee shop. There was a moment of silence and in the corner of her eye, Alex saw several people stop with strange looks on their faces as if they'd felt something odd. Shaking her head, Morgana picked up her coffee and took another sip as the rest of the world seemed to regain its proper rhythm.

"Well," Morgana finally said as she set down her coffee. "Before I headed here, I took the liberty of collecting all your passports and arranging six tickets to Paris. That's your lead and you kids have a week off school. The way forward seems obvious."

Alex barely held back a sigh as the others let out small gasps and in Jenny's case a short squeak of excitement. The only thing on her mind as she and Morgana stared at each other was the realization that in three thousand years her sister hadn't changed all that much.

12

Occupants of Paris

April 1942 C.E. Paris, France

Papers were spread out in front of him on the large desk with the faint breeze from the open window fluttering the edges slightly. The sounds of the city formed a pleasant background hum. His SS cap was placed just to the right of his hand and he glanced at it as he picked up a pen. A blank sheet of paper waited in front of him, but the words were not coming. The Nazi flag in the corner rippled in the light breeze and drew his eyes up to the photograph of Hitler hanging opposite his desk near the door. A silent watcher in the small office. There never seemed to be a shortage of those photographs.

He set his pen down at the top of the page and started with a sweet greeting and Ilse's name. Then he stopped. It was always so difficult to know what to write. It was too depressing to go on and on about missing her, the children, and Germany though it was all true. He had no doubt that she'd read parts of the letter to the children and didn't wish to bring them down. His earlier letters had spoken about Paris and some of the sights, but that was quickly losing any attraction for him.

Putting the pen to paper he started writing a little about his daily routine. He made sure not to put anything too detailed about locations and schedule in. Ilse wouldn't react well to a letter full of censorship holes. There wasn't much to say in truth. His role in intelligence was fairly minor compared to other officers. A knock on the door a moment later drew his attention up from the letter.

"Come in."

It was one of the younger officers who strode in. His Second Lieutenant uniform was perfectly pressed and judging from the shine on his belt all of the metal had been recently cleaned. He recognized him from a few of the French refresher classes, though with his neatly cut brown hair, small mustache, and blue eyes nothing about him really stood out. The man saluted him quickly.

"Hiel Hitler!" It was almost a yell.

Rising to his feet, he returned the salute automatically in at a much lower volume. "Hello, Lieutenant Baumann, what can I do for you?" He sat back down in his chair and folded his hands patiently.

"I apologize for the intrusion, Captain Eckstein." Baumann held out a letter towards him. It had no official markings and he quickly accepted it. "News from home, sir?"

Eckstein turned it over and examined the name and address. His shoulders slumped a bit despite himself. "Yes, from an old colleague. I haven't heard from him for a few months."

"From Cologne?"

"Yes." Eckstein had to force himself not to give the other officer an annoyed look. No doubt he'd seen Cologne marked on the letter. "I taught at the University there." The man didn't react to the statement. Baumann probably already knew that.

He watched Baumann for a moment before he pulled out the two-page letter. Baumann didn't move even as he began to scan the letter. Only a couple of lines had been blacked out and otherwise it was just news from the university. Apparently a few more of his former colleagues had been brought into service. There was a report on the marriage of a former favorite student of his and the birth of another professor's first grandchild. To his own surprise he was smiling a little, even if it wasn't the letter he'd been hoping for. Baumann however was still in his office and showing no signs of moving. Gritting his teeth for a moment, Eckstein watched Baumann shift towards the window.

"And your family do they live in the city?" There was a real hint of worry in the officer's voice that calmed Eckstein's nerves.

"No, our home is a ways outside of the city in a smaller village. A bit more peaceful so the Allied bombings haven't been a personal issue." The yet hung in the air and Eckstein almost shivered at the thought. Sooner or later a bomber would miss the targets by a greater margin or they'd simply run out of things to bomb in Cologne. "My family is safe."

"Barbarians the allies," Baumann almost growled as his face twisted into a sneer. "Cologne is one of our cultural jewels and they bomb it with no regard for all the history there."

Eckstein nodded in agreement though he couldn't help but feel that the same could be said of London. This twice damned war was destroying everything everywhere. All he could be grateful for was that when he'd been secure at the university, Ilse had insisted that she didn't want to the live in Cologne proper. The commute in for both of them had been long, but before the restrictions on women working, he'd rather enjoyed the time together it gave them. He couldn't fathom the worry others must feel daily knowing that loved ones were right in a target city.

Baumann had moved over to his open window, still making no move to leave. Eckstein narrowed his eyes suspiciously and glanced around his desk just to make sure that there was nothing he didn't want in view.

There wasn't of course, but paranoia had long since wormed its way into his daily life.

"It's sad sometimes. Watching the Parisians move about down below," Baumann suddenly said. "They're so angry, self-loathing about their own cooperation despite it being for the best. This resistance of theirs is useless. All it does is destroy more of Paris and French lives."

"Their city, their country no longer belongs to them," Eckstein observed carefully. He watched the other man's body language closely, but he gave nothing away. "I suppose I can't blame them. If the positions were reversed and I feared for the safety of my own children I would do anything to protect them, but I would resent it." Tilting his head slightly, he noted an uncertain expression on the other man's face. "But in time I'm sure that they will recognize that German rule is best for them."

"A fair point, sir." Baumann nodded and glanced at the photographs sitting on the side table. Eckstein stayed silent and gave the man a moment to take them in. His favorite was of the whole family with his wife Ilse smiling warmly as she held the six-year-old Elsa. There were more recent ones of the children, but none of them all together since then. The photo had been taken back in 1936, almost six years ago he recalled sadly. "You have a beautiful family. Four children?"

"Yes, that photo is a few years old I'm afraid. Two boys and two girls."

"A fine mix, sir, you and your wife must be proud." He picked up one of the more recent photographs that showed a teenager and a boy in Hitler Youth uniforms. "Your sons, Captain? Member of the Hitler Youth, I see."

"Yes, Enrich and Reinhold. Enrich is sixteen now. His brother is fourteen. My wife tells me that it keeps them very busy with different activities."

"Excellent, sir. I'm sure your boys will be fine additions to the army in a few more years." Baumann almost smiled, the expression was off putting on his features. Then Baumann put his hands behind his back. There was a flicker of hesitation on his features that Eckstein wasn't sure what to make of. The other man was trying to make his mind up about something, but what exactly he was uncertain of. "I'm considering marriage myself, but there are so few German women here in France. I would, of course, only start a family with a true ethnic German girl."

"Perhaps you will be transferred home soon." Eckstein shifted in his chair and pulled out a file folder from his desk, giving Baumann a pointed look.

"I can hope." Baumann merely moved over in front of the desk again and folded his hands behind his back. "When was the last time you were home, sir?"

"It's been over a year now."

"So, you used to work at a university? I heard you were a professor; did you teach French then too?"

"On occasion," Eckstein answered with a nod. "I was a linguist. I taught several languages in classes, but I occupied myself studying the proto-languages for the most part. Sometimes I consulted on lesser-known languages. It was interesting work."

"It's almost a pity then to have someone of your skill merely teaching soldiers and translating documents," Baumann said. There was a hint of something in his voice that Eckstein didn't trust.

"Well, it is important that our men are able to communicate with the French." He fought to keep his features neutral and added, "Bilingualism is important in gathering information and administrating such a large city."

"At least until they all learn German," Baumann added.

Eckstein looked up at the younger man, wondering how long he was going to linger. And if he'd been sent to make small talk and probe him. He couldn't think of anything he'd done to draw attention to himself. The instruction he was giving the locally posted soldiers kept him busy in addition to his duties assisting with reports. Eckstein couldn't even remember the last time he'd spoken to a local.

"That will be a long process and one I suspect many older Frenchmen will resist." Eckstein closed the folder on his desk and decided to be frank with the younger officer. "Is there anything else I can do for you, Lieutenant? I appreciate you bringing me my mail, but I don't wish to detain you further."

Baumann's features shifted for a moment between surprise, anger, and a hint of worry. Then the younger man squared his shoulders, apparently having made his decision. "Yesterday you and Captain Fuchs were having a conversation in an unknown language," Baumann said almost smugly. "I overheard you in the Officer's Mess. It wasn't German or French, but unknown."

"Low German."

"I'm sorry?"

"It's called Low German, it is a regional dialect." Eckstein tried to look calm despite the line of questioning. Had this younger lower ranking officer decided that yesterday's conversation might give him a chance for advancement? The idea made him angry and he tightened his twined fingers. "I'm guessing that you are from Eastern Germany yourself."

"Berlin," Baumann answered, straightening up proudly.

"Ah yes, then you wouldn't be familiar with it I suppose. Low German is mainly spoken in northern Germany and the eastern Netherlands. There are pockets of speakers in other areas of course, but I doubt you'd hear it much in Berlin, though there are certainly those who speak Low German.”

“It didn't sound like German.” Baumann looked younger than before, almost like a petulant child and Eckstein had to remind himself to be careful.

“Well, as I said it is also spoken in the Netherlands. To be frank while it is linguistically part of the Germanic language family it is descended from Old Saxon and shares similarities with Dutch. In the Netherlands they call in Low Saxon in fact. Even amongst my fellow linguists there is debate of how to categorize the language.” He chuckled in an attempt to defuse the tension in the room and added, “My father was very fond of it and my grandfather spoke it all the time. It is the reason I became a linguist.”

“I'm not sure it is appropriate for a Nazi Officer to be speaking a language other than German and that your fellow officers don't understand.” Baumann looked flustered and angry. Tipped his hand too quickly, Eckstein thought with amusement. Did the boy think he'd be paying blackmail? Clearly, he did. Been spending too much time around the Gestapo. “I should report it, sir. You are a Nazi officer!”

“Report what exactly? That a linguist is seeking to keep in practice with the languages he speaks?” Eckstein's amusement was washing away the earlier fear. “I'm in Paris for now due to my fluency with French, but at some time I might be needed in the Netherlands. Low German is also used by parts of the Polish population as well. And by ethnic Germans in the Baltic States.”

“And Captain Fuchs?”

“Also comes from an area in west Germany that dabbles in Low German. We discovered it a few weeks ago and he's agreed to give me a chance to practice. Before the war I made use of the dialect by teaching it to my children.”

“I see,” Baumann replied tightly. “What were you talking about?”

“Mostly the weather and the recent Black-Market report,” he answered calmly. That part was a lie, but Baumann had no way of confirming that. He could see that the younger officer knew it. “Captain Fuchs is working with Gestapo on the rationing problems and wanted my opinion.”

“Very well, sir. Thank you for putting my mind at ease.” He saluted quickly and all but ran out of the room.

Once the door was shut Eckstein allowed himself a sigh of relief. He’d have to let Fuchs know that they needed to stop taking advantage of their fluency of Low German for private conversations, no matter how innocent. He could hear the stomping in the corridor outside his office fading away. Leaning back in his chair, he looked towards the photographs of his family and felt a twinge of guilt. He’d allowed himself to forget the primary rule of living in Nazi Germany: someone is always listening.

Shaking his head, he set the blank sheet of paper to the side. He couldn’t write home with this on his mind. Instead, he opened his top desk drawer and pulled out a thick folder with the latest documents the SS had seized, along with an intelligence report from downstairs on the latest black-market findings. He scanned the first opening lines and almost grumbled. Did it honestly surprise anyone that farmers were directing part of their yields into the black market? At least they could make a decent living that way when the rest of France was only one level above starving.

He finished the report and set it to the side. That was the administration office’s problem now, not the SS. At least not yet. The Gestapo would probably be the ones that jumped in on that one. He picked up the next document, pulled out a fresh sheet of paper, and began to translate the poorly scribbled French writing.

13

The Earthen Cache

It was good to be back in Wales. Merlin breathed in the crisp air with a small smile tugging at his lips. Morgana would no doubt roll her eyes at the simple joy he experienced from being back in the land of his birth, but there remained a connection. No matter how much time passed, no matter how much the technology and landscape changed, and no matter how many places he lived, this would always be home. They could change the name, they could change the language, but the land still echoed with the world he'd known.

"I'm getting sentimental in my old age," Merlin said aloud as he followed the hiking trail up the hillside. "And now I'm talking to myself." That made him chuckle and eased his worry a little more.

Far behind him was a car park where he'd left the small rental car he'd secured in Cardiff. Around him the greening hillsides were damp with the remnants of an early morning rainstorm and he could smell the oil of the plants in the air. It was fresh and put a spring in his step despite the seriousness of his mission. The simple black backpack he was carrying was light with a bottle of water tucked in the side. His phone was tucked in his pocket and he knew it was only a matter of time until Morgana called him again.

He paused and turned his gaze towards the north where he now knew a Dragon slumbered. It was a touch embarrassing to know that it- Emrys had been there on his previous visits to the region. They'd dismissed too much all those centuries ago when it came to Gofiben, Bran, and Galath. It pained him to think of how many times the Iron Chalice could have changed the course of a life of another Iron Soul. Merlin wished there was time to find the dragon Emrys and speak with him. Alas, time was not on their side. He needed to find the cache and to return to Ravenslake to keep Alex safe until they decided the next course of action.

Of course, his plan was to return with a working option for them. Scáthbás and Medraut had both already proved themselves capable of returning from death and they couldn't afford this fight to drag on. They needed something permanent, something there could never be any coming back from no matter how distasteful it might be. Morgana... well he didn't want to think about the conversation this would trigger with her just yet. Merlin shook his head, dismissing such thoughts. This wasn't the time to be wool gathering. Pulling the map of the area out of the pocket of the grey coat he was wearing, Merlin examined the hillside carefully to see how far he was from the tunnel entrance.

It wasn't far, just another mile around the curve of the old mountain. Merlin fancied that the path he was on might have been the same one that workers used three thousand years ago. That was silly of course due to the years of soil deposit that had occurred, but he liked the idea. Up ahead was a small information sign next to a deep depression in the ground that formed a small entrance into the mountainside.

A heavy wooden door filled the opening with chains crisscrossing to keep it shut. Merlin allowed himself a fond smile. It was nice, he supposed, that archeologists were beginning to pay more attention to their native culture rather than just focusing on the Roman era. That and he was confident that the cache was hidden deep enough and well enough to have escaped notice. Moving his hand lazily, Merlin called on his magic. Small green sparks danced across his fingers before he flicked them at the chains. The sparks spun around the metal and there was a soft hiss followed by a crash as the chains fell to the ground.

He pulled open the door, noting that rot was already beginning to set in. If this door had been put in to stop local children from running wild in the old mining tunnels, then it wouldn't hold up much longer. Before him, stretched a dark tunnel that he knew from personal experience had been dug with rocks, antlers, and the first metal tools. He looked over his shoulder, searching the area for the sign of anyone or anything following him before he slipped into the tunnel.

Opening his palm, Merlin exhaled slowly and watched as the green of his magic collected into an orb and brightened to a warm white color. The light was welcome in the dark, tight tunnels and Merlin began walking forward slowly. Beneath him the solid trod dirt floor of the tunnel muffled his footfalls, but his breathing echoed slightly in the long empty corridor. His eyes were occasionally drawn to small bits of artwork on the walls. There were painted animals and several handprints scattered about. Small reminders of the workers from so long ago.

There was no copper to be found down here any longer. Merlin was certain of that as his hand traced over part of the stone. Back in the late Bronze Age the isles had enjoyed their position of power. Tin from Ireland and copper from Wales combined to make bronze which was moved by boat as far away as Rome. It was a far cry from the idea of a barbaric backward world that the uneducated thought it had been.

He walked slowly, barely paying attention to the change in the air as he focused on all the branches of the tunnel. It was a bit harder than in his youth to keep track of the turns. Glancing back over his shoulder, he shivered a little at the realization of how far he was from the surface. As a young man he'd never properly appreciated that his position as the son of the local priestess and a smith had protected him from working in the tunnels.

Merlin panted slightly and stopped in front of a small niche in the stone. It was just large enough that one of the children workers could have sat in it to stay out of the way. He gave himself a moment to catch his breath, summoning his magic and releasing it into the air with a stern wish for the air to be made fresher. Green sparks spun through the air and the staleness eased enough for him to recover. He was grateful that Morgana wasn't here to lecture him on how silly he'd been not to pay attention to the thin air.

With a shake of his head, he turned his attention back to what he came for. Touching the wall thoughtfully, Merlin frowned and pushed a spark of his magic into the stone. Nothing happened and his frown deepened. He looked around the junction in mild confusion. He knew too well that magic had kept his memory strong over the centuries, but now... He stepped away from the wall and looked down the tunnel, trying to see if anything was familiar.

"Arrogant old fool," Merlin groaned, rubbing the side of his face with worry.

Uncertain, he moved further down the tunnel and stopped when he came to another niche space. He wasn't sure if this was the spot, but it looked like it. Just like the last one, he inwardly sighed. Nonetheless, he raised his hand to the wall again and pushed some of his magic into the stone. It shifted beneath his hand. A small section of the wall shimmered and sank down, exposing a small hole.

Merlin reached inside and carefully picked up a small sealed earthen jar. His fingers cradled it gently and he drew it out with the greatest of care. There were two more such jars in the hole along with a rusted iron dagger that the magic had failed to preserve and a lump of iron ore. He shrugged out of the backpack and let it fall to the ground. Unzipping it with one hand, Merlin pulled out the first of several towels and began to carefully wrap the first jar up. There was a strange sound that echoed down the tunnel, a soft muffled thump that made him look up sharply.

His light dimmed in response and Merlin tucked the wrapped jar into the bottom of the pack. He reached up and took out the second jar and began to wrap it as a muted crunch echoed weakly down the tunnel. Merlin's movements were shaky, but he managed to get the small jar surrounded in the fluffy towel and shoved deep into the bag before another light appeared at the closest turn. Raising his eyes, Merlin shifted the backpack behind him and carefully pushed it back with his foot.

A Sídhe descendent stepped around the corner. Its violet eyes caught the light as the beam from the flashlight it carried settled on him. For a moment neither of them moved and Merlin took in the haggard appearance of the creature with its torn jeans and jacket. It was the sound of others coming up behind the first Síd creature that spurred Merlin on. Drawing his hand up, Merlin clawed his fingers and called on his magic. A worried voice that sounded like Alex at the back of his mind cried that these poor creatures were being controlled. Their free will had been stripped away. Guiltily, he said a silent apology to the memory of Frea before tossing the orb of glowing green magic in his hand forward.

It burst into tiny sparks upon impact with the creature. Merlin glared at them, focusing his magic with a mental command as the spark burrowed into the creature's flesh. An aborted scream ripped from it, only to be silenced as it dissolved into dust. The flashlight fell to the ground and hit the rock with a soft crack as the plastic broke. Light filled part of the tunnel, casting an eerie shadow as he summoned magic into both of his hands.

"Abomination," one of the back creatures hissed. The light of the flashlight revealed another three Sídhe just around the corner.

Merlin took an uneasy step back. There was a glint in the eyes of the advancing Sídhe that worried him. Suddenly it seemed all too clear that they weren't in control of themselves, but the knowledge that it was part of the power of the Iron Soul made him feel ill. The magic in his palms flared in response to his thoughts, but Merlin pushed the thought away.

One of the creatures lunged towards him, slashing with long talons. Thrusting his right hand forward, Merlin released the magic in a sharp wave that sliced through the air. The creature screamed as the magic struck its chest, cutting through the layers of clothing and into the flesh. Silvery blood splattered out against the walls and ground, catching the light. It vanished as the creature did leaving only flecks of dust. Merlin brought forward his left hand and release the leaf green magic in a small bolt at the second creature only for it to dodge out of the way. The blast hit the Síd creature behind it before Merlin could redirect the magic.

It took him a moment to realize that his enemy was right next to the opening in the wall and he froze in horror as the creature grabbed at the last jar. There was a flicker of something in its eyes, but Merlin's attention was drawn away from that as another two Sídhe descendants rushed around the corner. Throwing a hand forward, Merlin sent a wild shower of green sparks raining down on the advancing Sídhe while his eyes locked onto the jar.

The creature threw it towards him. Panic gripped Merlin's chest with an intensity he hadn't felt in over a century. Magic flared from his fingertips as he raised a hand up in a futile attempt to protect himself. The wave of green sparks rushed through the air, striking the jar and knocking it away from him. He could see the fragile earthen jar beginning to crack as it sailed towards the tunnel wall.

The jar smashed against the wall, splashing the liquid across the stone and onto the Síd. Hissing filled the air only to be drowned out by screaming. A shriek of agony and terror ripped through the tunnels. Skin was vanishing from the Síd as the liquid spread up its arm. It clawed at the arm, tried to tear off its coat as the others drew back in horror. Merlin's eyes moved to the wall. The stone was dissolving, being eaten away by acid as his heart dropped into his stomach.

He'd been warned it was a powerful poison. Cyrridven had warned him that the remains of the potion they'd brewed all those years ago to help him learn his magic and connect with the Iron Realm would be deadly. The affected creature spun towards its fellows, lunging at one with frantic sounds spilling from its mouth. To escape it, the second creature jerked away only to collide with the dissolving wall. Merlin saw a dark droplet fall onto its arm and grimaced as the process resumed.

The third Sídhe creature was frozen in place, its eyes wide with shock. Merlin summoned his magic and sent a bolt of bright green blasting through the air. The bolt struck the creature which dissolved with a cry of surprise. Those affected by the poison didn't even notice. The first one suddenly dropped to the ground, its body shaking and limbs twitching. Its mouth opened in a silent scream only for the body to vanish around the face. There was no dust, no ash as it vanished. Just nothing.

An uncomfortable wave of pity hit Merlin as he watched the last of the creatures fall to the ground. He summoned an orb of magic and tossed it towards the creature, ordering the magic to end the thing's life. But as it struck, the dark liquid flowing over the Síd's skin expanded and the magic vanished. Stepping back in horror and almost tripping on the bag, Merlin tucked his limbs close to his body and stayed completely still. The creature vanished, leaving no traces and then slowly the dark liquid faded away. It was a long time before he dared to move.

Merlin looked back to the wall. There was a new small opening where the liquid had eaten away the wall and floor. Thankfully it seemed to have finally stopped. There was no sound in the tunnels save his own breathing and Merlin licked his lips nervously. He dropped his gaze to his pack that had managed to remain out of the way of the fight. Two jars were wrapped up inside it. Two jars that he hoped would be the key to destroying Arthur and Scáthbás once and for all.

Picking up the pack, Merlin carefully slipped it on. His eyes moved back to the gaping hole in the wall and he grimaced. Part of him dearly wanted to stay and study it, an instinct he blamed on his profession in chemistry a few decades back, but a voice sounding like Cyrridven in his head warned him to stay away. He stepped around the area, taking care not to touch any of the edges and moved down the tunnel stopping just long enough to pick up the fallen flashlight. All he could do was seal up the area and hope that no one came poking around here for a long time. He just hoped that Morgana and the children were staying safely within the new protective blood spells.

14

The Departing

And they were back at the Portland Airport about to go to a whole other continent in order to find a magical artifact. Alex almost burst out laughing. Somehow her quiet and calm life had become one of Aiden and Bran's games. She'd heard them mention fetch quests in the past and this sort of fit. Find the Iron Chalice in Wales in order to heal Aiden so he will wake up. Find the Iron Hammer so they could hopefully break the magical connection between the Queen and all the Sídhe creatures. So that they weren't being hunted and didn't have to kill controlled creatures to survive. Alex's stressed amusement dried up as that thought processed.

She looked around the main foyer of the airport. It was clean and fairly modern. Nothing looked out of place and Alex relaxed a tiny bit. There were no Sídhe and no signs of Arthur. Still Alex couldn't help but scan everything. Her fingers clenched and unclenched as she lamented that she now had the habit to check her surroundings.

"I can't believe we're going to Paris!" Looking at her boarding pass fondly, Jenny shifted excitedly between her feet.

"Going to Paris with no time to see anything," Nicki added with a dark look and a grumble.

"Well, that may not be true," Bran pointed out with a reassuring smile. "If I was going to hide something in Paris, I'd put it near a landmark so it could be found in the future."

"We don't know that Eckstein ever meant for the Iron Hammer to be found," Aiden reminded them with a shake of his head. "He might not have been thinking that far ahead, especially without knowledge of magic."

"Aiden makes a good point," Morgana agreed with a nod, turning her attention back to Alex. She grabbed her hands and squeezed. "Remember that this life matters in the here and now. Try not to worry about who Eckstein was."

"I'm more worried about all the dreams," Alex confided. "What happens if I can't keep it all straight?"

Morgana's expression was conflicted and the older mage seemed to be struggling for what to say. Under other circumstances, Alex might have found it amusing or impressive that she could make Morgana lost for words.

"It may not be easy," Morgana finally conceded. "I won't argue with you on that. You're the only female life that I'm aware of and there have been many Iron Soul incarnations. I'm not sure how many exactly, but that's a lot weighing you down." She paused and gathered her thoughts for another moment. "Perhaps try writing it all down. See if that helps you create some distance. During the dreams try to think of them as movies."

"I'll try," Alex agreed with a forced smile. "Thanks."

Morgana nodded, but clearly wasn't fooled by Alex's brush off. Nonetheless, she reached into her leather satchel and pulled out a small wrapped package. Alex turned her attention to it, eager for anything else to focus on.

"Your passports," Morgana announced as she handed Alex the small wrapped bundle. "Do you have everything else you need?"

"I think so," Alex told her as she opened the packet and pulled out the passports. Flipping them open, she began to hand them out to the appropriate people. "It isn't a vacation; hopefully we'll get there and find the Hammer quickly."

"I hope so," Morgana agreed. "I dislike allowing you to leave Ravenslake again without me." The frown was back on her face and there were small lines between her eyes.

"We'll be fine," Alex assured her with a forced smile. "Besides, you said so yourself that someone needs to keep an eye out for the Sídhe returning. Even with the blood protection spells active they'll keep trying."

"Yes, they will and yes, I did say that," Morgana conceded with a slight frown. "I made one more attempt to call Merlin, but still no luck in reaching him."

"We'll keep an eye out," Alex offered weakly, earning her a dubious smile from Morgana.

"You do that," the mage replied dryly. "I will protect Ravenslake and relay information to you from Merlin once he returns." Morgana reached into her pocket and pulled out an envelope that she opened quickly, pulling out two credit cards. "Here you are, Alex," Morgana announced as she handed one to Alex. There was no name on the card, instead it was one of the prepaid cards sold in grocery stores. "I've taken the liberty of securing you kids some funds. Far easier than trying to arrange repayment to a lawyer who wants to know what is happening," she added with a teasing look at Jenny.

"Wow," Alex breathed looking at the card. "Thank you, how much is on it?"

"Ten thousand dollars," Morgana replied calmly as she pulled out a second one and handed it to Bran. "Try not to be ridiculous in how you spend it. I may have been diligent in long term investments, but it isn't easy to keep that much in liquid assets. I can't pull it again on short notice."

Bran was staring at the card she handed him with a stunned expression and shared a look of surprise with Alex. "Uh on this one too?"

"Yes, I can't imagine anything will occur that will require more than twenty thousand at one time, but if there is anything let me know at once," Morgana insisted, acting as if she hadn't handed them a year of college tuition. "But I don't want to risk you not getting what you need while you're in Paris. Hopefully the Hammer is there, but it is possible you'll be guided somewhere else."

Holding back a laugh, Alex risked a glance towards Nicki who looked torn between gawking at Morgana and near irritation. The expression on her face was a bit like a goldfish with her mouth opening as she tried to think of something to say. Some levity was nice and Alex inhaled deeply while the corner of Morgana's mouth twitched up. The professor clearly knew that she'd managed to put her a little at ease. It was a quiet sort of affection that left Alex reassured someone was looking out for her. And yet here Morgana was allowing her to go off on another 'quest' for a magical artifact without her. She trusted them and Alex thought that might be worth even more.

This wasn't the time to ponder her relationship with Morgana and she became aware that she'd been silent at least a moment too long. Thankfully the others either didn't notice or decided against saying anything. She looked down at their meager bags which consisted only of backpacks at this point which just fit the carry-on rules. They were ready to go through security and start the long trip overseas, but Alex didn't feel ready. Someone moved behind her and she started to tense.

"So why do Alex and Bran get the cards?" Nicki questioned, leaning around Alex and looking at the card with false disinterest. She relaxed as a long red braid fell against her arm and Nicki winked at her.

"I feel Alex and Bran are the most responsible," Morgana informed Nicki with a sly smile.

"You just like them better since they're former students," Nicki pouted, making Aiden laugh. "Darn reincarnation and playing favorites."

Morgana chuckled and Alex relaxed a little, not as thrown by the reincarnation joke as she expected. Then Morgana turned and looked up at her with a fond smile even as her green eyes hardened seriously.

"Stay safe," Morgana commanded her sternly. "Try to find the Hammer, but if you cannot, then return here and we'll work on another plan. No one's life hangs in the balance this time."

"Okay," Alex agreed, but the word sounded a bit hollow to her. Judging from the look on Morgana's face she'd heard it too, but honestly if they didn't find the Hammer then the dreams wouldn't stop and that was just... not okay. "We'll keep you up to date," she settled for promising.

"We'll go and get in line for security," Bran announced with a smile as he bent over and picked up her backpack. "It'll take long enough as it is."

Offering Bran a small smile, Alex nodded and watched the others file over to the roped off area. Portland security wasn't too bad, but he wasn't wrong that it would take some time. She turned her attention back to Morgana and allowed a soft sigh to escape her.

"What are you going to do?" Alex asked. "I mean are you really going to be okay in Ravenslake by yourself until Merlin comes back."

"I'll be fine," Morgana assured her with a fond smile. She reached up and brushed a strand of her blonde hair out of Alex's face. "Contrary to what you may think Merlin and I haven't spent three thousand years joined at the hip. And as for what I'm going to do, I'm going to sit down with Timothy and have a long talk with him over the current state of the Sídhe slave descendants. Once we break the power of the Iron Chain reaching out to them as potential allies could become a critical step. I know Scáthbás and she won't just give up."

"I wish we knew more about her," Alex said. "Arthur said that Elaine was just her vessel, but we still don't know how. If she was trapped in England then how did she get to California?"

"I don't know, but I'm looking into some options to learn more about her history," Morgana informed Alex calmly. "You're not the only one with questions and how she's managed all this may reveal how to stop her."

"Okay... well just be careful," Alex ordered with a weak laugh. "And if you need us then call and we could try-"

"Nicki is not ready to water travel," Morgana cut in firmly, giving Alex a stern look. "But I will be fine and Merlin will be back soon. He's failed to locate the Hammer and doesn't know yet that you've had a lead."

"He isn't going to be happy about that."

"It's his own fault for not checking in," Morgana reminded her, though her mouth was tight. "He's planning something."

"Merlin?" Alex almost laughed. "You sure?"

"Don't let the absentminded professor image fool you, Alex," Morgana scolded. "There are times that even after three thousand years he surprises me with his choices."

"Are you worried..." Alex trailed off, not sure how to finish the question.

"I'm not worried about his loyalty," Morgana answered softly before sighing and shaking her head. "Don't worry about it. Sometimes we just clash, but it'll be alright." She reached up and gripped Alex's shoulder, giving it a solid squeeze. "You focus on finding the Hammer. I know you're worried, but the memories are with you for a reason. You are the champion of the Iron Realm and as you protect it, so too will it protect you."

She had no idea how to respond to that. It was the sort of heavy thing she'd expect from a fantasy book and yet there was a ring of truth to it that hummed in Alex's bones. Offering Morgana a small nod and a half smile, Alex gestured over to the others.

"I should go," she said uselessly. "Please be careful."

"There are blood protections all over the northwest now," Morgana reminded her. "I think I'll be fine."

"They may not stop Arthur or his mother," Alex said. "And there... are other ways to hurt people. Or the Sídhe might break through the gate."

"I'll keep an eye out," Morgana promised with a hint of impatience. "Go on and stop worrying about me. I've managed this long, haven't I?"

"I suppose," Alex agreed, really wishing that she had something clever and witty to say. "Okay then."

She nodded and took a step back, fighting down the uneasy feeling of leaving Morgana. Something in her really didn't want to move away. Alex almost asked Morgana to come with them, but even the knowledge that her hometown and Ravenslake were protected wasn't enough for her to do so. Too much could happen and Merlin was in the wind. Sighing slightly, Alex walked over to the line. Bran smiled at her and shifted just enough for her to duck under the rope.

"You okay?" Bran asked softly, leaning towards her.

"Fine," Alex replied only to get a raised eyebrow from him. "I'm a little uneasy," she admitted softly. "Just worried."

"We'll be with you every step of the way," Bran promised. He reached down and squeezed her hand in reassurance. "If you need anything tell us."

"Right now, I need my bag."

Bran grinned and handed the backpack over. Shifting forward, Alex pulled her bag onto her back while Bran gave her a knowing look. She gave herself a moment to gather her composure before looking back toward Morgana, but the mage was already gone.

"Come on line," Aiden grumbled behind her making Alex turn to look at him. He was rocking on his toes and peering towards the front of the line. "We've got a plane to catch. Adventure awaits!"

"You are way too excited about this," Nicki laughed, tossing her long red hair.

"Hey I'm the one who missed the Quest for the Iron Chalice," Aiden groaned. "Forgive me if I'm excited about the Quest for Thor's Hammer."

"Doesn't have the same ring to it," Lance teased with a widening smile.

"Sadly, I must agree with you," Aiden grumbled dramatically. "But come on, let's get through security and get something to eat."

"Another international flight," Nicki groaned. "I'm starting to hate flying, why couldn't we just use water transport."

"Oh, do you want to be the one who makes sure that we end up in Paris," Bran countered with a raised eyebrow. "I don't know about you, but I remember Merlin mentioning something about mages who disappeared into the water tunnels and probably drowned."

"Touché," Nicki agreed with a tilt of her head before she paused. "I wonder if we'll ever find Cathanáil."

"Oh yeah," Aiden groaned. "I knocked it into Arthur's water tunnel, didn't I?"

"You did," Alex agreed, reaching over to squeeze his arm. "But trust me, lost to the water of the world is better than in the hands of Arthur."

"Still maybe that should be the next quest," Aiden suggested with a growing smile.

"Easy, boy," Alex said. "Let's get through this fetch quest first." She allowed herself to smile and added, "Though I have wondered if being the current Iron Soul would let me find it. Cathanáil was pretty awesome."

"Great, that's next on the to do list then" Bran gestured for them to move forward into the line. "But first things first."

The line moved forward and another sound of excitement escaped Nicki. Lance laughed and put his arm around Jenny with a soft smile on his face as she looked up at him. A rush of joy hit Alex at seeing Lance and Jenny smiling at each other. She breathed out slowly, a bit more easily this time. At least there was them. A bunch of lifetimes, but they had finally gotten together peacefully. That little hum at the back of her mind quieted a little at that thought and Alex tried not to dwell on the question of what that hum was.

15

Lady from the Waters

1 16 C.E. Sør-Trøndelag, Norway

Dusk was settling in and they still had yet to reach a decision. Overhead the first faint star was appearing and all their allies were still in his village, arguing with the locals about the fate of the Dvergr. Thor glared at his father and brother, not liking the way they and the other villagers were huddling together to talk. This had been going on for hours now and his head was pounding like someone had taken a hammer to it.

Narrowing his eyes on the others, he inwardly growled at all of them. Why were they making this a problem? After all, Brokkr had been a boon in the forge, finishing projects that Thor didn't have time for anymore because of his magic training.

"Don't be angry with them," Sif's soft voice said beside him as she sat down on the stone with him. "This is strange and unsettling to them. Asking them to house a whole group of unknown creatures is a lot to ask."

Sighing softly, Thor closed his eyes and rubbed at them, willing the returning headache away. "Am I that easy to read?"

"Your glare helped. I'm a bit worried too, but you need to remember that the people of this village have only seen the bad side of strangers from other worlds. Most settlements in this area don't have protective walls."

Thor conceded her point. The arrival of Morgana and Merlin had brought a lot of change to his small village. Before there had been a smooth if dull rhythm to life. Provided illness didn't take hold of you, then life was fairly planned out. It had been something he'd hated and one of the reasons he'd been pleased when he'd first discovered his own power. Even if he hadn't dared to reveal it to anyone.

"You're right. I should try to remember how this has affected all of them."

"Oh, don't frown so, Thor." Sif reached over and brushed a warm fingertip over the furrows between his eyes. "It isn't all bad. I have no doubt what they experience will become part of great stories and songs! Surely that is worth something."

"But I wonder how much they will get wrong."

"A great deal, I am sure. There are tales of a being called Loki-"

"I've been wondering," Thor confessed, "But I didn't want to intrude."

"Don't worry, there is no such being. Not to my or my father's knowledge. We wonder sometimes if he was a creation of human imagination or if another powerful being passed through here long ago." She nodded towards Baldr. "And I recently heard of a being called Hod. Supposedly he is Baldr's twin, though they have different mothers."

"Uh..." Thor puzzled it over before giving up. "How does that work?"

"I have no idea," Sif confessed with a laugh. Placing her hand on his arm, she smiled warmly at him.

A chuckle escaped him and he exhaled slowly. Sif had achieved her purpose of distracting him and he was grateful to see that his father was nodding in agreement to Odin. Straightening up, Thor stood from the rock and extended a hand to Sif. She took it and they quickly moved to join the others. His brother glanced at the others for a moment before he shifted and moved over to them. He was moving slowly, eying Sif uncertainly.

"Arvid," Thor greeted with a nod. "This is Sif. Odin's daughter."

"A pleasure to meet you, Arvid," Sif said with a smile while his brother stared in surprise.

"The pleasure is mine, Sif." Arvid's eyes were wide as he looked between her and Thor. "Uh... well, Father has convinced most of the villagers to trust you though they are still nervous about having them here."

Frea moved over to join them and Arvid shifted back from her. She ignored him and focused her eyes on Thor. "We will start preparing an area for them in our village," Frea promised. "Once it is ready, they can come to us. We would welcome their abilities with metal."

Thor nodded in agreement and saw Arvid relax in relief, though his brother still looked a touch overwhelmed. "Thank you, Frea," Thor said. "That will help tensions here." It occurred to him that he didn't know much about Frea's home. As a Sídhe descendent she was a bit sensitive to bright light so they probably didn't live on the surface. "At least we have a temporary solution and they want to help. Though I'm not sure what we're supposed to do about the Dark Elves now."

"I do not believe that Sídhean will welcome the connection to them," Frea said. "The problem is that we just do not know how the magic of the Iron Gates is going to react to their attempts."

Frea was about to say more but stopped with an alert shine to her eyes. Tensing up, Thor felt the hair on the back of his neck standing on end.

Fires were burning throughout the village and the guards posted near the torches at the walls were in place. Nothing was wrong. Yet he could feel something just at the edge of his senses. Frea caught his eye and nodded her silent agreement. Arvid was looking between them. His confusion was obvious, but he was waiting for them to tell him more. Thor strained his ears, trying to hear what had first gotten Frea's attention. Then a few tense moments later he heard something up the hill: a blend of footfalls, shifting rocks, and breaking branches.

"The Dark Elves are coming," Frea announced, giving Arvid an expectant look.

His brother nodded numbly to her, but Frea was already turning away. She drew her bronze sword in one smooth movement and stalked over to the Sídhe under her command. Merlin and Morgana looked over sharply when she shouted an order and a warning that the Dark Elves were coming. There was a pause that lasted only a heartbeat as the villagers digested her words. Those without weapons rushed for them while the armed readied themselves.

"We'll kill them all!" one of the Dvergr shouted, raising a small axe over his head.

His fellow Dvergrs cheered and Brokkr gestured for them to follow him. Thor's eyes widened as the group of nine small creatures plowed into his forge only to reappear moments later with each of them now armed. Glancing towards Frea and Sif, Thor was a bit worried at the small smiles on their faces.

Pulling his sword, Thor joined the others at the gate as the guards looked on in confusion. Merlin didn't wait and waved his hand, sending forth a rush of green sparks out that opened the gate. Morgana raised her hand and silvery magic formed a shining orb. She threw it out into the darkness, extending the light and illuminating the Dark Elves.

They rushed outside the gates as the Dark Elves began to crash down upon them. Behind them, the gates were quickly shut as the first of the Dark Elves slashed at Thor with a bronze sword. He avoided the blade just in time. Frea thrust her sword forward into the Dark Elf in one smooth motion. Her hood fell back, exposing her long pale hair as she spun and slashed at another Dark Elf. Thor looked up into the hills and tried to see how many Dark Elves there were. Adjusting his grip on his sword, Thor fumbled for Mjǫllnir with his left hand.

Another Dark Elf swung an axe clumsily towards him, but Thor brought his sword up to catch the axe head with his right hand. While it snarled at him, Thor swung Mjǫllnir, colliding the metal against the chest of the creature. Magic flared off the Hammer at the contact. Tiny bolts of lightning arched off the surface of the Hammer and across the Dark Elf's body. It was knocked back in a combination of force and power that made Thor grin.

But more were coming. Sif's golden magic was falling like rain on a trio of Dark Elves, Morgana's silver whip was lashing one attacking her with a sword, and Merlin's green magic was causing the earth to swell up around the legs of a few more. Odin was cutting the head off of a Dark Elf with his guards fighting one each. Frea had silver blood seeping from a cut on her arm even as she dueled one of the enemies.

Another lunged at him and Thor brought Mjǫllnir down sharply on its shoulder, sending it crashing to the ground. He thrust the sword into its prone neck and watched as it dissolved. The Dvergrs were attacking in small groups, knocking the Dark Elves over and stabbing them with swords, daggers, and axes. Everyone was getting swarmed. Worry churned in his stomach as his magic tingled over his fingertips in response to his desire to do something.

Then the world slowed down. An idea came to him. Dangerous, he had no idea how it would really work, but he liked it. Holding Mjǫllnir towards the sky, Thor grinned as the tightly restrained magic burst free. It rushed from the metal, arching into the air as small bolts of lightning. Overhead the sky began to rumble and clouds began to churn over the stars and the moon. His heart raced as a euphoric sense of power washed over him. Lightning flashes illuminated the sky and he didn't care how it was possible as he reveled in the fact that it was. His magic glowed, lighting up the triskelion symbol as he brought the Hammer crashing down on a Dark Elf.

The air was sharp around him. Magic was thrumming with every move he made. Pushing his magic through the wooden handle, Thor gasped as Mjǫllnir shook and the lightning surrounded him. The magic was lashing around him, spinning almost out of control as his muscles tightened painfully. Thor heard a roll of thunder exploding around him as he lost his grip on the magic.

Everything turned white. Uncertainty and outright fear over what he'd done filled Thor, consuming him for the long deafening moment of total silence that followed. Then the world dimmed and he heard people moving. At some point, his eyes had closed. He forced them open.

There were no Dark Elves. The others were on the ground around him, and there was a slight shimmer of silver in the air, but it vanished in moments. Overhead lightning was flashing, illuminating the face of Sif as she looked up at him in surprise. Thor lowered Mjǫllnir quickly and nervously.

"Sorry," he apologized. Thor extended a hand to Sif to help her to her feet. "I was just... I just wanted to get rid of them.

"And your magic reacted to that wish," Odin huffed as he leveraged himself up.

"Thor!" Merlin snapped, shaking his head as he stood. "Don't... try not to do that again."

"Agreed." Morgana shook her cloak which did nothing to remove the mud. "At least not until you've got some more control."

Raindrops began to fall from the sky and struck his face. The sudden chill made him shiver, but Thor exhaled slowly. The sword fell from his hand. Giving it up, he shifted Mjǫllnir into his right hand. Sif came up next to him and placed a hand on his arm.

"Thank you," Sif told him softly.

"I didn't hurt you, did I?" Thor asked her in a low voice, searching her for any signs of pain.

"It was odd," she offered carefully. "Something hit me, but it... rolled over me like it knew I wasn't the real target."

Sighing in relief, Thor nodded. "I'll work on controlling that better."

"Good idea, but it did work," Sif reminded him with a soft chuckle.

"We should return home," Odin's voice called out. "We've distressed the humans enough tonight."

"That's a wise choice," Merlin agreed with a nod before a strange look passed over his face. "We will contact you soon."

Thor glanced back at the village. The guards were standing in the open gateway and staring at them with fearful eyes. It took Thor a moment to recognize that the fear in them wasn't directed at the others, but at him. Sif squeezed his arm encouragingly before following her father up the hill. Merlin came up to stand next to him, shifting impatiently as the others vanished into the forest.

"Come with me," Merlin ordered in a low voice. Morgana sent a strange look his way. "I heard her calling me."

Thor looked at Morgana in confusion. Whatever surprise Morgana may have felt didn't stop her. She summoned another orb of light that illuminated their path as they headed down towards the shore. Thor was grateful that he didn't have to return to the village just yet.

"What is it?" Thor asked Morgana. He glanced between her and Merlin. "Is something wrong?"

"Hopefully not," Morgana answered quickly though she didn't look at him. "Stay close to me. There shouldn't be any danger, but... just stay close to me."

Thor frowned at the order. This had already been a long day and his patience was at an end. Just minutes ago, he'd proven what he was capable of in a fight. Grumbling under his breath, Thor followed Morgana closely and noted the excited spring in Merlin's step. They reached the rocky shoreline quickly. Around them, the sound of the waves crashing on the cliffs and rough coastline echoed beneath the stormy sky. The rain was beginning to ease, but the roll of thunder and occasional flashes of lightning continued.

Then water began to churn a few feet from the shore as if something large was bubbling up beneath it. Moving back from the water, Thor sent a frantic look towards Merlin and Morgana. They weren't moving away and didn't look worried. In fact, Morgana glanced his way with an amused expression.

Water burst straight up from the surface of the sea with a thunderous splash. It twisted into a column of standing water that after only an instant began to form into a humanoid shape. Waves of water swirled into a white gown covering what looked like a woman. Long black hair with a soft green shine to it hung over her shoulders. Bright sea green eyes looked at him, almost glowing in contrast to her bronze skin. Small droplets of water formed a small ring around her head that illuminated her face. She was utterly strange to him and yet Thor found himself calming down in moments.

"Thor, may I introduce Cyrridven. She is an old ally and friend of Morgana and myself." There was a fondness in Merlin's voice that was confusing and reassuring at the same time.

"Uh, it's a pleasure to meet you," Thor managed to force out.

"The pleasure is mine, Iron Soul," Cyrridven greeted in a smooth voice that had an echoing quality to it. She turned her eyes from him and looked around. "There are Sídhe nearby."

"There is a colony of the survivors of the war living in the area," Merlin confirmed with a nod. "They've... actually, they have been very helpful. They keep to themselves and don't bother the humans. These Dark Elves are a threat to them as well. We have an alliance of sorts with them."

Thor's eyes were drawn to a sword scabbard on Cyrridven's belt formed of gently flowing water. A golden hilt glimmered in the soft light of Morgana's orb. Without realizing it, he took a step towards her only for his feet to splash in the water. Cyrridven looked at him thoughtfully with a sad smile on her face before she turned her attention back to Merlin.

"The magic of the Iron Realm feels stretched thin," Cyrridven informed them softly. "Whatever is happening here is... affecting the greater whole. I was already on my way here when a great surge not long ago called to me."

"The Sídhe's actions have overcome Arto's magic in the Iron Gates," Merlin acknowledged sadly. "Breaking through the magical barrier has corrupted them."

There was a look of horror on her face and Thor's stomach turned. Once again, he had the impression that he didn't understand the full gravity of what was happening. Licking his lips, he considered asking the strange... woman what it all meant.

"I see," Cyrridven whispered. "I wanted to be certain that you were aware of the attack on the Iron Realm."

"We are," Morgana said. "Sadly, they are proving to be more of a problem than expected. Thankfully their numbers are manageable."

"Then they do not have a tunnel?"

"No," Merlin answered. "The Sídhe seem to have become aware of the corruption and are no longer sending their kind through."

"Possibly because of these Dark Elves, that's what the locals call them," Morgana added. "They are as much, if not more, a threat to them should they return to Sídhean."

"We're trying to sort out the best way to fight them." Merlin leaned heavily on his staff. "The effect of magic being... stretched thin is probably connected to their violent entrance into our world. It somehow pulled beings from a world unknown to us here."

Thor tried to focus on the conversation, but his eyes kept traveling back to the sword hilt. There was an odd buzzing in his head and an itch in his hand that he couldn't quite shake. Lowering his hand back to Mjǫllnir, Thor relaxed a little as the strange sensation eased.

"Then there is another people here?" Cyrridven questioned, looking mildly alarmed. "Indeed, this is complicated, more so than the war. Are these Dark Elves very powerful?"

"They seem to have some form of magic. Although that was only in the tunnel they were building." Morgana trailed off and Thor watched her features furrow in thought. "But they haven't used magic in combat. The Sídhe descendants don't seem to have magic either. They are cut off, but the Dark Elves were..." She straightened up and her eyes widened in realization. "They were somehow pulling magic from Sídhean. That's what we were seeing!"

"Morgana-" Merlin began.

"No, Merlin, think about what we saw. They were touching the stone. Somehow, I'm not sure how, they have reconnected to Sídhean."

"To what end?" Cyrridven asked, tilting her head slightly. "To gain some magic of their own? Bring more of their kind here or invade Sídhean?"

"I'm not sure," Morgana admitted, looking between Cyrridven and Merlin. "But the magical barrier..."

"Has already been breached once," Merlin reminded her darkly as a scowl appeared on his face. "We may have to consider creating a new gate."

"There is no point to that, Merlin!" Morgana waved a hand angrily in the air. "They've broken through once. It had consequences enough that it seems to have scared the Sídhe off, but the Iron Gates don't protect Earth from something within the Iron Realm already."

"She is correct, Merlin," Cyrridven agreed. "I wish I had news for you. I will try to call a vision and see if I can learn anything." In the corner of his eye, Thor saw Merlin tense up. "I'll return to the water. In the meantime, your attention should remain on Thor."

"And the sword?" Morgana questioned, her eyes dropping to the hilt.

"It is Thor's should you think that best," Cyrridven answered, her voice echoing around him. "But I see a weapon much like it at his side already."

His thumb brushed over the triskelion symbol on Mjǫllnir's side at the words. He almost smiled and Merlin nodded in understanding. A soft huff escaped Morgana, but she nodded. Thor wanted to say something, but the words were stuck in his throat. The sensation was back and made him shift as a dull tingle between his shoulder blades made it hard to stay still.

"I have faith that the Iron Soul has created what they need for the challenge they face," Cyrridven said. "I will protect Cathanáil until it is needed once more. Farewell mages of the Iron Realm. I shall return when I have news for you."

Cyrridven smiled at him. It was a warm expression and full of fondness that surprised and unnerved him. He had the feeling that she was seeing someone else, just like he sometimes did with Morgana and Merlin. Then the water spun around her as she sank below the waves once more. Thor nearly stepped forward again as the gold hilt vanished from his sight.

"What... what is she?" Thor gasped out once she was gone.

"Cyrridven is an Old One," Merlin explained with a soft chuckle of amusement. "She was exiled to our world a very long time ago. Unlike most of them, Cyrridven has fully accepted the Iron Realm as her home. It may seem strange to you now, but she is loyal to our cause and a great source of information."

"She didn't look like Sif," Thor pointed out carefully. Sif and her father almost passed as human while Cyrridven had been different. "Her skin was darker."

"Old Ones are not physical beings; they are energy and what we see is a form that they have created to survive in our world. Sif and her family seem to have favored the coloration of people from this area. Cyrridven probably resembles people from wherever she first entered our world. Though her use of water to form her body also sets her apart." Merlin paused and a slight frown appeared on his face. "To be honest I've never discussed it with her."

"There are usually more pressing matters when we see her," Morgana said. She looked a touch amused at Merlin's sudden discomfort. "Cyrridven spends much of her time sleeping in the waters of our world."

"Sleeping in water? Why?" Thor asked with a frown.

Merlin and Morgana exchanged worried glances and said nothing out loud, but a great deal at once. It was Merlin who began to explain, "Thor, the Old Ones are not beings of our world. Sif has explained the reality of their forms to you, but something you need to understand is that the magic of our world knows they shouldn't be here. Dwelling in our world causes... instability."

"They go insane if they don't cleanse themselves," Morgana said, giving Merlin an impatient look. "Water helps them, I'm not sure why, but it keeps the madness at bay. Someday, hopefully soon, Odin and his family will need to rest in the waters to avoid losing their minds."

"But Sif was born in the Iron Realm," Thor heard himself argue, the words springing to his lips. "Surely that changes things."

"I'm not sure," Merlin said a moment later. "You are correct that their birth here may impact things, but in the end, Thor, their physical nature is in conflict with the power of our world."

"I don't understand," Thor admitted, frowning at the older mage. "Here they're thought of as gods and have powers that ordinary humans don't have. Why would being sent here be a punishment?"

"Because the conflict that generates their powers hurts them," Morgana told him with a cold expression. "Think of it as a dull, but constant pain. They live with it. Live with a dull ache every day. Those like Sif are born with it. I doubt she even fully understands that those aches aren't normal."

His breath caught at the words and there was a pain in his chest at the very idea. Sealing his lips together, Thor struggled to gather his thoughts and keep control of his features. Merlin and Morgana were watching him. He wasn't sure what to make of it and even a few months ago he would have shouted angrily about it. Now he knew it would do no good.

"What about Frea and her people?" Thor finally asked.

"Frea and hers don't seem to have magic. Some of the other creatures from their branch of the Tree of Reality have magical powers, but only very slight abilities. It seems the further the world they originate from the more disconnect their descendants have. This... severing from the power of their home world seems to let them live a bit more peacefully in our world. Of course, they don't really look human and can't alter their appearances like the Old Ones can." Merlin nodded towards the water which was crashing on the shore. "There is a price it seems for living in a world that is not yours. Some pay it with more dignity and empathy than others, but they all pay it."

Keeping his hand on Mjǫllnir, Thor tried to process the words. Merlin and Morgana walked a little way up the shore speaking in low tones and staying where they could see him. The irritation once again flared up in his chest alongside a sense of unease at the reminder from Cyrridven that he was just one more warrior in a line of them. Underneath it, all was a nagging question and certainty that he hadn't understood something. Why if living in another world was so difficult would the Sídhe even want to invade?

16

Confrontation of Half Breeds

Water blasted forth from the small lake, rising in a pillar off the surface and beginning to spin in the air. Merlin kept his hand stretched out and watched in silence as the green sparks of his magic blended with the water. The swirling became stronger and stronger as the water spun into what appeared to be a vertical whirlpool. At the sight of the spinning water, Merlin felt a dull ache in his chest that confused him for a moment.

Cyrridven. The name echoed in his head and Merlin suddenly found it hard to breathe. Clenching and unclenching his fists, he struggled to inhale, and held the breath for a long moment before he slowly released it. There were tears gathering in his eyes and Merlin almost laughed at himself. Really, this was going to happen now? He was going to accept the idea that Cyrridven was gone now? A harsh laugh escaped him and the water tunnel shuddered in response to his loss of focus.

"I'm sorry, Cyrridven," Merlin said, watching the churning waves. "I'm sorry."

She'd always been there, distantly, but he'd known for millennia that in times of trouble she would help the Iron Realm. Her loyalty to the Iron Realm had been absolute to the point of confusing him and he knew that for years Morgana had waited for a betrayal that never came. Now he'd recovered the remains of the potion she'd prepared to help train him and Merlin realized that he'd never properly thanked her.

Cyrridven had given him the name Merlin. She'd teased of course that it was the name he'd be known by in the future. Myrddin had become a distant memory and if someone were to shout it, he doubted he'd respond. She'd trained him, named him, supported him, and now died due to his own mistake. Another long sigh escaped him and Merlin shook his head. There was nothing he could do now and the water tunnel needed his attention.

The churning magic had weakened due to his lack of focus and was sloshing around wildly. Raising his hand once more, Merlin pushed his magic into the pool and focused on a mental image of Ravens Lake. It was difficult, but he was able to push the memory of Cyrridven rising out of the water from his mind. In a rush of green and soft blue, the water shifted and the tunnel reappeared, beckoning him forward.

The bag on his back suddenly seemed heavier and Merlin paused to consider this decision once again. If anything went wrong and he was swept the wrong direction then he risked dumping the most dangerous poison he knew of into the world. He had no idea how far it could spread and had no desire to test it after what had occurred in the tunnel. Pulling off the backpack, Merlin clutched it in one hand and eyed the whirlpool carefully. He was lingering too long and, in the distance, he thought he could hear movement. Yet he unzipped the top of the bag and checked on the small wrapped jars once again. They were solid enough to keep the poison contained, but he'd seen one smash all too easily in the tunnel.

Behind him, the distant sounds were growing louder. The hairs on the back of his neck stood on end and he could feel a shudder in his magic as it responded to a coming threat. Yet he couldn't shake the fear of stepping into the water with the jars. Zipping the bag up, Merlin pulled it on and clenched the strap tightly with his left hand as he turned to look behind him.

Figures were marching towards him. They were slight of build and wearing a mixture of clothing though all had hats or hoods of some kind. All of their heads were tilted down away from the sunlight, but he could see white hair escaping their head coverings. Merlin moved towards the water tunnel only for the creatures to rush towards him in a startling burst of speed.

"Merlin!" A familiar voice shouted from beyond the figures. It surprised him enough that teamed with his lingering concerns over the jars he stopped in front of the water tunnel and risked a look back.

Everything came to a stop as the Sídhe creatures formed a half circle around him. There was no reaction on their faces to the sight of the sloshing water tunnel. The Sídhe creatures just stared at him, their violet eyes locked almost unseeing on him. Merlin was about to turn and rush to the water tunnel when another a more human figure appeared behind the ranks of Sídhe. Merlin froze in place, his limbs thrumming with anger at the mere sight of the boy.

Holding back a sneer, Merlin locked his eyes on Arthur as the familiar, hated figure approached. The young man looked completely normal with his short and slightly messy blond hair and dressed in jeans and a dark t-shirt. Nothing about him would alarm those that saw him, but Merlin was repulsed by the mere sight of him. He wondered, not for the first time, how he had ever been taken in by Arthur's deceit. For a moment he was completely silent as the young man sauntered over and the Sídhe parted to let him through.

"Professor Yates," Arthur greeted with a smirk. "Pleasure to see you again, sir."

"Medraut," Merlin growled, straightening up as the man approached.

"That isn't my name anymore." Arthur chuckled, his blue eyes glinting in amusement. "Though I suppose after centuries of the tales of King Arthur you might be a bit protective of that name as well. It is after all how your precious Arto is remembered."

"Don't speak of Arto," Merlin snapped. Straightening up, he glared fiercely at the young man. "You have no right."

"He was my cousin," Arthur reminded him with a lazy shrug and a nonchalance that did not reach his eyes. "I was family."

"Who you betrayed for power."

"I had my reasons then." Arthur took another step forward which made Merlin shift back. Water lapped around his ankles sending a shudder through his legs. "Don't assume that you knew everything, Merlin. I did care about Arto in my own way."

"Then you do actually remember that life?" Merlin heard himself ask with genuine curiosity coloring his voice. He hated it, but he had truly found himself wondering so he quickly added, "Or is that just your training from Scáthbás talking."

"Scáthbás told me many things about that life, but over time I've discovered those parts of me." There was a spark of something in his eyes that Merlin, even with his great experience, couldn't identify. "Just as I suspect poor Alex is discovering parts of herself." Then Arthur shook his head and the smug expression returned to his face. "But what are you doing here, Merlin?" Arthur demanded, striding forward with his hands in his pockets as he glanced around. "No Morgana and no Alex. You all alone in Wales." A suspicious look crossed Arthur's face as he narrowed his gaze on Merlin. "Why?"

"It's spring break and there are ancient gates to check," Merlin reminded him coldly. "Especially with them decaying and the Sword missing as you're aware, Medraut."

"You're here checking the gates?" Arthur repeated doubtfully. "They're a lost cause without Cathanáil. The only reason the Sídhe aren't breaking them down over here is old fears about lingering magic."

The remark made Merlin frown. He wondered how much Scáthbás knew about events that had occurred in the period between her imprisonment and return. Arthur was watching him, no doubt weighing his reactions so Merlin fought to keep his expression neutral. He wanted to demand an answer as to why Arthur was here, wanted to learn about their plans, but the boy was smarter than that.

"I suppose this is the time I'm expected to give you a grand speech about how it isn't too late," Merlin said, allowing himself a slight frown. "Remind you that I'm half Sídhe too, born from a rape, who found his way as a guardian of the Iron Realm and that you could do the same."

"You're the professor of literature," Arthur huffed, a cold look on his face. "You're aware of how cliché that would be. Besides you were allowed to come into existence by the power of the Iron Realm, I'm not sure what that says about whatever guiding force it is that you protect and revere, while I was created by Scáthbás."

"Indeed, which is why I won't waste my breath."

"I thought you were supposed to be the optimistic one. Always seeing the best in a situation. Believing that things will get better."

"There's a lot you don't know about me, boy," Merlin reminded him. "I'm very old."

"So am I."

"No, not like me," Merlin said calmly, meeting his gaze evenly. "I'm optimistic because I know how much humans can survive and recover from. I've seen so many wars, so much bloodshed, and so many days that seemed like the end. Yet the world kept going. I'm optimistic because I know that there is nothing you can do that will forever destroy the Iron Realm, but that doesn't mean I'm going to let you try."

Another dark look flickered over Arthur's features and the boy shifted, glancing at the water tunnel. "Don't think that blood spell will keep your precious Iron Soul safe," Arthur told him evenly. "I'm half human same as you and Morgana."

"But you have no loyalty to the Iron Realm," Merlin countered. He took another step towards the water tunnel. "You tried to kill Alex." Merlin gave Arthur a chilly smile as he added, "And I once saw a blood spell attack Morgana many years ago because of her torn loyalty and she was Arto's own sister. You're not safe, boy, not even close. You have no loyalty to the Iron Realm and it will destroy you."

"Loyalty to the Iron Realm," Arthur repeated, smugness and something else creeping into his voice. "Ah, Merlin, look around. The Iron Realm is now ruled by what exactly? Warring little states that are scared of their own diversity and unwilling to surrender any power despite global problems that threaten all of Humanity. And you and Morgana do nothing. For three thousand years you've possessed the power to shape the world, to guide more than just the Iron Soul and yet have done nothing. This world is dying and you don't care."

"Medraut, there is nothing you can say that would ever convince me you sincerely care about anyone or anything but yourself." Merlin gave a dark laugh.

"Perhaps not, but you were a child of the old times, Merlin. I doubt you approve of everything humans have done since then."

"Not everything." Merlin shifted the backpack as he debated his chances of getting one of the jars out. "And sadly, it isn't universal, but we have access to clean water and I won't argue against modern medicine." Merlin narrowed his eyes on Arthur. "What do you think you're going to achieve with this conversation, Medraut? Do you think you're going to kill me?"

"That is a possibility." Arthur's eyes flickered to the water tunnel still swirling behind him. "But given how close you are to the tunnel I doubt it." Arthur shifted and gave Merlin a searching look. "You never wonder do you?"

"Wonder what exactly, boy?"

"Why the Sídhe invaded so many worlds?" Arthur answered calmly his eyes never leaving Merlin's. "Why this all started? The Old Ones are banished here by a corrupt government... though not lately so perhaps Avalyen has finally stabilized, but what of the Sídhe?"

"Conquest and slaves appeal to some," Merlin said. He disliked the inkling of curiosity he could feel beginning to grow at the back of his skull.

"Morgana has a simple view of them." Arthur said with a shrug. "And I don't blame her for that. What happened to the children was harsh, but she's never questioned how a culture like that emerged. The Sídhe may not have the same emotional spectrum as us, but you have to admit that they aren't completely heartless. So why? What drives a people to take over other worlds and lose themselves in the suffering of others?"

"I daresay you're eager to tell me," Merlin scoffed with a doubtful frown. "But it won't change anything, Medraut. This is the Iron Realm. It is the home of humans and other creatures that evolved here, not another world for the Sídhe."

"Yet you tolerate the Old Ones. They have children and add to the frustration of the Iron Realm."

"We tolerate some of the Old Ones," Merlin corrected, faking a chuckle and stepping back again. Judging from the sharp look in Arthur's blue eyes he wasn't fooled. "Most of them are neutral towards us at best. Alex did just destroy Chernobog as I'm sure you recall. Those that move against mages are delt with."

Something shifted in Arthur's eyes at the mention of Alex and Chernobog. The smugness that had been in them faded, even if only for a moment. Merlin held back a smile, it seemed that Arthur for all of his boasting carried a bit of fear. Then again, he had seen her slay one of the worst of the Old Ones with Cathanáil despite never laying a hand on the Sword before in this life. There was no doubt in Merlin's mind that someday Arthur would have to pay either Alex or Jenny for his manipulation and betrayal.

"You're afraid of Alex," Merlin observed with a smile. "Good, you should be." He took another step back. "Though I'm not sure who you should be most afraid of: Alex, Morgana, Nicki, or Jenny. None of them are women I'd want out for my blood."

Arthur's hand twitched. Merlin braced himself for a magical attack even as he checked his own magic swirling in the water tunnel. It had been open far too long and he wondered if it was even safe to use anymore. Black sparks flared around Arthur's hand, a sharp contrast from the white magic that Merlin had seen him use in the past. One more part of the trick, he mused angrily as he brought his hand up and sent the green sparks flying forward to create a barrier.

The black bolts from Arthur's hand struck the green shield which shimmered in response. Merlin was weighing the odds of destroying Arthur here and now when the Sídhe began to rush forward once more. More black bolts weakened the shield and the green magic flickered. Taking a step back, Merlin dropped the walking stick and brought his left hand up. Green magic rolled out of his palm in a wave. The ground shook and rocks sprang up from the earth, tripping the Sídhe and sending them falling to the ground. A shout from Arthur at them made a shiver pass up his spine. Releasing another wave of magic, Merlin felt a twinge of guilt as more of the poor enslaved creatures were struck with green bolts and began to fade into dust.

Three of the creatures were back on their feet and almost upon him. Summoning more magic, Merlin blasted bolts of green straight into their chests. Behind him, he could hear the water tunnel weakening and feel his magic draining in an effort to keep it open. More Sídhe were closing in on him and Arthur's attack on his shield hadn't stopped. Gathering up as much magic as he dared, Merlin formed an orb and launched it towards Arthur just as his green shield vanished. He couldn't linger but heard a shout of alarm that almost made him smile.

Throwing himself into the water tunnel, Merlin struggled against the wild current as the magic around him shuddered and tightened around his body. Air was forced from his lungs, but he couldn't breathe the water. Summoning the image of Ravens Lake, Merlin tightened his hand around the strap of the backpack as the current tried to tear it away. The pressure was building, his ears were popping, and his limbs weakened. Magic rippled across his skin, a soft and silent warning that made him force his eyes open.

Up ahead a light was growing brighter and brighter. He pushed against the currents, driving himself towards it. Distantly he thought he could hear shouting. Strange magic washed past him, a shimmer of black against the twisting blue and green of the water and his magic. The light was just in front of him. Merlin pushed more of his magic outward, reaching for the light as the magic of the tunnel collapsed. Water splashed over him in an icy crash sending a jolt of panic through his heart. Then he was at the light and falling forward as the tunnel collapsed beneath him.

He hit the ground hard and coughed even as he tried to breathe. The chirping of nearby birds reassured him that he'd made the trip successfully. His pants were moist and sticking to his legs though he'd managed to keep his shirt dry. Behind him, Merlin heard a loud splash as the water tunnel collapsed back into the lake. Shaking his head, Merlin grimaced as water trickled down the back of his neck. Yet his fingers were still wrapped tightly around the strap of the backpack and he was back in Ravenslake. Rough trip or not, he had to consider it a success.

17

Life of Fear

The air was warm and a sweet smell of blooming flowers filled the air. Yet there was a chill down the back of their spine that Alex couldn't understand. Something was off, but she was at a loss to explain it as she sank further into the dream and her awareness that it was a dream began to slip away.

A sense of relief sank into their bones as they walked up the small drive leading to the two-story brick house. In the setting sun, the red bricks of varying shades gleamed and the green trim faded into the ivy growing up the east side of the house. A swing made of rope and a wooden plank hung from the largest branch of an old oak was occupied by a young girl in a plain blue dress.

The little girl laughed, a long brown braid slipping over her shoulder as she jumped off the swing. "Father's home!" She called loudly, rushing towards him with a giggle.

She hugged him tightly around the middle, earning a pat on the head and an affectionate chuckle in return. The front door opened and a woman appeared in the doorway, greeting them with a tired smile as the little girl released them. She was short with brown hair styled in a softly curled bob and intelligent blue eyes. Her dress hung loosely on her frame with an apron tied around her waist. There was a little girl, about four, with bright blond hair cradled in her arms half asleep. The smell of baking bread was carried on the air out of the house and mixing with the scent of the flowers in the window box.

"Welcome home, Gottfried," the woman said. Smiling widely, she leaned up to kiss their cheek.

"Hello, Ilse." They stepped inside and shrugged out of their coat.

"Father," the little girl in Ilse's arm cheered as she woke. "Hello, Father."

With a smile, they shifted the little girl from Ilse's arm into theirs and kissed the rosy cheek presented to them. "Hello, Elsa, how are you?"

"Good, Father," she repeated, looking pleased with herself. "We had a nice day."

"I'm pleased to hear that." They chuckled, bending over to put the girl down as more children joined them.

There were four of them in total. All young. The oldest was a boy who couldn't have been older than ten, and healthy looking. The chill at the back of their spine vanished for a moment before flaring worse than before. Nonetheless, they knelt down and proceeded to accept hugs from the children. The oldest boy was a bit more formal but still smiled widely at them.

"And how are my children?" They placed a hand on their knee to steady themselves as they remained on the floor.

"I had a very good day at school," the oldest boy announced, straightening up proudly. A strand of blond hair fell into his brown eyes, but he ignored it. "I did very well on today's test."

"Excellent, Enrich." They gave the boy a wide smile. "I'm pleased to hear that." They turned their eyes to the second boy. "What about you, Reinhold?"

"I have a test on Friday," the younger boy said. He shrugged his shoulders a little, earning a displeased look from his mother.

"I had a good day too," Gisela told them eagerly. "And I helped Mother with the bread when I got home."

"Yes, she did," Ilse agreed though she didn't look as pleased as her daughter.

"I like having Mother home," Gisela announced with a giggle. "It's better than before.

Ilse grimaced at the words, but her smile faded for only a moment. Their six-year-old daughter didn't seem to notice how her words had affected her mother. When they opened their mouth to say something Ilse shook her head. Staying silent, they nodded and everyone moved further into the house.

The entry was small but had a place for coats and boots. Small paintings and a few black and white photographs hung on the wall giving it a homey feel. Yet that odd chill was still present despite the warmth that filled the house. There was a small table by the door and they set their case down on it with a soft thump. The others were moving further into the house and gathering in the kitchen. They followed a moment later, rolling their stiff shoulders as they walked.

Warm sweet smells hit them as they entered the kitchen, which was filled with natural light from the late afternoon sun through the numerous windows. Pots and pans hung on racks along one wall and some herbs were hanging to dry above the sink. A doorway to their right led into the small dining room.

"How was the university?" Ilse leaned over and pulled the pan of bread from the oven.

"Same as yesterday," they answered. It sounded like a calm answer, but judging from the small nod Ilse gave them, she understood what they weren't saying.

Ilse set the bread down on the counter with a small thump and forced a smile as she turned her attention to the four children who were watching them. "Children, it will be dark soon. Go out and enjoy the sunshine," Ilse ordered the children with a blend of sternness and affection.

None of them argued and they all moved quickly to the back door. They glanced out of the largest of the kitchen windows and admired the small yard for a moment. There was a small garden on one side and they could see the remaining green produce that had yet to be harvested. A few moments later the children moved into view and the two boys went for a red ball waiting beneath a tree.

They turned their attention back to Ilse as she shut the back door securely and made a ragged exhale. She leaned against the doorway for a moment and they crossed the room quickly. Resting a hand on her shoulder, they were silent and tried to think of something to say.

"You're distressed," they observed. Ilse shifted off the wall and turned around. "I'm sorry about what Gisela-"

"It isn't that," Ilse cut off. She shook her head. "I went to the market for a bit today. At home, it's a little easier to ignore... everything." They waited silently while she gathered her thoughts, sensing there was more she needed to say. "The rumors aren't good," she murmured, looking out the window into the yard where the children were playing. "Edith's cousin was hanged yesterday. He was a little too vocal and now that you're being pressured-"

"It will be alright." They sought to reassure her, putting a hand on the small of her back. "It will be alright."

"It's horrible, but sometimes I miss the old days," Ilse said.

"What when we could barely afford food and my job was in constant jeopardy?" they pointed out, ignoring the sick twist in their stomach at the reminder.

"I know, but at least I was able to work then and help," Ilse all but spat at them, giving them an angry look. "Elsa doesn't even remember that and you heard Gisela."

"She doesn't understand."

"No, she doesn't, and thanks to her teachers she never will," Ilse groaned and rubbed her eyes for a moment. "I know that things were bad before and that maybe I should be grateful that I don't need to work anymore, but..."

"You miss it."

"I do and watching the children come home each day with more of these ideas in their heads is horrible, but we can't do anything."

They fell silent, neither knowing what to say nor willing to simply change the subject. Sometimes it was easy to pretend that everything was alright. The infrastructure of Germany was repaired and working, there were functioning hospitals, and work could be found for those that needed it. Yet there was the constant onslaught of posters and movies telling everyone what to think and how to feel. And in the schools, it was even worse.

"I miss it too sometimes," they confessed. "It was harder to survive, but this..."

"I know," Ilse whispered. She reached over and took their hand. "I hate hearing the dark whispers. I hate... it's just hard, Gottfried. Pretending all the time."

"This too will pass," they murmured weakly.

"Those are the words of a professor," Ilse agreed sadly. "But what effect will it all have on our children."

"They're good children, decent and healthy," they protested weakly.

"Yet Enrich is old enough now that we don't have much choice but to put him into the Hitler Youth. I've heard of children who aren't in it being harmed by small gangs or facing trouble from teachers. Then it will be Reinhold's turn and then the girls will have to go into League and they'll listen to more of those horrible things." She shook her head, real anger flashing in her eyes. "What about the university? No changes?"

"More and more are joining the party," they admitted uncomfortably. "But we're fortunate thus far. Most of the curriculum changes have been focused in the lower schools."

"I'm aware," Ilse replied tightly, focusing on slicing the carrots. "Enrich was more than happy to educate me on identifying Jews when he came home today. Apparently, they have a textbook on it now: the differences in their noses, ears, lips, and chins and even their speech." Her words may have been factual, but there was an underlying hint of fear. "He's only ten years old, but I've been asked why he isn't in the Hitler Youth yet. He's even complained about not having a uniform to wear."

A groan escaped them as they risked a look out the window. Enrich was chasing after Reinhold in a little game of chase while Gisela and Elsa played with the dolls at the side. Enrich had their blond hair and Ilse's brown eyes and was growing like a weed. His younger by two years brother favored his mother with brown hair and a slimmer build. Gisela had a long brown braid and bright blue eyes that almost matched the ones of her favorite doll.

They were so young and innocent, but forces in the school were beginning to have more of an impact than they liked. Dread tied a knot in their stomach and a wave of helplessness crashed over them. Still, they and Ilse were silent, just taking in the sight of the children playing for several long minutes. Then with a pained sigh, Ilse pulled away and stalked across the kitchen.

"I can't, Gottfried!" she all but shouted, her limbs shaking.

"Ilse." They sighed, following her across the room. "It will be okay."

"You can't promise that!" She wiped at her eyes. "We can afford bread again. Unemployment is plummeting and the streets are safe, but there's this fear, Gottfried. I can't shake it!"

"I know, but we need to survive. We need to focus on the children."

"So, we're just supposed to play along?"

"It's what everyone else is doing," they reminded her. "Hitler didn't win the election with a majority; the Nazis don't have the universal support they pretend to."

"Mother, Father," a young voice called from the kitchen door making them both turn around quickly. They found Enrich frowning at them with a curious expression on his face. "What are you talking about?"

"You shouldn't sneak up on your parents," they told their son calmly as Ilse shifted uncomfortably.

"Yes, sir, but what were you talking about," the boy pressed with sharp brown eyes focused on them.

"Signing you up to join the Hitler Youth program," Ilse answered after a moment's pause. "You're a bit young, but the program-"

"Truly!" Enrich gasped, his suspicious expression replaced with utter joy. "Thank you, Father! Thank you, Mother! Wilheim is already a member and has been wearing his uniform every day!" He puffed up his chest and stood at attention the best he could. "It will be marvelous."

They nodded, exchanging a worried glance with Ilse. Whatever had been occupying Enrich's mind when he'd first appeared at the doorway was gone. Instead, he dashed forward to hug his mother and them quickly before returning to the yard. Before the door was even closed, they could hear Enrich telling Reinhold his good news. There would be no escaping it now.

Slightly stale air replaced the smell of the fresh bread and the image of the kitchen, Enrich's grin and Ilse's worried face slipped away from her. Groaning softly, Alex flexed her fingers and felt them curl around the warm edge of a blanket. Her whole body was cold and tense, like the time she'd gone out camping and half froze in the too light sleeping bag after the cold front moved in. Licking her lips, Alex told herself to open her eyes, but didn't. It was like there was a weight on her that was slowly lifting off and she just had to be patient.

"Alex," a familiar voice called softly to her right. "You okay?"

"What?" She groaned, turning her head towards the voice, but still not opening her eyes.

"You were speaking German again," the voice offered and she finally recognized it as Bran. "Are you okay?" he asked in a lower voice

"I just..." She forced open her eyes and found herself lounging in an airline passenger seat that had been extended. "Uh..."

"We're on the plane," Bran said. "Morgana in an act of benevolence put us in first class for the ocean leg so we could sleep."

She looked up at him and he slowly came into focus with his green eyes betraying some worry. He was kneeling in the aisle and talking in a low voice. The cabin was dim with only a few low lamps and the floor lights still on. Sitting up, Alex looked around in mild confusion as the last images and emotions of the dreams lingered. Her stomach tightened and she shivered, remembering the fear that had been filling Eckstein. There had been a chill present throughout the whole dream, she realized with a grimace. An underlying fear that he'd almost become used to.

"Right..." she said slowly. Shaking her head, Alex told herself to focus on the present. "How far out are we?"

"Not too much longer. We'll be landing first thing in the morning," he told her. "But you were starting to toss and turn. Everything okay?"

"It wasn't about the Hammer." Alex pressed the button and stayed still as the seat slid back into the sitting position. "Just a memory."

"You okay?"

"I'll be fine," Alex said, slumping back in her seat. "I'm not sure it was useful to us," she admitted even as she reconsidered the words. "It... that may have been just to reassure me if that makes sense. I... I don't think Gottfried was a bad guy. I mean just based on first impressions, but nothing yet about where he hid the Hammer. I think... I think the dream was an earlier memory. Early in the Nazi period."

"Not ideal, but hopefully that will help you find the Hammer," Bran said, looking a bit uneasy at the conversation.

To distract them both, Alex leaned over and looked around at the others. Aiden was sound asleep with bright orange earplugs visible. Nicki and Jenny had both put on the eye covers and seemed to be asleep, but Lance had been behind her with Bran and she couldn't see him.

"Lance is fine," Bran assured her with a small smile.

"Don't tell me you've got mind reading powers now," Alex teased, smiling a little.

"No, still just telekinetic with the minor spell abilities," Bran said. "Was thinking about trying lightning, but that seems to be your thing."

"I'm pretty sure everything has been my thing at some point," she teased. "You could try plants or earth like Merlin."

"Morgana mentioned that plants were the other Bran's natural power," Bran reminded her calmly.

"Uh right, sorry."

"Don't worry about it," Bran said with a more honest smile. "I haven't sorted out my feelings on the reincarnation issue either, but I think I'll wait on trying to use magic with plants. Crazy as it sounds maybe I'll experiment with darkness spells."

Alex's confusion must have shown on her face because Bran laughed. "Darkness, Alex, not the dark arts or whatever else is going through your head. Think about it, Morgana's magic takes the form of light and while my power manifests as yellow, I bet I could do some spells to make things dark. Might be a useful way to blind our opponents or hide us."

"The Sídhe have night vision," she pointed out.

"But magic might work differently than normal darkness," Bran argued before shrugging. "Just a thought. I want to try something that others don't use. That way we keep a variety of abilities on the team."

"I can't argue with that," Alex said, closing her eyes for a moment. "And who knows what else we'll have to fight before this is over."

Grimacing at her own words, Alex's lungs constricted as if a metal band was being tightened around her chest. She was suddenly light-headed and on edge despite knowing that there was nothing danger-ous around them. Alex gripped the edge of the seat, hoping that Bran wouldn't notice even as she swayed slightly. There was a tentative hand on her shoulder a moment later that steadied her, but Bran said nothing. Slowly the shaking stopped, leaving Alex to wonder when it had even started. She eased her death grip on the armrests as her heartbeat slowed to normal. Bracing herself, Alex waited for Bran to say something about it or offer some advice, but he didn't.

"So have you got any thoughts of what to do first when we get to Paris?" Bran asked her quietly, glancing around for any of the flight attendants. "It'll be morning when we arrive."

A wave of gratitude washed over Alex. Her eyes teared up a little though she wasn't sure if that was shame, fear, or gratitude and didn't dare look up at Bran. "The only thing I've seen in Paris so far is the Eiffel

Tower," she reminded him through a very dry mouth. "We probably have to start there."

"Well, we could grab some food and have a picnic on the lawn around it," Bran suggested. "That wouldn't look too weird and we could try combining our powers and see if that triggers anything."

Alex hesitated for a moment but nodded. It was their best option even if it made her uncomfortable. "I'm just not thrilled with all the visions," Alex acknowledged. "But it is the fastest way to find the Hammer. I just hope that it is in Paris."

"Well since your dreams aren't showing you anything else then it probably is," Bran said, trying to cheer her up.

"You have a lot more faith in how magic works than I do." Alex chuckled darkly, giving him a doubtful look. "But I hope you're right."

"It'll be okay, Alex," Bran promised. He squeezed her shoulder gently and offered her a soft smile.

Alex knew he wasn't just talking about finding Mjǫllnir, but she nodded in agreement anyway not trusting herself to speak.

18

The Professor of Languages

March 1938 C.E. Cologne, Germany

Professor Eckstein was not a particular fan of the new Main Building of the university. It was only four years old and yet he still found it hideously modern and prison-like. The windows might have been bigger than the average prison to be true, but the structure was flat with no personality at all. While it provided more office space than older styles, he continued to prefer the more traditional and dignified gothic style. Of course, today with the students eagerly and happily talking about the glorious addition of Austria to the Fatherland it was an uglier sight than usual.

They were all so excited and happy. He scanned the crowd of students searching out any signs of discontent, but found none. Holding back a sigh, he kept his own features blank and nodded to several of his students as he walked into the main building. Around him, the voices echoed with pride in the achievement of their troops. Gottfried had to hold back a snort. What achievement? It was a surrender to protect citizens without a fight. He didn't blame the Austrians of course when staring down an army of fanatics survival instincts were bound to kick in, but he didn't have to be pleased with the German side of things.

Walking inside, Gottfried nodded in greeting to both students and colleagues. The mad excitement was everywhere, but something on the wall was also drawing attention. He paused for a moment and his eyes widened as he made out a poster on the wall that was condemning the annexation of Austria. Gottfried looked around and noted with relief that no one was lingering nearby with pleased looks on their faces. A few students were already rushing away with nervous expressions and Gottfried noted the wisdom in the action. He started walking again, all too aware that Gestapo would be on campus soon to investigate.

Thankfully there were no more distractions between him and his first lecture. He entered the hall and found many students already waiting and talking in groups amongst the desks. Walking to the main desk before the blackboard he pulled off his jacket and set his hat on the edge of the desk. He put his briefcase down on the desk and opened it with a loud click to retrieve his notes for the day. A glance up at the clock indicated there were a few more minutes until his lecture began. Gottfried made a point of ignoring the conversations and writing the primary lessons for the day on the board until the clock struck the appointed hour. He set down the chalk and clapped his hands together to both clear off the dust and draw the students' attention to him.

"Ladies and gentlemen," he called out. "I understand and recognize that the recent news is very exciting, but normal life still goes on. Please focus on your lessons." Gesturing to the board behind him, Gottfried was pleased to see that he had captured their attention. "Language will matter a great deal as the world marches on."

"The whole world will speak German soon!" One young man near the back shouted which made others cheer.

There was a moment of hesitation on his part. His chest tightened with worry about saying the wrong thing. Then he smiled slightly and gave a fond nod to the students. "You'll find that language changes take a great deal of time and if you have plans to join the army and assist in that dream then knowing another language will be of great use to you."

His stomach turned as his eyes swept across the students. They were so young, so full of potential and he knew that there were some who disagreed with the Nazi machine. There were plenty who did and suffered in the same silence as him thanks to the threat of the Gestapo and their re-education programs. Still, there were others who were all too eager to throw themselves into the ideology. Too many men in this class would vanish into the army and too many of the clever women would become relegated to being housewives no matter what ambitions and talents they possessed.

Pushing the thought away and noting that his class had finally settled, Gottfried turned back to the blackboard and began to lecture about verb changes in French. The two hours slowly ticked by and he felt the weight of the students' eyes on him heavier than usual. It wasn't inspiring and energizing as it usually was. Fear that he'd said the wrong thing and someone behind him was stewing on it was churning in his stomach.

Then class was over and he forced a friendly smile as the students began to pack up. A few returned the warm smiles and most didn't seem to care at all. The knot began to loosen and Gottfried began to feel like he'd dodged the bullet that the energy of the annexation news was bringing. He'd just have to be mindful this week until all the celebrations and excitement died down, just like most of the population. With a slight smile, he followed the students out into the hallway and began working his way towards his office.

"Professor Eckstein."

Gottfried turned around and searched for the source of the voice amongst the students, but his eyes were quickly drawn to the small mousey man walking towards him. He was towered over by the students, but they dutifully parted for him. Gottfried stepped to the side of the hallway and waited patiently.

"Mister Grubber."

"Professor Eckstein, the department chair wants to see you in his office at once." There was no emotion in his voice and Gottfried was reminded why the students called him a robot. Gottfried almost smiled at the thought, his mind reminding him that the source of the word was an old Slavonic word, rabota. It meant forced labor and hadn't originally had anything to do with the new ideas of mechanical men. "There is an SS officer here."

Gottfried's amusement was gone in a moment. He managed a nod and kept his back straight, desperately hoping that there was no panic on his face. Reminding himself that it was an SS officer and not Gestapo, he struggled to relax the tension in his spine. He followed him upstairs and noted with a hint of relief that they were headed to the Linguist Department chair's office. This was just a meeting, he told himself and he had a strong suspicion of the topic.

The Department Chair's office was only slightly larger than his own and had a window overlooking the front of the school, but was typical in every other fashion. Bookshelves stuffed with books lined one wall interspersed with keepsakes from his travels. A small name plaque with Professor Schneider was front and center on the desk in front of an older gentleman who was completely gray and balding. Near the desk stood a tall man in the uniform of an SS major who eyed him as he entered. His escort didn't enter and closed the door behind him with a soft thump, trapping him in the situation he'd been avoiding.

"Professor Eckstein there is concern that you have yet to join the Nazi party." Professor Schneider folded his hands on the desk in front of him. Thankfully he looked just as nervous. "Questions that I'm sure you understand are better left unspoken are being directed towards our department, both from local officials and students," he added carefully as his eyes urged Gottfried to understand the seriousness of what he was saying. "Is there something we should be aware of?"

"No," he answered quickly. It was difficult to stay still in the chair. He'd known it was coming. Of course, it was coming. Popularity with the students had protected him for a time, but as the Nazi mindset sank deeper and deeper into the generation that wouldn't be enough. "Nothing of concern." He forced a chuckle. "I've just always avoided politics I'm afraid, always hesitated to burden a party with my participation."

The joke was a bit flat, but it had the needed effect of easing the tension a little. Gottfried's heart clenched, but he stayed calm even under the weight of the officer's gaze. "I am a family man who has always been content with my wife, children, and classes, but if you feel this is an important step for me Aldman then I will of course officially join."

"Thank you, Gottfried." Aldman sighed in relief with his shoulders visibly loosening. "I know that in the academic world we prefer to focus on our students and classes, but solidarity with the outside world is important too. We want students to be able to see that their university supports their efforts for the future."

Translation: we can't dare be seen as opposition. Gottfried studied his colleague, but he couldn't tell how much of it Aldman actually believed.

"Thank you for bringing the concerns to my attention," Gottfried replied politely.

Standing up, he shook hands with Aldman who looked as relieved as he felt. It reassured him a little that Aldman hadn't been planning to throw him to the wolves. The weight of the officer's gaze on his back was still heavy, but it wasn't as frightening. Turning to the officer, Gottfried gave him a respectful nod and waited for a beat to see if he would leave first. He didn't and Gottfried ushered himself out the door.

Releasing a soft exhale, Gottfried kept moving away from the office on shaky legs. He debated the wisdom of going to his office to grade but doubted his own mental state. A quick mental review of his schedule confirmed he had only the one lecture today. If he took the earliest train in tomorrow, he'd be able to catch up on his work.

"Professor Eckstein," the sharp voice of the officer called behind him.

Gottfried stopped at once and turned to face the officer. He didn't smile in greeting. It didn't feel appropriate as he found himself facing the SS officer. The man's eyes swept over him and he made a tiny nod. Gottfried knew he'd just been judged and inwardly prayed that he hadn't been found wanting or lacking.

"Your language skills are highly regarded by your colleagues. Fluent in what ten languages?"

"Yes, though that includes German. I had the advantage of learning Latin as a young man which made the Romantic languages much easier." He stopped himself from saying more despite the instinct to ramble.

The officer hummed thoughtfully and nodded once again. "Excellent. Someone of your skills could be of great use to the Fatherland."

There it was. Join the Nazi Party to show unity and loyalty, but he was already being considered for something more. The knot in his stomach managed to tighten as the officer nodded to him once more. Then the man walked past him calmly as if he hadn't just twisted another man's world around. Breathing in slowly, Gottfried forced his trembling legs to keep moving. Ahead of him, the SS officer had been stopped by a group of male students who were asking him questions with bright, eager eyes. Gottfried kept walking and didn't even slow down until he was outside the building.

He allowed himself to get lost in thought as he made his way towards the train station, grateful for the chance to stretch his legs. With a sigh of defeat, he shook his head. That was that now. Part of him railed against the idea, arguing that he was an educator and had to stand up, but the faces of his children flashed through his head. If he had been younger when this all happened and they hadn't been born yet... Shaking his head, Gottfried dismissed the fanciful idea. It was easy to fall back to ideas of what if, but at the end of the day he had a family and was choosing them. He'd always choose them.

The echoing sound of in time footfalls began to resonate around him and finally pulled him from his thoughts. People were beginning to stop and gather in lines along the street. Cheers were already bursting forth from the small crowd. He walked forward to join them and silently peered down the street. They were marching again. He stopped to watch the lines of Hitler Youth boys' parade with their Nazi flags and in their neat uniforms down the street in their lines. It was a drill, just like the one that soldiers used and it made his stomach turn. They were just children yet the looks on their faces carried a hint of something darker. People were coming out of the buildings and cheering on the small parade. Women with special medals around their neck marking how many children they had produced for the Fatherland cheered the loudest. A few of the younger boys broke from the military procedure long enough to smile and give a small wave before they were reined in by their fellow little soldiers.

That's what they were, Gottfried reflected with a grimace, little soldiers. The German army was expanding every day and no one with any brains was foolish enough to think that Austria was the end of it. Even his own students already knew the dream. Even they were aware of the true dream that all the world would speak German. The leaders kept marching, their eyes front and center and any smiles they might have once had stubbornly kept repressed. This was what Enrich wanted for himself, it was a bitter idea and another one he had no power against. Frustration and anger flashed through him and Gottfried grit his teeth to the point of pain.

He waited until the parade was past to start walking again and kept his head down. Right now, he didn't trust himself at all. The train station seemed too far away and every step along the same street where the boys had been playing soldiers was uncomfortable. Gottfried looked around at the businesses thoughtfully. Most were doing better under the Nazi party for sure. He couldn't argue with some aspects of their success. The public works program had already built more new infrastructure than they'd seen since before the Great War.

Shuddering, Gottfried kept walking. He didn't want to think about that war or its aftermath. The anger was still there below the surface of Germany. The unfair treaty, the financial burdens on a destroyed country and the humiliations of it all were all still here. Everyone had struggled under the weak democracy. Money had been all but worthless. There'd been too many parties and too many problems without cooperation to fix. Anger at each other, the government and the rest of Europe had been simmering below the surface for years.

The Nazis had tapped into that and made it the fuel of a new fire. They hadn't needed a majority to get Hitler into office or public support. Fear and anger had been their instruments with Hitler's Stormtroopers spreading them through Germany. Now there was no end to it all. They had their economic recovery, they had reminded the world that they weren't a dog to kick and had an important position on the world stage, but what came next? Far behind he thought he could hear the boys marching in their lines. A shiver went down Gottfried's spine, he had his answer.

19

Vision in Paris

Alex frowned at the display, trying to muster up her admittedly rusty French and sort out exactly what they wanted. Next to her Aiden and Nicki were loading up the canvas shopping bag with bread and some plastic cutlery. She could hear Lance and Jenny in the next aisle over discussing sodas and how to chill them.

"Honestly, Alex," Nicki suddenly laughed. "Just grab some meats. It'll be fine."

"I'm trying to remember-"

"If it looks like lunch meat, we're probably safe," Aiden said. "Come on, it'll be fine."

Sighing, Alex conceded that they were probably right and grabbed packages of what she was pretty sure was ham turkey. She tossed them into the shopping bag and hoped that she hadn't gotten it wrong. It was a bit funny that she could hold a basic conversation in French but hadn't ever learned anything beyond core foods. She knew pineapple, pie, and cake, but not turkey.

"Relax," Aiden said as they headed for the front. "We're getting something to eat and then we'll go to work."

Alex nodded but stayed silent. She wasn't sure how to even begin to explain the nervous excitement teamed with dread that was building up in her stomach. Around her the sights and smells of Paris blended together, but she only felt distant from all of it. This was a dream come true, a dream that had caused her to take French in the hopes of one day being able to come to Paris and read old French literature. It was all a bit empty now.

There was a faint hum at the back of her mind, but Alex couldn't focus on it. A dull headache trying to start, her mind suggested though Alex wasn't sure she believed such a simple explanation. Pushing it to the side, Alex moved to the front of the group and greeted the cashier in slow, but precise French which earned her a smile and a small look of approval. Something about the expression helped even as a feeling stirred at the back of her mind that she'd forgotten something. It passed quickly as the cashier turned her attention to the next customer and Alex's friends steered her outside.

One nice thing about heading for the Eiffel Tower was that it was easy to know which direction to go. Around them were shorter historical buildings and tourist markers directing the flow of foot traffic as they navigated their way around the busy streets. As they came closer and closer to the famous landmark, Alex looked around for anything that seemed familiar. Unfortunately, she wasn't certain what might be familiar from another life or what was just familiar from books and movies.

Then they reached a stretch of road and park that gave Alex a clear view of the Eiffel Tower. Her heart skipped in excitement at the sight of the elegant metal structure, but not as much as she'd always imagined it would. Everyone stopped and enjoyed the view for a long moment. A soft sigh escaped Jenny and Alex turned to find her friend resting her head against the side of Lance's arm while they held hands. Alex looked back at it and tried to summon her relish for finally seeing it in person, but it just wasn't there.

Some of the locals were still wearing jackets, but to Alex, it was warm and pleasant as they found an empty spot of grass. Alex looked up at the tower again, trying to picture it with the Nazi flag flying, but found the idea too distasteful. Thankfully she was distracted from the echo of the past by Jenny beginning to lay out their associated meats, bread, and condiments. Lance handed her a small can of soda that she took with a soft thanks. The others had everything in hand while Alex felt lost. It was rather like being in a boat on the water without a line, anchor, or captain the literature major in her thought. She just... lacked something to grab onto. She frowned at the thought, unsure of what to make of her own stream of consciousness.

"Alex," Bran's voice called. "What kind of sandwich do you want?" Blinking her eyes, Alex focused on him. The others were watching her with soft sympathetic looks that made her feel even worse. "Turkey?" Bran pressed, never taking his eyes off her. "Ham?"

"Uh turkey," she answered, shaking her head, and forcing a smile. "Sorry, I'm a bit... out of it."

That statement earned her worried glances from everyone except Bran who merely nodded. Forcing a smile, Alex looked back at the tower for a bit. There was a hum at the back of her head again as her eyes traced the iron lattice structure and she wondered how effective the metal would be against the Sídhe.

Then her eyes shifted to the thick hedges that lined the lawn. Beyond them were elegant buildings and all the clichés of Paris with postcard facades on the buildings, flower boxes, bright signs, and music. In contrast to Wales where even the newer buildings had an old feel to them, almost everything here seemed young and new to Alex. Suddenly a sandwich wrapped in a napkin was thrust towards her by Jenny.

"Thanks," Alex murmured quickly. She took the offered food. Around them, the thrum of Paris and the voices of other tourists churned into a mess she couldn't make out. "Looks good," she added absentmindedly before taking a bite.

The sandwich didn't have much of a taste, but then again, she didn't feel hungry. Instead, she watched Jenny take a few selfies with herself and the Eiffel Tower. Then she handed the phone over to Nicki and tugged Lance over to be in a picture with her. There were other tourists moving around the lawn, pointing up at the tower, and taking photos so no one paid them any mind. A few officers were patrolling nearby and everything seemed very normal with a hint of familiarity.

"Alex?" Aiden called softly. "You ready to try?"

Try? She blinked in confusion as she automatically swallowed the last bite of the sandwich. Then her brain caught up as Bran gave her a pointed look. Right, they were going to try and trigger a vision if nothing happened when she got here.

"Yeah." She cleaned her fingers off on the paper napkin. "Nothing so far... just all a bit familiar in a weird way."

"Well, that's something," Bran said. "So, I'll give you some of my magic and see if we can help you view something specific."

"Right," Alex agreed with a small smile. "Worked in Wales." She giggled a bit nervously. "We found a Dragon."

"Wonder what we'll find this time," Lance murmured with a look to Jenny who gave an anxious laugh.

Alex crossed her legs and rolled her shoulders trying to shake off the building tension. As expected, no one was paying any attention to them. Bran offered her a reassuring smile as he sat opposite to her. In the corner of her eye, Alex saw Nicki move her fingers and a few sparks of her blue magic appeared. She offered Alex a wink and Alex nodded at the silent promise to watch over them.

Bran held his hands out towards her, resting his wrists on his knees that were almost touching hers. Alex hesitated and formed her fingers into a fist as she noticed they were trembling. There were a dozen thoughts zinging through her head and fighting to be heard, but they were all fearful. Her stomach turned and her lungs compressed as if something was being pushed against them. The edge of her vision blurred and a rush of fear flashed through her.

Grabbing Bran's hands before the fear could descend into another panic attack, Alex kept her eyes down so he and the others wouldn't see her reaction. Bran squeezed her hands and Alex felt a flush of shame, certain that he knew what was happening. Still, he stayed silent and Alex focused on her desire to see more of Eckstein's life. It was impossible to visualize the desire, realizing that she had only a rough idea of what he looked like due to his children.

Alex could feel the magic creeping over her. It was like stepping into a warm mist as it settled over her. Her own glittering dark silver, iron colored, magic flickered over her skin so faintly that she suspected only she could see it. Bran's yellow magic was barely visible in the sunlight and she watched silently as it blended with hers, changing into the color of her own magic.

"Never going to get used to that," Alex said.

"Yes, you will," Bran said gently. "It'll be okay, Alex," he whispered in a low voice. "Just keep breathing."

She wanted to snap at him. Alex could feel the words rush to the tip of her tongue, but somehow, she kept her jaw shut and the words inside. Bran just squeezed her hands again and the flow of magic eased a little as he gave her some more time. Closing her eyes, Alex exhaled slowly and began to repeat the name Gottfried Eckstein in her mind over and over. She wasn't sure if it would work, but she could feel something happening as the magic flared in her chest. Her head was heavy. She tried to open her eyes only for the world to drift away.

Awareness returned in an instant as if they had just blinked. There was a moment of confusion and a sense of déjà vu that they didn't understand but easily dismissed. They were walking towards the house again, but they could see tiny changes that marked the passage of time. Part of the fence and the front shutters were in need of fresh paint. Flowers in the window boxes were beginning to bloom and the sound of birds drifted down from a tree. Yet the chill that they'd been living with seemed worse than ever. They glanced back towards one of the other houses on the street.

One of the neighbors was out by their garden watching them with sharp eyes, but looked down quickly. Moving forward, they shifted the leather bag they were carrying to their left hand and tried to ignore the sense of being watched. The wind began to pick up and above their head, the leaves rustled. In front of them, the door opened and Ilse stepped into view. There was a tired smile on her face and they offered her one in return. As they stepped through the doorway and into the entry, they let out a soft exhale. Ilse's hand came up to cup their cheek spreading warmth into their face. It was pleasant and they closed their eyes for a moment.

"Welcome home." Ilse leaned up to kiss their cheek.

"You alright?" they asked as the door closed behind them and they read the tension on her shoulders.

"Mister Fischer was taken today," Ilse answered in a low voice. "For reeducation."

"Oh..." they gasped, uncertain of what to say.

"Someone heard him make a comment about business being bad," Ilse began to explain in an almost frantic rush. Locking the door, they quickly escorted her deeper into the house and hopefully away from any eager ears. "They can't do this!" Ilse snapped. They entered the kitchen and she slammed her hands down onto the counter. "He's a good man! He shouldn't have to-"

"Ilse," they scolded in a low voice. "Quiet! Everything listens now, you know that."

She lowered her eyes, a look of defeat that made their heart clench and ache. Stepping forward to wrap their arms around her, they closed their eyes and breathed in the smell of the earth from the back garden. Her head rested against their chest and for a moment the lingering chill eased.

"We're luckier than most," Ilse admitted a few moments later. "We could be living in the middle of the city rather than outside of it. At least we have some privacy. We don't have to be as afraid as others. But, Gottfried, I'm so tired of being afraid."

"I know," they answered softly, kissing her forehead. "I know, Ilse. If there was a way..." They sighed and closed their eyes, letting the wish go silent. Now they weren't even sure what to wish for. "I've...." They released her and took a step back, trying to take a deep breath, but failed. Stumbling for a moment, they fell back against the table in the kitchen. It rattled slightly, the plates and silverware shifting. "I've got to join the Nazi party. There was an SS agent at the university today."

"They-" Ilse gasped and then she covered her face with her hands. "What... what are you going to do?"

"There really isn't a choice," they reminded her weakly.

"But, Gottfried, you don't approve of this. How can you put your name on this?"

"We have four children to feed, to clothe, and care for," they finally said. "If it were just me, Ilse... but no one questions government acts. You can't. There won't be anyone who will help us and you aren't allowed to work anymore." Head sinking and shoulders slumping in defeat they added, "I'll agree. Happily, of course. Leave no room for anyone to question and report us."

"Enrich will be pleased," Ilse forced out, her lips trembling slightly, but that was as close to crying as she got. "He's been asking about why you weren't a member already."

"I never considered myself a man who would ever strike his children, but..."

"I know," Ilse reassured him. She slotted her body against theirs and laid her head against their chest. "I almost struck him myself two days ago when he said that it was right and good to rid ourselves of the Jews." She sniffed and they thought the tears might now come. "They've taken our children from us. Taken out all the ethics and reason we tried to give them and poured blind loyalty and cruelty in its place."

The wind outside was howling just enough that they didn't feel terror at her saying those words out loud. Enrich was out at one of the many activities, Reinhold was with his friends, and the girls were upstairs. There was a hum in the air, a vibration that danced across the back of their neck. This wasn't what they were supposed to be seeing and that strange thought made them frown, but they didn't move. The odd feeling grew and there was a zing of energy down their arm that made them shift suddenly as the world and Ilse faded.

Opening her eyes, Alex stayed completely still and let the sunshine warm her suddenly icy skin. For a moment she was confused. The air suddenly smelled and tasted different. The faces around her were strange until her memory of them suddenly snapped back into place. She kept her lips sealed and stayed silent, afraid of what she might say if she allowed herself to. Her stomach was tied in knots and she regretted that sandwich.

"Alex?" Bran called softly. "Did it work?"

"I connected," Alex said quickly.

"Did you see the Hammer?" Nicki asked with a glance around. "Anything useful?"

"No," Alex forced out. "We need to go later. This was too early again." Alex closed her eyes for a moment and almost savored the fear and dread she could still feel lurking in her body. It was strange to be grateful for it, but she understood why at least. On multiple levels. "Just give me a few minutes," she said. "Then we can try again."

"Do you think it'll work?" Lance asked her with a frown, drawing her attention to him. "Is this helping?"

"I still don't know when or how Gottfried found the Hammer," Alex told him as a real smile began to tug at her lips. "But I can tell you that he was absolutely trying to protect it from the Nazis."

"That may be why you saw that," Bran told her softly. "You needed to know that first."

Pausing, Alex considered the words and gave him a sheepish nod and smile. "Yeah," she agreed a moment later. "I think you're right. Let's try again." Alex held her hands out towards Bran, drawing a look of surprise from him.

"What? Are you sure?" Bran asked, his lips twisting into a worried frown.

"Yes," Alex insisted. "I was focusing on him and not the Hammer. I'll focus on the Hammer this time like I did the Chalice. Either I'll see where it is now or learn more about how it got from Norway to France."

She could see the hesitation on Bran's face though the others all looked fine with the idea. Nicki even looked excited. "Relax, Bran, she'll be fine," Nicki told him. "Unless... are you okay?"

"Yeah, I'm fine," Bran answered with a nod. He looked like he was going to say something more, but instead held his hands out towards Alex again. "Once more unto the breach."

"I'm not sure Shakespeare is appropriate here," Alex replied. She focused her attention on his hands and held onto the relief she felt from seeing Eckstein. Underneath it was more of that nervous dreading energy that she didn't know what to do with.

"I disagree," Bran replied softly. They linked their hands together and the magic began to flow.

20

His Partner

Wet was not a state that Merlin enjoyed. His shoes sloshed on the pebbly beach of Ravens Lake as he forced himself to walk towards the street. Thankfully there wasn't any traffic on the northern side of the lake and no one around to witness Professor Ambrose Yates soaked from the belt down. He hummed thoughtfully to himself, lamenting the loss of control over the tunnel while reminding himself to be grateful that he'd made it to Ravenslake at all. He had warned the children about water travel in the past and had lost students to the swirling depths before. Calling on his magic, Merlin opened his hand as green sparks began to illuminate his skin. With a simple command, he dried his pants and boots, removing the unpleasant moisture from his person.

When he reached the road, he looked around to get his bearings only to sigh. Morgana's home was much closer than his own. Shaking his head, he started to walk up the road and watch for the turnoff to his fellow mage's residence. He gripped the strap of the backpack tightly in one hand and kept an ear open for any sound of the jars being disturbed.

Soon enough he was walking up the drive of Morgana's home with the gravel shifting beneath his feet and the Victorian style home towering over him. Thankfully, her red car was in the drive and Merlin trudged up onto the porch. Ringing the doorbell, Merlin reached up and rubbed the back of his neck, trying to loosen the tension gathering at the base of his skull. The door opened, just a little at first, but then all the way as Morgana saw who it was.

"Ambrose." Morgana raised an eyebrow with a curious glint in her green eyes. She took him in quickly as she stepped to the side of the door and gestured him inside. "What happened to you?"

"Good to see you too, Morgana," Merlin greeted. He was suddenly aware of the dried lines of mud across his pants and boots. "I had a slight problem with the water tunnel on my way back. Your home was closer."

"You'd better have more than that as an explanation." Morgana huffed as she closed the door. He heard the telltale sound of the lock and latch as he headed into her living room. "I can't recall the last time you had that kind of trouble with a water tunnel."

"It happens." Merlin waved a hand dismissively. "I assume my spare clothes are still in the guest room."

"They are," Morgana answered with a nod. "But what distracted you so badly?"

"I will explain," Merlin promised as he looked at a nearby clock. "Oh dear, it seems that I was in the tunnel for some time." He shook his head, trying to place exactly what time it would have been here when he entered the tunnel. "I'll explain after I clean up."

He could almost hear Morgana beginning to argue but headed back to the spare bedroom determined not to give her a chance. Once the door was shut behind him, she fell silent apart from one last grumble. Merlin carefully pulled the backpack off and set it on the floor. He wasn't willing to face Morgana's wrath if he dirtied her linens despite her ability to clean them with magic.

Changing into fresh clothing quickly, Merlin sighed at not having a chance to shower, but he was testing Morgana as it was. After living almost three millennia she really should have been more patient. He dismissed the spare jacket and rolled up the sleeves of his button-down shirt before picking up the backpack. Entering the bathroom, he washed his hands and face before looking thoughtfully at his reflection. He looked tired and the worry lines that the centuries had given him were more pronounced than they had been for some time. Shaking his head, he dried off his face and headed out towards the living room.

He could hear Morgana in the kitchen and in his mind's eye could see her making tea for them. There was a tension in the air that he was certain she had sensed and while neither of them were modern British, they had both long embraced tea.

"Morgana," he called. He sat down on the sofa, placing the bag next to his feet. He unzipped it and looked down at the wrapped jars with a mixture of dread and relief. "If you have a moment."

"Ambrose," she returned coolly, walking into the living room from the kitchen with the expected tray of tea. "Where have you been and what happened?" She set the tray down on the table and sat in one of the armchairs.

"I had some things to take care of," Merlin explained calmly as he zipped the bag closed. He was aware of Morgana eyeing the bag carefully and knew that a thoughtful frown would have taken over her face by this point. "I had confidence that you and the children would be alright."

"That was cryptic, Ambrose," Morgana observed, narrowing her sharp green eyes on him. "I'm not in the mood."

"I'm a literature professor," Merlin protested with a slight pout hoping that she'd let it go. "I'm allowed to be archaic and cryptic."

"No," Morgana said with an even more suspicious look. "That's all professors." She crossed her arms over her chest and watched him suspiciously. "What have you been up to?"

"I'm afraid that I was checking on some things after failing to find Mjǫllnir. Sif woke at my call, but she has no information about the Hammer. I'm afraid that she is going to wake her family."

"Lovely, more Old Ones," Morgana grumbled.

"Indeed, but they liked Thor for the most part and with luck, they will return to sleep once the Hammer is found." Merlin groaned and rubbed his forehead as he looked towards the bag. "Well, I should be getting home."

"You will not." Morgana's eyes narrowed on the bag. "You just got back and haven't explained anything, Ambrose."

"I'm not sure that it is wise-"

"No," Morgana snapped. She leaned forward in her chair, setting her dark eyes on his. "You don't get to do that, Merlin! We've known each other too long, been through too much. Three thousand years of living, war, and loss so don't you dare try."

"Morgana..." he trailed off and swallowed the lump in his throat. "It's complicated."

"Then explain in small sentences. Use our native tongue if you need to," Morgana said. "Where have you been and why?" Her eyes darted over to the backpack. "And what is that? What are you trying to hide from me?"

"Nothing," he insisted weakly before sighing and shaking his head. "I'm just... struggling with how to begin, Morgana."

"Let's start with what is in the bag," Morgana suggested, her voice softening to the point that Merlin wondered how worried and stressed he looked.

He unzipped the backpack and reached inside, poking around until he found the solid mass of the first jar amongst the towels. Pulling forth one of the old earthen jars, Merlin gently ran his fingers over the long-dried clay. He marveled that they had remained so intact. The weight of Morgana's eyes was impatient, but she remained silent as he carefully set the jar on the table before them.

"You know the story of Taliesin and the magical cauldron I assume?"

"The story where the boy brews a potion to grant wisdom with the first few drops and the rest will be poison?" Morgana asked with a furrowing brow. "I've heard it."

"It is one of those tales that I wonder about the origin of." Merlin tented his hands together in front of him. "Rather like the Fisher King, I suppose. I wonder if there was a mage who had visions of the past or future and told them as stories, unaware of their real meaning and significance. Someone who didn't understand what they saw and dismissed it as entertaining dreams."

"Ambrose," Morgana called sharply, pulling him from his thoughts. "I believe that the myth of Taliesin has become connected to the stories about you over the years." There was cunning in her eyes as she waited for him to confirm what she must already be suspecting.

"Indeed, it has, and with the same odd twist as the tale of Guinevere and Lancelot being connected to Arthur. It is true in a fashion. The first year that I was training as a mage, Cyrridven brewed a potion for a year and a day just as the story goes. The first few drops contained within them such a strong concentration of magic that they triggered my vision of the birth of the Iron Soul and reinforced my connection with the Iron Realm. I have never wavered since then." He breathed out slowly, his mouth dry and his lips feeling ready to crack. "But the rest of the potion was poison. It was completely free of even a flicker of magic and thus could destroy whatever it touched. I stored the poison in earthen jars and hid them away to keep them from ever being used as a poison on the world."

There was shock in her wide eyes. The tale was old, but it was a strange one with only a glimmer of truth. He wasn't sure what Morgana had expected him to say, but the way her eyes were locked onto the jar told him that this hadn't been it. Fear and worry replaced the shock and she eyed the jars carefully which assured him that she understood the weight of what he was saying.

"There were three jars," he explained softly. "I hid them long ago. There was no way to destroy the poison and I feared the consequences of using it. When I was retrieving them a group of Sídhe descendants attacked me. The poison eroded the walls and destroyed the creatures. Thankfully when released it doesn't work for long."

"Why did you never tell me?" Morgana asked in an emotionless voice. "Did you not trust me?"

"No, I trusted you, but this..." Merlin trailed off and placed a hand on the jar. "At the time the idea of it frightened me, but over the years that fear has transformed into a terrified clarity of the danger these pose. I never spoke of them, Cyrridven never asked of them, and we both tried to act as if they did not exist. It is why neither of us ever entertained the notion of making that potion again: not for Arto or any other Iron Soul. The danger is too great. I wanted to forget."

"And yet here it is," Morgana said.

Merlin noted that she did not reach for the jar and was staring at it with a hesitant expression. "A poison completely free of magic... I found myself wondering if it might be able to corrode the connection between Arthur and the power of the Iron Soul," Merlin said softly.

"You kept it stashed as a weapon," Morgana all but hissed. "How many caches do you have, Merlin, of things you've never told me of?"

"There are a few," Merlin heard himself admit as he raised his eyes to meet Morgana's. "And there are things in place to inform you of them should I fall."

Her face betrayed no reaction to his words. He suspected she was not surprised. It would not surprise him if Morgana had arranged something similar. Their slow aging, eternal purpose as it was had sustained them for a long time, but they had avoided accidents and grave injuries. The extent of their lifespans was unknown to them both though he had often wondered. Still, they had their duty and both were devoted.

"What is your plan then?" Morgana asked, moving the conversation forward. "We'd have to find Arthur or the Iron Chain to even try with the poison. And how could we safely deploy it? If it is as dangerous as you suggest then we need to be precise."

"There are many aspects to consider I know," Merlin agreed wearily. "Sadly, I'm not sure how to weaponize the poison beyond just throwing the jar."

"These jars... how were they made?" Morgana questioned, ghosting her hand around the small vessel. "If this poison is so powerful how does this small thing contain it?"

Merlin chuckled lightly. "There's nothing special about them, Morgana... we just put the poison in them as soon as the potion was used. I don't know if there is a delay before it stabilizes or something else." He paused and closed his eyes, straining to pull the memory from so long ago. "We poured it directly from the cauldron."

"But the jars?"

"I made them myself out of clay," he said. "It seems strange, Morgana, but what keeps the poison, has kept it safe all these years is some sort of magic. Something beyond…" He trailed off and shook his head before looking towards her with a smile. "Strange isn't it. After all these years there are still things we do not understand."

"I suspect that will always be the case," Morgana said before turning her eyes back to him. "I don't like this, Ambrose, but we will not resolve it today. I expect that you will not store them with the Iron Chalice."

"Never," he assured her quickly. "I will not risk the Chalice."

"And keep them away from the children," Morgana added sternly. "Clearly you're going to do what you think best, but don't risk the children."

There was no small amount of anger and judgement in her voice. Merlin might have laughed at the reversal of roles, but it wasn't funny. "Where are the children?" Merlin asked, rubbing his eyes as exhaustion threatened to overwhelm him.

"I'm uncertain of their exact location at the moment, but somewhere in Paris," Morgana answered him with a hint of smug satisfaction. "I saw them off from Portland with their passports and plenty of funds."

His head snapped up and Merlin looked at Morgana in unconcealed horror. "What?" he gasped. "Morgana, what have you done now?"

"They have a lead on the Iron Hammer," Morgana informed him, raising her cup of tea to her lips and taking a long sip. "It made sense to send them to Paris. Well Alex and Bran at least, but they're safer together."

"But Arthur-"

"Arthur is unlikely to be looking for them in Paris," Morgana countered quickly, giving him a warning look. "They placed the blood protection spell in Spokane and Portland before departing. Ravenslake is now barred to those that mean harm to the mages," she added with a smirk. "Timothy remains able to move around without discomfort."

"Arthur found me without any issue!" Merlin protested, slapping a hand on his knee. "I'm not sure how, but that's why I lost focus on the water tunnel, Morgana." He shook his head and began to stand up. "Somehow he found me!"

"Ambrose... Merlin," Morgana started as she licked her lips nervously and considered him carefully. "What is this about?"

"We need to stop them," Merlin answered as calmly as he could, but the look on Morgana's face made him stumble. "They aren't safe!"

"No." Morgana's eyes dropped to the jar on the table. "This is more than that. You never told me about these even during the first war."

"We weren't fighting strange half-Sídhe creatures like us back then!" He ran a hand through his gray curls and tugged at the hair in frustration. "Alex is in danger! We have to bring them back here! Arthur could find them or something else!"

"Alex is fine, Merlin!" Morgana shouted. Silence dominated the room and Morgana exhaled slowly. "She's alright," Morgana repeated. "It bothers me too, Ambrose. We failed to see the threat. We let him close to her, close to us, and he nearly got the Sword. Aiden only survived because we were lucky and that had nothing to do with us. We had nothing to offer except money after the fact!"

"And yet you've sent them off once again with just money!"

"They can handle it," Morgana answered in a cold voice.

A wise man would drop the topic at that voice, but Merlin was stubborn. "They're children, Morgana!"

"Not by the standards of our time," Morgana said, her green eyes narrowing on him. "Everyone is a child to us, Ambrose, but they've already proven that they can handle a threat."

"We had to rescue them at Stonehenge."

"They could have handled it." Morgana crossed her arms and glared at him. "Are you going to tell me what this is really about?" She gestured to the jar and his bag. "After all this time you go and retrieve these jars, and now you're hovering even worse than me."

"I..." Merlin faltered, suddenly aware of a weakness in his knees. Morgana's gaze softened. She stood up and came around the coffee table, sitting next to him on the sofa. Their fingers entwined as she put a hand over his. "I feel old," he finally answered.

"You are old," Morgana reminded him with a chuckle.

"So are you."

"But you'll always be older." Morgana squeezed his hand warmly. "I know what you mean," she admitted a moment later. "We missed something big and it almost... but we can't just lock Alex in Ravenslake. She's got to make her own choices and so far, she's doing a pretty decent job."

"But so much could go wrong," Merlin protested weakly. "And we..." He shook his head. "I'm just not sure what we're dealing with now, Morgana."

To his relief, she said nothing in response to that. They just sat there for some time as he tried not to wonder about Alex, where the Iron Hammer was, and what they were supposed to do next. Finally, he turned his gaze back to the small earthen jar and wondered how he could use it to destroy Medraut and Scáthbás once and for all.

21

Sympathy for Old Enemies

16 C.E. Sør-Trøndelag, Norway

The sun was creeping towards the horizon and Thor was trying to stay still. His breath wafted up into the air forming tiny shapes in front of them. Adjusting his fur cloak, Thor held back a shudder at the chill beginning to seep into his bones. Northman or not, winter was setting in too quickly for them to be dawdling around outside.

Across the snow-covered glen, Sif gave him a smile that sent a flash of warmth through his chest. He barely held back a silly grin even as her brother Baldr caught his eye with a warning glint. Merlin and Odin were speaking in low voices to his right and Morgana was scanning the forest impatiently. A layer of snow covered the ground and only the subdued sound of critters moving in the trees disturbed the peaceful scene.

"Where is Frea?" Morgana asked out loud as she glanced towards the sun. "She should have been here by now. We even met later in the day for her sake. At this rate, it will be dark before we can return to the village."

"Not to mention the cold," Merlin added with a chuckle. "Peace, Morgana. They may have gotten turned around. We can afford to wait a bit longer. We have magic after all."

The Dvergrs made impatient noises from where they sat together sharpening their weapons on a fallen tree they'd dusted off. The slink of metal on the stones was strangely comforting and Austri, one of the Dvergrs he's learned to tell apart from the others, looked up and nodded to him. Thor peered into the trees as he debated just going over to talk with Sif despite Baldr's presence. Her tall brother kept giving him looks from time to time and Sif looked flustered. Thor hoped it was a good sign.

Suddenly a scream filled the mountainside making them all tense. The chirping of the birds and the sounds of small creatures moving around them all seemed to go silent. Thor strained his ears, desperate to confirm that the high-pitched shrieks weren't coming from the direction of his village. Another scream reassured him that they were coming from further inland only to have a rush of guilt hit him at the relief he'd felt. Without waiting for the others, he began to move.

"Stay together!" Merlin ordered sharply behind him, but Thor didn't slow down. "Mind the snow, Thor!" Merlin shouted after him.

The warning was enough to make him slow a little as his feet tried to slide out from beneath him. Blood was pounding in his ears at the sudden silence which seemed unnatural. Rushing through the trees, Thor found himself both hoping for and dreading more screaming. There were a few faint game trails for him and the others to follow as they fanned out. Another shout filled the forest followed by the clanging of metal on metal. There was a battle nearby and Thor sped up his pace as the ground began to slope towards a valley.

Rocks lined the way, dropped there by landslides and other disasters, confusing him as he looked for the source of the noise. A steep valley began to open ahead and he caught sight of smoke curling up through the air. Tracks in the snow ahead of him were coming towards him and then suddenly turned back around. Racing forward, Thor followed the narrow trail they marked down the slope of the valley.

A rocky outcropping and woven wood wall created a large shaded space from the rays of the sun up ahead. Smoke was pouring out from underneath the sheltering shelf of rock and for a moment he was stunned at the sight. He'd known Frea's people lived nearby, but he hadn't imagined it was so close and yet undiscovered. Thor stopped in his tracks and looked down in shock at the sight of small burning buildings and Sídhe creatures running from Dark Elves. Smoke billowed up into the air and the smell of burning hair and flesh filled his nostrils. The woven walls were collapsing in flashes of fire and only the rocky terrain kept the flames from spreading. Steam hissed as burning fragments of wood rolled down into the snow and half obscured the scene.

Pulling out Mjǫllnir, Thor marched forward as a small Síd ran screaming from the village and began to climb the rocks towards him. The rays of the sinking sun cast long shadows all around them and the small Síd stopped and looked at him with terror filled eyes.

"I'm not here to harm you," Thor assured her quickly. "Hide until this is over!"

She nodded weakly and dashed off into the valley, huddling behind a rock where he caught sight of a few more Sídhe hiding. Behind him, he could hear the others catching up before another set of shrieks echoed in the valley. He kept moving forward towards the smoke and the once hidden village. The last rays of the sun were vanishing behind a mountain causing the temperature to drop and Thor barely held back a shiver.

A flash of silver magic from behind him illuminated the area. Moments later shining silvery orbs shot past him and settled in the air, casting a soft light through the smoky war zone. Dark Elves looked up sharply, their black eyes glittering in the magical light with expressions of surprise on their faces. Sídhe creatures with their translucent skin used the distraction to flee. The Dark Elves froze and the screams died down leaving the howl of the wind through the rocky valley and the sound of footfalls.

Then the strange peace of the scene was broken as the Dark Elves turned their attention to him and the other new arrivals. Gone were their rags and simple clothing, now they all wore full leather armor with bronze accents and carried bronze weapons. Five began to march out of the village towards him, sending a jolt of fear through Thor. One of them snarled and he began to move as battle instincts took over. Swinging Mjǫllnir to the right, Thor struck the nearest Dark Elf with a hard blow as magic leapt from the metal and into the creature. It began to dissolve as screams tore from its mouth, but he was already moving on. He thrust the Hammer forward as he willed the magic thrumming within it to release on a group of Dark Elves a few feet ahead. They were moving towards him as pale blue lightning arced through the air and struck them. As he pushed further into the small village, Thor found more and more small Sídhe creatures that some part of his mind recognized as children to his own shock hiding and trying to flee.

Green magic bolts blasted past him and collided in a flurry of light with the chest of another Dark Elf. It swung its sword wildly at him before another bolt threw it backward and it began to dissolve like the others. Thor kept moving into the village, catching the attention of another Dark Elf that threw a spear towards him. Deflecting it with Mjǫllnir, Thor jumped forward and swung the Hammer against the being's head. There was a cracking sound and it began to dissolve, but Thor didn't linger.

Two more Dark Elves charged him. He swung Mjǫllnir, releasing another blast of lightning that took one down in seconds. The second swung a sword at him. Thor slammed Mjǫllnir against its arm sending it stumbling to the side, grasping the arm in pain. Before the Dark Elf could recover, he opened his left hand and sent a wave of pale blue sparks flying forth to form an arrow in the air. It screamed and began to vanish.

There were more coming out of the darkness. Thor couldn't see far into the village that followed the cliff. He stayed his hand whenever he caught a flash of frightened purple eyes and struck whenever the sickly dark skin appeared. Grabbing a Dark Elf around the neck and holding it in place, Thor's eyes widened as he took in the creature's appearance. The blackness that had been seeping into their skin was all but solid now with a shimmering black shade having overtaken their entire complexion.

Pulling on his magic, Thor grimaced as the sparks swarmed around the creature and burned wildly against his own skin in reaction to his uncontrolled emotions. He shoved the creature away and spared it only one last glance before swinging Mjǫllnir at the next Dark Elf to rush him. Silver and green magic flared in the corner of his eye and he caught a glimpse of Odin slamming a glowing staff into another Dark Elf. With a grunt, he hit one more Dark Elf with Mjǫllnir and straightened up sharply to find only the empty burning village around him.

"Thor!" Odin's voice called from behind him. "Are you alright? Do you see any more?"

Holding up Mjǫllnir, Thor turned around quickly and searched the area. There were no more Dark Elves to be seen, but his heart was still pounding. Then slowly he lowered his Hammer and exhaled as the cold air settled on his sweaty skin.

"No," he called back. "I think that's all of them." He began to look around more closely at the houses that were still standing. "But be careful."

At his words, the Sídhe began to come creeping out of their hiding places. They looked around carefully and he watched them in silence as they gathered their children close to them. The last remains of the woven wood wall separating the village from the open air collapsed onto the rocks and released a hiss of steam as the flames were doused by the snow. Morgana's light orbs remained in place but illuminated a sad scene. Several small houses, built half of stone and half of wood, were still smoldering. Members of the village were moving around them with dazed and sorrowful eyes as they sought out each other and picked through the remains of the houses. Other buildings were still intact and more Sídhe crowded around them.

Turning to look at the others, Thor noted that even Morgana was staying silent as she studied the scene. Her face was devoid of any harsh satisfaction and instead, there was a pained expression of familiarity on her features. He almost sighed in relief at the silent reassurance that she wasn't going to say anything cruel, at least not today.

"There may be more Dark Elves nearby," Merlin announced as he withdrew to the opening in the rocks and began to investigate. Morgana followed him out a moment later.

Thor watched them go and was silent as Odin, Sif, and Baldr lingered out in the night air. Sif bent down to speak with some of the children in a low voice and after a long moment, Thor forced himself to start moving again. He pushed some more magic into Mjǫllnir and smiled when it began to glow softly, illuminating his way.

The village was built tightly against the cliff side, huddling underneath the rocky ledges which kept it in the shade with one narrow road separating the inner and outer buildings. None of the residents were paying him any mind beyond a quick glance. With his bleached hair and pale skin, he couldn't be mistaken for a Dark Elf, not even in the darkness.

"We need to get the fires out," a familiar voice ordered up ahead to an unseen person. "And post guards!"

Speeding up, Thor followed the voice around another small house and sighed in relief. Frea was leaning heavily against the stone cliff face with an exhausted expression on her features. Silver blood marked a wound on her left arm and a long scrape on her right cheek. Another one of her people was in front of her and gave Frea a deep nod before rushing off. Frea groaned and stumbled to the side before nearly collapsing.

"Frea," Thor greeted carefully, He took in the female Síd seated on what remained of a burned-out pile of wood. "Are you hurt?"

"I'm fine," she replied in a low voice. "Just a flesh wound."

Thor shifted uncertainly as he took her in. Without her hood and cloak, she looked so very small with her long and slight limbs. Her long pale hair was a tangled mess with ash and dirt streaked through it. Vacant violet eyes looked around the remains of the village and Thor frowned in sympathy for her and all her people.

"I'm so sorry this happened," Thor told her gently as he moved in front of her. Kneeling in the dirt and ash, he took her hand and gave it what he hoped was a reassuring squeeze. "I'm so sorry, Frea."

"We don't belong here," Frea murmured. "Shouldn't you be grateful?" The words were weak and lacked spite so Thor didn't take them personally. "They did the job for you."

"I've never planned on harming any of you," Thor promised her softly. "You can't help what you were born as or that you were born here."

A soft pained laugh escaped Frea, but she also nodded at his words. For a moment they didn't speak and Thor looked around as more of those who had fled began to return. They joined the others in starting the cleanup and gathering of supplies. Thor watched them, wondering if he should join in and help or if that would be going one step too far.

"Where did they come from, Frea?" Thor finally asked. "The sun was still up so they couldn't have-"

"They came..." She hesitated for a moment and frowned. Instantly she became more alert and jumped to her feet.

Frea was already disappearing into the shadows when Thor climbed to his own feet. Hurrying after her, he barely noticed the houses and Sídhe who backed away from them. He had to push more magic into Mjǫllnir to brighten its glow as the darkness swept in around him. Then he froze as up ahead a crack appeared in the cliff face. It wasn't large, but small stones were still falling away from it.

"They swept in," Frea gasped in front of him. "They tunneled through the rock and attacked us at our back!" She suddenly screamed in rage, her voice echoing off the cliff. Behind them there was panicked shouting at Frea's outburst and he heard others approaching.

"Thor!" Morgana's voice called.

"I'm alright," he assured her without turning around as he moved up next to Frea. "What is the point of all of this?" Thor asked as he gazed into the dark tunnel before them. "Why do all of this? What are they hoping to achieve?"

"They took some of my people prisoner," Frea informed him with sad eyes. "I saw some, when the attack first started, being bound... I started to fight, but there were so many."

"And dragged them into underground tunnels," Morgana muttered darkly behind him. Her words sent a chill down his spine that made him frightened to even turn around.

"Thor?" Merlin's voice pressed with worry which finally made him turn to face the elder mages.

"But why?" Thor repeated urgently as he looked to Merlin. "What use do the captives have? More slaves or are they hoping to make them Dark Elves as well?"

Frea made a sound of alarm and Morgana's eyes widened dangerously. He could feel the mood shift from one of confusion and sorrow to near panic. Gently, he laid a hand on Frea's arm to keep her from running into the tunnel.

"Could they do that?" Frea demanded, looking at Merlin with frantic eyes.

"Perhaps..." Merlin started uneasily before pausing and grimacing as the others looked to him. "Perhaps they are able to make a way back to Sídhean because they are still connected. While the tunnel may be gone if they did create a hole in Arto's defense then until that hole is closed something may still be lingering."

"So, they might still be being corrupted," Thor remarked thoughtfully only to tense as all three turned to look at him. He stuttered for a moment before recovering his train of thought. "Maybe that's the key here. That connection must be broken before the Dark Elves can be stopped. They seem to be getting worse. They started out with only small parts of black on their skin, but it's been spreading."

"They might be seeking to corrupt my people," Frea realized in horror. "If they've managed to rebuild some sort of connection, then they might use my people to increase their army."

"A good observation." Merlin straightened up and looked out towards the sky in thought. "Then we need to look at breaking that connection. If the Dark Elves are gaining enough power to reconnect to Sídhean and Thor is right that it's getting stronger, then we need to stop them quickly."

"Not just quickly," Morgana said, nodding towards the tunnel. "We haven't time to lose. It's a solid theory, Merlin."

"We should go now!" Thor gestured to the tunnel with his Hammer.

"I understand your worry, Thor," Odin cut in as he and Sif came down the small path. "I have sent Baldr to rally more of my people and our family. If we are reentering their domain we should do so with force."

Thor glanced towards Frea, noting the torn expression on her face. Her violet eyes turned towards the tunnel and then moved among the injured around them, clearly weighing her multiple concerns.

"We cannot afford to lose or withdraw once again," she finally conceded. Thor tightened his grip on Mjǫllnir to hide his frustration. "We should wait for more forces," Frea agreed.

Odin nodded and Sif offered him a small reassuring smile before she shifted over to Frea. Thor backed away as the Old One began to gently tend to the wound on Frea's arm. Merlin and Morgana moved closer to the tunnel, each summoning magic in their hands. Silver sparks burst forth first and spun into the air. They settled like a wall made of fog over the small tunnel entrance. A moment later a layer of green was added, casting a soft light through the village as the pair of mages settled themselves on either side of the tunnel.

Thor stayed close to Frea and pretended not to notice the slight tremor in her shoulders as she began to turn her attention to the wounded. The new opening in the rock loomed behind them ominously. It was still and silent for the moment, but Thor could feel a shudder in the air around them. The air carried a hint of something foul and he knew in his gut that a storm was building.

22

The Ahnenerbe

Shivering, Alex closed her eyes and breathed out slowly. Around her, the noise of Paris was distracting with honking and chattering floating through the park. She could still feel the warm weight of Bran's hands around hers. Yet despite her relative discomfort, Alex felt a little better, more than a little to be honest. It was like she'd been standing too close to a sudden drop and had suddenly been able to take a step back.

"You sure you want to try again?" Aiden asked at her side. "You don't have to, Alex."

"Yes, I do," Alex said with a slight smile as she opened her eyes. Everyone was looking at her and she visibly relaxed. "Really guys this isn't so bad. Gottfried wasn't a bad person, not like..." Alex trailed off and shook her head. "Anyway, I'll be fine."

"Gottfried may not have been a willing Nazi," Nicki told her. "But he probably saw a lot of stuff that you won't like, Alex."

It was a quiet, but powerful reminder. Alex's stomach turned as she thought back to some of the photos in her old history textbooks. "Fair point." She caught Jenny giving Nicki a dark look. "But we need to find the Hammer. I'll try to focus on it this time," she promised. "Hopefully that will be everything we need."

Nicki didn't look convinced, but Jenny offered her a supportive smile while Lance nodded. Alex returned her focus to Bran and he gave her a tiny nod of agreement. He breathed out and closed his eyes. Yellow magic flared around their joined hands and Alex focused on the slight tickle of it against her skin. Reaching out with own magic, she focused on Bran's magic and watched for a moment as the soft yellow began to darken. Alex's fingers twitched with the desire to touch the ground and she carefully detached one of her hands. Bran's eyes opened in surprise, but he shifted his hand down to the ground as well.

Gripping the grass, Alex closed her eyes. There was a burst of energy up her hand and arm, sending a shiver across her skin. She repeated the words Iron Hammer over and over again. Straining her memory, Alex tried to remember if it had a name like the sword, but nothing came forth. Magic was trickling over her arms like water running upwards and her back straightened of its own accord. Alex shuddered slightly as the magic rolled over the back of her neck and breathed out slowly. A sense of dizziness washed over her. Alex's body began to sway. Someone gripped her shoulder as her awareness slipped away.

They rolled their shoulders as the door closed behind them with a soft thump, leaving them alone in a small conference room that had pale yellowing walls. A framed black and white photo of Hitler hung on the wall between a pair of Nazi flags in stands. As the wooden door opened, they jumped to their feet. Two officers in dark charcoal uniforms of the SS strode in, their hats tucked protectively under their arms. The one in the lead was a Colonel with a Major two steps behind him. A pair of civilians or at least ununiformed Nazis entered after them.

The Colonel was a tall man with neatly combed dark, almost coal black hair and pale blue eyes. Deep lines surrounded his eyes which were sharp as they swept the room and took them in. The Major was shorter with brown hair and dark brown eyes that had a hardness to them. Something about him was a touch frightening.

"Heil Hitler," they greeted quickly, their back straight and thrusting their arm forward with the palm open. The gesture was forced and uncomfortable as always, but their neutral expression remained intact.

The Colonel and Major returned their salute quickly though the Major's was more energetic than the Colonel's. They waited for instructions and resisted the urge to fidget. The collar of their own SS uniform was stiff around their neck like a plaster, but then thankfully the Colonel sat at the table.

"Be seated gentlemen," the Colonel told them all imperiously. He gestured to the waiting empty seats.

They glanced towards the ununiformed men distinctly, trying to understand who they were. The Major went to a small cabinet in the corner of the room and returned with several glasses and an old looking bottle. They fought to keep a neutral expression as alcohol was poured and passed around.

"Thank you," one of the other men said carefully. "My apologies, but I don't believe I caught your name."

"He is Major Berger and I am Colonel Voigt," the Colonel informed the men in an even polite tone before gesturing towards them. "This is Captain Eckstein of the SS." He took a sip of his drink with a slight smile. "Gentlemen you have been selected for an important task, one that will allow our glorious Reich to demonstrate our superiority and place in history to the world."

The men glanced towards them in curiosity and they tightened their grip on the glass nervously. One of them looked far more comfortable than the other, almost excited in contrast to the worry churning in their own gut. He was tall with blond hair they suspected might not be completely natural and beginning to bald with sharp brown eyes. The second man was shorter with gray hair framing a large bald spot. His frame was a bit pudgy and he had a pleasant looking face with obvious nervousness written on his features.

"Good to see you, Colonel Voigt," the first man said. "Please tell us why we're here. I've heard some rumors about a new expedition."

"Indeed, Professor Weber," the Colonel said. "Captain Eckstein is an expert in history and languages," Colonel Voigt explained. "He's been busy teaching our men in Paris French, but this is a better use of his talents. You, Professor Dietrich, are an expert in mythology," he added gesturing towards the man who'd asked their names. "And Professor Weber is one of Ahnenerbe's resident archeologists."

"Ahnenerbe?" Professor Dietrich repeated incredulously as he looked around the bare room. "I didn't realize that this was their office."

"It isn't," Major Berger corrected with an oily smirk. "This is an SS office."

"This mission will be something of a secret, I'm afraid," Colonel Voigt informed those gathered. "It is a mission of personal importance to Himmler."

"What area is the focus this time?" Weber asked eagerly. "Africa? Asia?"

"No, you'll be focusing in Europe," Voigt said as he looked down at his drink. "In Norway to be precise."

"Norway?" Dietrich repeated. He adjusted his glasses and frowned. Weber looked confused and a bit disappointed.

"Himmler is convinced that Thor's Hammer is in Norway," Voigt answered the unspoken question almost dismissively. "So, you'll be going and tracking it down."

"Thor's Hammer?" they repeated doubtfully as their eyes jumped between the officers. "You can't be-" They cut themselves off and coughed. "Surely it is just a story. Thor is a myth after all."

They received a warning look and instantly silenced any other doubts they might have offered. Sharing a look with Dietrich, they were aware that the other man wasn't any more impressed than they were.

"Several of Ahnenerbe's scholars have been tracing local myths and have found some interesting stories that hint at a protomyth, an origin point for the stories if you will."

"So, you have a location?" Weber asked, looking much more eager now.

"There is an area that you are to check," Major Berger explained. "It will take some time, but if you are successful then the expedition will be a remarkable success!" There was a gleam in the man's eye that they didn't like at all. "Should the stories be true then imagine what such an object could help the Third Reich achieve!"

"First things first," Voigt cut in looking distinctly unimpressed with Berger. "There are many details to sort out first: transport and staff, but Himmler is eager to see the expedition begin."

Leaning back in the chair, they couldn't believe this was happening, but the more they thought about it as Voigt and Berger brought out files for them to look at, the better it sounded. Their placement in France was comfortable in theory, but living in an occupied city full of people who had every reason to hate you carried its own problems. Norway wouldn't be much better thanks to the occupation and the King being in exile, but at least an archeological expedition would keep them isolated.

They looked down as another folder was slid over to them and opened it quickly. There were a few maps of the Norwegian coast with notes scrawled on the edges, pages of interview questions and answers, several photographs from the area, and copies of several drawings of Thor's Hammer. Their eyes lingered on the image of the iconic Hammer and for a moment there was a strange sense that it didn't look right. The feeling passed quickly and they turned their attention back to the Colonel. This may be a fool's errand and no doubt one more attempt of the Ahnenerbe to rewrite history to suit Hitler, but at least he could stay away from the worst aspects of the war.

That thought echoed in their mind. Images of camps with piles of corpses and people who looked like the living dead flashed through their mind. There was a bombed-out Berlin and a burning Dresden. Around them, the room flickered as the strange images overtook all thoughts. Blinking, they tried to force the strange premonition away as the Colonel turned towards them. They heard a question and some kind of answer came forth even as the... connection frayed.

What followed were flashes of faces, places, and voices. They sailed past too quickly for any meaning to be gained. Then it all slowed down and the Eiffel Tower appeared. That then changed to a long dark tunnel that stank of decay. A light illuminated a wall built of bones. The connection pulled apart further as a shining weapon made of metal appeared. It was some sort of hammer with the triskelion symbol engraved on the side. One end was wide and flat while the other tapered into a smaller edge. Something snapped and she flinched at the sharp rush of magic back into her chest.

Everything was suddenly different. She wasn't in a chair in a closed room or in that strange tunnel. There was a soft pillow beneath her head, soft music playing in the background, and someone was holding her hand. It took her a long moment to come back to herself as Eckstein faded into the backdrop. Not moving she just listened to the soft voices she could hear distantly.

"Guys I think she's coming around," someone female whispered. "Does she need more magic?"

"Let's see if she wakes up on her own," another voice, also familiar, but this time male answered. "We don't want to overwhelm her."

"At least she's coming around," another female voice interjected. "I would've hated to call Morgana about this."

Groaning, Alex forced her eyes open. Her shoulders ached from sitting in a hunched over position too long. Something cracked slightly and Alex grimaced with a soft groan. Turning her head, she found a smiling Jenny seated on the edge of a bed next to her. Alex frowned in confusion and looked up towards the bottom of the upper bunk.

"Hostel?" she asked softly.

"That's right, private room with our own bathroom," Jenny answered, squeezing her hand. "You were gone a long time, Alex. Bran had to stop giving you magic."

"He's okay right?" Alex asked, suddenly more alert as she started to sit up.

"I'm fine," Bran called from across the room. "Sorry we had to move you, but we were attracting attention."

Alex shifted again and Jenny leaned back to give her more space. Every muscle in her back protested as she sat up. A yawn escaped her before she could stop it, earning a soft chuckle from Jenny. She looked over towards where Bran's voice had come from. He was seated at a small round table in the center of the room with Nicki. Four bunk beds lined the wall and their luggage was stacked up near one of the two wooden doors. The furniture looked solid and fairly new. Orange light was pouring in through the one large window and Alex frowned as she recognized the glow of a sunset.

"How long?" she forced out, suddenly aware of how dry her throat was.

"We stayed at the tower for three hours," Jenny informed her. Leaning over, Jenny retrieved a bottle of water. "Then Bran broke the connection, but you just kept sleeping."

"How'd you get me here?" she asked as she gestured around the room. "What happened?"

"I was sharing magic with you," Bran reminded her gently. "But I felt myself growing weaker... I disconnected from you and we tried to wake you up."

"You wouldn't wake up," Nicki took over a little too calmly. "We were freaking out, but then you started mumbling in your sleep."

"So, we brought you to the hostel in a cab. Told the front desk you'd blacked out from drinking," Jenny added, looking a touch embarrassed. "Sorry about that part."

"We were going to call Morgana if you hadn't woken up in another hour," Bran finished looking very relieved. "The others tried giving you magic, but you didn't change it so we hoped it meant you were just in a deep vision."

"I wouldn't wake up," Alex repeated in surprise as she looked at their faces. They all looked relieved now, but she thought she could still see shadows of worry. "Sorry about that, didn't mean to scare you." She paused and licked her lips. "It didn't feel like I was gone that long... except at the end... there were all these flashes."

"Don't worry about it," Jenny urged, reaching out to brush a strand of blonde hair from Alex's face.

"How'd you get me to a cab?"

"Lance is pretty strong," Jenny reminded her with a grin and a slight blush that Alex didn't want to think about.

"Where is he?" Alex asked as she looked around the room. "And Aiden?"

"Downstairs making some dinner and some calls," Nicki answered. "Aiden wanted to check in with his folks."

"Oh, that's fair," Alex agreed, wondering if she should call her parents.

Falling silent, Alex stretched out her arms as she waited for everything to... settle. It was an odd thought and her heart jumped uncomfortably at it, but thankfully a panic attack didn't follow. Jenny offered her a smile and withdrew back to the table where she leaned over something the others were looking at.

"So do you know the future yet?" Jenny asked Bran with a soft chuckle.

Alex straightened up enough to see the series of cards spread across the surface of the table. She couldn't see them clearly but recognized enough from the brightly decorated pieces of paper that she chuckled.

"Tarot cards?" Alex asked, looking at Bran.

"Blame Nicki," Bran muttered as he shook his head. "When they ran out for dinner stuff, she picked some up."

"I thought they might help," Nicki huffed as she waved her hand. "Another medium for you to use. Need I remind you that you are the party seer." She tapped the final card in the spread that was still face down. "So, what do you see?" Nicki asked with a widening grin.

"And your outcome is-" Bran turned over the last card and revealed the image of a burning tower. Grabbing the small book he'd been reading earlier he flipped through it for a moment and grimaced slightly before quickly perking up. "The Tower, but it could be good."

"It's the Tower," Nicki repeated doubtfully, giving Bran a look.

"But it's not inverted," Bran insisted as he leaned over to look at the book.

"There's a man jumping out of a burning room." Nicki leaned over and pointed at the card. "Jumping out of the Tower, how is that good?"

"Maybe tarot cards isn't the best way to do this." Alex turned on the bed and set her feet on the floor. "Too vague for one." She noticed that her sneakers had been removed and were on the floor next to her feet.

"Oh, give him some time," Nicki teased with a grin toward Bran. "He'll probably sort it out."

"We'll see." Bran paused and examined the cards thoughtfully. "It might be something that mages have used in the past so maybe I should try it again and actually use some magic."

"So, I can disregard the Tower?" Nicki asked eagerly. "Okay, I officially disregard the Tower."

Smiling a little, Alex breathed out a bit more easily. She tried to remember the last parts of her vision when everything had gone strange, but there were only a few images that stood out to her. There was the dark tunnel and the Hammer. Alex frowned and tightened her grip on the sheets. There might have been bones. Something nagged at her memory, but she couldn't chase it down.

"How about some food?" Nicki asked her, suddenly much closer. Alex looked up to find Nicki right next to the bed with a hesitant smile. "Shall we go downstairs and get something to eat?" Nicki offered more gently. "You should eat something, Alex."

"Yeah," Alex agreed with a nod, reaching down for her shoes. A wave of dizziness hit her and she froze in place.

"Alex?" Nicki gasped. "You okay?"

"I'm fine," she snapped more harshly than she meant to. "Just back off!"

"Hey!" Nicki started to protest.

"Give her a minute," Bran said from nearby. "We'll meet you down-stairs, Nicki."

Alex kept her head down, trying to ignore the trembling beginning to take over her hands. Slamming her eyes shut, Alex tensed as Arthur's smirking face appeared before her. There was a bloody sword in his hand and her stomach ached. Opening her eyes, Alex stayed still and tried to push the rush of terror and the images away. She flinched as the door closed with a soft thump. A moment later she heard a chair being moved. A pair of shoes appeared in the corner of her eyes as someone sat down.

"Alex, it's Bran," he announced calmly. "You're in a hostel in Paris. The others are downstairs and are safe." There was a long pause. "What can I do right now? Do you need anything?"

"No," she growled, clenching her jaw and trying to take a slow breath. "I mean- sorry."

"You've got nothing to apologize for," Bran reassured her. "Just try to breathe. Focus on my voice if that helps." It did help a little and Alex raised her eyes towards Bran. He was sitting in the chair, slumped forward and just watching her with a neutral expression. "Lance was making sandwiches of some kind. I didn't go out shopping with the others," he explained as he opened a small book and began flipping through it. "I'm wondering where they went shopping that they found a tarot set in English. Maybe Paris has more interesting shops than I thought." He chuckled lightly. "I think I was just guilty of stereotyping. You'd think I'd know better."

"You're entirely too calm about all of this," Alex muttered, half accus-ingly as she tried to unclench her fists.

"Contrary to what might be going through your head this is a com-pletely normal reaction," Bran told her. That just made her angrier. "My Uncle George had PTSD."

"PTSD," Alex repeated stunned. The anger slipped away as shock replaced it. "That's something for soldiers!"

"Post-traumatic stress disorder," Bran lectured as if he hadn't heard her. "You're not wrong, it is often found in soldiers, but like the name suggests it is tied to traumatic experiences. And while you may not like to think of it that way, you've had plenty of those, Alex. The Sídhe capturing you, Chernobog, Arthur, and now your other lives have all put you under a lot of stress and pressure." He paused and offered her a small smile. "This isn't your fault, Alex, so don't think it is. Please just keep in mind that you've got us, Morgana, and Merlin if you need us."

He went silent and Alex lowered her eyes, unsure of the different emotions fighting for dominance in her chest. The irrational anger she'd felt towards Nicki had faded and guilt and embarrassment were taking over. Part of her asked why this was starting now and tried to remember what she'd heard about PTSD in the past. Weren't there triggers or something? Wasn't it usually after a bad event so why now and not right after Arthur had stabbed her? Her mouth was dry and she wasn't sure what to do now.

"Your uncle?" Alex repeated as she searched her memory. "I don't think you've ever mentioned him." She wanted Bran to start talking again and give her something else to focus on.

"He wasn't my actual uncle," Bran confirmed with a soft smile. "But he was my dad's best friend in their unit." Bran paused and seemed to be gathering his thoughts. "He was there when the car bomb killed Dad. It hit him hard and when he came back..." Bran trailed off and shook his head. "Mom and I tried to stay in touch even though Dad was gone and we were dealing with that." Alex wanted to ask what happened, but there was a sad note in Bran's voice that worried her. "And after the accident,

Mom sent me to counselors to try and make sure that I didn't end up the same way."

"Did they help?"

Bran shrugged. "Hard to say. I don't know how I would have coped with the initial inability to walk otherwise. Maybe I would have been fine, maybe not." He smiled a little. "Course I didn't try to explain the vision that saved our lives. I knew even then that it would make me sound crazy."

A rough chuckle escaped Alex and she found herself smiling a little bit. Bran offered her a soft smile in return and shifted in his chair. Alex's stomach grumbled a moment later and he outright laughed while Alex grimaced. Reaching down for her shoes, Alex breathed out slowly as she started to pull them on. She wasn't sure what she was supposed to say now. Thankfully Bran merely stood up from the chair and extended a hand to help her stand up from the bed. Her legs shuddered and she almost stumbled. Bran kept her upright and slowly released her hand. With another smile, he looked towards the door and Alex nodded, grateful she didn't have to speak quite yet.

23

Living in Another's Memory

The familiar ring of metal against metal echoed around her in the small smoky space. Large hands were holding a glowing sword in place against an anvil with tongs and she could feel her right hand tightly gripping a hammer. Magic was coursing over her skin as the hammer crashed down. Alex could see a glowing triskelion on the side of the hammer which pulsed as the magic flowed from the hammer into the sword.

Mjǫllnir.

The word, the name sprang to her head. It wasn't exactly what she was familiar with from mythology, but close enough with a sense of rightness settling around it. The Hammer was raised out of her view for a moment only to smash down once again on the sword, a soft pale glow shimmering across the metal's surface.

Alex was grateful for the glimpses of the Hammer and the chance to familiarize herself with it. Unlike what she expected, the Hammer had one large flat side like a normal hammer, but the other side narrowed into a smaller flat edge. Alex supposed that it allowed the Hammer to be more versatile. The symbols on the side made it look a bit more like the mythological object she was expecting, but it didn't match any of the images she'd seen in the books they'd gone through.

Feeling at ease with the clanging sound, Alex drifted in the dream unaware of the passage of time. Her initial confusion faded, though part of her wondered why she was seeing this. This was the Iron Hammer without a doubt, but she wasn't with Gottfried. The Hammer smashed down again before they used a set of tongs to put the sword back into the hot coals of the forge. Heat rolled over Alex and she could almost feel the hairs on her arms being singed.

Then the man shifted, rolling his shoulders, and releasing a low sigh. He paused and turned towards the doorway giving Alex a chance to see their surroundings. It was a small wooden hut with woven walls. Tools were scattered around near the forge and anvil on long benches that lined two walls of the space. It was cramped and chaotic, but also oddly comfortable to Alex. She had no power over where to look and their focus narrowed on the doorway.

"You can come in," they called sounding more amused than anything else in a deep and smooth masculine voice.

A beautiful woman stepped into the small hut with a gentle smile on her face. For a moment Alex was at a loss as she stared at the newcomer. Something about her was different. She looked human, but an instinct warned Alex not to be fooled. Long golden hair framed an unnaturally symmetrical face with large green eyes.

"I didn't want to disturb you," a soft high voice answered.

"Sif," they greeted suddenly sounding a touch nervous. "Everything alright?"

"Yes," Sif answered with a soft sigh. Moving further into the workshop, she turned her head to examine an axe blade on one of the benches.

"Baldr is just being…" She shook her head and looked back towards them. "He doesn't like me visiting you, Thor."

Alex would have gasped or smiled under other circumstances. She'd wanted to see the Iron Hammer and it had apparently worked. A bit late, but it had worked. They glanced back towards the forge for a moment before smiling and looking back to Sif.

"We knew that would likely be the reaction," they chuckled in response.

Sif offered them- Thor a soft smile as she slipped further into the hut. She didn't fit in at all. The tools, furs, and benches were all dark thanks to years of use and exposure to the smoke while she was fair in every sense of the word. Nonetheless, Sif seated herself on the edge of the wooden bench and waved towards the forge. Alex could feel Thor's features shift into a warm smile as he turned back to the fire.

He worked quickly, hammering the red-hot iron blade with Mjǫllnir. Sparks of pale blue magic arced off the Hammer and into the iron where they glistened and settled into the metal. Alex watched mesmerized by the display, partially in awe that Thor had used Mjǫllnir as a smithing hammer. She would have expected it to be used just for battle. Alex found herself wishing there was a mirror nearby so she could see the mythological figure that she once was.

There was a loud hiss as Thor slid the blade into a tall vessel of water. It shuddered in Thor's hand, but he kept it steady and Alex could see the last glimmers of Thor's magic fading. It wasn't magical like Mjǫllnir or Cathanáil or the Chalice, but she knew it would last longer and be a little stronger against beings from other worlds.

Then Thor turned his attention back towards Sif. She smiled at him as he crossed the small hut and submerged his hands in a large bowl of water. It was cold in contrast to the heat still rolling out of the forge.

He splashed some of the water on his face and tugged at his hair as he loosened the leather band holding it out of his face. Alex caught a glimpse of blond hair but noted it had a hint of red before Thor tied it back once more.

Sif shifted right in front of them-him and brought a hand up to touch her-his chest. Alex wanted to look around and see if there was a good reason she was still in this memory, but Thor's eyes were fixed on Sif's. There was an uncomfortable flutter in her stomach as she was forced to stare into the shimmering green eyes. Then soft lips pressed against her own. A soft pleased hum escaped her and Alex knew if she'd been in control that she'd be blushing.

This was worse than losing herself in the memories she decided as Thor's lips shifted against Sif's. His arms came up to rest on her backside. There was no sense of belonging here. She just felt like a voyeur, but she couldn't leave. Thor's eyes closed, blocking the view of Sif's golden hair, but the sensations remained. Lips opened and Thor's tongue brushed across Sif's lower lip sending a flush of heat and horror through Alex.

Alex tried calling on her magic, but there was only a strange fluttering sensation in her-Thor's gut. She tried again, repeating over and over that she didn't want to see this. She didn't want to know this part of Thor's life. Had she been in her own body, Alex would have been frantically apologizing and blushing. Sif's hand came up and tangled in Thor's hair.

Then she heard her name. It was distant, but Alex focused on it. The hut and the... sensations dimmed slightly. Someone called her name softly once again and Alex let the dream fade away. There was tugging ache in her chest as she began to wake.

The soft glow of a cell phone illuminated her bunk and Alex blinked rapidly. Her heart was still pounding from the dream as fight or flight instincts kicked in. Blushing she shifted in her bed, suddenly very aware of the tightness in her stomach and the jumble of thoughts in her head. It took her a moment to realize that without explanation or introductions, she'd known Sif at once. She'd known Sif's face and touch. Her shock cut through the lingering sensations and Alex exhaled slowly as she turned her attention back to the cell phone. There was just enough light to see Jenny's face and the slight frown on her face.

"You okay?" Jenny asked with a soft flush as she adjusted the phone and sat on the edge of Alex's bed. "You were tossing and turning really bad."

"Yeah," Alex said, her voice cracking a little. "Just... an odd dream." A rush of embarrassment washed through her. "It was nothing."

"Didn't sound like nothing," Nicki teased lightly with a cat who got the canary grin, leaning over the edge of the top bunk to join the conversation. "Nice that you're having something other than nightmares."

"It wasn't like that," Alex insisted, ducking her head as her cheeks heated up.

"Sure," Nicki said doubtfully.

"It was a memory," Alex confessed, bringing her hands up and covering her face. "And... well, I..." A hysterical giggle escaped Alex. "Uh let's just say that there are some problems with all my previous lives having been men. It makes them a bit awkward." A horrified look of realization took over Jenny's face. Forcing a chuckle, Alex shook her head and softly added. "I'm fine, go back to sleep." There was a snort from Nicki above her head, but when she looked up Nicki offered her a soft understanding smile.

Thankfully what she'd revealed seemed to be enough to get the other girls to drop it and Alex was overwhelmingly grateful that none of the boys had woken up. Soft snoring was coming from their side of the room and she quickly pulled her blankets back over her head. There was a soft thump above her as Nicki settled back into her bed and near her feet, she could hear Jenny climbing back into her bed.

Alex lay silent and still under her own blankets, trying to push away the lingering emotions. She was aware that her face must have been insanely red and the mere thought flooded her with embarrassment and nervousness. As her eyes adjusted back to the darkness, Alex pulled back the blanket and looked around. She could see the vague outline of the table and chairs and the bunks against the far wall. There was some faint light spilling into the room from the street beyond through the curtains that let her see their luggage which was still mostly packed and waiting near the bathroom door.

Sighing softly, Alex listened to the soft sounds of Jenny's breathing evening out. It was a familiar sound from when they'd shared a room freshman year. Things had been simpler then. Alex almost laughed or cried as she remembered how scared she'd been of magic and yet a little hopeful and excited. Arthur had been so... he'd been one of the most beautiful things she'd ever seen. Their brief magical connection had made some small quiet part of her hope. Alex shook her head and rolled over, burying her face in the pillow. She couldn't think about him. Even now her hands began to shake and her chest tightened. Tears gathered in her eyes and Alex tried to think of something else, anything else, to avoid another panic attack.

Shifting onto her back again, Alex brought her hand up and tried to examine it in the darkness. She could see her fingers, but no details and wiggled her hand in a small wave to herself. She was afraid to go back to sleep, Alex conceded darkly with a flare of anger in her gut and afraid to lay awake thinking of things. Soft snoring sounds floated down, assuring Alex that Nicki had fallen back to sleep.

Alex tugged softly on her magic. The horizontal and prone position felt strange as the magic began to flow through her body. It was a little ticklish as it spun over her skin and sparked off the edge of her fingertips. The dark gray sparks lingered in the air on her command, casting a soft glow. It wasn't bright and she considered the color carefully. She'd never given much thought to the various colors that their magic took. In the early days, Alex had figured it was some sort of symbolism about their magic or personality, but that didn't really fit. Colors meant different things around the world. Aiden's red magic could obviously link to his natural fire, but he'd used ice in the past as well. Nicki's magic was blue like water appeared to be, but again she could do more than just control water with it.

Arthur's magic had been white. Soft and beautiful, looking like it came out of a movie. It had certainly fit his White Knight persona that had lured them all in. Alex clenched her fingers as her chest tightened again. Sadly, trying not to think of Arthur just made his face swim before her as she slammed her eyes shut. Alex could feel the chill of the snow as she fell to the ground. Her mouth went dry as weakness overwhelmed her. One hand flew to her stomach, but there was no wound.

Trembling, Alex rolled onto her side and curled her body into the fetal position. There was no wound, she told herself as she looked towards Aiden's bed. He'd saved her. Aiden had arrived just in time to use a fireball to knock Cathanáil from Arthur's hand into the water tunnel and had nearly killed himself saving her. She looked frantically around the room trying to find something familiar to ground herself in the present. There was nothing and her fingers itched to rub the soft fake fur of her stuffed dog Galahad.

A smile tugged at Alex's lips and the tightness in her chest remarkably eased at the thought of the old stuffed dog. She turned her head slightly and giggled into her pillow. Closing her eyes again, Alex tried to summon what the little dog looked like with its old faded fur and torn right eye. The image was soothing and Alex rolled onto her back as the pain in her gut faded. Breathing slowly, she debated trying to go back to sleep or meditating. While the meditation often helped her relax Alex was afraid of it summoning up other memories.

Her magic flared over her hand, thrumming almost painfully against her skin as she called on it without instruction. The slight pain helped Alex focus on the present and she stared at the dark sparks. They were the color of wrought iron she reminded herself as she released a small stream of sparks. Spinning through the air, they sailed over the table and lit up the surface. Alex narrowed her gaze on a long scrape across its surface and tried to envision the scar repaired. The sparks of magic floated down to the surface of the table and the surface shimmered for a moment. Before the last sparks vanished, Alex could see the scar disappearing as the wood shifted and grew up to fill the empty space. She smiled and relaxed into the mattress once more.

She called on more sparks of magic and toyed with them in silence. Slowly she created a floating image of a smiling face above her, but it wasn't enough to dispel her worry. Stretching out her fingers, Alex concentrated on the magic and conjured an image of an orb. The sparks of magic turned into a stream that rushed into a single point of light. It expanded and thrummed softly, casting a brighter light around the room. There was a slight groan from Jenny's bunk and Alex waved her hands, silently ordering the magic to disperse. The room went dark again.

Alex's eyes were heavy and she let them slide closed. The soft hum of her magic was fading, but she could still feel the lines of heat across her skin. Folding her hands over the blankets, Alex practiced inhaling and exhaling in time with her heartbeat. Her mind was proving harder to quiet so she whispered the words: Iron Hammer and Mjǫllnir over and over to herself. Gradually it became harder to remember the words as the heat across her skin cooled and the weight of the day pressed her into the mattress.

It was dark, almost impossible to see even with the beam of the flashlight moving around. The beam stopped suddenly and a chill raced down her spine at the sight of a skull. She recovered from her shock only for the beam to shift down and illuminate a wall built out of tightly packed human bones. Stumbling forward, she caught herself on a wall and her fingers wrapped around a small shelf crafted from thigh bones. Horror flashed through her chest and drove her on. She ran like someone was chasing her, but there were no sounds behind her. Tears were slipping from her eyes and her fingers tightened around the handle of a heavy leather case she was carrying.

Then she stopped as she came to a junction. Both corridors were lined with bones and pitch black. She shined the flashlight both ways, but it didn't provide enough light to truly see anything beyond the maze of bones. Stepping forward, she slowed down now and listened. There were soft sounds around her like small creatures were moving in the dark. It provided no comfort and her legs were beginning to ache. Coming to a stop, she found herself looking at a small niche in the wall where bones had fallen and scattered. She knelt, set down the case, and brushed aside the bones to find a small hole. Using her hands, she scraped small piles of rubble from the hole with hands too large to be her own. She was dreaming again Alex realized, but then whoever she was turned the flashlight on the case.

The too large hands opened it. A heavy looking iron hammer with a top that was wide on one end and narrowed on the second filled the leather case. They didn't touch it, but there was a small shock up her arm. Then, without a word, they closed the case and slid it down into the hole. It just barely fit.

With a shuddering sigh, she pushed the bones up against the wall, stacking them gently into a façade of the carefully constructed medieval walls. It was enough to hide the hole. There was a moment of hesitation, but then she stood up and began to walk away. The flashlight beam shining ahead as she followed the dark walls to a destination she didn't know. Alex tried to figure out what was happening, but there was a torrent of sorrow, hope, regret, and resignation pounding in her chest that she just couldn't understand.

"Alex," someone called. "Alex honey, are you okay?" It was Jenny, she realized as she struggled her way back to consciousness.

The room was bright now with sunlight pouring in through the windows. Her eyelids were heavy, but the rush of adrenaline from the dream helped her wake.

"The Catacombs," Alex said as she started to sit up almost desperate to voice the thought before anything swept the dream away. "He came back to Paris to hide it. The Hammer is in the Catacombs."

24

Dangerous Discovery

March 1944 C.E. Sør-Trøndelag, Norway

As a German, Gottfried had always considered himself fairly sturdy stock and that had been before all the eugenics and propaganda. He'd been just old enough during the Great War to serve during the last days and had survived. In the aftermath, he'd married Ilse and started a family despite the struggles in Germany at the time, proving that they could overcome whatever the world threw at them.

But Norway was cold. The wind picked up the moisture from the sea and carried it to the dig site in icy, biting blasts that cut down to his bones. Gottfried was having to reassess his view of his strength and sturdiness. While the situation with the locals was a little warmer than it had been in Paris, the wind and lack of services made it less than a pleasant location. It was harder to send and receive letters and while the view was impressive, he felt like he was at the end of the world.

A sigh escaped him and he grumbled at himself. He was complaining over nothing. This was a waste of time for the Nazis and kept him away from the ugly operations. Still, Gottfried had a strange sense of dread in his gut. It made no sense. He hadn't been this nervous since he was officially brought into the SS and taken away from his teaching post.

He hadn't even been this concerned since the news of the first Cologne fire bombing. People he knew had been killed or lost everything and his children could have been in the city. So why did this place leave him so on edge?

It didn't help that their small camp consisted of tents for the workers and a few small buildings for the Ahnenerbe officers. It was all too exposed and he worried about the day that a local rebel group decided they were an easy target. A knock on the door drew his attention away from his thoughts. He didn't wish to speak with anyone, but called for them to come in.

Weber walked in, his dark long coat managing to flutter around him as he slammed the door shut. Displeasure was all over his face and he eyed the papers scattered across Gottfried's desk. "Have you found anything?"

"I'm afraid not, Weber. I've located the old reference that probably drew Himmler's attention here, but beyond that nothing." He shook his head and straightened up the documents. "I'm afraid there just isn't much to place the Hammer here beyond that old oral story."

"The tunnel excavation is going too slowly," Weber grumbled. His blond hair was fading back to a dark color and was messier than Gottfried had ever seen it. "We need results."

"Honestly, I'm impressed that we even found the tunnel. We're on the trail of something interesting."

"That's not good enough for Berlin. Himmler firmly believes that Thor's Hammer is real. That means that it must be found for the Third Reich. It is part of our great history and will be part of our glorious future!" Weber's eyes were wide and gleaming. "Imagine what something like that could do!"

Gottfried wisely just nodded and kept his mouth shut. Tunnel or no, his opinion about the Hammer hadn't changed. It was a myth and

Himmler's local story suggesting that it had once been in the area hadn't changed his mind. It made him wonder what else the Ahnenerbe were out doing in the world. Were they trying to find the Ark of the Covenant or the Spear of Destiny as well? It sounded ridiculous, but the way the Ahnenerbe had latched onto an old story and was convinced it might be real was also ridiculous.

"I'm not an archeologist, but surely these things take time."

"Yes, but we've been out here for three months."

"And already located a cavern system with clear signs of human habitation."

"We both know it could be completely unrelated!" Weber was twisting his hands and Gottfried had to wonder why the other man had even come to speak with him. He obviously didn't really want to be comforted. "You're not really part of Ahnenerbe, you can't understand."

A knock on the door drew both of their attention and Gottfried called for them to come in. He was half expecting one of the workers, but Professor Dietrich entered and nearly jumped at the sight of Weber.

"Oh, I do apologize, Got-Captain Eckstein."

"It's not a problem, Professor Dietrich," he assured him quickly. "Weber and I were just discussing the tunnel."

"Ah, yes, it is rather interesting," Dietrich agreed. "Part of a small natural cave network though with clear mining marks. Though I'm not sure what they were mining for."

"Iron perhaps," Gottfried suggested only to earn a disapproving look from Weber. "My apologies. Geology was never a talent of mine."

"No, I suppose not." Weber was standing completely straight. "I've taken enough of your time, Captain Eckstein." He looked to Dietrich with a distasteful expression. "Professor Dietrich." He gave them both a quick nod before he headed out of the door of the small building.

Gottfried turned his eyes to the other man. The professor had taken off his glasses and was cleaning them with a corner of his suit. He always looked a bit nervous to Gottfried, but now he just looked tired.

"He hates me," Professor Dietrich despaired. "He at least pretends with you."

"A benefit of rank." Gottfried managed only a slight smirk before shivering at the lingering draft Weber had let in. "Not that it really does much good out here."

"I'm not sure what they think they found," Dietrich said. He slumped into the spare chair and tightened his coat around him. "It's so cold here. They tell me that it's spring and flowers are starting to bloom, but I still think it's cold."

"I can't tell you anything about if this is really spring, but the area does have a few interesting variations of Norse stories." Gottfried glanced at one of the papers he'd been translating. "But nothing I would think worth the time, money, and effort for this dig." He picked one of the papers up and shook his head. "I'm not sure what they're thinking honestly."

Dietrich gave him a warning look and Gottfried nodded his understanding. Inhaling slowly, he reminded himself that Norway was under Nazi occupation. They were no safer here than they had been in Paris or Germany. In fact, it would be easier to just vanish and get shot. Looking towards the photographs of his family on the edge of his desk, he sighed. Dietrich came part way around the desk and patted his shoulder.

"I know." Dietrich tightened his grip for a moment. "I know, Gottfried."

"Thank you, Adalard."

They settled into the comfortable silence, each getting lost in their own thoughts. Gottfried was very aware of how Dietrich was looking towards the photos of his own family. He knew that something had happened to Dietrich's family, but had never pressed to know the details.

"Car crash," Dietrich said suddenly as if reading his mind. "Three years ago. Just a car crash."

"I'm sorry." He didn't know what else to say. Thankfully Dietrich just gave him a slight smile and nodded.

Shouts from outside made them both turn sharply towards the door. Gottfried listened to the noise in confusion. They were happy, excited noises not ones of disappointment. Someone was shouting for Weber. He looked back at Dietrich as they both jumped to their feet. Dietrich rushed for the door and Gottfried paused long enough to grab his SS long coat and pull it on.

He stepped outside on the rocky terrain. Some grasses were beginning to push their way up through the soil, but much of the area had been trod down by people. Across the camp was an opening into the hillside with a large scaffold structure around the entrance. Men were standing just outside the entrance and Weber was rushing over. Weber stopped at the entrance and spoke with one of the workers as their hands gestured wildly. Exchanging another look with Dietrich, Gottfried began to walk over to join Weber.

"We found a chamber!" Weber's chest puffed out as if he'd done the deed himself. "They're clearing the rubble. It's very old by the looks of things."

"What makes you think this is special?" Dietrich asked. The other man took off his glasses and cleaned them as Weber gave him a dark look.

"Clear tool marks! Mining efforts weren't at this scale in this area. Yet these tunnels were carved into natural caverns. That is significant and an actual chamber must be important."

Another man came out with a load of rock in a wheelbarrow that was dumped to the side. He looked stunned and a little shaken, but Weber ignored him and pushed past. Gottfried fell into step behind him and entered the tunnel. Lights were hung along the tunnel wall on small hooks illuminating the path. Much of the tunnel was still intact beyond the entrance which had been caved in with rocks and dirt. Gottfried walked slowly, mindful of his footing and studying the tunnel as a whole. Staring at the carved walls, Gottfried slowly raised a hand and touched them. There were bits of carved graffiti scattered about and his heart jumped with excitement. However, ahead of him, Weber made an impatient noise.

"We're here for the Hammer."

It was Dietrich who gave him a dirty look and for a moment Gottfried feared that the smaller man would hit Weber. Thankfully he just gritted his teeth and followed Weber further in. They reached the junction in the tunnel where the worst of the collapse had been. The rubble had been shifted largely to one side and Gottfried could see evidence of tool marks on the walls. He wondered just how aggressive Weber's workers had been. Up ahead the tunnel opened into a larger space and Weber was vibrating with excitement. He kicked a bit of the remaining rock out of his way, inhaled deeply, and stepped forward into the chamber.

Exchanging a look with Dietrich, Gottfried followed Weber into the small room and gasped. A pedestal of stone in place of honor held a strange looking hammer made of dark metal. One side had the iconic flat head that he was familiar with, but the other side tapered into a smaller surface.

"That's not Thor's Hammer!" Weber glared at the hammer, gritting his teeth. "It looks all wrong."

"Now, now, Professor Weber, mythology is complex!" Dietrich dashed forward and bent over so he was at eye-level with the hammer. His voice was quivering with excitement as he explained, "This was a tool. Legend may have made it a weapon, but a hammer is a tool first and foremost. The craftsmanship is impressive."

Weber was clenching and unclenching his fists as he stared at the hammer. Dietrich had already pulled out a notebook and was sketching the thing even as one of the workers stepped forward with a camera and took a photograph. Gottfried frowned and leaned forward to get a better look at the symbol. He shifted his flashlight and smiled slightly when the triskelion gleamed as his excitement returned. It wasn't the symbol he'd been expecting to see, but it fit. This artifact was so unexpected, so remarkable. He might not have been an archeologist, but even he could recognize that someone had held this item as very important.

"It hasn't even rusted, it really looks like iron to me," Dietrich said frowning slightly. "What do you think, Gottfried?"

"I'm not sure."

He reached out to brush one finger across the surface of the metal. His eyes widened when a pale blue glow appeared beneath his fingertip. Lightning burst forth from the Hammer in a wave of electricity forcing them all to drop to the ground. His heart was pounding and Gottfried grabbed at the rock beneath him as thousands of images and sounds were suddenly dumped into his brain and the cavern faded away. Strange creatures were bearing down on him. The sky was ripped open with lights and colors spilling forth from it.

There was a beautiful woman with long hair and a sorrowful expression. He could feel her holding his hand and shivered at the strange ghostly sensations. Tears were slipping down her cheeks even as she tried to smile. She was saying something about a hammer, but the words were distant and hazy. A sense of guilt, happiness, and sorrow welled up in him, but he couldn't understand it. More faces flashed before him. They were unfamiliar to him and yet there was a flicker of recognition inside his chest. He could feel a weight in his hand and somehow knew it was the Hammer. It was being swung down on metal and heat rolled over his hands. The vision shifted again in a burst of bright blue light that darkened to gray.

Another woman appeared, this one younger than the last. Her image was foggy for a moment, but as it cleared Gottfried could see more of her features. She couldn't have been much older than Enrich. She had long blonde hair pulled back out of her face and sharp gray eyes. Their eyes seemed to meet and hers widened in surprise before her features twisted into a scream. Electricity jolted up through his arm accompanied by grief and growing panic. It was wrong, it was all wrong. There were more faces, more people nearby. They looked more like the people he was used to though the girls were all in pants. They were someplace dark with floating lights. It was too much, too quickly.

Gasping for air, Gottfried's chest was burning and his hand ached. Someone was beside him and calling to him even as others moved around them. The sounds had an echoing quality and beneath his hands and knees, the ground was cool and hard like tile, but uneven.

"Gottfried!" Someone was shouting his name and it echoed through the chamber. "Gottfried, can you hear me?"

It was Dietrich he realized slowly as his sight returned. They were back in the cavern with flashlights illuminating the space. He could remember it now. He'd touched the Hammer and there'd been some kind of explosion. It was darker than before. The small lights hung in the tunnel were dark, probably blown out by the lightning. His body ached, but he slowly pulled himself up onto his knees as Dietrich kept a hand on his shoulder.

"I'm alright," he said.

"Just take it slow," Dietrich insisted. "You were hit by that blast." Dietrich shook his head and looked towards the Hammer. "Remarkable, I'm not even sure what to think."

Gottfried forced his eyes back to the Hammer. Mjǫllnir, a strange voice provided in his head. It sent a shiver down his spine. Weber was reaching for the Hammer with a pair of leather padded tongs and wild excitement on his face. Another man was holding open a box with a nervous expression as the Hammer was moved through the air. A sense of dread overcame Gottfried as the tingle in his hand finally began to recede.

"Easy, Gottfried," Dietrich said. His hand was on Gottfried's shoulder, keeping him from moving and he realized with a jolt of surprise that he'd been moving for the Hammer.

"We found it!" Weber cheered as he set the Hammer in the box. Gottfried saw the poor worker's legs buckle under the weight. "Himmler will be thrilled! You saw the lightning come from it! Just imagine how we could use it."

The dread in Gottfried's gut intensified painfully. Something in him twisted and rallied at the very idea. Again dozens of images flashed through his head leaving only a strange mixture of emotions in their wake.

"Weber, you saw what it did to Gottfried!" Dietrich's body trembled with rage.

"We'll be cautious of course." Weber's tone was dismissive and he ran a possessive hand over the box. "But this could be a source of electrical power for the whole country! We have to study it! This is what we've been working for. It is divine intervention that we found it at all!"

Weber glanced toward him only once on his way out and made a quick promise to send in the medic. Dietrich stayed next to him as he recovered the feeling in his legs. Yet Gottfried kept staring after the Hammer as a deep fear took hold. He wasn't completely sure of the source, but he knew that something terrible had just occurred.

25

Timothy Talks

Stepping out of the bathroom, Merlin rubbed his hair vigorously with the towel. His home was quiet and there was the slight smell of waffles in the air. Merlin let the towel fall around his neck and shoulders and sighed softly. His bare feet curled into the thick crème carpet of the hallway as he began to head back to his room. It would have been a lazy day for grading if not for the lingering worry.

He shook his head and tossed the towel back into the bathroom. It hit the tiled floor with a soft thump and Merlin headed for his bedroom. His shirt was waiting at the foot of his bed along with his socks and shoes for the day. There was a tension in the air was unsettled him, but Merlin couldn't put his finger on the source. After pulling on his socks and shoes, he moved over to his dresser and gingerly opened the top drawer. Two earthen jars were snuggly packed in rolls of multicolored socks. They were still safe.

Trying to dismiss the feeling, Merlin pulled on his shirt and moved back towards the living room. Merlin paused in the doorway and peered into the kitchen as he buttoned up his shirt. His Brownie guest was up and moving about. The small creature still astonished him a bit. Over the years he'd been very aware of the descendants of the creatures the Sídhe enslaved spreading across the world and hiding from humans. Brownies retained a little magic that they were known to use in the homes they took shelter in.

Timothy wasn't half a foot tall but had a humanoid form. His pudgy face was bright with contentment and his little dark eyes caught the sunlight pouring through the windows in a rather interesting way. Merlin honestly still wasn't sure what to make of the little creature. He'd been freed from the power of the Iron Chain the prior week and had been content to remain. Morgana was even entertaining the idea of allowing him to live with the young mages. On one hand, it might be useful to have the little creature around, but part of him couldn't shake his worry. Timothy had gotten close enough to wound Alex while bound to the Queen's order to kill mages.

"Don't worry about it, Timothy," Merlin called over to the small Brownie as it moved around on the kitchen counter cleaning up bits of dried batter. "I'll clean it up later."

"It's no problem, Professor Yates," Timothy gave him a bright little smile, flashing his teeth.

"You can call me Merlin you know," Merlin pointed out only to see the small creature shudder. Frowning, Merlin wondered what sort of tales were told amongst the Fae creatures to convince their children to stay hidden. "Or Ambrose." He offered Timothy a reassuring smile. "It's my modern first name."

"Yes, Ambrose," Timothy agreed with a smile. "That will do, sir."

"Thank you for helping with cleanup."

"I enjoyed breakfast greatly," Timothy said with a glowing smile. "Very tasty."

"Yes, though you hardly ate any." Merlin headed to the counter and picked up the mug of coffee waiting for him. It was still warm. "Hardly seems fair."

Timothy ignored him and gestured towards the dishes in the sink. The faucet turned and water began to pour over them before the soap bottle levitated. A few drops of soap hit the water and Merlin contented himself with watching Timothy's small acts of magic. Of course, it was more than the mages had managed in their first months.

The sweet ding of the doorbell drew his attention away from the Brownie. Merlin hesitated for a moment before deciding that Timothy and his magic were well out of view. As he approached the front door he relaxed as he saw a familiar figure through the window. He opened the door with a slight smile, holding back a sudden yawn.

"Morgana," he greeted calmly, grateful that he'd managed to get dressed before her arrival. "Good morning."

"Good morning, Ambrose," Morgana said. He stepped to the side allowing her to stride inside. She was dressed neatly with her hair over one shoulder in a braid, but there were bags beneath her eyes conflicting with her otherwise composed appearance. "I heard from Aiden a few hours ago."

"And?" Merlin questioned as he closed and locked the door.

"They're alright and safe. Alex's dreams are a bit... out of control, it seems," Morgana informed him carefully. "I got the sense that she isn't handling the stress well. Aiden indicated that everyone has been keeping an eye on her."

"All the more reason for us to retrieve her," Merlin said, brightening at the convincing argument for bringing the Iron Soul back to Ravenslake. "She shouldn't be alone."

"She isn't," Morgana reminded him. Merlin got the impression she was reminding herself of that more than talking to him. "They're heading to the Paris Catacombs today. Alex had a dream of hiding the Hammer in tunnels lined with bones."

"The Catacombs?" Merlin repeated in alarm. "But Morgana the Catacombs are a mess of bones, pitfalls, and cave-ins! The place is a maze."

"Which is why it fits that this Gottfried Eckstein hid Mjǫllnir there," Morgana said shifting into the living room. "Even the locals only know part of the Catacombs. Nazi occupiers wouldn't have had a chance. Eckstein was stationed in Paris for a time so he would have thought of it as a place to hide something away."

Merlin studied her expression and held back a hum of irritation. Morgana had that cold vacant look on her face. She wouldn't budge against any argument he could make. Glancing towards the kitchen, Merlin debated calling Timothy to join them but decided against it. Reaching out, he gripped her arm and directed her into the sitting room. Sunlight was pouring in through the windows creating a pleasant atmosphere. Merlin released her arm and went over to the front facing window to open it. The air outside was still a bit crisp, but fresh and carried a light scent of the new grass and coming flowers.

As he turned back to Morgana, Merlin froze in place from shock. There was a lost and exhausted expression on Morgana's face. Her eyes were distant and she seemed somehow smaller and younger than she had in years. It took him a moment to notice that Morgana's shoulders were shaking. She had wrapped her arms around herself and was far too quiet.

"Morgana?" Merlin whispered, half afraid of scaring her.

Morgana's dark hair was hanging into her face. Her green eyes were dull with the shine of tears illuminating them. She wasn't crying yet, but it was the closest that Merlin had seen in decades. He moved forward to her, giving the woman a soft understanding smile. Without a word, he wrapped his arms around her. After a heartbeat, Morgana dropped her arms and brought her hands up to grip his shoulders.

"I'm so worried for her," Morgana whispered. "All those memories, somehow Arto's funeral at Stonehenge caused something to change. Some spark of magic to go into Alex and unlock her past lives. I don't want her to have to remember all of that!" A muffled cry escaped Morgana and Merlin brought a hand up to gently cradle her head. "Merlin, humans can't cope with that! We've barely lived with it and we're half Sídhe!"

"Morgana, you need to calm down," Merlin said. "You're becoming too invested. Alex is a lovely girl, but..." he trailed off and swallowed. The words stuck in his throat. He understood her worry. "I understand. I was arguing for her to return myself yesterday," Merlin reminded her with a forced chuckle.

Morgana pulled back and looked at the floor with flush red cheeks and a few tear tracks visible. A hand came up to brush them away and Merlin thought he saw a flash of silver magic.

"I remember," Morgana said as she looked up at him. The tear tracks were gone with a hint of silver fading into her skin.

"It's dangerous to care too much." Merlin rubbed at his eyes, frustration gathering in his spine.

"It's worse not to," Morgana returned softly. "Then what would we be?"

"Sídhe," Merlin admitted. "I suppose." He collapsed back into his armchair. "Sometimes I miss the simplicity of the first war."

"It was easier," Morgana agreed. She sat down on the sofa across from him. "We knew our enemy without emotional complications." She must have heard Timothy in the kitchen because she glanced knowingly towards the doorway.

"Yes, the emotional complications have rather piled up haven't they," Merlin observed as he looked at his hands. "The questions... the moral grays."

"Lieven, Elizabeth, Peter..." Morgana shook her head and trailed off. "They kept me sane when the world wanted me to vanish into the background."

"They were fine children," Merlin agreed gently. "And they grew up to be fine men and women. They have descendants out there in the world, Morgana."

"Who know nothing of me besides old myths." Morgana shook her head. "We're just ghosts, Ambrose. We train the mages, but we're losing our ability to adapt."

"I don't know about that," Merlin protested with forced cheer. "I'm managing the computers and smartphones just fine."

"It's not about that," Morgana countered giving him a stern look. "We..." she trailed off and bit her bottom lip lightly. "We don't question why anymore."

"Course we do," Merlin huffed, frowning at her.

"No, not really. We've paid attention to technology and learned to live and work with it, but take Bran for instance. He's trying to understand the real basis of magic. He's looking at the physics of it. Alex is trying things with her magic that I've never seen before."

"You're saying we're not creative."

"When was the last time we figured out a new use for our magic?" Morgana asked. "And now I'm not sure how to help Alex. These memories and dreams... it's new. It is something actually new and I have no idea of what to say to her and how to help her."

"Do you want to die?" Merlin asked gently.

"Not right now," Morgana assured him, meeting his eyes with a clear and intense gaze. "Alex... she needs us. More than most of the others did. Too much is happening right now for us to leave her, but I'm getting tired again, Merlin."

"Well, let's not dwell on it," Merlin suggested as he stood up. "I'll make some tea and let's work on those jars. I fully intend on making sure that Scáthbás dies and has no refuge this time."

"I still wonder how she managed it all." Anger flashed in Morgana's eyes.

"That like many things, I suspect we will never have an answer to," Merlin said sadly. "Life never reveals all, not even for a mage."

His remark drew a slight smile and a nod of agreement that reassured him as to Morgana's mental state. Heading into the kitchen he found Timothy levitating the plates and griddle back into their respective positions. He opened a cupboard and brought down two mugs before picking up the kettle.

"Timothy, thank you for taking care of that," he told the Brownie gratefully as he began to pour water into the kettle. "Though at this rate I'll be sad to see you go."

"I would prefer to remain and help the young mages," Timothy told him, standing tall and straightening his small jacket that had been made from dolls clothes. "The Queen... her powers are dark and twisted. Bad things for all if she takes this realm."

"I agree." Merlin set the kettle on the stove. "Do you know anything about her plan?"

"No, she sent her will through the binding," Timothy explained with a visible shudder. "Anger, rage, and smugness. It pulled at us, hurt us when we tried to disobey, and then we were just puppets to her distant will.

She… it is hard to explain, I'm just a Brownie," Timothy said nervously. "But there is dread in my heart."

"And what of the Sídhe still in Sídhean? Do you know anything about them?"

"There are old stories, my family carried them with us to this part of the world," Timothy offered with a tilt of his head. He blinked his black eyes which gleamed in the light. "But the stories of the Sídhe, I don't know. Even now… we don't mix much."

"No, I suppose thousands of years of slavery are hard to overcome."

"We all carry burdens not our own," Timothy agreed seriously. "But Iron Soul, Alex… her magic tastes old and yet fresh."

The words almost made Merlin jump and he narrowed his eyes on the Brownie. "What do you mean by that?"

"Not sure," Timothy squeaked. He drew back from Merlin's thunderous expression. "Like the Chain that bound, but also different."

"I see." Merlin sighed in a strange blend of relief and disappointment. He licked his lips, feeling a touch foolish. "I suppose that makes sense."

"Feel stronger now too," Timothy said. He gestured at the cupboards. They all swung open at once and he giggled. "We Brownies use our powers for housework. It's simple and straightforward, but this feels better." He rocked on his heels and began to look around.

"Timothy, do you think that's because of the Iron Chain?" Merlin questioned quickly before Timothy became distracted.

"Probably," the Brownie agreed even as his eyes focused on the door to the small pantry. "Our magic has never been strong. The Sídhe don't have any, probably because they were true enemies."

"Or your home world was closer to ours," Merlin suggested thoughtfully. "Sídhean is one of the outer worlds from what I've learned."

"Yes, that fits the stories," Timothy replied distantly. "My magic feels stronger now."

"That may be because of the binding," Merlin said. "You only feel stronger."

"Maybe." Timothy shrugged. "Guess we'll find out if it lasts."

The Brownie jumped off the counter in an astonishing bound. He hit the floor with barely a tap and rushed over to the slightly ajar door. Merlin watched with a curious look as the Brownie vanished inside.

"Wonder if they're all like that," he muttered. His mind whirled with the bits of information Timothy had given him. "I wonder if he is stronger... no, that would be ridiculous," he told himself, but there was a small doubt at the back of his mind.

The whistle of the kettle drew his attention back to the matter at hand. As interesting as Timothy and his kind were, they had the pressing problems of Scáthbás and Arthur to deal with. There was no doubt in his mind that the pair would already be plotting their next move. Placing his hands around the mugs, Merlin sent a small jolt of magic into the ceramic to heat them up. His hands moved quickly through the familiar motions and soon he had two warm mugs of tea, each one made to their preferences.

Sparing one more glance towards the pantry, Merlin chuckled as he heard Timothy talking softly to himself. He felt a moment of pity for whoever's house Timothy had formerly lived in. The small noises would have been very distracting and worrying to an ordinary human.

"I see you found the jars," Merlin said as he reentered the sitting room. Morgana had a notebook open and pencil in hand and the pair of jars on the coffee table.

"Your top dresser drawer," Morgana said without looking up at him. "Where else would they be since you can't put them in the safe with the

Chalice? You still are under the delusion that I would shy away from your underwear."

"It is rather rude, my dear Morgana." Merlin held the cup of tea out for her.

"Really, Ambrose." Morgana chuckled as she accepted the drink and gave him a look. "After all the time we've known each other? You really think thoughts of your nether regions are going to be what bothers me."

"Not to change the subject," Merlin cut in before the conversation could go any further. "I believe that we have another item to address."

"What's that?" Morgana asked, sitting up and taking a sip of her tea.

"Do you remember what Thor told us the last time we saw him?"

"I recall that boy trying to lecture us on a great many things," Morgana pointed out as she raised her eyebrow. "I don't recall what the last one was."

"I can't recite it word for word," Merlin admitted with a shake of his head. "But he said that we were too stubborn about being enemies with the Sídhe."

"Not everyone is comfortable befriending ancient enemies of the realm," Morgana grumbled, looking towards the window. "I'm not sure what I would have done if he'd taken up with Frea instead of Sif. That was bad enough."

"Still Thor may have had a point," Merlin said earning him a look from Morgana. "Timothy and the others were connected to Scáthbás through her use of the Iron Chain. When you bind something to you then you are bound to them as well."

He could see the realization in Morgana's eyes. Neither of them said anything for a long moment. Then Morgana carefully set down her tea and picked her notebook back up.

"Well then," she finally forced out. "Let's start with how to open these jars safely and once the children are back, see about setting up some peace talks."

"I agree," Merlin returned with a smile. There was something building in his chest that he couldn't put his finger on. It was part excitement, part dread, and part something else. Something new was coming, potentially answers to questions he'd long forgotten or perhaps even more.

26

The Mines of Paris

Lance was the calmest as they gathered outside the hostel. Night had fallen once more and the thrum of Paris around them was both exciting and terrifying. Neon lights blended with the softer glow of the street lamps to create multicolored lines across the glass of windows on passing cars. There was something magical and romantic in the air that Alex knew they wouldn't get to enjoy. Alex adjusted her small backpack nervously as the bottles of water and snack bars shifted inside of it. Licking her lips, she watched as another group of young tourists headed out of the hostel. They were laughing and joking, no doubt on their way to a bar or club. She hoped their attire and supplies didn't give away their plans.

"Nervous?" Bran asked as he stepped up next to her.

"Well, we're about to combine our powers in a spell to track the Iron Hammer and hopefully help us navigate the Paris Catacombs," Alex replied softly, fighting to keep her tone even. "Yeah, I'm a bit nervous."

"The good news is that we're mages," Aiden said. He tugged at his own backpack nervously. "The bad news is that it has been illegal to enter the Catacombs without official permission since 1955 and they have special police that patrol everything."

"We could plead American ignorance," Jenny pointed out with false cheer.

"I think that would just get us into more trouble," Bran said. "Look we don't have time to find a guide and we'd never be able to sneak away from an official tour."

"But we need to get to the normal official area," Nicki said quickly. "Alex saw bones and those are mostly in the tourist area. The rest of the catacombs are old quarries."

"Yeah, except those police will probably be near the official area. Plus, we can't say for certain that things haven't been moved," Aiden reminded them. "And Eckstein probably didn't hide the Hammer in the main tourist area."

"According to what I was able to find online there are small tombs scattered in the tunnels," Bran added. "Beyond the main tourist area. That's probably where it is."

"Not much to go on and we can't safely just wander around." Lance shared a worried look with Jenny.

"We're going to use magic like we did with the Chalice," Bran assured him. He nodded down the street. "Maybe in the park? That'll give us some room."

They walked down the sidewalk in silence towards the small patch of grass that Alex hesitated to actually consider a park. There were two benches on either side of the triangular area, but a couple trees at least provided some illusion of privacy. Lance and Jenny shifted back from them as the mages gathered in the center of the area and in the corner of her eye, Alex saw Jenny take Lance's hand. The simple action caused a sharp pang of relief and grief to mix together in her chest that Alex quickly pushed away.

Taking Bran's hand with her right one and Nicki's hand with her left, Alex breathed in and out slowly. Aiden stood opposite of her in the small circle and offered her a reassuring smile. Alex could see a faint glow of magic gathered around each of their hands and tugged gently at her own magic. Beneath her feet, she could feel a soft hum in the ground and found it comforting. There was a tingle of magic through her body and she pulled gently on the spark in her lower chest. It flared to life like a flame exposed to fuel.

The dull gray color of her magic blended with Bran's yellow and Nicki's blue. Slowly both began to darken to the color of iron as the energy flowed into Alex. Her eyes moved to Aiden as his own red magic flowed into Nicki and Bran as she pulled on the offered power. It was gathering in her chest, growing sharper and hotter with each passing moment. Alex could see the pulsing mass of dark gray magic as it gathered the energy surrounding them.

She closed her eyes and focused on the Iron Hammer. The dream from the prior night sprang to mind and she could feel herself in the dark catacombs. There were bones that she was shifting in order to hide the Hammer in a maze where the Nazis would never find it. She didn't know the whole story yet of how Eckstein and the Ahnenerbe found it, but his desperation echoed in her. Somehow, something had made him believe in its power.

Magic jumped off her fingertips. "Guide me," she said out loud, pushing that thought to the magic, trying to imprint that wish onto the magic. "Guide us."

"Alex, it worked," Nicki said a moment later. "Just look."

Opening her eyes, Alex blinked in surprise and then smiled. There was an orb of softly glowing light in the center of their little circle. Small wisps of pale light, almost like smoke surrounded it as it waited in the air. Releasing Bran and Nicki's hands, Alex reached out towards it and watched the wisps of magic reach for her fingertips. A giggle escaped her.

"I can see it too," Bran said and he looked at Aiden who nodded.

"See what?" Jenny asked. She looked intently at the space between Alex's hands. "Is there something there?"

"So, the mages can all see it this time," Bran said thoughtfully. "Well, that's easier than just one of us seeing it. I wonder what we did differently. Last time Alex couldn't see it."

"Maybe because it went through Alex and used a little bit of all of our power," Nicki suggested.

"As interesting as the theory of magic is we do need to get moving." Aiden gave a pointed nod at the orb.

"Right," Alex agreed, dropping her hands and focusing on the orb. "Uh... show us the way."

She felt silly saying that and must have sounded it based on the chuckle that came from Lance. Nonetheless the orb pulsed for a moment before beginning to float away. Alex's feet followed. It hung in the air just a short way in front of them, always a little ahead, but never moving off more than a few feet. They followed it down the road and around a couple of turns before coming to a sudden stop on a side street just above a manhole cover.

"Down down to goblin town," Nicki sang softly.

Alex looked at her in confusion before dismissing it as a reference she didn't understand. "Okay, Bran, you're up," she said. Alex glanced around at the people on the sidewalk and the cars on the street. "Hurry."

Yellow magic flashed in the night and the manhole cover lifted out of its snug position. Lance grabbed it with both hands and looked down into the dark hole. There was a collective intact of breath and Alex's legs began to shake. Nicki acted first and opened her hand, forming an orb of softly glowing light which she then dropped down the hole. It floated down gently, illuminating the hand rungs of a ladder set into the stone.

"I'll go first," Aiden volunteered. Turning around, he shifted his position and found the first rung. Then he laughed weakly. "Maybe I shouldn't be so sad about missing the quest for the Holy Grail."

"Don't be," Lance said. "But hurry up. Illegal, remember."

"Be careful," Nicki added.

Aiden nodded and began to descend into the hole in the ground. Nicki went next as a cold sweat broke out across the back of Alex's neck. Bran gestured for Jenny to go next and the girl grimaced, but gingerly began to lower herself down the ladder. Alex slowly followed. The metal rungs were icy to the touch and each movement to lower herself made the hole seemingly convulse around her. Sheer terror hit Alex and her fingers clamped around the rungs desperately. Raising her eyes, Alex looked up towards the light of the street.

"Alex?" Bran called down. "You okay?"

"Fine," Alex said. "Just..." she trailed off and fought back a tremble. "Don't worry I'm not claustrophobic." Alex paused at her own words. She had never been before at least, but that sudden sense of terror had been overwhelming.

Slowly, she made herself let go and focused on the rock face in front of her. She tugged at her magic to illuminate her hands and carefully descended into the tunnel. After what seemed like an eternity her feet touched down on a solid rock surface and Nicki gently tugged her away from the wall. Alex's legs trembled a little, but the sense of terror had passed as suddenly as it had come. The guiding light was shimmering in a tunnel before them next to the softly glowing orb of Nicki's that Jenny was huddled nearby.

"So, you can't see the guiding orb or any light from it?" Alex asked as she joined Jenny.

"No, all I see is this orb," Jenny said, pointing at the one made by Nicki.

Alex nodded thoughtfully and started to look around as Lance touched down in the tunnel with Bran right behind him. Both shook their hands and Bran glanced at the light orb and the guiding light. Then he opened his hands and his magic formed a second one. Jenny and Lance gave him a grateful smile. Bran then turned his attention up and the manhole cover slid back into place, blocking the light from the street above.

"Okay," Lance said, shifting to the front of the group. "Stay together and keep your flashlight at the ready just in case. Mages be careful using magic for more than light around here. There is a chance of cave-ins, small, but real so let's not help things along." He paused and looked down the long stone tunnel stretching before him. "Stay aware of support points in the walls and caverns should anything happen."

Everyone nodded and carefully swung off their backpacks to retrieve their flashlights. Alex slipped hers into the pocket of her hoodie, grateful that they'd thought to dress warmly down here. A dank chill hung in the air and the hum of Paris was already barely audible. Lance looked like he was going to say something more, but shook his head.

"I'll lead," Aiden offered. "Since I can see the guide. Lance, you know the most about rocks and caves in general so you should probably be next."

"Yeah," Lance agreed, shifting to the side to let Aiden through.

They slowly started walking with Alex taking up a position right behind Lance. Jenny was behind her with Nicki's orb hanging just over her head. Bran was behind her with Nicki at the rear. Aiden summoned his own light orb for Lance's benefit and Alex was almost amused by the dual lights floating down the tunnel in front of their small group.

It was slow progress. The tunnel was wide enough for them to pass through, but the floor was uneven with small dips and holes. Around them, the walls were marked with graffiti and carvings left by centuries of explorers. Even Lance looked uneasy as he examined the walls. Alex was paying attention the graffiti and carvings, but she was certain that Lance was probably paying more attention to the rock. He'd be aware of what it all was and maybe even how much it could hold up. Alex shivered at the thought and did her best to banish it.

"I can't believe I'm down here." Nicki sounded like she just might faint or start jumping around insanely. "The actual Paris Catacombs!"

"It's so creepy," Jenny whispered, shining her flashlight around. "Look at all the graffiti."

"Lots of people come down here," Nicki said. "They're called cataphiles. They actually found a movie theater down here a few years back. And there are Nazi bunkers and-"

"Maybe not now," Aiden interrupted. "Let's get moving."

They began to slosh through some standing water and Alex cringed. These jeans and shoes would never be worn again. She could hear the others behind her and the sound of them struggling through the water, but the silence around them was unearthly. Every movement seemed to echo and Alex had to look back to remind herself that everyone was still there. Her legs were beginning to ache and she wondered how long they'd been walking.

"Why are these tunnels even here?" Jenny asked, breaking the heavy silence.

"Oh, these are old mines actually," Nicki informed her cheerfully. "No one is really sure when it all started. I think the first real mention of the mines was in the 13th century. After they took out the stone they wanted for buildings, they found they could use the caverns for other things." They followed the light past a small tomb-like room piled with brown bones that made Jenny hiss in alarm. Nicki grimaced slightly, looking less impressed with her surroundings now. "As for the bones those were brought down here because the cemeteries of Paris were full and the tunnels were collapsing," Nicki said. "After one major collapse, the city created a special office that inspected and tried to map the tunnels. They filled in some areas beneath streets, but they also used millions of bones to reinforce the tunnels."

"And made it a tourist location," Jenny said. "Creepy."

"Actually, not all the bones are in the ossuary," Nicki corrected. "There are lots of bones in other tunnels that aren't as organized as the main ossuary."

"Do you think Mjǫllnir would be there?" Alex asked.

"Mjǫllnir?" Nicki repeated, giving her a curious look. "Possibly. It depends. I can't imagine that Eckstein hid it in the tourist area, but maybe nearby if he came into the catacombs that way."

"The find the path will take us there," Aiden said confidently from the front.

"Find the path?" Jenny repeated.

"It's a reference," Alex told her with a chuckle. "Just go with it. They like to do that."

Then the light turned, moving away from the more open tunnel and slipping into a smaller tunnel with a much lower roof. The whole passage dipped lower and Alex paused as she caught sight of the water filling the lower section. Aiden glanced back at them before he began to press on. As he sloshed into the water the sense of dread hit Alex once again, her eyes locking on the low ceiling as the light kept moving forward.

Bran grabbed her hand and kept her upright. The tightness in her chest increased. Around her, the old tunnels of Paris vanished and she could see the white neat stone walls of the Sídhe tunnel. She could hear crying and musical voices echoing against the stone. Someone said something, but their voice was far away. Her body was too heavy and it was hard to breathe. Then she connected with the wall behind her, the cold chill of the stone seeping through her clothes.

"It's okay, Alex," Bran's voice called to her. "We're here. It's okay. Everyone is safe." The short sentences made it through the haze a little and she tried to focus on Bran. "That's it, good job. Focus on your breathing. Come back to the present."

Slowly the white stones faded away and were replaced with the rougher rock of the mine walls. Alex's eyes focused on a small worn carving of a horse across from her. She closed her eyes for a moment before looking at Bran. He smiled at her and she realized that she was collapsed against the wall at the edge of the water.

"Good job," Bran said gently. He offered her a smile and glanced down the small tunnel. "Do you need more time?"

"No," Alex forced out through her dry mouth. "Let's find the Hammer. I'll be okay."

Bran nodded and said nothing more. He stood up and offered Alex a hand. It was then that she noticed the others were a bit ahead of them and flushed with embarrassment.

"Don't worry," Bran told her. "It wasn't long."

"This isn't the place," Alex growled. She took a tentative step forward into the water. The chill hit her hard and she clenched her teeth. "We aren't safe down here."

She followed the wet passage and sighed in relief when it began to slope up a little more. The water receded and there was only the barest amount beneath her feet. None of the others had turned to look at her and Alex wasn't sure if she was grateful or hurt by that. Bran followed her closely and she joined the others waiting for them up ahead. Nicki gave her a beaming smile and Jenny reached out a hand to her. Alex took the hand and Jenny gave it a reassuring squeeze. That helped.

The long passage stretched out past the edge of the light. Around them, the rounded walls were marked with graffiti and small carvings left by other people. Alex swallowed thickly, struggling to ignore the tightness of the space. There were no bones, just tiny passages, and grottos that had been carved from the rock.

Ahead of them, the tunnel opened into a large room and Alex sucked in a sharp breath. The air was stale, but she didn't feel the weight of the stone all around her. Up ahead gargoyle-like figures were carved into the stone surrounding a rough limestone pillar. Alex's stomach turned at the realization that the pillar was one of the only things keeping the rock above her head from collapsing onto her.

Bones were piled up around them. They lacked the elegant arrangements of the photos she'd seen in the past. Instead, they were pushed up against the walls and neatly stacked in only a few places which were collapsing. Brown with age, they were a mix of different types of bones and Alex heard Jenny make a sound of terror behind her as they spread out. Unlike other areas, there were only a few signs of modern explorers. The light shimmered and dropped closer to the floor.

"I think this Find the Path spell is broken," Nicki groaned.

Alex frowned and moved closer to the guide, kneeling onto the cold ground. She touched the ground as she bent down to get a better look at a shadowy patch of wall. A jolt traveled up her arm. There was a hole at the lowest point in the wall, barely two feet across and not even a foot high. Alex waved her hand. Her magic burst forth and formed an orb of light that she pushed towards the hole. Somehow out of this whole maze-like place this was familiar. Before she thought about it, Alex shrugged off her backpack and leaned it up against the wall.

"Alex?" Bran called.

"Just a second," Alex said as she crawled forward. "This is... familiar."

Moving to the hole, Alex ignored their protests and began to crawl down the hole. The guiding light moved ahead of her. This didn't match her vision, but Alex could feel her heart racing with every inch she managed. She could hear Jenny telling her to stop and Bran urging caution, but she kept shimming her way through the small opening. Then beneath her hands was empty air and Alex turned her attention to the floor. She fell out of the hole with a yelp and into an ungraceful pile. The light orb illuminated the whole small grotto, but Alex's eyes instantly focused on a figure on the other side of the room.

It was a body, a skeleton that was collapsed amongst a pile of rubble. There were fragments of clothing left and a dark stain on the rocks surrounding the bones that made bile rush into Alex's throat. Scattered on the ground were bits of metal and Alex gasped as her eyes found a small stylized cross on the ground.

"Alex!" Nicki called through the wall. "You okay."

"Yeah," Alex said, raising her eyes back to the skull. There next to his head was carved a small German eagle. A discarded skull pin sat on the rocks below it, one side badly bent.

"What is it?" Nicki demanded. "Alex!"

Tightening her hands in fists, Alex scooted away from the body and pressed herself into the far corner. Tears pricked at her eyes and she slammed them shut. She had stumbled through the tunnels and crawled into here. She couldn't breathe, she was starving and so hungry, but the light was gone. There was just darkness and silence. Terror clawed at her insides, sobs tore out of her throat, and tears ran down her cheeks. Alex couldn't help it. She screamed.

27

The Jǫtnar

16 C.E. Sør-Trøndelag, Norway

1 The stars were brightening up the sky in an arch of light that should have enthralled Thor, but it was all he could do to keep from pacing. He was trying to stay out of the way of the Sídhe as they carefully organized themselves. Thor leaned against the rock face and watched a small Síd child that he thought might be a girl pick through some shards of pottery. His eyes shifted over to where Sif and Odin were waiting and looking up the valley. Baldr would be back soon with reinforcements and they could investigate the tunnel.

Shifting impatiently, Thor looked back towards the tunnel in question. Small torches illuminated the Sídhe village just enough for him to see Merlin and Morgana by the opening. The Dark Elves had gone to a lot of trouble for this raid and the knowledge that the prisoners might be undergoing some sort of transformation made him feel ill. The sound of someone approaching made him turn sharply and his eyes were drawn to Sif as she climbed up the rocks towards him. Thor extended his hand and she took it with a grateful smile.

"Thank you," Sif said as he helped her up onto the flat area. "How are things?"

"I'm not sure, to be honest," Thor confessed. "They seem to be moving things into the intact houses, but with the tunnel..."

"So, what is the plan?" Sif pressed. "When my brother returns and all the Dvergrs are here? Are we planning to destroy them all?"

Tensing up, Thor wondered if this was a trick question. Was there a right answer to this? He couldn't see how that was possible. "The Dark Elves are dangerous," he finally said. "I don't like it, but I don't see how they can coexist with us."

"I'm sure Merlin and Morgana once felt the same way about the Sídhe who were trapped in the Iron Realm," Sif pointed out with a hint of curiosity in her voice. "They didn't kill all of them."

"No," Thor admitted. "I'm not sure what happened there. Merlin and Morgana talk a lot, but they rarely truly say anything." Rubbing his eyes, Thor frowned at the headache beginning to form. "I'm sorry, Sif. I don't have an answer for this. The Sídhe were a military with a clear goal: an ugly one, but Merlin and Morgana have been clear on that front. When that fell apart, they scattered and hid."

"How are the Dark Elves different?" Sif only half asked. She sounded as uncertain as him which allowed Thor to relax.

"Indeed, what are Dark Elves at their core?" Thor asked with a frown. He stared into the dark tunnel beyond the ruins of a small house. Merlin and Morgana were still guarding the entrance, still as stones themselves. "Why do they do these things? They enslaved the Dvergrs to make them armor and weapons so they have that in common, but why come after Frea's people?"

"I'm not sure," Sif admitted softly. "The Sídhe... they've long been enemies of this world. Long ago they started small raids to take humans into their realm. When the Gates were made those trapped on this side scattered. Whatever happened to the Dark Elves has driven them onto another path."

"Yes, but Frea and her people are peaceful. From what Morgana and Merlin said their ancestors were not."

"Their ancestors were warriors, they were trained to be raiders," Sif reminded him. "Perhaps their culture taught them not to view humans as real living things or taught them that they didn't matter. I suppose anyone that disagreed with that never would have been given access to the tunnels."

"So only the worst came through," Thor murmured, his frown deepening. "And their descendants don't have magic and just keep their heads down. I suppose that makes sense."

"You're not convinced," Sif said, smiling slightly. "And Baldr thinks you're just a foolish warrior."

"I'll try not to be offended by your brother's view of me. We know the history of the Sídhe and on the surface, the Dark Elves aren't so different..."

"But their actions are different," Sif agreed. "They seem to have some sort of lingering connection to Sídhean that Frea's people lack." Sif tugged at the end of the braid thoughtfully as she nibbled on her bottom lip. Thor watched her with a growing smile despite their topic of conversation. She looked so human and pretty. "What?" Sif asked him a moment later, frowning up at him with narrowed eyes. "What is it?"

"Nothing... you just looked..." Thor shrugged weakly as a blush rose to his cheeks. "You just keep surprising me, Sif."

Sif's eyes widened in surprise and there was a slight smile on her face for a moment. Then she sighed regretfully. To Thor's surprise, she stepped closer to him and leaned her head against his shoulder.

"Why'd you have to be like this?"

"Like what?"

"Smarter than you look," Sif teased wistfully.

Acting on instinct, Thor wrapped his free arm around her waist. Sif was so warm beneath his hand, warmer than a human and he was once again reminded that Sif was something else.

"I'd apologize if I understood the problem," Thor said.

"You're human," Sif whispered. "I'm not."

"I'm aware," Thor said, tightening his hand around her waist.

He looked down at her and admired her beautiful features though it was the gleam in her eyes that he admired most. Thor slowly brought a hand up to her cheek. It was warm beneath his hand and he had to inhale sharply. Sif's eyes widened, but she leaned into his touch and brought her own hand up to his cheek. Her fingers brushed over his skin for a moment and the thoughtful expression returned to her face.

"We're a tragedy," Sif murmured sadly.

"We don't have to be," Thor protested, holding her tighter. "Can't you let us try?"

"You'll grow old and resent me," Sif argued weakly. She pulled his hand away from her cheek though she left his hand on her waist alone.

"And I'll be reborn, I'm the Iron Soul," he reminded her. "I just keep returning in new lives. Maybe-"

"Don't," Sif interrupted sharply. "Don't promise me anything. You haven't the right to bind your future lives to me."

He wanted to say something, but Sif's words settled heavily on his shoulders. She gave him a sad and almost pitying look that he hated, so he quickly looked back towards the tunnel. Morgana was watching them and he felt a flash of anger at her knowing expression like she knew exactly what Sif had just said. The knowledge that he'd had other lives hadn't really bothered him before, even though he disliked the idea of just being one in a long line.

"I'm sorry," Sif said. "I wasn't trying-"

"I know," he interrupted quickly. He didn't look at her. "I... I'm sorry too." Sighing he scrambled for something else to say. "What do you want to do, Sif? When this is over never see each other again?"

She flinched and Thor had the bad feeling it was the wrong suggestion. Her eyes were sad, but she didn't cry. He wondered if Old Ones even could cry.

"No," Sif sighed. "I suppose not." She looked up at him and offered him a forced smile. "I'm... I'd like us to try, Thor, but please be aware that we are different species. We can't have children and you'll age, but I won't."

"I don't think having children would be a good idea for me. The next threat that comes along could go after a human wife and children. Seems like a big risk."

"The Dark Elves may be the only threat in your lifetime."

"Maybe, but maybe not." Some of his confidence returned. Sif gave him a warning look and despite how much he wanted to kiss her, he settled for brushing his lips against her forehead. A soft sound escaped her, but she didn't pull away. "You're assuming that I'll die years from now, but either of us could be destroyed." Thor's chest tightened at the idea. "I mean-"

A scream from outside the village cut him off and made them jump apart. His eyes searched outside and noted a faint glow reflecting off the snow. More shouts from beyond the village made Thor rush for the edge of the cliff with Sif on his heels. The rocks were slick from the snow, but the trail was worn enough they navigated their way beyond the rocks safely. A group of Sídhe was huddled together with a strange light spilling over them and the snow.

Thor looked up only to gasp. Above their heads, a patch of dark night sky was shimmering and rippling. The stars vanished from sight before a strange jagged line of bright blue and purple appeared in the middle of the strange darkness. It swelled across the sky, blocking more stars from view. A strange hissing sound was wafting through the air like a torch had been thrown into the snow.

"What is it?" Thor asked Sif in a low voice.

"I'm not sure..." Sif whispered back with audible shock. He could feel her hand trembling in his before she seemed to recover herself. "It may be an opening into this world."

The lines of blue and purple were growing larger, their jagged edges more pronounced and reminding Thor of tearing fabric. All the hairs on his arms and the back of his neck were rising and his hand flew to grip Mjǫllnir hanging from his belt on instinct. Drawing it forth, Thor held it out before him and pushed some magic into the metal. The soft pale blue glow stretched out around them, but the light was swallowed by the strange tear in the night sky.

A dull hum began to fill the air and sent a shudder up Thor's spine. His instinct was to cover his ears, but he stayed firm and kept Mjǫllnir at the ready. The Sídhe were quick to fall back and Thor heard one of them running off and shouting Frea's name. Thor lifted Mjǫllnir higher. Lightning flashed into the air just as several large forms fell from the hole and crashed into the ground.

The rippling light from the hole brightened and illuminated the lumps as they began to move. The first of the large creatures unfolded itself with a loud snarl. It was tall, standing at least seven feet, with pale blue skin and thick patches of white hair that resembled fur more than anything else. Wild dark blue eyes peered out from a misshapen humanoid face at them all. The other figures began to stand, looking much the same as the first and roared sending the remaining Sídhe scattering. Thor eyed the nearest creature, but it was completely unfamiliar to him. Its large form towered over him as it stood on two legs. Another form fell from the hole and another and another making Thor's eyes widen in alarm as he lost count.

"Uh greetings," he shouted. "You're in the Iron Realm. Can you understand me?" Thor could feel a tingle of magic running over his body and his tongue suddenly heated up painfully.

"Jǫtnar!" the creature bellowed, exposing a double row of teeth.

Thor paused in confusion, but then the creature reached up behind its shoulder and pulled something off of a heavy looking holster. It was a large hammer made of unfamiliar gleaming metal. Taking a step back, Thor exhaled and began to call forth more of his magic as the bad feeling shifted into outright alarm.

It swung the hammer at him, once again shouting "Jǫtnar" with the others behind it taking up the battle cry. Thor grunted, rolling out of the way of the massive Jǫtnar hammer as it crashed into the ground. The beast growled at him and began to pull up its hammer. Jumping to his feet, Thor thrust Mjǫllnir into the air and pulled on the magic he could feel gathering in his stomach and the air. Overhead lightning flashed in the sky and the strange hole began to shimmer again.

There were more of them crashing around in the shadows. Thor gathered his magic in his left hand and tossed an orb of bright blue light into the distance. At least ten more of the Jǫtnar looked at him sharply. Their eyes caught the light and reflected it like animals. A few spun away and began to run while others roared and added to the echoing mess of noise.

Silver magic lashed out to his right and wrapped around one of the creatures. Thor noted that the creatures were wearing rough metal plates strapped together. He could just make out strange designs engraved on the plates. The craftsmanship hinted at intelligence, but the eyes that met his were wild as another swung at him. Thor pushed Mjǫllnir forward and sent a wave of magic rushing into the metal. It lit up like the sun and lightning arced off the metal towards the Jǫtnar. It tried to dodge, but the lightning caught its body and illuminated the area.

One of Odin's foot soldiers rushed past him and struck at the leg of the nearest Jǫtnar, hitting a patch of blue skin on its leg with his sword. A blended snarl and scream echoed against the rocks and it swung a large hand at the Old One, batting it away like an insect. Risking a glance over his shoulder, Thor saw Odin raise his spear and send a shimmering wave of gold rippling through the air.

The attack signaled the onslaught of chaos. Jǫtnar charged at him and he lost sight of Sif. Beneath him, the ground rumbled. Rocks jutted out of the ground, and silver bolts blasted the creatures down. As one descended on him, Thor swung Mjǫllnir and felt bones crunch in the creature's leg. Thor brought the Hammer down on the creature's head as it crumbled. The Jǫtnar shimmered and vanished into pale dust.

More were coming forth and his eyes jumped up to the strange hole. The violet color was pulsing and the dark blue color was fading away. He had no idea what that meant, but it was bad. A strand of his bleached hair fell into his face and Thor grunted in irritation. The spark in his gut grew stronger. It was vibrating against his rib cage as the power pushed up through his arms. Mjǫllnir's metal surface sparked and overhead the sky brightened with lightning. Thor raised the Hammer towards the sky and pulled on his magic and the power he could feel echoing from the sky into Mjǫllnir.

"Get back!" he shouted to the others.

In the corner of his eye, he saw the smaller figures of his allies falling back. Lightning blasted down and struck Mjǫllnir, sending a thrum of power through Thor's body. He smirked as the nearest Jǫtnar roared and began to run towards him. The ground trembled under the force of the massive creature's movements, but Thor stayed in place. He swung Mjǫllnir down and sent a bolt of lightning flashing forward. The Jǫtnar roared as the world burst into light and the arcing bolt struck it in the chest. The roar turned into a pitiful cry, the Jǫtnar's body convulsed and fell to the ground. Lightning kept flashing, jumping from Jǫtnar to Jǫtnar. Around them, the bodies vanished in flecks of pale dust that the wind carried away like snow.

For a moment Thor was disoriented. His senses were all enhanced, but it was overwhelming. He was overheated, but there was a pleasant thrum throughout his whole body. Strength raged through him and a feeling of utter invincibility coiled around his bones.

Then another Jǫtnar came charging out of the darkness. Thor's eyes settled on it and the world snapped back into proper focus. He brought Mjǫllnir up in front of his chest and braced himself. Odin shouted something that Thor couldn't hear over the pounding of blood in his ears. Around them the wind was billowing, creating waves of snow in the air that threatened to blind him.

The Jǫtnar swung at him with its hand. Thor smashed Mjǫllnir into its large palm sending a rush of magic through the metal. It cried out and collapsed backward, but didn't vanish. Thor's leg's trembled, but he rallied and brought Mjǫllnir down once again. The Jǫtnar tried to roll away, but Thor caught it in the back. There was a crack that made his own muscles flinch and a pitiful cry as the body vanished. Beyond him, he could hear crashing in the trees as the surviving beasts fled into the darkness.

"What were those?" Thor asked Sif as she rushed up to him. "You alright?"

"I'm fine," Sif assured him. "And I'm not sure. I've never seen creatures like that."

"The Dark Elves must have done something." Thor raised his eyes to the strange rip in the night sky overhead. "They fell into our world just like the Dvergrs."

"Then more could be coming or something even worse could happen," Sif said, sounding out of breath as she lingered at his side.

"What do we do about this?" Thor asked as he gestured at the hole. "We need to stop it before anything else comes through. Between the Sídhe, your people, the Dark Elves, and Dvergrs we have enough different peoples trying to survive in one area." He turned and looked into the group of allies until he found the smaller Dvergrs pushing their way to the front. "Brokkr, any ideas?"

"Don't know," Brokkr answered gruffly. "The hole behind us closed up after a bit. We were trying to reach it and debating if it was safe to go through when the Dark Elves found us."

Adjusting Mjǫllnir in his hand, Thor eyed the distortion with a deep frown. It was almost like he could smell something slipping into his world that didn't belong there. He hated it and flexed his fingers around the handle of Mjǫllnir.

"Thor?" Sif asked.

"Even Mjǫllnir doesn't like it," Thor tried to joke, but it fell flat. "It isn't closing like the last one. It must be stronger..."

"Or go further in the Tree of Reality," Sif suggested. She brushed a strand of golden hair out of her face and for a moment Thor admired the way the strange lights illuminated her features.

"Their connection is too strong, we need to break it somehow," Thor said. "But how?"

Mjǫllnir's steady hum and the sound of thunder rumbling overhead drew Thor's eyes up to the sky. A raindrop hit his cheek as it began to rain. Lightning flashed and an idea hit him. A quiver of excitement raced through his body and he gestured for Sif to get back.

"Thor?"

He didn't know what to say or how to explain. All he knew was he needed to act fast before the idea deserted him. Thor raised Mjǫllnir towards the sky and closed his eyes. Breathing deeply, he dug his toes into the ground beneath them. A cold wind raced across his hand and the rain began to turn to snow. Beneath his feet, the steady pulse of the Earth was speeding up. Magic was flowing up his legs making them lock in place and tremble all at once. It was too much and yet he kept pulling. A vicious crack in the sky made his eyes open.

Snowflakes were gathering in his hair and beard as a bolt of lightning flashed down and struck Mjǫllnir. The Hammer glowed the brilliant blue of his magic as he pushed the gathered power from the Earth into the metal. Small bolts arced off of the surface and the triskelion symbol lit up like the sun. Thor pushed Mjǫllnir towards the lights. Lightning erupted from the Hammer but formed a solid beam of light and magic. There was resistance. Air was forced from his lungs. Magic washed over the rip and the strange lines of blue and purple flashed through a rainbow of colors.

He could feel the resistance fading. The magic coursed easier. Then with a snap that echoed in his bones, the resistance was gone. Surprised,

Thor pulled back on the magic and stumbled. He sucked in a greedy breath, suddenly feeling the pain in his chest. Around him, he heard low voices and someone caught his arm.

"Thor?" Sif's voice called to him.

Thor opened his eyes, not sure when he'd closed them. He met Sif's gaze before turning his head towards the tear. Thor watched silently as the hole in the sky shimmered once more, but this time his lightning danced over it. He grimaced and grit his teeth as they all waited. Then it rippled like fabric in the wind and the wound began to seal as a wave of gasps rolled through the gathered crowd. The light dimmed and the colors faded into the blackness of the night sky with only the tiny pinpricks of the stars left overhead.

"Well, that's gone at least," Odin said with visible relief on his features. His eyes moved over to Thor for a moment before looking out into the darkness. "But several of those creatures escaped."

"Let's hope that they will calm down now," Sif said, touching her father's arm gently. "Perhaps they were just in a panic. They attacked rather viciously after falling through the portal."

"Maybe, my lady." Brokkr shifted over by Thor and shook his head. "But I doubt it."

Thor rather doubted it too, but the ground beneath them suddenly began to tremble. Turning quickly, he looked up the hill towards Merlin. The older mage was looking back towards Sif's village and the abandoned tunnel entrance. A white mist of magical sparks appeared high in the air above them, spreading through the sky like a blanket of glittering stars. It was beautiful, but terrifying to Thor as his own magic began to flare in his limbs and chest. His whole body ached, but his instincts spurred him to action.

"Come on!" Morgana shouted. "Gawking won't do any good."

They began to retrace their steps up the slope. Above them, the points of light began to gather together, spinning into a thin pillar that grew higher and higher into the dark sky. Thor paused and looked up at it in time to see beams of light growing out of the main pillar and stretching out into the night sky. It was a tree, he realized with a start. The branches were stretching out across the night sky and fading into stars. Thor was frozen in place, his magic humming almost painfully in response. Certain points on the tree were gleaming and shining brighter than all the rest as the branches extended out all around them.

"They've-" Morgana gasped next to him. "But what-"

"It's the Tree of Reality," Merlin growled. "The fools, what do they think they are doing?"

"What does it mean?" Sif asked as her eyes darted between the nearest glowing branch and Merlin.

"They're pushing magic out along the lines of connection," Merlin explained in a rush. "That's what is causing the tears. It's unstable!"

The ground trembled again and bile surged up Thor's throat. He clamped his jaw tightly shut and gripped Mjǫllnir. He wasn't sure what was happening, but every instinct was screaming it was bad. He caught Merlin's eye. The older mage nodded and they began to rush back towards the tunnel. There were a few Sídhe standing guard nervously at the edge of the passage with their spears and swords at the ready. Frea was waiting for them, a stern expression on her face, and her wounds bandaged up.

"Frea, perhaps you should remain with your people in case those creatures return," Merlin suggested as he summoned an orb of light.

"My warriors are prepared to fight," Frea said sternly. "I am going to help rescue those I can."

Merlin said nothing, merely nodding and taking the first step into the tunnel. Thor met Morgana's eyes as she fell into step beside him. Already he could feel his chest tightening in response to going underground.

"Be careful, Thor," Morgana told him. "You were lucky back there. Very lucky it worked, but it took a lot of your magic. You need to be careful that you don't collapse."

Nodding, Thor turned his eyes forward and focused on the orb of light being cast by Merlin. Behind him, he could hear the others following them and hoped that numbers would be enough to overcome whatever magic the Dark Elves had conjured. If he still believed in the gods, he might have even prayed that the whole host of Sídhean wasn't waiting for them.

28

Land of Bones

Screaming filled Alex's ears and drowned out the sudden rush of noise in her head. It did nothing to stop the flow of images, smells, and emotions bombarding her. Part of her was aware that she was still underground, that there was an old body only a few feet from her, but most of her mind was occupied swimming through the faces. She recognized the two boys playing ball in the yard and their sisters sitting to the side with books as Eckstein's children. Alex recognized the brown-haired woman in an old-fashioned gown as Gwenyvar. There were several images of Merlin and Morgana with different emotions accompanying them all.

But most she didn't know. Most were being pulled from deeper in her mind like long forgotten memories. She fought back, clawed at it, and repeated her own name: Alex over and over. It brought forth other images and she switched to her full name, repeating it and willing the magic to recede. Everything slowed down and the shocked face of a living Eckstein floated in front of her. Hundreds of emotions crossed his face and she screamed again as the flesh melted away and decayed into the vacant skull across from her.

Slamming her eyes closed, Alex shook her head as if that would dislodge everything pounding through it. Hands grabbed at her shoulders. Someone was right beside her and making low soft sounds. Another voice shouted for them to be careful. Her whole body was trembling. Cold was seeping into her bones. She was dying again, all over again back on that shore with Arthur smiling in victory.

"Alex, it's okay," a familiar voice said. "We're here. It's Bran and Aiden."

The names cut through the fog a little. Alex wanted to open her eyes, but they were so heavy. Images kept flashing beneath her eyelids. So many faces and names. They all triggered a different set of emotions, but it all blurred together. Her chest ached. Was she still breathing? No, she was dying.

"Alex, focus on my voice," Bran commanded. "Focus on me and keep breathing."

Her lungs burned at the words. She hadn't been breathing. Alex gulped for air. The haze began to lift. She became aware that her whole body was shaking. Aiden was kneeling by Gottfried's body, studying it with a strangely blank expression on his face. Alex didn't want to look, but her eyes moved of their own accord to the corpse. The bones were browning with age and Alex thought she could still see signs of decaying flesh. His uniform was decaying and the bits of metal were all that truly remained. Yet Alex couldn't help but see flickers of his face. She'd seen it only a moment, but it was already lodged in her brain. He'd had a very normal face, intelligent and kind even if not handsome. Graying blond hair and blue eyes that were long gone now.

"Easy, Alex," Bran whispered to her. "Easy."

"I'm okay," Alex tried to reassure him though it fell flat. "Really. I'm okay."

"What do you want to do?" Aiden asked her gently. "Just leave it or take it with us?"

"I... I don't know." Alex swallowed thickly and forced herself to study the body, careful to keep taking slow and steady breaths. "How would we explain it?" She remembered that they weren't supposed to be there. "And I have no idea where our- his kids are at now," she forced out the words, fully aware of how she stumbled over the description.

"We could cremate it," Bran suggested, keeping a hand on her arm.

"Yeah, with my fire I could do that quickly." Aiden looked back at her and waited. "Take the ashes and you could decide what to do later."

"He died down here alone," Alex suddenly heard herself say. "He knew he had to disappear. There was someone else who helped him..."

"Don't try to think about it right now," Bran cautioned her. "One thing at a time, Alex."

"Right, sorry."

"It's not your fault," Aiden assured her before Bran could. "Why don't you go back with the others? I'll take care of the cremation."

"Do you think it's safe to do that down here?"

"I'll use my magic to help clear the air and keep things under control," Bran promised. "But the others are worried about you."

Alex nodded, suddenly realizing that she came in here alone. The others must have heard her scream and scrambled to get through to her. She gave Aiden and Bran soft thankful smiles which they returned.

"Think you can get back to the others now?"

Nodding to Bran, Alex turned back towards the little opening and inhaled deeply. "Guys I'm coming out," she called out to the others.

In response, Alex could hear movement in the small tunnel and slid her arms inside. It was tight and dark leaving her to wonder how she'd gotten through before. As she began to crawl though, Alex struggled to breathe.

The position of her arms was tight against her chest. She was closed in, a problem she'd never had before. Gottfried had crawled in there to die all alone either by starvation or maybe he'd used his service firearm. The idea made everything seem tighter and darker. She stopped moving for a moment and tried to catch her breath. It wasn't all that long of a tunnel, only about seven feet so she couldn't understand why she was struggling.

"Keep going, Alex." Aiden's voice was muffled behind her as the voices of her friends at the other end of the crawl space became louder. She could see light up ahead and movement at the opening. "Keep going."

Her hand reached out into the cavern and someone grabbed it in a large warm hand. Alex tightened her grip around the hand, relishing the contact and sense of security. Lance's face appeared overhead as she pulled her upper body out of the crawlspace. He was kneeling down and began to gently pull her forward. With a soft groan, Alex managed to get to her own knees and let Lance guide her into a standing position. He offered her a soft smile and released her only to have Alex's knees start to buckle. Vertigo hit her, she began to fall, but Lance caught her quickly while Jenny made a small sound of alarm.

"I've got you," Lance assured her. "Come on let's give the others some room."

Leaning against Lance, Alex let him lead her a couple of steps away. He gently set her against the wall and Alex took in a long, deep breath. Closing her eyes, she tilted her head back, not even caring when her head met the tunnel wall. Through the small opening, she could hear low voices and energy flared in her chest. She paused and realized that Aiden must have started the cremation. That feeling was new. Or was it? She wasn't certain now.

"What's the delay?" Nicki questioned, bending down and looking through the opening. "Guys, everything alright?"

"We're taking care of Eckstein's body," Bran called back. "Just give us a few minutes."

The others looked at her and Alex tried not to flinch away. Jenny stepped up next to her and wrapped her in a hug. It was a little awkward since Jenny still had her backpack on, but Alex leaned into the embrace and breathed in the scent of Jenny's shampoo. Jenny made soft comforting sounds and Lance's presence at her back was warm and reassuring. A bittersweet feeling welled up inside of her that Alex couldn't fully distinguish the source of.

A few minutes later she could hear the others crawling back out, their grunts mixed with words of encouragement from Nicki. Pulling away from Jenny, Alex wiped at her eyes and turned to look at the others. Aiden straightened up and dusted himself off a little. It didn't do anything for the layers of mud collected on his boots and jeans from the flooded areas. She watched Bran pick up his backpack and slip something into it before pulling it back on.

"Okay, so Eckstein stashed the Hammer and got lost down here." Bran looked towards her sympathetically before continuing, "So we still need to find the Hammer."

Alex nodded her understanding and looked around for the light orb. In her... confusion she'd lost track of it. There were still light orbs from the others illuminating the room, but a soft glow of light from the crawlspace alerted her that it was still near the remains. Swallowing, Alex closed her eyes and tugged with her magic. She could feel the pulse of magic swirling in the air and reached for it. A few thin wisps of magic began to be drawn towards her. Closing her eyes, she pushed the rest of the world away.

Holding out her hand, Alex twitched her fingers and felt more of the magic following. The soft blend of all their magic shifted and began to turn a darker gray color. Alex tried to focus on the memory of Mjǫllnir, its unexpected shape, and the triskelion that she'd seen through Eckstein's memory. The resonance of the magic shifted and Alex opened her eyes.

The orb hovered before Alex for a moment before it began to move once more, drifting towards the way they'd come earlier. No one said anything about Alex causing them to backtrack. Everyone got their things, took gulps of water, and pulled their backpacks on once more. Aiden took the lead again with Lance right behind him.

They followed the guide orb in silence. No one seemed to want to talk and Alex was just fine with the quiet. The steady rhythm of their footfalls was enough to reassure her that she wasn't alone. Around them, the tunnels continued to turn and vary in how intact they were. Another section was flooded and Nicki and Aiden made small sounds of displeasure as they waded through while Lance helped keep them steady. There was less modern looking graffiti and markings now as the tunnels became rougher and less sculpted.

"Hey guys look at this," Jenny called. Her flashlight was shining into a small room just off the hallway.

Curiosity warred with Alex's desire to keep moving. Her legs were beginning to ache and her chest was sore from screaming and crying though she didn't want to say anything. Sharing a look with Bran, Alex stepped forward and looked inside. The room resembled a cave, but there were candle chandeliers hanging from the ceiling. Smaller candles were scattered around in small niches and a large flatter stone had been shifted to the middle of the room. She stepped all the way inside and the others followed, bringing their light orbs in with them. Around them the walls were painted in a variety of colors with different symbols, pictures and names overlapping in a chaotic mural.

"These chandeliers look modern," Nicki observed with excitement creeping into her voice. "This is a break room."

"We didn't bring any candles so let's leave those alone for the next group," Lance said as he looked around in slight awe. "I wasn't expecting anything like this."

"Well, it is a society," Aiden said, sitting down. "Let's take a break for a bit."

"Alright," Lance agreed as he shifted off his backpack.

Alex looked towards the entrance to the room. Their guide light was hovering just beyond the doorway, just waiting for them to continue. She shrugged off her pack and sat on one of the rocks that had a slightly worn patch from other visitors. Pulling out a granola bar, Alex focused on eating the small meal and not the weight of the rock overhead or the memory of finding her own former body.

"Eat," Jenny urged her. Alex looked over at the other girl who nodded towards the granola bar in her hand. She'd only taken a single bite. "Eat something, Alex."

Nodding, Alex brought the granola bar up and quickly finished it off as Jenny watched. She could see worry in Jenny's eyes, but the other woman was staying silent. Alex wasn't sure if she was grateful for that or not. The others all seemed to be just as uneasy and only Aiden and Nicki managed a soft conversation. Lance moved to leave first, hoisting his bag back on and silently signaling them that it was time to move on.

They followed the light and Alex licked her lips nervously. It was hard to tell, but she didn't think they'd been detoured too far for Eckstein's body. She must have been thinking of him too much when they cast the spell. Everyone was dragging despite the break and exhaustion was setting in, but they couldn't stop. They didn't have the supplies to be down here too long. Hopefully, they were close.

Alex took a shuddering breath and lowered her eyes. She watched her feet intently, putting one foot in front of the other for a long time. It was too hard to look down the tunnels. Even with all the light orbs floating around them there was a deep lingering darkness always at the edge. There was the weighty silence of being buried underground far from the hustle and bustle of Paris and the knowledge of how much stone was above them.

The front of the line stopped as they entered a small tomb-like room. Piles of browned bones lined the wall and formed a large mound of remains at the far side of the room. Alex looked around with a frown. The bones were right, but this wasn't the place. The light shifted towards the ceiling and sailed over the bone pile leaving her gaping in disgust.

"Oh god no!" Nicki groaned. The redhead shuddered and looked at Aiden desperately. "Not over the bones!"

"We can't abandon the quest now," Aiden said though he looked a bit pale.

"Okay enough references," Lance said. Despite his stern expression, he looked a bit ill himself. "You're sure it's going that way?"

"Yeah," Aiden took a couple steps forward. "Right over the bones. Guess there's enough space to get through."

"But they're bones," Jenny protested. "We can't crawl over human remains."

"Technically, we desecrated a grave back during Christmas break," Bran reminded her.

"Please tell me this isn't going to become a thing we do on breaks." Nicki was eying the bones with a mixture of morbid glee and disgust. "Because I didn't sign up for that."

"None of us 'signed up' for this." Bran sighed and shook his head. "Come on, the Hammer is this way. We need to keep moving."

"Why do I keep coming on these adventures with you people?" Jenny asked. No one answered her.

Lance began to carefully crawl over the pile. Muffled noises escaped him and Nicki grimaced, taking a step back from the bone filled corridor. Alex wondered if Eckstein had come over them or if the detour had made it necessary. Jenny went ahead of her across the bones and Alex followed only a few feet behind her. It was difficult to move up the initial slope as the bones shifted beneath them. The pile almost reached the ceiling meaning that Alex quickly had to drop to her knees to keep going.

"Oh God, I want hand sanitizer," Jenny all but whimpered.

Alex understood the sentiment as her fingers slipped into the eyeholes of another skull. Holding back a grimace she kept crawling across the uneven surface. Every so often there was a soft crack of bones breaking from deep in the pile, but they all kept moving over the pile. Up ahead it began to drop from the roofline and Alex turned so she could slide feet first after the others. She nearly fell over upon reaching the other side, but Aiden caught her arm. Nicki was doing a small dance and frantically shaking her limbs. Jenny made the sign of the cross and shuddered.

It took them a few minutes to recover mentally enough to keep going. Alex felt dirty, sweaty, and dehydrated from her earlier tears but wasn't willing to say anything. The guiding light kept moving, guiding them around turns and through another flooded corridor. There were fewer signs of modern access now with the only graffiti being old carvings in the wall. Alex lost track of time and Lance called them to stop for another water break before resuming the trek. Her legs ached and Alex was beginning to fear that they would never find the Hammer.

Then the guiding light stopped and Alex dropped her eyes to the pile of bones. Around them were half organized bones, neater than the rough piles they'd been around earlier, but not as neat as they were in the tourist area. It was depressing and also very familiar. Alex slowly dropped to her knees and with trembling fingers began to shift the bones. They were brown from age like all the others, but as her fingers brushed them aside there was a strange hum that traveled up her hands. She pulled the bones away to expose a hole in the rock floor.

Lance's flashlight shined into the hole and the beam fell on a cracked leather case. Reaching into the hole, Alex carefully navigated the heavy box through the opening. Alex's hands trembled as she opened the case. She smiled when the beam of the flashlight reflected off of smooth metal and revealed an engraved triskelion symbol. There was no rust or signs of age. The dark iron metal gleamed in the light and shimmered when Alex reached out to touch it. A hum filled her arms, traveling from the Hammer through her whole body. It was a marvel and matched her memories.

"Mjǫllnir." Alex beamed and a laugh escaped her. "The Iron Hammer."

"What is it with you Iron Souls and putting the triskelion on everything?" Aiden asked earning him a look from everyone. "What it's true!"

Alex shook her head and the guiding light flickered out. "Uh, I guess we better cast another spell."

"Yeah, this time focus on the nearest exit," Lance said. "We can navigate on the street."

"And then call Merlin and Morgana," Alex added. Her eyes were still locked on the Hammer. A small smile tugged at her lips as the other mages gathered around her. Yet the sense of relief and satisfaction was quickly drowned out with fear that the Iron Hammer wouldn't be enough and the mess of lingering emotions left behind from Gottfried.

29

Bated Breath

Merlin had always considered himself a patient man. At almost three thousand years old it should have been easy to await news, but he was quickly finding that was not the case. Today Morgana had met him at his own home. She'd said it was convenient, but Merlin was aware she'd gone to the workshop and checked on the Iron Chalice while he made them tea.

"The children have been underground a long time," he said uneasily.

"Finding Mjǫllnir will no doubt take time," Morgana reminded him. She was looking at papers in a folder spread across his coffee table with an intense expression. "They will contact us when they return to the surface."

"The Paris tunnels are dangerous. Anything could have happened: a cave in, an attack or a flash flood."

"Stop it, Ambrose," Morgana commanded. She looked up at him with stern green eyes. "Honestly stop trying to make me worry. You know I can do it just fine on my own."

"It's a nine-hour difference," Merlin muttered as he began to pace along his living room. "It's almost three o'clock here. It's almost midnight there."

"Which really isn't that late for Paris. The children took food and water down with them. Four of them are mages and I'm confident that they will not allow themselves to be split up. They located the Chalice without help from us and have found Mjǫllnir when you could not."

Merlin didn't grimace at the sharp reminder. He hadn't liked the Hammer being put in the old tunnels. Once the Dvergr died off there hadn't been much there any longer.

"I can't believe Nazis found it," he grumbled.

"Well, there isn't much to find on Gottfried Eckstein and what I have is very sterile, but I'd say he wasn't a bad man."

"I'm surprised all records of him weren't destroyed."

"That's the interesting thing. He went missing after returning to his post in Paris after assisting the Ahnenerbe and was listed as missing in action. There isn't anything in his old records about him stealing the Hammer."

"Is it possible he used magic?" Merlin was surprised at the idea. "The levels thankfully weren't high then, just the usual low level."

"I'm not sure. Alex might learn eventually from her dreams, but it isn't a priority," Morgana said. "There are no records of his family being questioned by the Gestapo at least."

They settled into silence; the only sound was Morgana gently turning the pages in the folder she'd secured from Germany. There wasn't much there, but then again Captain Eckstein of the SS hadn't been anyone truly important. Not to the Third Reich and not to the Allies. Just another soldier, just another German trying to survive. Merlin wondered how he'd managed to secure the Hammer without suspicion falling on him and his family. If the SS had suspected he was part of it, then the Eckstein family no doubt would have been questioned.

The sudden ringing of Morgana's phone almost made Merlin jump and his fingers grabbed at the air for his staff. It took him a moment, but he located the noise as Morgana pulled out her phone. She eagerly answered it and he saw her shoulders relax.

"Speakerphone," Merlin ordered.

The command earned him a dark look from Morgana, but she adjusted the phone and set it on the coffee table between them. For a moment all Merlin heard was Bran's voice and a wave of relief washed over him. Morgana gave him an understanding look.

"Say again, Bran," Morgana told the young man.

"We just got out of the Catacombs and we have the Hammer. It'll take us a little bit to get back to the hostel, but we're going to clean up and go from there. Anything you need from us?"

"Merlin and I will discuss what to do next." Morgana nodded slightly and smiled triumphantly. "We may water tunnel to you to retrieve Mjǫll-nir."

"Sounds good, just let us know." Bran sighed through the phone and there were muffled voices on the other end. "Everyone is pretty beat and filthy so if it isn't an emergency maybe give us a couple of hours."

"We can't promise anything, but look after each other," Merlin said loudly.

"Yes, sir. We'll call in a little while to discuss the plan."

Merlin hummed thoughtfully and stared at the phone for a long moment before looking at Morgana. She closed the file in front of her and shifted to the side of the sofa to give him room to sit. His limbs suddenly seemed very heavy and exhaustion he hadn't known he was carrying weighed him down. Morgana gave him a knowing look once more as he sat down and he wondered just when he'd become so old.

"We should retrieve Alex quickly. A water tunnel is the best option," Merlin suggested quickly, already impatient to travel to the children.

"I'm not sure about bringing them all back by water tunnel," Morgana countered thoughtfully.

"Oh?" Merlin questioned, feeling a hint of irritation with her hesitance. "We managed it last time and it isn't safe for Alex to remain in Paris too long."

"Last time it was necessary with the spike of magic caused by activating and using the Chalice. I'm not sure that either of us is really in the mental condition to maintain a water tunnel that long. You know the more people you're taking through the harder it is."

Merlin could do nothing but nod in agreement. He'd almost lost control of the water tunnel he'd recently used himself. Closing his eyes, he inhaled deeply and then let it out slowly to rein in his emotions. Everything was piling up faster than they could process. They'd gotten used to having decades to adjust and even with as long term adaptable as they were, Merlin feared that he and Morgana were proving too slow now. He opened his eyes and looked back at Morgana.

"The Hammer may prove difficult to get on a plane. None of the children have really mastered that level of control," he reminded Morgana. "Security would notice it the moment they lost concentration on keeping it hidden."

"Plus, I wouldn't trust putting Mjǫllnir on a plane." Morgana agreed with a frown. "They say that cell phones can interfere with the instruments."

"I'm not sure that's actually true, but I see your point. One wrong spark and Mjǫllnir could bring everything crashing down." Merlin nodded and hummed to himself. "If we were to just retrieve Alex and the

Hammer then it won't be too difficult. We could bring them both back here and the others could follow on more normal transportation."

"I admit that I am becoming anxious having her away. Paris has no blood protection around it and while them finding the Hammer didn't trigger a spike in magic, Arthur still might be aware of it. I just don't like having her so far away."

"You were confident yesterday." Merlin felt a little better knowing that the unease wasn't just him. There was something in the air, he realized. Something heavy like a fog hanging over them: not evil or threatening, just present. "Why the change?"

"I've just got a strange feeling," Morgana replied. Merlin nodded his understanding. She sensed it too then. "Bran's been hinting that she's struggling with the memories of her other lives. They're slipping in as dreams and visions more frequently. I can't imagine what that's like."

"Separating her from her friends might not help."

"Yes, but three of those friends are reincarnations of people she used to know," Morgana pointed out. She was pressing her lips thoughtfully. "Who knows what confusion that might cause?"

"She's known us in dozens of lives," Merlin told her gently. "We may be no better."

Morgana nodded a little but stared down into her coffee. Her distress and worry were clear even as she tried to stay focused. "Let's ask Alex," Morgana finally said. "See what she thinks. At this point, she may agree that being separated from the Hammer is a mistake." Morgana picked her phone back up and dialed a number quickly. Merlin leaned back into the sofa, settling into his worn spot and listened. "Yes, Alex, sorry to bother you. Merlin and I think it would be best to bring you and the Hammer back to Ravenslake as quickly as possible."

There was a moment of silence on Morgana's end. Merlin almost used his magic to heighten his hearing, but he'd never been very good at that. Morgana nodded at something that Alex said.

"Yes, Alex, one of us will come and get you through a water tunnel," Morgana told Alex. There was a pause. "No just you. Water tunnel travel is difficult and it would be safer if I was just focusing on you." Another long pause almost made Merlin stand up and pace. "Oh, excellent. Yes, that's one of our concerns."

Merlin wondered which concern Alex was talking about: lack of blood protection, Arthur, or getting the Hammer onto a plane. Probably the last one. Relief was obvious on Morgana's face and he almost smiled. It had taken three thousand years, but Morgana finally had an Iron Soul that she cared as much about as Arto. The thought both filled him with warmth and dread for the future. The inevitable loss of Alex would be difficult for them both. Something about her had wormed its way in. Then Morgana pulled the phone away from her ear and looked over at him, drawing him from his thoughts.

"Where should we meet them? It needs to be specific."

"The Seine by Norte Dame," Merlin suggested after a moment of consideration. "That area is accessible even at night."

"Good thought," Morgana agreed before relaying the information to Alex. "Alright then, two hours. Be careful until then."

"I should go," Merlin said as soon as Morgana set down the phone. "I've always been better at water travel than you."

"You almost lost control just the other day."

"That was different." Merlin huffed slightly and gave Morgana a stern look. "I explained that to you. Arthur had found me and the tunnel was breaking apart. I managed to get myself here safely despite that," he argued.

Morgana tilted her head in agreement. He could tell she wasn't happy about it, but he was grateful that she wasn't fighting him on it. The unspoken argument that she was too close to Alex hung in the air, but he hesitated to use it. They were both fond of Alex, more so than they had been of an Iron Soul incarnation in a long time. Merlin groaned and sank into the back of the sofa, toying with his fingers. He didn't like this unease. It made him feel like an old man.

Merlin hoisted himself off the sofa after a few minutes of silence and busied himself in the kitchen making sandwiches. He wrapped a few up and put them in the fridge for Alex to eat later and took the rest out to Morgana. There was nothing to do but wait for the two hours. That wouldn't give the children long, just enough time to get back to their hostel and clean up. Hopefully, no one would stop them in their present state. If he remembered correctly, the Paris mines were off limits. Shaking his head, Merlin picked up one of the sandwiches and forced himself to eat while he planned.

His home wasn't as conveniently located to the lake to make a water tunnel as Morgana's house was being at the western end of town. However not all water tunnels had to be made in large natural bodies of water. When almost two hours had passed, Merlin led Morgana out to his yard with a spring in his step and unlocked the workshop, gesturing her inside.

The workshop hadn't changed much since he started teaching the younger mages the basics of blacksmithing. He hadn't had the time for many projects lately so it was cleaner than normal with the tools all put away. A few feet away from the door, a large floor safe in the foundation contained the Iron Chalice and was covered by a heavy woven mat. Morgana's eyes dropped to it, but she said nothing and made no move to check on it.

"We'll need to consider where and how to store Mjǫllnir," he said.

"That's a conversation to have with Alex," Morgana answered. There was a bite to her tone as if she was concerned he'd argue. "Given the threat of Arthur, it may be something she should keep on her."

"Then you and Nicki may need to explore that magical bag idea further. If memory serves Mjǫllnir wasn't a small thing."

"I would be deeply impressed if Nicki could figure out how to make that bag of holding she keeps dreaming about."

They came to a stop in front of the side door of the workshop and Morgana glanced at him with a slight frown. She was confused as to where he was going Merlin realized and he barely held in a smile. He unlocked and pushed open the back door revealing a small side area that was almost completely filled by a small stone square. A set of pipes connected the gutters of the workshop to a small opening in the wooden cover. Merlin stepped forward and pulled the cover off revealing a two feet deep cistern roughly half filled with water.

"You want to use this?" Morgana asked doubtfully. "It's rather small, Merlin."

"It's the middle of the day, if we keep using magic down at the lake then sooner or later someone is going to notice. We were lucky there weren't any stories about a demon on the water from when Chernobog came here."

"Why didn't you use it the other day?" Morgana countered with a raised eyebrow though she couldn't hide the fact she was considering it from him.

"The cover was on." Merlin opened his palms and green magic sparked to life. "Any other objections?" he asked her pointedly.

"No, you have a point," Morgana conceded with a slight nod. "I expect you'll be able to return without difficulty."

"I know my own backyard well enough I think," Merlin agreed with a smile. Morgana's shoulders relaxed and she offered him another nod and a smile. They were both feeling the strain, he reminded himself. "Stay safe until I return," he told her. The words weren't really necessary, but they served as an apology.

Green sparks turned into a stream of glimmering magic that flowed into the cistern. Merlin's magic spread across the surface of the water. Briefly, he worried that there wasn't enough water to make this work. Then the water began to rise out of the cistern in a small column. It began to swirl in a tight formation and twisted from horizontal to vertical. Closing his eyes, Merlin focused on the memory of Notre Dame. He hadn't been to Paris for some time, but the majestic cathedral sprang to mind easily. Merlin opened his eyes and found that the spinning water tunnel was larger as it pulled water from the Seine. Stepping over the concrete block wall of the cistern, Merlin reached towards the water tunnel and stepped inside.

Water tugged at his clothing but didn't seep into the fabric as he walked across the current. He was being swept across the globe as his magic tingled across his skin and protected him. In the swirling blues and greens around him, Merlin caught flashes of other places, people, and animals, but ignored them all as he focused on Paris. The green color around him intensified as he pushed more of his magic into the water tunnel. He began to slow down in speed and the images became clearer and clearer.

The water tunnel opened slowly along a dark riverside. Merlin stepped out onto the small platform built along the pale brick retaining walls that lined the Seine's path through Paris. Soft lights glimmered against the water and sparkled off of the churning water tunnel. The rush of the water was too loud and above him in the darkness loomed Notre Dame.

Merlin looked up towards it even as he waved his hand and the water tunnel fell apart with a splash. Humming softly, he climbed up the small staircase that led up to the bank. A spring chill began to seep into his skin and he looked overhead, but the lights of Paris allowed only a few dim stars to be visible.

There was a distant sound of voices and Merlin looked around as he reached the top of the stairs. Stopping in place, Merlin's body trembled in relief at the sight of the children. They were standing in a group with Alex, all smiling even though they all looked exhausted. He wondered for a moment how long they'd been underground. Only Alex had anything. A backpack was strapped to her back and she was clutching at the straps tightly. Merlin could almost feel the hum of Mjǫllnir and smiled.

"Alex," he called. Merlin started walking as they all turned towards him and used it as an opportunity to check them all over, even Lance and Jenny. No one was injured as far as he could see. "Good to see you all." Putting a hand on Alex's shoulder, he gave it a slight squeeze. "Ready to go?"

"Yeah, just..." Alex looked at the others. He could see that she was nervous. Their little group hadn't been separated much lately.

"We'll be fine, Alex," Jenny assured her. "We've got tickets booked tomorrow night." Jenny slipped her arm through Lance's and beamed up at him. "Time to rest and maybe even see some sights."

"We'll get you something," Nicki promised with a smile. "And let us know if you need anything."

Alex nodded slowly and Merlin almost sighed in relief. For a moment he'd been concerned that she'd change her mind. He looked them all over one more time. "You still have money, correct?"

"We've barely touched what Morgana sent us with," Bran answered. Then the boy grinned. "Maybe a fancy dinner tomorrow before we go to the airport."

"Oh, I like that, I vote for that!" Jenny was almost jumping with excitement. Then she gave Alex another smile. "See? We'll be fine."

Merlin offered the girl a real smile. Her eyes widened and she looked uncertain. There was a tug of guilt in his gut and Merlin knew that Arto would be very distressed that even the reincarnation of Gwenyvar would have reason to fear him. She and Lance had gone with the mages after both the Iron Chalice and now Mjǫllnir. It was a different sort of loyalty and one he wasn't sure he completely trusted yet, but it was loyalty all the same.

As he led Alex towards the river, Merlin was aware of the others watching them. He was grateful they were hanging back so Alex didn't second guess herself. It took him a moment to realize that the slight hum he'd been feeling in the air was stronger around Alex. Merlin looked at her in the corner of his eye. She was frowning thoughtfully as a strand of blonde hair hung in her face. She wasn't using any of her magic at the moment, but there was a distinct sense of power radiating from her that connected to the odd feeling he'd had earlier. It wasn't even Mjǫllnir in her bag, but Merlin was sure that finding the Hammer had something to do with it.

Alex was silent and still as he formed a new water tunnel. He almost considered having her help, but her silence and the far off look on her face instantly killed that idea. Reaching over, Merlin took her hand and gave it a soft squeeze of reassurance. Alex's gray eyes met his for a moment, flashing with something, but exhaustion swept it all away.

"I promise you can rest soon."

They stepped into the water tunnel and Alex's grip on his hand became iron. His fingers ached at the strength of her fearful grasp as images flashed by them. Gray magic began to flow from her free hand and mix with his own green magic though Merlin doubted Alex was aware of it. She gasped softly behind him as an image of Yellowstone appeared for a moment before they rushed by. It made him smile.

Merlin focused on his memory of his backyard and the cistern. He'd built the thing to ensure he'd have water for forging and any accidents years ago but had never really used it as his little neighborhood had a well. The water tunnel opened before him, creating a thin layer of magic between them and his back yard. He could see Morgana waiting though her image was blurry. Stepping forward, Merlin tugged Alex out after him and caught her when she almost tripped over the edge of the cistern.

Alex was a bit shaken on her feet as she stepped over the wall and he let go of her hand. Morgana surged forth and wrapped Alex in a tight hug. The blonde young woman looked surprised for a moment and her eyes flashed with something Merlin couldn't identify much to his surprise. Then Alex smiled and returned the hug, her shoulders relaxing. They led her back into his house quickly. Alex shrugged off her backpack and pulled out an old leather case.

His eyes dropped to the case as Alex set it on the table of his living room. "I'm still amazed it was found in Norway."

"Honestly I'm not sure how they did," Alex said. "I didn't see any of that. I wish I knew."

"Sadly, it is impossible to always know." Morgana shook her head. "There's always something that you can't explain. The source of a legend that is true in too many ways. I usually assume that someone with a little magical ability had a vision as a dream and just told it as a story. It really doesn't take much."

Alex nodded vaguely and Merlin shared a worried glance with Morgana. Judging from the way the other mage was watching Alex she sensed that something had changed. The energy in the air was sharper than before, like a building storm, and Mjǫllnir was thrumming with power in the case. Merlin wasn't certain what was going to happen next, but it seemed the world was waiting with bated breath for it.

30

Thieves in the Day

April 1944 C.E. Hamburg, Germany

There was only a brief window of time when Weber's hotel room was accessible without guards inside. Every step of the journey back to Germany, Weber had become more and more paranoid. But now there was a tiny hint of opportunity that Gottfried found himself pursuing despite the voice telling him not to. Gottfried carefully hoisted himself over the side of the fire escape and placed his feet on the narrow ledge running around the back side of the hotel. He moved his feet slowly and carefully as the sounds of the world were drowned out by the pounding of his heartbeat.

Relief made his knees tremble as he reached Weber's open window and he carefully climbed through, glancing around to make sure that no one was insight. He avoided contact with any of the furniture around the window and crept towards the hotel room safe. In his right hand, he was carrying a small sturdy leather case that he hoped would be large enough.

Gottfried knelt beside the safe and licked his lips nervously. His gloved hands were trembling as he reached out and carefully began to enter the combination, mindful of the sounds of the guards outside the door. Part of him was angry that Weber had left the window open after their meeting this morning and angry at himself for noticing while another part was relieved. The safe clicked and he eased the door open. Why hadn't Weber put the combination of the safe straight into his pocket when they first arrived? Then Gottfried wouldn't have memorized it against his own will.

His hands were shaking worse now as he pulled out the leather covered case from the safe. He set it on the floor and opened it, needing to see the Hammer one more time. The Hammer gleamed brightly in the case. Gottfried could feel the electricity sliding over the surface of his skin and leaving standing hairs in its wake. There was power here, it could be felt the instant you got too close. That was the problem.

He'd been trying to ignore it. All of it. For the last week as they checked over every last inch of the tunnels to make sure there were no more lost treasures, he'd had terrible dreams. The Hammer was always at the center of it. There was a whisper at the back of his head urging him to touch it once more, but Gottfried couldn't obey it. The visions had haunted him, made it impossible to hide from the dark reality of what he knew had to happen. When they'd gone to Oslo to get on the plane, the feelings of dread had only gotten worse.

Gottfried pulled the Hammer from the case and quickly transferred it into his own. The Hammer barely fit, but he was able to close and secure the case. He glanced around the room and spotted a small German eagle statue on one of the bookcases. Standing up, he tiptoed across the room and grabbed the statue. He slipped it into the larger case and closed it up before carefully sliding it back into the safe. With any luck, the weight would keep Weber from checking inside.

Sounds from the hallway made his heart jump to his throat and Gottfried stood up with the heavy case in hand. He returned to the window and carefully climbed out onto the ledge once more. Every footfall against the stone sounded too loud and he turned up the collar of his long coat only to almost lose his balance. He grabbed the rail of the fire escape with his right hand and stayed still for a long moment as he fought to recover his breath. Then he eased himself over the rail and almost collapsed.

Wiping the sweat from his brow, he began to slowly walk down the fire escape steps, trying to be quiet. Two stories down, his own window was open. There were no soldiers waiting for him as he slipped inside the hotel room. Gottfried turned around and closed the window behind him, releasing a long sigh of relief. His legs were shaking and Gottfried crossed the room to where his trunk was waiting by the door. Setting the case down on top of it, Gottfried looked down at his trembling hands.

What had he done? The thought was terrifying and cut through the adrenaline rush. He'd stolen from the Third Reich, from the SS and because of a few nightmares. There was a tug in his gut that drew him towards the Hammer, but he shook his head and went into the bathroom. Taking off the gloves, Gottfried ran the water over his hands and splashed it on his face. He didn't dare look at his reflection, too frightened of what he might find in his own eyes. Unease churned in his stomach and he feared he might be ill.

A knock on the door made him jump. For a moment he couldn't move, but the knock came again. He forced his feet to work and they carried him to the front door. Gottfried looked nervously down at the case and squeezed his left hand and the gloves within it tightly. Opening the door, Gottfried found only one of the hotel staff.

"Your car for the train station is here, sir," the young man said. "Shall I take down your trunk?"

Gottfried nodded blankly. His heart was finally beginning to slow down but jumped as the young man reached for the case. He grabbed it and forced a little smile. "I'll keep this with me if you don't mind."

"Of course not, sir."

As the young man hoisted the trunk onto his cart, Gottfried set down the case and pulled his gloves back on. A leather satchel was on the table by the door and he slung it over his shoulder before picking up the case. It was heavy and he could feel the thrum of electricity still. Gottfried just hoped that no one else could. He followed the young man down to the nondescript black car. Around him people on the street nodded respectfully, reminding him that his rank insignia was clear on his coat. As his trunk was loaded in the car, Gottfried slid into the back seat and sighed softly when no one came bursting out of the hotel.

Weber would be getting back to his room from his 'meeting' with the pretty young woman from the bar any moment now. Hopefully, he'd merely check that the case was in the safe and go about writing his reports. The car began to move and Gottfried clutched at the case on his lap. He could still feel it and almost begged the thing to stop giving off that low energy. No one else was reacting to it and no one else had been shocked by it, but he couldn't stop feeling it. At least the Hammer wasn't the mythical weight that the legends described.

They slowly came to a stop and Gottfried looked out to find the train station to his right. Opening the door, he climbed out with the case still tight in his hand while the driver unloaded his trunk. One of the train staff came over and Gottfried pulled out his orders. The man nodded quickly and gestured for the driver to follow him with the trunk. Gottfried followed them at a distance while he looked around the station. It was busy with people coming and going. Patriotic music was wafting through the area through the loudspeakers and the Nazi flag hung overhead. He was back in Germany with all the good and bad that brought.

"Gottfried!" a voice called over the crowd. "Captain Eckstein."

He turned to find Professor Dietrich heading towards him. The man was dressed in a suit that was a bit baggy from his weight loss in the north. There was a smile on his face that Gottfried couldn't quite return. Their eyes met and Gottfried watched as the smile faded into a slight frown. Swallowing thickly, Gottfried repressed the urge to run.

"Do you have a private car?" Dietrich asked calmly.

"Yes."

"Then let's speak on the train. It isn't due to leave for a bit."

There was nothing he could do. His trunk was being loaded and Dietrich gestured him to the end of the car and climbed up in front of him. He waved off one of the attendants who looked towards him. Gottfried nodded and followed Dietrich inside, speaking only to inform the other man of his car number. They found it easily enough and Dietrich sidestepped to let him inside before firmly closing the door behind them. It did little to muffle the sounds of the platform and Hamburg.

Dietrich was frowning at him. His eyes dropped to the case in his hand knowingly and Gottfried felt the world trying to fall away from him. "That was stupid, Gottfried," Dietrich said, sounding a lot like his grandfather. "I expected more from you."

"I don't know what you mean," he forced out only to get a sharp look. "Adalard... I just can't." Gottfried was at a loss, uncertain as to how Dietrich seemed to know what he'd done.

"Tell me you have more of a plan than this?" Dietrich all but begged. The man was looking around them carefully, his eyes suddenly sharper and more alert than Gottfried had ever seen as he scanned the crowd outside the window.

"I've been ordered back to Paris," he informed the other man. Gottfried inhaled slowly and tried to calm his pounding heart. He wanted to pace and release the nervous energy building up in his limbs, but the train car was far too small.

"I know." Dietrich's voice was gentle and resigned. His shoulders were slumping and Gottfried could see just how worried the other man was.

"I was going to hide it in the tunnels under Paris, the old mines, and catacombs," he explained. It sounded like a decent idea. "Not even the locals know their way around down there."

Dietrich's expression changed and he glanced towards the train door with clear worry. Gottfried could do nothing but wait and hope that the SS wasn't about to arrive. He had a long trip from Hamburg to Paris and there would be plenty of time for something to go wrong.

"Weber will discover the theft. While you were on a schedule set by the main office, they will still be suspicious."

"What else can I do?" Gottfried asked. He hoped that the older man had a real suggestion. "It can't go to Berlin."

"I don't leave for a few more hours," Dietrich replied. He exhaled slowly and his jaw tightened. "I'll fake suspicious behavior so that when the theft is discovered they come after me. Maybe even leave Weber a confession."

"What?" Utter shock filled Gottfried along with confusion. He had to be hearing wrong. "You can't be serious, Adalard!"

"We need to pin it on me," Dietrich repeated. The other man shook his head and slid a trembling hand into his pocket. "I don't like the Nazi regime, Gottfried. Never have, but like you and others I'm just trying to survive, but if they get this Hammer...." He shuddered. "It will take them time to use it, but they will fight to buy that time and do horrible things." Gottfried looked at him with sad eyes. "You've heard about the camps?"

Gottfried swallowed and nodded, feeling the hole in his stomach opening wider. "Yes, I know." They weren't much of a secret.

"You're right that we can't let the Hammer go to Berlin. It is far too dangerous."

"But-"

"You need enough time to get to Paris. And you know what will happen to your family if they discover it is you."

"You can't-"

"I haven't got a family to worry about," Dietrich reminded him. He reached over and gripped his shoulder. There was moisture gathering in both their eyes. Gottfried knew he should argue and protest, but he didn't know what to say. "They chase me for a bit, I make a show of getting rid of a case that the Hammer is supposedly in and they don't go after you and your family."

"They may suspect anyway."

"They might," Dietrich agreed sadly. "But it is the best option. We both know that this artifact can't reach Berlin." Dietrich looked down at the case sadly. "I only regret that I'll never know what it really was."

The words confirmed that Dietrich planned to die. Gottfried's throat tightened, but there was no real option. Capture by the SS would lead to torture and execution. It was all so ugly and he took a shuddering breath. He wanted to thank the other man, wanted to say something more, but in truth, they'd been together too long as it was. Dietrich held his hand out and Gottfried shook it gratefully. It was a mad plan that by rights should never work, but Dietrich might buy him enough time to get to Paris, check in, and get the Hammer into the tunnels. They held their hands together for a long moment before Dietrich pulled his away.

"Farewell, Captain, meeting you was a bright spot in this whole business."

"Thank you, Adalard."

He wished they had more time to talk and plan, but they were out of time. Gottfried wished he'd been brave enough to speak with Dietrich on the boat back or during one of those chilly nights in Norway. If he had then they might have had time to make a better plan. Maybe even have had the courage to just throw the thing overboard and let it sink into the sea. Outside the noise was increasing as more passengers arrived. The train would depart soon and it would become a question of how far he got before the SS looked his way. Dietrich's plan while suicidal might just give him the time he needed.

Dietrich turned to give him one last smile though it fell short of his eyes. The man's hands had stopped shaking and he nodded. Then he put on his hat and turned up the collar of his coat before moving out of the car. The door shut behind him with a soft click and Gottfried collapsed into the seat. His legs were weak and his chest was too tight. There were no tears, but grief welled up inside of him. Gottfried regretted stealing the Hammer for a moment, wondering why he couldn't just keep his head down and ignore it. The Hammer seemed to hum in response to his thought and Gottfried put the case on the seat next to him, unwilling to touch it any longer.

Time passed slowly and he avoided looking out the window. He didn't want to see if SS agents were coming or worse Gestapo. The sounds of Hamburg and the station washed over him like a steady tide of waves and then finally the whistle blew and they started moving. Gottfried looked out the window, but there were no officers and soldiers rushing to catch the train and no sign of Dietrich. A sigh escaped him and he offered a prayer to the heavens.

He gave himself an hour of watching the countryside roll by. The trains wove in and out of small towns that were full of flags. In a few places, children ran after the train and waved up at it with dogs on their heels. Gottfried's lips lifted into a tiny smile. At least all the good and innocence in Germany hadn't been destroyed. Not completely. He inhaled and straightened up. No matter what happened now something would survive. The war might drag on years more, but at the end, there would be people to start rebuilding again. With any luck and wisdom, they'd all learn from the mistakes of the last post-war era and do things better.

Gottfried adjusted the small fold up table in the car and set his satchel on it. His hands trembled a little as he reached inside and retrieved a pen and a sheet of empty paper. He spread it out in front of him. There was one more thing he needed to do, one more thing that needed to be done just in case. Swallowing, Gottfried looked out the window once more. The landscape was rushing by as they picked up speed after the latest slow down. His mind wouldn't settle. Everything that could go wrong was running through his mind, but worst of all was the question of what happened if everything went right? Could he really just walk into his office the next day and act as if nothing happened?

The blank sheet of paper was taunting him. It was to be his last letter to his wife, to his children, but it couldn't seem like he meant it as such. When the SS discovered the theft, they'd go after Dietrich but would look at others in their expedition no doubt. They'd check on him and his last letter home. It couldn't echo with a lost and sad sentiment. He picked up the pen and wrote his usual warm greeting even as his chest tightened.

Fear threatened to make his hands shake, but he managed to carefully write out a general greeting to his family. He wrote that he was on the train back to Paris and expressed his wish that he could have stopped to see them in Cologne. The words began to flow a bit easier and he wrote about being grateful to be home in Germany and about how lovely everything looked beyond the window. It was wistful but hopefully, would echo his love for his country to anyone who might come and read the letter.

The train jolted slightly as they slowed for the next station and the case with the Hammer knocked against his hip. Gottfried reached out and steadied it on impulse, but the thrum of electricity seeped into his fingers. He looked down at it. This was so crazy. He almost laughed, but his chest shuddered with a growing sob. Tightening his fingers into a fist around the pen, Gottfried struggled to breathe for a moment and was grateful he was alone. The reality of what he'd done was settling in. As much as he wanted to hide the Hammer and return to his life it wouldn't happen that way.

He would die down there. Gottfried knew it in his bones. To find a truly good hiding place he'd have to wander for hours, maybe even days to get away from the path of the Resistance. He'd have to keep the Hammer away from them too. Once it was hidden, he doubted he'd ever find his way out. Swallowing, Gottfried trembled with fear. Yet he was filled with a strange sense of pride and accomplishment as well. He just hoped that Dietrich's sacrifice would be enough to keep his family safe. He hoped that with every fiber of his being.

31

First Attempt

Alex wasn't so sure about this now. It had seemed like a good idea, well no the only idea, when they'd left for Paris. With the Iron Chain in the hands of the Queen and Arthur, they could use the power of the Iron Realm itself and bind other Sídhe creatures to their will. Alex still wasn't sure just how far that power could extend, but she didn't want to give them any longer.

The goal was to break the spell, but Alex couldn't help but feel nervous as she followed Merlin into his back yard. The thick lilac bushes and fence hid them from any curious neighbors and created a sense of isolation, but it just made Alex wish the others were here. Mjǫllnir was paradoxically heavy and light in her hands all at once and seemed far too large for her. She imagined that Thor must have been a large man with bright red hair though that image didn't feel right.

She adjusted her grip on the Hammer, trying to sort out what she had to do. This wasn't the same as before when the Sídhe had been present. Somehow, she needed to reach all the way to the Iron Chain and break the connection to all the Sídhe creatures. That or destroy the Iron Chain. Neither of those really sounded very possible right now.

"Try not to worry," Morgana said next to her. The older mage reached out and gripped her shoulder gently. "This is the first attempt."

"You think there'll be more?" Alex asked nervously. The reassurance helped a bit but made her wonder how many times she'd be attempting this.

"Alex, you're turning the magic of one magical artifact against another, the Iron Hammer against the Iron Chain. This isn't a simple thing. Merlin and I don't know what to expect here."

"So, what should I do?"

She turned her head to watch Merlin come out of the workshop. He was carrying a length of iron chain that looked solid but lacked the magical quality of the real Iron Chain. Alex frowned as the chain clinked with every step, but stayed silent. Merlin offered her a slight smile and dropped it on the grass with a thunk.

"I thought it might help you visualize," he explained. Merlin actually sounded a little sheepish and Alex smiled. "This is different than anything you've done before."

"That's not completely true," Alex said. She looked over towards the patio set where Timothy was balanced on the back of a chair. "I've done it before once."

"Yes," Morgana said a bit slowly. The older mage sounded uncertain but rallied quickly. "Would it help for Merlin and I to release magic for you to use?"

"Uh, no not yet," Alex answered uncertainly. "I'm not sure how this will work just yet."

Merlin and Morgana exchanged a look that left Alex feeling even more uncertain. Yet neither of them argued and they both took a step back to give her some space. Sitting down on the grass, Alex lowered one hand to the ground. The blades of the grass tickled the palm of her hand, but Alex pushed past the distracting sensation. She closed her eyes and breathed slowly, trying to meditate and calm herself. The world tilted a tiny bit as a jolt of vertigo hit her, but Alex could feel the spark of power beneath her heart beginning to pulse. Under her fingertips, a small wave of energy began to lap at her fingers. Alex almost smiled as she tugged gently at it and her own magic. Both began to flow up her limbs, filling her body with a rush of warmth and a pleasant tingle of power.

Alex tried to stay still as she carefully pushed a small spark of magic into the Hammer. There was a rush of magic out of the metal and it began to hum in her hand, sending small jolts of electricity up her arm. Inhaling slowly, Alex was hit by the smell of ozone and shivered at the tingle going down her spine. It was different from holding Cathanáil had been, but despite the size difference between her current hand and Thor's, the Hammer seemed to fit now. Looking down, Alex finally smiled as the metal began to glow a dark gray color, though the triskelion symbol took on a bright, almost white, blue color.

"The color of Thor's magic," Merlin offered from the side.

Alex nodded in response, not feeling any surprise. The blue color was fading quickly as the gray magic seeped into Mjǫllnir. Closing her eyes, Alex focused on the flow of magic she could feel. Her own magic was pouring into the Iron Hammer while older stored magic was flowing out into her limbs. Alex's eyelids tightened and her brow furrowed as she focused on her goal of collecting the energy into one location in front of her.

Slowly she opened her eyes and sighed in relief. An orb of glistening gray magic was hovering before her. There was only the tiniest glow from it. There was no command for it to give light, it was just waiting. Magic gathered and waiting for a command. In the corner of her eye, Alex could see Merlin beaming and Morgana thoughtfully studying the orb. More and more magic was being drawn into it and Alex's vision went a bit hazy.

She could now see small glistening strands in the air like spider silk wafting in the sky. They were difficult to make out, but as she focused on them the soft hint of color became clearer. Tiny sparks gathered together, flowing out of the trees, sky, and ground to form the white, green and, blue strands. As they flowed into the large sphere, Alex's own magic seeped into them.

Alex pushed the gathered magic out slowly as she envisioned a fog spreading out around her. Sinking her fingertips into the dirt, Alex swallowed and focused on the Iron Chain. Sending her magic out, Alex ordered it over and over again to find the Iron Chain. Her chest tightened as the magic stretched out and she held in a grimace. She was being pulled and stretched out in too many directions. A soft huff of pain escaped her and she closed her eyes, focusing all her might and will on the Iron Chain.

The blackness of her inner eyelids began to brighten. She was beginning to see something and pushed the magic towards it. Vertigo hit her and Alex gasped for air, feeling like she just been pulled harshly. Her vision cleared though she didn't open her eyes. She could see the Iron Chain. It was draped across a table over rich dark purple fabric gleaming in the low light. There was no sign of Arthur or his mother. Alex tried to reach for the chain, but she couldn't reach. Her chest ached as the magic stretched. She could see black lines shimmering off of the chain, reaching out into the world, and binding living creatures to the will of its holder.

Fighting to reach it, Alex split her focus into the real world. The weight of Mjǫllnir reminded Alex of her purpose. Alex hoisted the Hammer above her head, but the strands of magic twisting and turning through the air were too indistinct. She reached out her left hand and tried to grab one, pulling it closer, but it slipped through her fingers. Her legs trembled and her knees buckled. Wasn't she sitting? She swung the Hammer down, trying to catch the Chain.

It broke. Magic rushed back and struck Alex in the chest. Everything whited out. Distantly she heard screaming. Her throat ached and someone grabbed her shoulder. Mjǫllnir fell from her fingertips and she forced her eyes open. Confusion hit her, overpowering the pain radiating from her heart. She was sitting down on a lawn and looking towards a set of iron wrought patio furniture.

"Alex," someone called. Alex frowned and tried to move away. "Alex!" She recognized the voice as Morgana's now and started to relax.

There was a bottle of water at her lips, gently being tipped up and as the first drops hit her tongue Alex began to greedily drink. Someone was talking, but she was having trouble understanding the words. Shaking her head helped a little, but also sent a jolt of pain through Alex.

"Easy, Alex," Merlin said gently. He was on her other side.

Morgana gently took her arm and slung it over her own shoulder, helping Alex to her feet. Keeping her eyes down, Alex didn't want to see any disappointment on Morgana's face, but her teacher shifted slightly and kissed her forehead.

"It was a good try, Alex," Morgana said. Her voice was warm and reassuring. "Rest now and we'll try again later."

Alex nodded but didn't think it would help. Blinking cleared the last of the haze and Alex looked over at Merlin as she stabilized on her feet. He knelt down and picked up Mjǫllnir carefully. Morgana walked her to the back door and all but dragged her inside. Once they were in the living room, Morgana eased her into an armchair.

"Alex, are you feeling alright?" Merlin set the Hammer down on the coffee table.

"I just... I couldn't reach," Alex groaned. "I can see a bunch of the magical bindings, but I just can't reach. It isn't like when they were here and those Sídhe were so close to me."

Then Timothy appeared in front of her, leaping onto the table from the floor in a single bound. He pushed a mug of tea towards her and then picked the lid off the cookie container. With large dark eyes, he looked up at her imploringly. Alex tried to smile and lift her arms to take one of the cookies, but they were too heavy. A flash of dark gray magic spun through the air and surrounded one of the chocolate chip cookies, lifting it out of the tin. It sailed to her mouth and a confused Alex took a bite.

"Well, you're physically exhausted, but all that magic is still inside you," Morgana observed with a chuckle.

"There was some backlash," Alex admitted uneasily. Her arm finally listened to her and let her hand come up to take the cookie. The gray aura around the cookie faded. Alex was aware of them watching her and swallowed thickly, grasping for something. "I thought our magic was supposed to be weird around Brownies." Alex glanced over at Timothy who was already dusting off the mantel. "That's what you said before."

"And it is or at least it normally is," Merlin agreed, sitting down across from Alex. "However, I've been observing Timothy and he believes that he is stronger now than before and I haven't felt any reactions between my magic and his."

"What does that mean?" Alex nibbled on the cookie nervously. "Do you know or have any theories? Was it because of what I did?"

"I believe it could be due to his exposure to the Iron Chain. While a darker incarnation of the Iron Soul created it, the Iron Chain was still connected to the power of the Iron Soul. Also, it could be due to you seeking to spare Timothy when you cast the blood spell. He may be in a state of grace within the area. I can't say for certain, but those are the theories that have come to mind."

"Oh." Alex took another bite of the cookie and chewed it thoughtfully. "I'm not sure about this, Merlin. If there are side effects like with Timothy-"

"The Iron Chain cannot remain in the control of Scáthbás." Merlin's brown eyes met hers with an icy firmness in them. "She's not a creature of the Iron Realm, Alex, and she's caused so much havoc with it."

"I know, I'm just not sure I can break the spell," Alex said. She lowered her eyes as shame bubbled up in her chest. "The Hammer is powerful, but I'm not sure it's enough."

"You'll get it," Timothy said. Alex looked up in surprise as the Brownie bounced off the mantel, sailing through the air and landed on the coffee table with a soft tap while Alex gaped at him. "I have no doubt that you will break the spell."

"Thanks, Timothy, but what if I can't. The others could be attacked and hurt. The Queen's mage kill order is still in effect."

"They are mages too, have faith in them." He reached out and patted her hand with his tiny one. "You broke the spell on me and the others. You just need to find the right pathway and I know you'll break this one too."

"Maybe," Alex said. She was glad to hear that the Brownie had faith in her, but she was uncertain herself. "That was different though."

"Different yes," Morgana agreed gently. "But that doesn't mean it isn't possible to work another way. This is a big thing we're asking you to do, Alex, but you just gathered a huge amount of magic and used it to find the Iron Chain. For a first attempt, it was quite amazing."

"Yes, were you able to see the Iron Chain?" Merlin asked.

"Yeah," Alex said. "But I couldn't reach it."

"We'll try later and Merlin and I will help, maybe that will make the difference," Morgana said. "But you need rest. You've been on the go too long." Morgana looked at Merlin and gave him a stern look. "No attempts until you've had at least eight hours of sleep."

Alex didn't argue as Merlin agreed to Morgana's condition. She looked down at her hands, shifting her fingers together. For a moment she barely recognized them, they just seemed too small. Morgana stood up and touched her shoulder gently. Nodding, Alex forced a little smile and stood up.

"I know the way to the bedroom," Alex told them both. "I'll get some rest."

"I'll retrieve some of your things from your dorm room," Morgana said gently. "As you left your luggage in Paris."

"Ah yes," Merlin rubbed his beard sheepishly. "Sorry we didn't think about that."

"We did and decided it wasn't worth the risk," Alex assured him. "And thanks, Morgana, some fresh clothes would be nice."

Heading down the hallway, Alex let her fingers run across the smooth wall. Merlin's house wasn't as grand as Morgana's Victorian, but it had a cozy feel to it that soothed her a little. The guest bedroom was fairly dull with plain white walls, a full bed next to a nightstand and a small dresser. Simple, but comfortable. Alex sank down onto the forest green comforter and stretched out on the bed without bothering to remove her shoes or get beneath the blankets.

Her mind was racing and wouldn't quiet. Alex tugged at a strand of her blonde hair absentmindedly and traced the faint patterns she could see on the ceiling paint. She briefly wondered if Merlin had used magic to do the job. Magic had been at low levels before, but Alex had suspicions that at this point Merlin and Morgana could do a lot with just a little bit of power. Alex flexed her fingers again carefully as the built-up magic in her chest fluttered. It was almost painful, like a pool of hot iron around her heart.

Sitting up, Alex opened her palm and pulled on the magic. Sparks appeared around her hand and after a moment turned into a stream of dark silver. Alex's hand tingled as the magic escaped, looking for its purpose. Unsure of what else to do with it, Alex directed it over into the corner of the room. The stream of gray magic spun together into an orb that just floated in the air. Alex moaned gratefully as the pain in her chest eased at expelling the magic. Apparently, there was such a thing as holding magic too long. She eyed the orb curiously and pulled out her phone to note the time. It would be interesting to see how long the magic would linger before dissipating.

Then Alex was distracted by her phone and a text message from Jenny. It was a photo of her and Lance on the Eiffel Tower together. She couldn't help but smile at the happy expressions on their faces. There was a tiny jolt of jealousy, but it was about them seeing more of Paris than her. That was a relief at least. Alex closed the message after sending a quick reply and flicked past her various apps to her contact list. She debated calling Jenny or Nicki, but then spotted her mom's name on the list.

Alex hesitated for only a moment before making the call. She drummed her fingers against the bed as she waited for someone to answer. Nervousness was growing in her chest. What if something had happened while she was in Paris? What if the Sídhe had broken through the blood protection? A terrible sense of dread slid down her spine and settled in her gut.

"Hello, sweetie," her mom's voice said a moment later.

"Hi, Mom," Alex greeted as she lay back down on the bed. The worry vanished as quickly as it had appeared. Stretching out, she closed her eyes and tried to envision her mom's face. "How are you?"

"We're fine, Alex," her mom answered. "What about you? We haven't heard from you all week."

"Uh well, there was an artifact that we had to go and collect."

"An artifact." Her mom's voice was a touch disbelieving and a bit amused. "Oh, the life you live, dear." There was a moment of uncomfortable silence and Alex wasn't sure what to say. "Did it go okay?" her mom asked.

"Yeah, we have it. Actually, you'll appreciate what it is, Mom, Thor's Hammer."

Her mom laughed, the sound sweet and soothing to Alex's strained body and aching mind. She hummed happily and listened to her mom laugh for a few moments. There might have been a slight note of hysteria in the laughter, but she ignored that.

"Really?" Her mom sounded out of breath. "You aren't toying with your mother, are you?"

"I told you that I was Thor in another life," Alex reminded her. She even smiled despite the uncomfortable subject. "But another life of mine found it and hid Mjǫllnir in Paris."

"Sounds like there's a story there."

"I'll tell you next time I'm home."

"Sounds good, dear, we'll talk over ice cream when you come home." There was a long pause. "So, what happened that you needed to call?"

Alex grimaced a little, apparently, she didn't call often enough that her mom wouldn't suspect something was wrong. "I tried to use the Hammer to... break an enemy spell, but it didn't work."

"Are you okay? You aren't hurt, are you?"

"No, just tired and disappointed I guess," Alex answered honestly. She looked over at the shining orb of magic. "We have to do this, but I'm worried it can't be done."

"I don't know much about magic," her mom said slowly. "And I want to better understand this life of yours, but I do know you, Alex. You can do it, just be patient. It may take a few tries, but in the meantime, you're still protected by that blood spell, right?"

"Yeah, we are," Alex agreed. "Thanks, Mom."

"Of course," her mom paused before continuing, "And I meant what I said about understanding this. Your dad and I are thinking that we are overdue to properly meet Merlin and Morgana." Alex felt a jolt of dread once again. Her parents meeting Merlin and Morgana didn't sound like a good idea. The pair didn't have the best history with her family in other lives. "Alex? Is that okay?"

"I suppose," she agreed slowly. "Just... remember that they're really old and tend to see the long game."

"Well, that's ominous."

A laugh escaped Alex. "Yeah," she said around another giggle. "I suppose so, but maybe it would be good for you guys to see more magic." A yawn escaped her. "Sorry, anyway when were you thinking?"

"This summer," her mom replied. "Once school is over. You've hinted that you'll be staying there this summer."

"It's safest," Alex said. "We're talking about renting a house so we're all in one place and off campus."

Her mom made a soft thoughtful sound that Alex couldn't read. It sounded unhappy, but also understanding. Guilt washed over Alex. Her parents deserved a normal child that didn't drag them into a magical war. Sometimes she could understand Merlin's decision to take the young

Arto away from his parents. Another yawn escaped her and her mom laughed.

"Get some sleep, sweetie. Sounds like you've got quite the project. Please just remember to put some of your energy into schoolwork when you finish breaking the spell. Spring break is almost over."

"Yes, Mom."

"And you will get it. I know you will," her mom added. "You're the greatest sorceress I know."

"It's mage, Mom, and you've never seen my friends use magic." Alex was smiling again.

"Then what's a sorceress?"

"No idea where that came from. Never heard Merlin or Morgana say it though."

"Fine mage then." Her mom sighed dramatically. "You'll get it, but in the meantime rest. Call if you need to and remember that we love you very much."

"I love you too."

There were tears gathering in her eyes as the need for sleep and the desire to keep listening to her mom's voice warred. She rolled to the side and settled against the pillow even as she kept the phone to her ear. Her mom seemed to pick up on her hesitation because after a moment she started softly humming through the phone. It was a familiar soft and slow tune. A homesick tear slipped from Alex's eye and rolled sideways down her cheek. She kept the phone against her ear listening to the soft humming until sleep finally won out.

32

Cauldron of Ice

Eleven hours of sleep had helped, but the sense of anticipation and nervousness hadn't faded. The others were on a plane back and Alex was mostly synched up to the schedule of Oregon once more. Stretching her arms, she looked out the window at the sun which was working its way to the midpoint of the sky. Nervous energy bubbled up in Alex and she looked towards the corner of the room where a small orb of magic was waiting. Through the night some of the energy had dissipated, but there was still far more than Alex had been expecting.

Kneeling next to the orb, Alex slowly reached out and touched it. The whole orb was only about the size of a basketball and just hanging in the air. She could feel a thrum against her skin, similar to how she'd felt when she touched Mjǫllnir. Just the thought of the Hammer made her heart jump and Alex was gripped with a sudden urge to rush to the living room and check on it. To make sure that it was safe. Shaking her head, Alex stood up and tried to ignore the impulse. It wasn't really hers, at least that was what she told herself, but now there was an insistent little voice at the back of her head that wanted to see the Hammer.

Alex opened the door and smiled as she found a grocery bag hanging on the doorknob. Inside was some shampoo and fresh clothes. Taking the hint, Alex went to the bathroom to clean up all the while ignoring the desire to check on the Hammer. She could hear other people moving around through the wall and wondered if Morgana had stayed through her sleeping. It wouldn't surprise her if the older mage had.

After getting dressed, Alex carefully combed out her hair the best she could with her fingers and pulled it back in a braid. Her reflection still looked tired and Alex couldn't help but notice that her gray eyes seemed darker. She leaned closer to the mirror and frowned as she studied her own irises. The soft gray color she'd inherited from her dad's side of the family seemed the same as always, but there were small flecks of dark gray that she hadn't noticed before. It was like the color of her magic. Alex sighed and leaned back from the mirror. She didn't know if it was really new or something she'd only just properly noticed.

Her reflection stared back at her blankly. Alex didn't know what to think. There was a young woman with long wet blonde hair, an oval face with pale skin, and gray eyes. Nothing about her showed any hints that she was special. It had been half a semester and she still hadn't really processed being the Iron Soul. That was a hero's job.

Alex closed her eyes and shuddered as different faces flashed across the back of her eyelids. Shaking her head, she opened her eyes and looked down into the sink. Her teeth were furry and she turned on the water to rinse out her mouth. A shiver rolled down her spine and Alex almost choked on the mouthful of water. Coughing, she leaned over the sink as another shiver hit her and a tug in her gut made her grimace.

The magic was flaring inside her gut and Alex could feel it creeping up into her chest. Taking a slow breath, Alex closed her eyes again and focused on the feeling. It was odd and she thought she heard something. Like a whisper, just at the edge of her hearing. She opened her eyes and stepped out of the bathroom, her bare feet padding along the floor. The noise from the kitchen was normal, but she could still hear something. Alex returned to the guest room to retrieve her shoes and pull on socks.

In her chest, her heart was beginning to beat a little faster and harder. A sense of urgency took hold, but to Alex's surprise, there wasn't any dread or worry connected with it. Magic flowed across her skin, just a soft brush. She couldn't see it and glanced at the orb still hanging in the corner. Alex considered it for a moment before tentatively stepping towards it. Her fingers danced across the outer layer of energy and a jolt shot up her arm. It wasn't solid, but there was something beneath her fingers. Bran or Aiden would probably know.

The magic didn't need instruction, her will projected more clearly than Alex knew her own thoughts. In a blur of dark gray, the magic flowed into her hands and swirled into her chest. Alex gasped. It wasn't truly painful but created a slight ache like she'd been exercising too long. There was a shimmer of gray across her skin that quickly faded, but Alex could still feel it there.

In a daze, she headed out of the guestroom towards the front of the house. Easing the front door open, Alex stepped outside into the fresh air. Merlin's house was at the end of the road in an area much more built up than Morgana's neighborhood. Alex stepped off the porch and walked to the road. She could just catch a glimpse of the lake from here. The magic was pulling her again and Alex started moving before she even realized it. Behind her, the door of the porch opened and Morgana called after her. The first question was calm and curious, but when she didn't respond Morgana's voice became more frantic.

Picking up her speed, Alex let her feet fall into a steady jogging rhythm. Merlin's driveway led out to the street and she kept running down the shoulder. Behind her, Alex thought she heard a car starting up. She didn't slow down and the pull just kept tugging. There were a few cars out and Alex caught glimpses of the other houses along the road.

She embraced the rhythm of the jog, letting her muscles stretch and tighten. Alex couldn't remember the last time she'd gone on morning runs. They'd just fallen to the wayside like a lot of other things. Nicki hadn't discussed them doing soccer next year and fencing club had stopped being about fun. Breathing in slowly, Alex focused on the beat of her heart and her feet against the road. These weren't her running clothes or shoes, but they still did the trick.

The sound of a car behind her was picking up and Alex chuckled. Merlin and Morgana were no doubt coming after her. Up ahead the road forked to the right and left with the lake straight in front of her. A small barrier along the road proved no obstacle and Alex jumped over it. Adrenaline and satisfaction rushed through her as her feet hit the ground. Morgana shouted something from the car. Part of her wanted to stop and reassure her, but the magical pull was becoming stronger. There was something in the air. She could almost taste it.

Beneath her feet, the small rocks shifted as Alex slowly worked her way down to the shore. She shivered as a cool breeze carried a few droplets off the surface of Ravens Lake that landed on her bare arms. The pull of the magic suddenly eased and Alex gasped for air, her chest feeling tight as the magic expanded. It was fluttering and waiting for something. A soft hiss escaped Alex and she looked around uncertainly. Alex could barely hear Merlin and Morgana behind her on the shore over the hum in her head.

"Alex!" Morgana shouted. Alex glanced back to find Morgana all but sliding down the hill towards her. "What are you doing? What happened?"

"I-" Alex stopped, unsure how to explain it. "I felt... heard something."

A splash in the water made them all turn and Alex heard Merlin gasp. The water rippled before them and Alex sucked in a sharp breath as she watched the small waves. It was so similar to Cyrridven and yet some instinct told her that it was not quite the same. She could remember the Old One with her bronze skin and dark hair turning on Chernobog and battling him to her death. Alex shivered at both the cold and the memory. That huge black form rising from the water and grabbing Cyrridven. She had fought back, but Cyrridven's real focus had been on throwing Cathanáil to her. Guilt hit Alex once more. Their ally had died giving her the Sword and she'd just handed it over to Arthur. She doubted that she'd ever forgive herself for that.

Water spun up into the air forming a water tunnel. Morgana grabbed her arm and pulled her back from the shore as silver magic appeared around her hands. Alex blinked in surprise. This was different from what she'd been expecting. The water tunnel shimmered with golden magic that was quickly swallowed by the churning water.

A figure burst from the water tunnel, half stumbling upon the shore and clutching a strange looking cauldron formed of ice in her hands. There was a slightly domed top over the opening and Alex blinked in surprise. Her eyes shifted up from the cauldron to the one carrying it and froze as the air rushed out of her chest.

It was Sif. She knew that face too well from her dream. The shining pale face and intense green eyes were older and sadder than they were in the memory, but it was her. Sif's long golden hair was styled in a long braid that hung over her shoulder and a dark green long coat fluttered around what was otherwise a very modern outfit of blue jeans, boots, and cream blouse. Alex was frozen in shock as she took in the Old One, her mind trying to connect the being in front of her to the memories.

"You're..." Sif gasped, staring at Alex with the same intensity only to shake her head. "I apologize." She cleared her throat and turned her eyes towards Merlin. "I'd greet you, Merlin, but this is of grave importance."

"Sif? What is that? Where did you find it?" Merlin questioned as he moved forward, walking right up to Sif and bending over to look at the ice cauldron. "It looks-"

"I was seeking other Old Ones who might help and found a trace of Cyrridven," Sif explained in a rush. "It led to a small cavern where I found this." She looked towards Alex and her expression turned slightly nervous. "I can only assume that she meant it for you."

Merlin nodded slowly and stepped closer to the cauldron while Alex stood on her toes and tried to peer over the rim. Wafting his hand over it, Merlin inhaled the scent of the potion with an odd expression crossing his face.

"That's the potion," he agreed. "It hasn't been used, but I'd say that it is complete." He frowned deeply. "Has been for a while."

"Is it still safe?" Morgana asked. She was eying the cauldron suspiciously.

"I think so," Merlin said slowly. He didn't sound confident. "It hasn't shifted to its poisonous state yet."

"The cauldron is made of ice," Sif offered, shivering a little. "It may have kept it safe."

Merlin nodded again and carefully ran a finger over the edge of the cauldron. "This isn't magical ice," he declared, frowning even deeper. "Why would she have-" He cut himself off and swallowed, shaking his head. "Maybe she knew." A sad sigh escaped Merlin and Alex dropped her eyes.

Hugging herself, Alex tried to stay still as guilt rolled through her. Cyrridven dying to save her had been bad enough before, but the idea that the Old One had known made it even worse. Merlin stepped back from Sif and glanced up the hill in the direction of his house. Then he looked back at Alex and Morgana.

"I'm not sure what Cyrridven had planned, but given what we are trying to do…" Alex could feel the weight of his gaze. "Alex… this potion intensifies the magical connection between a mage and the Iron Realm. Not for long, but it gave me a vision of the birth of your soul long ago. It may be the key to helping you."

"Is it safe?" Alex asked Morgana softly. She turned to the older mage who looked uncomfortable.

"I don't know," Morgana answered. "I've never used the potion myself."

Alex looked towards Sif. The Old One looked torn. Their eyes met and Alex's stomach twisted and fluttered. Horrified, Alex looked down at the cauldron and nodded.

"Okay," she said. The word surprised her, but she focused on the odd blooming certainty in her chest. "Cyrridven died for me. If… if she did know then she wouldn't have left something that could hurt me. I trust her… and Sif."

Both Merlin and Morgana looked nervous for a moment, but their expressions quickly became resigned. "We shouldn't do this here," Morgana said. She stepped forward as her hands began to glow silver and touched the bottom of the cauldron.

"Careful, Morgana," Merlin cautioned. "You mustn't allow your magic to interact with the potion. It is a very precise mixture."

"Yes, well, we can't have the potion dripping all over the shore either," Morgana snapped, giving Merlin a warning look. "Can we?"

"In the car," Merlin sighed.

He gestured to his SUV and Morgana nodded for Alex to go ahead. She hesitated for a moment but forced herself to look away from Sif and climb back up the shore towards Merlin's blue SUV. She got in the front seat while Sif and Morgana carefully climbed into the back. Sif asked Morgana a soft question about how safe cars were that almost made Alex laugh. Once this was over, she'd have to ask Sif about how long she'd been asleep and how much of the world she'd managed to see. Enough to update her clothes at least.

Merlin turned the SUV gently and took them back towards the house. Alex twisted her hands in her lap. Around her the magic relaxed, almost seeming satisfied with the turn of events which only confused her. There were times that magic seemed so lifeless like it really was nothing but energy and at other times it was as if an intelligence was driving it all.

They came to a stop back at Merlin's house before Alex could think about it too much. With wide eyes, Alex looked back at the cauldron being held by Sif and Morgana. Her heart clenched in anticipation. Alex stomach twisted as she climbed out of the SUV and hung back while the cauldron was rushed inside. Magic pulled on her again and Alex opened her fingers to release a few sparks. The pressure eased only a tiny bit and with a sigh, she directed the magic down to the hem of her jeans. Gray sparks spun around the bottom hem that was beginning to wear thin and a moment later the fabric looked good as new. Forcing herself to move, Alex was hit by a wave of dizziness that made her grip at the rail of Merlin's porch. She almost tripped over one of the gargoyles and looked down at it.

"The ones at Notre Dame are better," she muttered to it. Then she realized she was talking to a statue and hurried inside. She got inside just in time to see Merlin and Sif vanish into the kitchen.

"I have some jars," Merlin said. "Under the sink. Nothing special, but…" he trailed off for a moment. "Neither were the others." Merlin all but ran into the kitchen and Alex could hear cabinets opening.

"Let's hope it really is just a matter of getting the liquid contained quickly," Morgana muttered. Her green eyes were dark with worry and Alex shifted nervously as the older mage stepped over next to her. "You don't have to do this." Morgana reached up and caressed her cheek for a moment. "We can keep trying."

"This is the best chance," Alex replied. Her voice sounded a bit too weak, but she forced a smile. "I'll be alright. Merlin was after all and I'm the Iron Soul." She waved her hand towards the door. "And anyway, something pulled me towards Sif. I don't think there is really an option here."

Morgana shook her head. "You do have a choice, Alex. You don't have to do this if you don't want to." Morgana's green eyes cut into her with a sharp intense gaze. "We don't know how this will affect you. Who knows what it might make you see or expose you to."

The warning made Alex's stomach turn. She considered calling her mom and dad, but judging from the almost panicked sounds coming from the kitchen they didn't have much time. It made Alex wonder just where Cyrridven had been making the potion. Her eyes dropped to where Mjǫllnir was waiting on the coffee table.

"You just left it here?"

"We were more than a little concerned about you running off," Morgana replied dryly. "I feared that Arthur had managed to use the Iron Chain against you."

Alex shuddered at the suggestion, but it seemed to be what she needed to hear. Reaching out she gripped Mjǫllnir and sighed in relief as some of the built-up magic flowed into the Hammer. It started to glow and

Alex ignored the way Morgana's eyes widened. Without another word Alex walked into the kitchen

There were several jars waiting on the counter and Merlin was digging through another drawer. The cauldron was in the sink with a faint mist rising off of it. Spinning dramatically, Merlin held up a long glass stirring rod which earned him a strange look from Morgana though she stayed silent.

Sif's eyes met Alex's and she nodded quickly, not trusting herself to speak. Nodding in return, Sif turned and plucked the stirring rod from Merlin's hand. Both he and Morgana took a step forward, but Alex waved them back. She prayed they wouldn't protest or say anything. Alex was sure she'd throw up if someone tried to talk to her. In her chest the gathered magic was jumping around like an excited puppy and the air smelled like ozone. More magic was gathering and judging by the expression on Sif's face she could feel it as well.

Alex was silent as the stirring rod was dipped into the potion. Sif pulled it out slowly letting a few drops gather. Alex didn't have Nicki's memory for mythology, but she was pretty sure she remembered something about only the first few drops being magical. The rest was poison. Despite the urge to look at Merlin and Morgana, Alex kept her focus on Sif. It was hard to meet the Old One's gaze and Sif seemed just as uncertain as she was, but neither looked away. Alex awkwardly opened her mouth. Sif touched her head and tilted it back slightly, bringing the stirring rod to her lips. Alex gasped in shock when the sweet first drop hit her tongue. Her fingers tightened around Mjǫllnir as the magic ripped through her.

33

Realm of the Dark Elves

1 16 C.E. Sør-Trøndelag, Norway

If he survived this Thor was never going underground again. All around him, the rough tunnel was closing in and it was only Sif's hand on his arm that kept him calm. She said nothing despite the sweat breaking out on his forehead and merely stayed next to him. Everyone was as quiet as they could manage with Merlin and Frea in the lead. There was a distant sound of metal against stone and a hum in the air that felt unnatural. It was pressing against his skin and making his stomach turn.

The air tasted wrong against his tongue. It was too metallic and sharp with a hint of something organic that he couldn't name. Alien and uncomfortable smells were wafting up through the tunnel. He heard Morgana make a small sound that was a blend of alarm and recognition. Her speed increased and she hissed something at Merlin.

Overhead the rock rumbled and crashes ahead of them echoed up the tunnel. Everyone moved faster and Thor's heart was pounding as he eyed the roof. They entered an empty cavern with signs of discarded weapons and tools. None of it was familiar, but Thor thought it all looked ready to collapse. Up ahead the tunnel narrowed and it was a challenge for him to slip through. His shoulders banged against each side and ached, but he refused to let go of Mjǫllnir.

The tunnel opened into the cavern that was partially exposed to the outside where Frea's people had made their home. The village was in near ruins. Dark Elves were screaming and running towards them, waving weapons in the air and releasing long shrieks that made Thor shudder. Bringing up Mjǫllnir, he shifted to the side to give Sif room as she drew her sword. Then the Dark Elves reached them in a flurry of blades, talons, and screams.

Thor swung Mjǫllnir into the chest of the first Dark Elf sending it crashing back into another pair. Before the group could right itself, Thor pushed magic through the Hammer and released a bolt of lightning straight at them. It arced through the air and struck the first Dark Elf, transferring to the other two. They screamed and the first one turned to dust while the other two collapsed. A gold flare flashed through the air and struck another of them.

In the corner of his eye, Thor saw Sif's long braid spin in the air as she moved and he smiled. Another Dark Elf was nearing the downed injured one and he released another lightning bolt. They dissolved into dust and he barely dodged a set of long talons lashing out towards him. Thor swung Mjǫllnir and brought it sharply against another Dark Elf's chest. There were more of them coming and the sound of distant screaming.

Silver magic flashed in the darkness as a rain of small sparks showered down on a group of Dark Elves. They tried to run only to trip over each other. The bolts weren't enough to destroy them, but green magic from Merlin rolled past him and crashed over the Dark Elves. Their bodies began to turn to dust though a few crawled out of the way. Thor shoved Mjǫllnir forward and lightning lashed out to strike down two more Dark Elves.

His eyes searched the darkness. They'd never gotten a good estimate of how many there were. Morgana's light orb brightened, but the shadows between the stalactites and stalagmite seemed much darker than before. Frea moved forward, her face frantic with worry. Thor sped up his pace to stay close and noted gratefully that Sif was staying nearby. It didn't take Frea long to find the captives near one of the collapsing buildings.

Several of the Sídhe were bound to the walls in rough metal chains. Frea was at their side in an instant, tugging at the chains with her hands. Merlin and Morgana moved past them, orbs of magic at the ready for the next attack. Moving over to Frea, Thor tapped her shoulder and gestured her back. The Sídhe pulled tightly on their chains and closed their eyes, turning away as he brought Mjǫllnir down against their bindings. The chains fell away instantly, breaking open with a clatter. Links fell on the floor and Frea helped the first few to their feet. Thor moved to the next group and repeated the process, all the while keeping his eyes scanning the darkness.

"Take them back to the surface, Frea," Thor told her. His eyes traced over one of the younger Síd who looked terrified and was clutching at one of the women. "They shouldn't be down here. We don't know how the magic the Dark Elves are doing might affect you."

Frea looked ready to argue, but then she nodded to him. Thor tried to hide his nervousness as Frea waved for her warriors to join her. They were losing some of their help. Thor's stomach tightened nervously, but the taste of the alien magic in the air solidified his worry. He could hear something still echoing up from the next cavern. Sif was at his side and helped up a younger looking Síd. He watched them go over to Frea but didn't linger. A quick glance towards the roof sent a jolt of cold through his gut, but there was something off about the rock. It shimmered in the light of Morgana's orb in a strange way.

"Hurry," Merlin said. "We need to keep moving."

They followed the slope of the tunnel down into the cavern that the Dark Elves had been in last time. Every breath sent more and more shivers through Thor's body as the wrong taste in the air grew worse with every step. He found himself struggling between the urge to find the source and stop it and desire to run from it. A shriek from the darkness made him tense and he drummed his fingers on Mjǫllnir's handle as Sif took a step away from him.

Three Dark Elves rushed towards them. Merlin swung his staff which flashed a brilliant leaf green color and bolts of magic flew from it. The first two Dark Elves were blasted back and struck the far wall. Odin waved his hand sending a wave of gold magic at the last Dark Elf, sweeping it up in the gold sparks. It was crushed a moment later by the magic and turned to dust.

More came out of the darkness. Terrible high pitched shrieks and clicking sounds escaped them as they brought up their swords and axes. He sidestepped a clumsy axe swing and slammed Mjǫllnir down on the creature's back as it toppled forward. Magic flared off the Hammer and there was a crack just before the body vanished. Silver magic mixed with gold and green ahead of him as Sif and the others fought them back.

Thor kept moving. With a swing of Mjǫllnir, he destroyed two more Dark Elves and in the corner of his eye saw Sif stab another before releasing a blast of magic into its chest. It made him smile. Up ahead the slope evened out and they found themselves back at the mysterious tunnel that had been dug into the wall. Thor's heart beat raced and the energy in the air changed once again. Around him, the world seemed almost hazy, like looking through a column of heat. A glow of purple light illuminated the cavern, spilling out of a smaller tunnel and making the world seem all wrong. Thor's knees trembled. It was too much for his senses. Between being underground, the wrongness in the air, and the hazy world he feared that he'd collapse at any moment.

There were more Dark Elves here, standing guard over the tunnel and baring their teeth. Morgana moved first, sending a rippling wave of silver magic washing through the air as she, Merlin, and Odin's men charged down. Thor rushed to join them, reaching the first Dark Elves as the silver magic threw them all back. He slammed Mjǫllnir down on the nearest one and was moving before the lightning dissipated and the body finished vanishing. Dark Elves were ganging up on Odin, but Morgana sent a series of silver bolts into the crowd. Thor just hoped that she paid some attention to who their allies were.

His stomach turned once more and Thor stumbled, almost crashing into the blade of a Dark Elf. Catching himself on the side of the cave with his left hand he pushed magic through Mjǫllnir in a panic. Lightning flashed off the Hammer and exploded outward, knocking the Dark Elves back. The light in the tunnel was increasing and Thor grit his teeth as a high-pitched whine echoed in his skull. He pushed through the line, using Mjǫllnir to force some of the Dark Elves back. Panting for air, Thor smashed the Hammer into another guard and looked into the tunnel.

Several of the Dark Elves were ignoring them. Their hands were set tight against the rough stone walls with a soft violet glow surrounding them. Magic flowed across the stone like water, all being drawn to the wall at the far end of the tunnel. Violet, purple, and other shades blended together above the dark stone in a swirl of power that made the air hum. Thor's hairs were all on end and every instinct was screaming, crying, danger. The urge to run battled against the need to fight and he was frozen for a moment. Fight won out as one of the Dark Elves turned and noticed him.

It pulled its hands off the wall and charged without so much as a knife. Shock hit Thor first. Something was driving these beings, some mission or sense of purpose or maybe revenge that he couldn't understand. Instinct kicked in and he swung Mjǫllnir, catching the Dark Elf in the side. Another Dark Elf was knocked into his back, reminding him that he was ahead of the main battle line. Morgana shouted something and the weight on his back vanished.

Thor sent a lightning bolt at another Dark Elf who abandoned the wall and charged him. They were all looking between him and the wall as green and silver bolts blasted past them. Another two Dark Elves were destroyed without even leaving the wall, leaving only two more. Both of them snarled at him but did not leave the wall. Thor hesitated, confused by their decision and looked at the tunnel walls in alarm.

The swirl of magic across the stone was becoming clearer. He could see a large chamber made of cut white stone and filled with figures that were drawing back in horror. There were so many bright colors visible even in the low light and flashes of violet eyes as the figures ran away. Thor grit his teeth as the pitch of the whine changed, becoming higher and more painful. Musical voices echoed out of the swirl of magic, shouting with fear-filled voices. Something about them was familiar, like Frea's voice, and yet the alien quality set him further on edge.

He didn't move. The wrongness of it all rolled over him and pushed him to take another step forward. One of the Dark Elves left the wall, but before he could react Sif stabbed it through the chest. Her sword gleamed gold and the Dark Elf shrieked as it began to turn to dust. The other moved to attack her, spurring Thor into action and he swung Mjǫllnir at the Dark Elf's head.

They were all gone, but the wall continued to shimmer and the vision on the tunnel wall did not vanish. Sif walked towards it, her face slack with shock. Beyond the veil of magic, a couple of the figures stepped forward curiously. Then Sif shook her head and lashed forward with her sword. There was a clang as the metal struck the back of the tunnel and crashed against the stone. Sif stumbled back, gaping between her sword and the vision. Thor caught her with his left arm and shifted her protectively behind him. More Sídhe were appearing, these ones in elegant golden armor. They had long horns that curved up from their foreheads unlike Frea and her people.

Thor couldn't help but stare. This was another world. He was seeing into another world. Magic shimmered over the image, forming a perfect veil that he could have reached out and drawn back. Something tugged at his senses, it was familiar and yet he couldn't name it. The magic in his chest was flowing through his limbs faster and stronger than he'd ever felt before.

"The worlds are touching!" Merlin shouted with alarm in his voice. "We have to stop them!"

Merlin's words echoed through Thor's head. They were correct, but he was at a loss. Then his own magic pulsed in warning, pulling sharply on the ground below as more tried to gather. Kneeling down, Thor placed his left hand on the stone floor. There was a soft pulse of magic that reached for him, soothing him, and countering the harsh whine in the air. Thor held out his Hammer, pushing all of his magic into the metal. His skin was raw and his legs trembled. More and more magic rose from the ground into his hand and traveled through him to the Hammer. Breathing was a struggle; it was like being stuck in that small cave all over again.

But he forced himself to move, shifting to his feet and jumping forward. The magic leapt through his limbs, giving him a boost of speed and power. Smashing Mjǫllnir into the wall, Thor gasped as light exploded out from the impact point. The veil of magic rippled and shifted beneath the force of the blow. His bright blue magic spread over the veil. The hum in the air became a high-pitched whistle. Thor grit his teeth, fighting to ignore the pain in his spine and head that the sound generated. A roar of frustration escaped him and he pushed more magic forward. Then the view of Sídhean began to fade. There was shouting and screaming around him and beyond the veil.

Magic pushed back against him making Thor's stomach turn. It wasn't his magic. It was all wrong. Sídhean his mind provided as nausea hit him. He sank to his knees and tightened his whole pained body. His limbs were too heavy. His chest was aching, burning and raw. There were a few flickers of magic remaining, but every spark hurt. Mjǫllnir slipped from his fingertips and hit the ground with a metallic thud. Overhead the cavern rumbled. Adrenaline jolted through him, pulling him harshly out of the haze.

"Thor!" Someone was shouting his name.

Thor tried to stand, but even the adrenaline wasn't enough. The cavern roof trembled above him and his eyes widened. Small hands grabbed his arms and started hoisting him up. Thor blinked in surprise when he looked down and found Sif throwing his arm over her shoulder. Mjǫllnir gleamed in the dying light as the magic dissipated and Thor managed a small grunt. Sif shifted them just enough to grab it herself. She pulled him out of the tunnel where they found Merlin and Morgana striking down one last Dark Elf.

Behind them, the cave rumbled. Already the air was clearing, allowing Thor to become even more aware that he was in a collapsing cave. Rocks were falling around them as the ground shook. Sif kept a tight grip on him, pulling him along as they joined the others in a dash up the tunnels.

Thor's eyes landed on the Dvergrs who despite their short stature were making the best time of any of them.

As long as it had taken them to come down, it felt like they reached the surface in moments. Thor gasped for the fresh air, shivering as the winter chill settled over him. Sif led him away from the opening and he risked a look back at the mountain. It looked intact and the rumbling had stopped. A sigh of relief escaped him. With any luck, the Dark Elf area was collapsed, but neither his nor Frea's village would be at risk of rockslides.

"Don't do that again," Sif said. There was a hard promise to her voice that really should have worried him, but he was too relieved to find it anything but adorable. He smiled and she scowled at him. "I mean it, Thor."

"I'll do my best, Sif."

"Thor, I wasn't sure what you were doing. There was this glow around you and I thought-" she stopped herself and released his arm, letting him stand up. "Never mind. It's over now I suppose."

"Would it be alright if I kissed you now?" Thor asked.

Sif looked at him sharply. Her eyes were wide with surprise, but it quickly turned to amusement. There was still a spark of sadness in them for what he knew would be their eventual end, but it was muted. He waited as hope grew in his chest that maybe she'd agree it would still be worth it. Then Sif nodded with a small smile.

Grinning, Thor leaned down to quickly press his lips to hers. He'd meant for it to be a quick kiss, but Sif's hands came up and gripped his face as she pressed her body against his. Fumbling for a moment, he slipped Mjǫllnir back in his belt and wrapped his arms around her. The kiss was soft and over too soon, though Sif didn't pull away from him.

Thor closed his eyes and just breathed, enjoying the little bubble of peace he found himself in.

The sound of someone approaching finally forced him to look up. Odin was a few feet from them with a soft little smile on his dirty face. "Well, I suppose I should welcome you to the family," Odin said. The Old One fixed his good eye on Thor and would have looked intimidating if not for the slight smile on his face. "You did well, lad."

Thor nodded, keeping an arm around Sif as she leaned her head against his shoulder. He was grateful that no one was protesting. He was grateful that no one was pointing out that he was a mortal and Sif was an Old One. Odin's smile was a bit forced and Baldr was frowning a little, but they both backed away to give them space.

"What happens now?" Frea asked. She nervously stepped over to join them and eyed the tunnel. "I'm not sure about leaving all those tunnels empty. What if there are still Dark Elves down there?"

"We'll check the tunnels out," Brokkr offered. He stepped towards the tunnel and looked down it. "We're happier underground, your world is too bright and open."

"I suppose the Dvergrs living in the tunnels wouldn't be a problem," Merlin agreed slowly. He looked thoughtful and turned his eyes towards the horizon. It was too dark to see them, but Thor knew Merlin was looking at the nearby snowcapped mountains. "There are still those new creatures to contend with."

"We'll keep an eye out for them," Thor promised. He nodded and looked up into the night sky. It was cold, but the stars were clear and the magical form stretching into the sky was gone. "Do you think they'll be any other openings?"

"There shouldn't be," Merlin answered. "That was the result of the Dark Elves trying to reach Sídhean. I somewhat wish we'd had a chance to learn how they did it."

Morgana gave Merlin a dark look that clearly said she was fine with their destruction. "That isn't something we need to know."

Thor silently agreed with Morgana. There were plenty of beings from other worlds here now as it was. Merlin turned to look at him. The old mage had a thoughtful expression that made Thor feel nervous.

"And what of you, Thor? What do you plan to do now?" His eyes shifted to Sif who was still tight against him.

"With all the other world beings here, someone needs to keep the peace," Thor replied. He met Merlin's gaze straight on. "It isn't their fault they're here, but I won't let them cause harm to the Iron Realm."

He'd been sure that Merlin or Morgana would argue, would try to dissuade him, or say something about Sif. Instead, Morgana simply shook her head and sighed softly. Merlin nodded and stepped away from him, going across the snow to speak with Odin. Shifting slightly, he kissed Sif's forehead and let her presence wash over him. Maybe he couldn't stay with her forever, but then again maybe they'd get other chances in other lives. Sif sighed a little and he knew their conversations and worries weren't over yet, but he couldn't bother with that as a warm happy feeling settled in his chest. Thor rested his chin on the top of her head and closed his eyes. The sounds and smells of the Iron Realm surrounded him, soothing the last of his fears and leaving him satisfied.

34

Iron Touched

The potion seeped into her tongue sending some shivers down Alex's throat. Her whole body and tensed and braced itself. A dozen questions about what was going to happen that she should have asked before ran through her head. Alex glanced to the side and saw Merlin watching her. He didn't look worried exactly, just on edge and curious. Nothing happened at first and she was about to ask if something went wrong, but then a wave of dizziness struck her. The world went a bit fuzzy and the colors started to brighten, overwhelming all the small details. Alex wavered, tightening her grip around Mjǫllnir as she tried to find something to ground her. It was worse than that time at Kayla's party in high school. She tried to say something, but her mouth wouldn't mov
e.

Panic clawed at Alex. She couldn't see straight. Maybe the potion was too old and had expired. Maybe it was all poison now. Before that thought could send Alex fully into panic mode a rush of magic swept through her. It righted the dizziness and filled her chest with energy. It pulsed in time with her heart and Alex regained a little control. She looked around.

Sif's human appearance was completely gone. In her place was a column of vibrating golden energy hovering off the floor. Alex was surprised, but it didn't linger and her eyes shifted to Merlin and Morgana. They still looked human, but a glow of green surrounded and filled Merlin while a glow of silver radiated from Morgana's chest. A small sound at the side of the room that was far too loud made her spin sharply. A tiny, dark purple shape was moving across the counter. There was a faint red and gray mixed glow around it in a swirl of energy, covering the form protectively like a shield. Timothy her mind provided.

The taste of the potion sank further into her tongue and her surroundings faded further with the four forms vanishing. She breathed out, almost sighing as the world drifted around her. Images of places trickled past like water as the resonance of the magic around her changed. It grew stronger and thicker. Alex didn't fight it. She could feel the magic churning and coming to life. Something was summoning it and calling it even if it wasn't her. There wasn't anything she could do and her fears that she'd been poisoned eased. A strange calm settled over her.

There were faces again. The same ones she'd seen at Stonehenge and in the Paris tunnels. Alex recognized a few: Arto's was first and his gaze locked with hers. Then more came, flashing past her in a line of the people she'd once been. Names, voices, and images of places washed past her like a slideshow moving too quickly. Mjǫllnir sparked against her palm and Alex's eyes narrowed on a tall figure with long bleached blond hair. She might have called Thor's name, but then he was gone.

More lines of magic were appearing. Most were black, stretching across the world, but Alex was surrounded by a red glow that pushed the black threads away. In the distance were more patches of red. The Blood Protection spells, she distantly realized. It didn't matter, not really. She was floating on a cloud. More threads of magic appeared in different colors. There were silver and green that she thought might have been lingering traces from Merlin and Morgana. Faint red, yellow, and blue nearby for Aiden, Bran and Nicki's last spells. There were more in the distance in even fainter colors, yet she could feel them.

Her magic spread further and further. Alex's eyes slipped shut, they had no use here. She shivered as her awareness extended to more points of magic, some familiar and some not. There were more Old Ones like Sif, some of them much darker colors that left her uneasy. More and more flickers of magic appeared and brushed past her, a slight introduction that Alex knew she wouldn't remember. She was moving or at least it seemed like she was. The vision blurry, running down in soft colors like rains around her with another scene slowly taking its place. All Alex could do was wait.

She was underground. The heavy smell of dirt, metal, life, and decay hit her all at once. It wasn't a Sídhe tunnel though, the feel of it was too different. All around her was a steady thrum of magic, familiar magic, that caressed her with soft warm brushes against her skin. Like a steady heartbeat, it surrounded her, soothing her. Alex turned and tried to see in the darkness that surrounded her. There was only a soft glow from Mjǫllnir allowing her to see the smooth stone walls of the cave, but a moment later the Iron Hammer went dark.

Alex was only in blackness for a moment. Something bright orange erupted in front of her, magic spinning together into an orb that looked like a hunk of red-hot metal. Heat rolled off of it and filled the whole cavern. But then the surface of the orb hardened. A dark gray color like her own magic overtook the orb giving it a metallic shine. There was silence around her. Alex reached out slowly with her left hand, barely noticing as sparks of magic glittered around her fingertips. Her hand brushed across the surface of the orb only for Alex to pull it back in alarm as a sharp brutal heat hit her palm. Pain flashed across her skin and Alex looked down in apprehension at red hot skin.

Red light filled the cavern, coming from the orb as the metallic shell cracked. In a shimmer of heat, it returned to the prior red-hot state. Alex stared at the orb in confusion, her unburnt fingers tightening around Mjǫllnir as her thoughts about the Iron Chain tried to push forward through the haze. There was push back against her as the magic pressed her forward. A sharp metallic clanging echoed in the chamber around her and drew her eyes back to the molten orb as a sharp pang reverberated through her own chest.

Alex gasped. There was a dent in the orb. She hadn't seen a hammer, but something had struck it. The hot metal flowed back into place a little, but another clang echoed around her and Alex saw the hot metal bend. It was cooling, turning darker once more even as the new shape held. Heat flashed through the chamber and Alex could see the flickering light of flames around her as the orb was reheated. Another blow struck it a moment later followed by another. Then it cooled.

The cycle continued as the orb was lengthened. It was turned and twisted in the air by an unseen hand and Alex caught herself reaching towards it twice more. The ground rumbled, almost throwing her off balance. A section of the rocky floor rose to create a long pedestal that was almost an anvil. The long hunk of metal was lowered to it. Rapid rings of metal being struck surrounded Alex as the shape was refined. Parts of it were narrowed and the roughly rectangular shape was slowly being beaten into a new one.

Time lost meaning to Alex. Mjǫllnir hummed softly in her hand and the burn in her free hand eased. Her eyes scanned the shape with each new strike and finally, she realized what it was. A human was being formed with a head, neck, torso, arms, and legs all taking shape. Spurred on, Alex stepped closer and leaned forward to examine it. Magic was shimmering across the surface, smoothing out the rough work of the unseen hammer and smith.

The shape was imperfect with only a hint of hands and no fingers or toes, but now that she saw it Alex had no doubt that would be the finished product. A memory tugged at her. Something she was supposed to be doing, supposed to be worrying about. Instead, she found herself reaching her left hand out again and cautiously touching the metallic form. The metal shimmered beneath her fingertips with her own gray magic radiated out across the form. It had no distinguishing male or female features. Instead, it was rough, but as her magic seeped into the metal and another ring of the hammer sounded the features of the face began to glow. Alex's eyes jumped to the face and she moved closer. But as the nose shrunk and the jaw shifted her eyes widened

Taking a step back, Alex almost dropped Mjǫllnir. The features kept shifting into place, but Alex knew the face she was seeing. It was her own. Shaking her head, Alex trembled and pushed at her magic, a sudden panic gripping her. But her magic swirled back to her, surrounding her in a wash of dark gray sparks. Closing her eyes, Alex chanted for the Iron Chain. That was what she was needed to do. She didn't need to see this. Alex wasn't even sure why she was seeing it.

"The Iron Chain." Alex's words echoed in the chamber. Taking a step back she repeated them once more. The magic began to loosen around her and her mind began to clear. "I need to find the Iron Chain." Tightening her grip on Mjǫllnir, Alex brought it up to her chest and hugged the ancient Hammer as if it were her stuffed dog Galahad. "I just need to find the Iron Chain. Please."

Closing her eyes, Alex fought back the shivers beginning to overtake her. There was a knot forming in her chest, a twisted mix of fear, anger, awe, and plain overwhelmed. Faces flashed in front of her again, threatening to sweep her back into the vision. Tugs at her magic made her whimper and clutch the Hammer tighter. Her mind jolted with a sudden headache so strong that she forced her eyes open, certain that something had hit her. The metallic form in front of her was glowing brightly. Alex took another step back.

"The Iron Chain," she said.

Alex pushed and pulled at her magic, trying to find some way to make it do what she wanted, but the pressure of the more wild magic around her made it impossible. While it felt a lot like her own magic it wasn't under her control. The pressure on her head was growing. Small gray spots danced over her vision and the faces started appearing again. There were more places too and things and more people. Strange emotions fired through her brain in a jumble she couldn't hope to understand. Slamming her eyes shut, Alex moved further back. She pulled on the magic around her, calling it to her and trying to take control of it. This was too much. Her head was pounding.

"I need the Iron Chain!" she screamed. The words echoed and the resonance of the magic changed all at once.

Collapsing around her, the magic rushed across her skin and left goosebumps in its wake. The temperature around her shifted and Alex was hit with a wave of vertigo. She inhaled sharply, the air tasted different and there were soft muted sounds around her. The images were slowing down now and the ache in her head wasn't so bad.

Merlin hadn't told her about this. He hadn't prepared her. Alex hoped that he hadn't been trying to mislead her. Maybe it was different for her because she was the Iron Soul. Maybe magic was just trying to show her too much at once. The rationalization helped and she slowly opened her eyes only to gasp softly. She was in a modern room. It looked a bit like a hotel living room with a sofa and two armchairs near a television. But most importantly was a long wooden box on the coffee table that was open. The Iron Chain was right in front of her on a cushion of dark purple.

Alex stared at it in shock, almost dropping Mjǫllnir as her hands fell to her side. After the cavern, she'd almost expected to... wake up maybe back in Merlin's kitchen. Confusion over what was happening took over for a moment, but then she noticed the black shimmer of magic around the Iron Chain and remembered why she'd wanted to find it. Alex reached towards the heavy looking chain, remembering the visions of it binding captive men and women as slaves in the hold of a ship. In another life, she'd created the thing to bend others to her-his will. As her fingers brushed over it, the Iron Chain's magic flared to life, sending out a wave of magic that hit her in the chest.

More faces flashed before her. These ones had dark skin, were crying and were screaming, but then their eyes turned lifeless. Snapping back to reality, Alex looked down at the Iron Chain. Bile pushed up into her mouth as she glared at the thing. Mjǫllnir hummed in her hand as the black lines spread out around her, threatening to tangle her in their grasp. The Iron Chain whined, more ripples of power pulsing out and traveling along the black strands. Raising her hand, Alex brought Mjǫllnir over her head. The world solidified for a moment, the magic tightening in her chest; holding her here. Mjǫllnir's magic pulled at her and Alex answered, giving the Hammer more of her own magic. It glowed overhead and she brought it down. A shout escaped her, echoing around her just before a sharp metal clang deafened her.

The Iron Chain gleamed as the black magic thickened. It was fighting back. Alex pushed more magic, pulled on everything around her. The black threads began to snap. Black whiffs of magic sailed over her, turning gray and flowing into Mjǫllnir. Alex raised the Hammer again, watching as the magic shimmering across the Chain flickered. Black magic spun around her as more threads faltered, seeping into the Hammer as she reclaimed all of it. Her chest was hot, her limbs quivered, but she slammed Mjǫllnir down once more.

Another deafening metallic ring surrounded her. The black magic exploded outward, striking Alex in the chest, but the Iron Realm's magic kept her in place. Below Mjǫllnir, the Iron Chain was beginning to shatter. Lines of bright gray were breaking across the black surface. The link that Mjǫllnir had struck suddenly burst apart and the black magic running across the surface of the Chain vanished. Around her, the remaining black threads snapped and the black magic dissipated.

Magic shuddered around Alex and she stayed perfectly still. The hum in the air shifted and she lifted Mjǫllnir away from the Chain. There was still magic running beneath the surface of the metal, but the color had lightened from pitch black to a softer gray. Rather like the color of her own magic, bur fading quickly. Distantly she heard shouting and a door being slammed. Alex wasn't sure if this was real or not, but she reached out with her left hand and grabbed the two lengths of the Iron Chain. A sharp jolt traveled up her arm, making the hazy world around her shudder.

The magic closed in around her and the cocoon of energy resettled as she hoisted the Chain off of the table. Those distant sounds were coming closer and Alex exhaled in relief as the weight of the Iron Chain seemed to fade away even though she was still carrying it. Magic swept around her and the disorientation was back. The burn and ache in her chest were getting worse and the world was blurry, like a running watercolor painting. She looked around, but could barely see anything except vague colored shapes around her. There was a soft rocking feeling that told her she was in a car.

"Do you think Alex is going to be okay?" her dad asked. Alex straightened up in surprise at the voice. She tried to speak, but nothing came out.

Around her, the magic thrummed so loudly that Alex was amazed her parents didn't hear it. Then it eased and the world came more and more into focus. Her father was driving their SUV down a familiar Spokane street with her mom in the passenger seat. They were dressed nicely and Alex wondered if they had some sort of function or if it was just date night. With a slight smile, she took in her mom's profile.

"I'm not sure," her mom replied. Worry filled her face and Alex opened her mouth to reassure her, but once again nothing came out. She pulled at her magic, wanting some way to interact with them, but it was sluggish and tight. Like it was caught on something. "She sounded tired when I talked to her, but I'm hopeful everything will be alright."

"Sometimes I wake up and tell myself that it must have just been a dream." Her dad shook his head and took a hand off the steering wheel to quickly push his glasses up the bridge of his nose. "It all seems so crazy."

"I know. It messes with the world view."

"I'm a reporter who knows magic is real, but for the safety of my daughter I can't break the story."

"Yes well, one of Alex's fellow mages is studying physics. He's sitting on a Nobel Prize discovery and can't do anything with it."

Her dad chuckled and smiled at her mom. "It does help knowing that she's not alone. I just wish we could do more."

"I know." Her mom sighed and shook her head. "I feel helpless. I'm her mom and there's nothing I can do."

"I know we said no, but maybe we should look at moving again."

"I'm tempted," her mom agreed. "Very tempted, but I'm not sure that would actually make things easier for Alex. There's a lot to be said for her being able to return to her childhood home away from Ravenslake. If we moved there, she wouldn't have that."

"But she'd have us there." Her dad's hands tightened around the steering wheel. "She comes home less and less. I'm not even sure if she'll be home this summer. Kind of invalidates that point if she never comes to visit."

"I don't know." Her mom smiled at her dad, she looked tired. "When school gets out, we'll talk to Alex about it. Ravenslake isn't an ideal place for us. I mean I could find work I'm sure, but it would be harder for you."

"Maybe, but maybe not. I've worked so much in interviews, writing, and social media that I could probably find something in marketing."

Alex's chest tightened and loosened all at once. There were tears gathering in her eyes. She felt a bit silly, but it had never sunk in how much her parents probably worried about her. Opening her mouth, she tried to say something and reached for her mother. But her hand passed through the chair like she was a ghost.

A sigh escaped her, but she smiled a little. The pressure of the magic was easing and Alex whispered a soft thank you to it for letting her see them. She let the lull of their voices wash over her as the conversation turned to work and Ed's law school progress. Then there was another voice. It was distant, but Alex's eyes widened. The familiar voice of Arthur rang in her ears.

"Make sure that you hit them in the front. I want them both dead."

Looking around frantically, Alex tried to find the source of the voice. It echoed around her, but there was no sign of Arthur. Then in the corner of her eye, she saw a large shape coming down the side street. It was moving too fast and she tried to shout a warning. Her mom gasped as a large truck came plowing through the stop light. Alex screamed once more, but the truck collided with the passenger side. Metal cracked and crumbled in a terrible shattering sound. The magic in her gut flared. There was a sharp tug in her stomach right before everything went dark.

Grief. There was grief as the feel of two people faded away, snuffed out and she was left in the dark. The grief was sharp and overwhelming and yet already fading. More faces. Landscapes swept past them again. The ache in their head returned worse than ever. Their skin was too tight. It was tearing, stretching, and tearing again as it became too small. An iron figure appeared with a shifting face that kept changing. Magic pressed in tightly, surrounding and suffocating. They were dying again. No, it was too soon to die again. Too much danger, no time for rebirth. They had to keep going. Fighting back against the crushing weight, they started to breathe again and forced open their eyes.

35

Vacant

The vision faded away slowly. Their eyes opened and they looked up at a plain white ceiling. The smell of the room was familiar and they had no sense of danger. Inhaling slowly, they tried to pull together the thoughts and emotions of the last few moments. The vision had been strange and there was a churn of pride, fear, excitement, worry, and grief in their chest, but no way to even begin sorting it all out. Soft whispers filled their head, dozens of voices in different languages and yet all understood.

They shifted slowly, blinking as the memory of the truck bearing down on the car pushed its way to the front of their brain. Closing their eyes, there was a ripple of grief. It drown out all the other emotions for a moment. There were multiple shivers of pain, shared and spread amongst the whole. A tear gathered beneath their eyelids and slipped out a moment later. As it ran down their cheek the magic began to finally recede like the tide going out. The voices began to fade until there was only one.

Alex took a shuddering breath. The sense of the others eased and retreated. She was alone. She was just her again. It was both reassuring and terrifying. Yet part of her still felt a lingering echo of the others filling her head. An ocean of unfamiliar and familiar whispers churned, drowning out everything. She was stronger and in a weird way heavier. It was odd and Alex had no context for it.

Her fingers twitched and brushed against something warm and solid. Shifting her hand, Alex exhaled as her fingers wrapped around the handle of Mjǫllnir. She noted the weight of the comforter across her chest and arms and shifted a little, letting the blankets adjust to her new position. Alex wanted to believe it was a just a strange dream, but something in her chest settled and told her it wasn't. Turning her head slightly she looked towards the window, noting that it was dark outside.

"Alex is awake," a soft voice called from her other side. It was familiar, but she couldn't place it. "Welcome back."

Alex turned her head to look at the nightstand. Timothy was standing on the top of the night table, still dressed in his mended doll clothes and shifting uneasily at her gaze. The Brownie offered her a small smile that didn't reach his eyes. Something about the dark creature inspired an odd rush of different emotions. He was worried and Alex focused on that fact, trying to push aside the strange response she'd had to the sight of him.

She tugged on her magic, letting it flow through her and focused on the Brownie. A small aura of barely there purple magic appeared around him mixed with a fuzzy impression of gray magic, but there was no sign of any black magic trying to reach for him. Alex said nothing and just stared at the small creature. She wanted to smile and say something, but her brain was as far as the desire went. Her muscles were all limp and everything was muted.

Sitting up slowly, Alex's eyes dropped to the green comforter spread across her. The green color looked sharper than before and much more vivid. A soft glow from Mjǫllnir was barely visible beneath the blankets.

Alex pulled it out and set the Hammer on her lap before releasing it. Her fingers ached, but she slowly traced them over the surface of the blanket. Tingles traveled up her fingers and sent a rush of goosebumps up her arm. Yet something still felt muted and wrong. The image of the truck flashed through her head. She saw her mom smiling and her dad laughing from the last visit home. Her eyes teared up again, but there just wasn't... something was missing.

"Alex." She looked up to find Morgana in the doorway. The other mage's eyes were dark with worry even as a sigh of relief escaped her. "You're alright."

Morgana sat on the edge of the bed and reached over to take her hand. The skin-on-skin contact was strange, but Alex kept herself from pulling away. Morgana's hand was warm and her fingers comforting as they wrapped around hers. Alex's eyes settled on Morgana and she waited in silence as the woman collected herself. Morgana's long dark hair was in a braid over her shoulder, revealing her pale features and pained green eyes. Alex watched as Morgana took a deep breath, bracing herself for something and tried to speak, but no words came out.

Footfalls in her doorway drew Alex's attention away from Morgana. Merlin stopped at the threshold of the room, looking every bit as tired and worried as Morgana. He met her eyes for a moment before dropping his brown eyes away from her. He walked into the room and sat on the bed opposite from Morgana. Following Morgana's lead, he reached over and placed his hand over theirs for a moment, squeezing gently. Then he pulled his hand away and set it on his lap, clearly at a loss. Alex waited for them to say something.

"Alex," Merlin forced out in a weak voice. "There are things you need..." He trailed off and shook his head. "You were successful in breaking the power of the Iron Chain. We've been contacted by two groups of

Sídhe. They described it as a tether being cut so you were successful on that front. Now I can't say for certain that it is permanent-"

"It is," Alex interrupted. "I targeted the Iron Chain itself with the Iron Hammer. I felt the magic in it destroyed." She frowned as her mind tried to unravel the tangle of thoughts and memories. The Iron Chain had been sitting in a box and she'd smashed it with Mjǫllnir. "I thought I was there... I picked up the pieces."

"You never left here, Alex," Morgana told her softly. "We were in the kitchen when you took the potion. You moved around a little, but then you just collapsed." Morgana's hand tightened around hers. "We brought you in here right after that. Timothy's been watching over you."

Nodding, Alex dropped her eyes to her left hand, still hidden beneath the blankets. She shifted her fingers and brushed something heavy and cold. There was a lump next to Morgana that somehow the other mage hadn't noticed. Her fingers wrapped around the thick links. Magic brushed over her fingers and Alex held back a shiver. Automatically she reached for it and began to pull it into her chest letting the energy gather. With a soft grunt, she pulled out the Chain, barely noticing the look of shock on Morgana's face or Merlin's gasp of surprise.

The Chain seemed too short. Alex remembered how long it had been when it connected to the other chains in the hold of the slave ship. Yet the main chain that had been infused with magic was only about three feet long and while heavy and sturdy wasn't all that awe-inspiring. Alex draped the first piece that was just over a foot long over her lap next to Mjǫllnir before dragging out the second half.

"I broke the Iron Chain," Alex said. There was nothing in her voice. No excitement, no pride or relief. She didn't feel anything though she knew that she probably should. Raising her eyes to Morgana's she watched the green eyes flicker with worry and uncertainty for a moment. "Mom and Dad are dead, aren't they?"

It wasn't really a question. She knew it. There was a cold weight in her gut. It might crack or burst at any moment. Morgana's eyes widened and the older mage swallowed thickly. Alex just looked out towards the window. Deep in her chest, something hurt, a tight twisting, but it was small. There was too much else. It was just too small. She blinked, wondering why she was so calm. That wasn't normal, right? She wasn't sure now.

"I already know," Alex said. She exhaled, the sound loud in the silent room. "Did my brothers call while I was asleep?"

Merlin and Morgana exchanged surprised looks but remained silent. There was worry, almost panic, and fear in their eyes. Morgana looked the worse of the pair, almost like she might start crying for her sake. Alex wasn't sure, but her mind nagged her that she wasn't reacting properly. Alex lay back against the pillow and looked up at the ceiling. She followed a small crack with her eyes as she listened to them shift on the bed.

"You're probably exhausted," Merlin said carefully. "It's been a long time since I used the potion, but it was... an experience."

"I'm not tired," Alex answered automatically. "I'm fine."

"Alex," Morgana said softly as she squeezed her hand. "Yes, your parents-"

"Morgana," Merlin hissed.

"She already knows," Morgana whispered. There was a pained sound from Morgana and Alex almost looked at her. "There was an accident in Spokane. Your parents were killed. Your brother Matthew is on his way back to the city to look after Edward."

"It wasn't an accident," Alex said, still keeping her eyes on the ceiling. "They were killed. Arthur arranged it."

"How do-" Merlin gasped only to cut himself off.

"I saw it," Alex answered without any hint of emotion. She almost frowned at herself. Her parents were dead, gone, and destroyed because of their connection to her. It was Arthur lashing out at her and the other mages and yet she just... "I'm okay," she told them.

"I doubt that," Merlin said. Alex looked at him. There was a dark expression on his face, almost thunderous. He looked down at the remains of the Iron Chain. "Alex, you're not alright. You loved your parents, don't you care?"

The words hit her in that small twisted spot. For a moment it was hard to breathe. Suddenly she did hurt a little, but the feeling was swallowed up in the ocean of everything else. Still, images of her parents' faces and a memory of them all laughing together at something sprang forth. She did feel something and her eyes prickled a little. Licking her lips, Alex tried to consider it. Merlin said this wasn't right and she trusted him, but...

"I'm not sure," she finally said. "I feel something, I do and I'm a little sad."

"A little sad!" Morgana's grip on her hand tightened. "Alex, what happened?"

"Indeed, the potion must have given you some sort of vision." Merlin made a small noise and Alex heard the Iron Chain being moved. "And you were able to reach and destroy the Iron Chain." Merlin hummed in thought and Alex could hear the soft clink of the links being shifted against each other. "Remarkable."

"But you never moved," Morgana said. "So how in the world could you have moved the item here without a water tunnel?"

"No water tunnel," Timothy said quickly.

Alex just kept looking at the ceiling crack. It reminded her of something, a river somewhere maybe. Strange thought, but it made her smile a little.

"Alex?" Merlin called. "What else happened?"

Frowning, Alex tried to remember all of it. There'd been so much going on, but she slowly found the words. "I was in a cavern underground and there was this body being made. There was magic being smithed like it was metal, but there was no one there but me."

"Ah, I saw that same thing long ago." Merlin's tone was a bit warmer now, but there was still an undercurrent of worry.

"It had a bunch of faces... or at least I saw a bunch of faces like Arto and Gottfried. Then it turned into my face," Alex explained. "It was a bit overwhelming so I kept asking to see the Iron Chain. Then I was in a room with it. I broke it and picked it up. Not sure how it got here, but Mjǫllnir was able to break it." Alex tapped the Hammer thoughtfully. "Then I was with my parents..." There was a twist in her chest again that she pushed past. "I heard Arthur's order. The driver was about to hit the car when I woke up. What happened to the driver?"

"He died an hour ago in the hospital," Merlin answered. Morgana made an irritated noise. "Your parents died almost immediately; they didn't suffer."

The pang returned, but once more it was swallowed up. Morgana's grip on her hand tightened and Alex was worried that she'd keep trying to talk about it. However, the professors stayed quiet and Alex was sure they were having one of their silent conversations. Already her mind was trying to process what would happen now.

Matthew was the oldest so he'd probably take custody of Eddy. It wouldn't be too hard for him to transfer to a Spokane law school so that Eddy could stay in the same high school. She knew her parents had life insurance so they'd be able to pay off the mortgage and pay for college. Her parents had mentioned offhandedly once that information on their plots was in the family safe, but Alex had the strong desire to make sure they were cremated. It made her think of Arto's bones and Bran's skull and something lingering rather than moving on. There was a shift in the emotions in her chest. Alex closed her eyes and tried to pin down something in the mess.

There was too much and instead, she turned her attention on the building magic in her chest. It was warm and reassuring, but beginning to twist too much. Alex ignored Merlin and Morgana for a moment, exhaling slowly and pushing the magic out. She kept her eyes closed and focused on feeling the magic seep out. Around her, it created a thin layer of mist letting Alex feel the other points of magic. While not as strong as it had been with the potion, Alex was very aware of the glowing presences of Merlin and Morgana. Like a spider web, it slowly spread out and let her become aware of things beyond the room.

She could feel the imprint of Merlin's workshop. There were tiny flickering points of magic where they'd poured magic into iron items. Beyond the house in the hills, she could feel the iron gate. It hummed in response and she almost smiled. Further away were more glowing presences and her muscles relaxed in relief. The others were back in the United States, maybe Portland. Small ripples of magic met hers even as it became harder and harder to see. Then the magical connection snapped and Alex gasped softly at the twinge in her chest.

"Sif's gone," Alex murmured, suddenly aware that she hadn't sensed the Old One.

"She wants to check on some of the other Old Ones," Merlin told her. There was a look of surprise and curiosity on his face, but he didn't ask how she knew that. "She'll be in touch. Sif seems to have decided to aid us."

Nodding, Alex opened her eyes and looked between the two older mages. Worry was still etched on their features. Alex knew that she wasn't reacting like they expected, but she just… couldn't. The knot in her chest pulsed a bit at the thought, but the pressure of everything else around it dulled the pain. A tiny part of Alex was a bit worried, but for now, she accepted the soothing presence that kept the ache at bay.

"Alex." Morgana shifted closer to her, pushing aside the Iron Chain and wrapping her arms around Alex. The hug was a bit awkward and Alex couldn't help but tense up, suddenly uncertain. "When you're ready and everything hits you, just remember that I'm here."

"I know, Morgana," Alex said. She relaxed into the hug and laid her head against Morgana's shoulder. "You've always been a good sister." Morgana tensed at her words, but Alex didn't notice. Instead, she closed her eyes as the emotions finally settled a little. "I need more rest."

Part of her wanted to call her brothers, just to check on them. Surely, she should be worried, scared for them, but the emotions didn't come like Alex expected them too. Alex briefly wondered if this was part of her panic attack problem, but she didn't feel fear this time. Merlin and Morgana got up from the bed. She heard Morgana start to say something to him as they left the room quickly. There was an urgency left in their wake, but Alex ignored it. Settling back into the bed, she let her eyes trace over the ceiling crack once more.

Alex could still hear Merlin and Morgana talking in the hallways. Their tones were low and too muffled for her to understand anything they were saying. Rolling onto her side, Alex ignored Timothy and closed her eyes. The sight of the truck coming towards the car reappeared and a shudder rolled through her body. That tightness in her chest stung again and Alex squeezed her eyes together tightly. Slowly her body relaxed even as the whispers began to return. Their soft voices caused memories of places and faces long gone to dance across Alex's mind. Magic spun up around her, its gentle hum blending with the whispers. Alex began to drift off to sleep, letting the memory of the truck and her worry fade away as the voices and magic gently cradled her.